ZEPHYR'S HOPE

**RELEASE DAY SAGA
BY RYAN MATTHEWS**

RELEASE DAY

KANO'S GRASP

ARJUN'S PATH

ZEPHYR'S HOPE

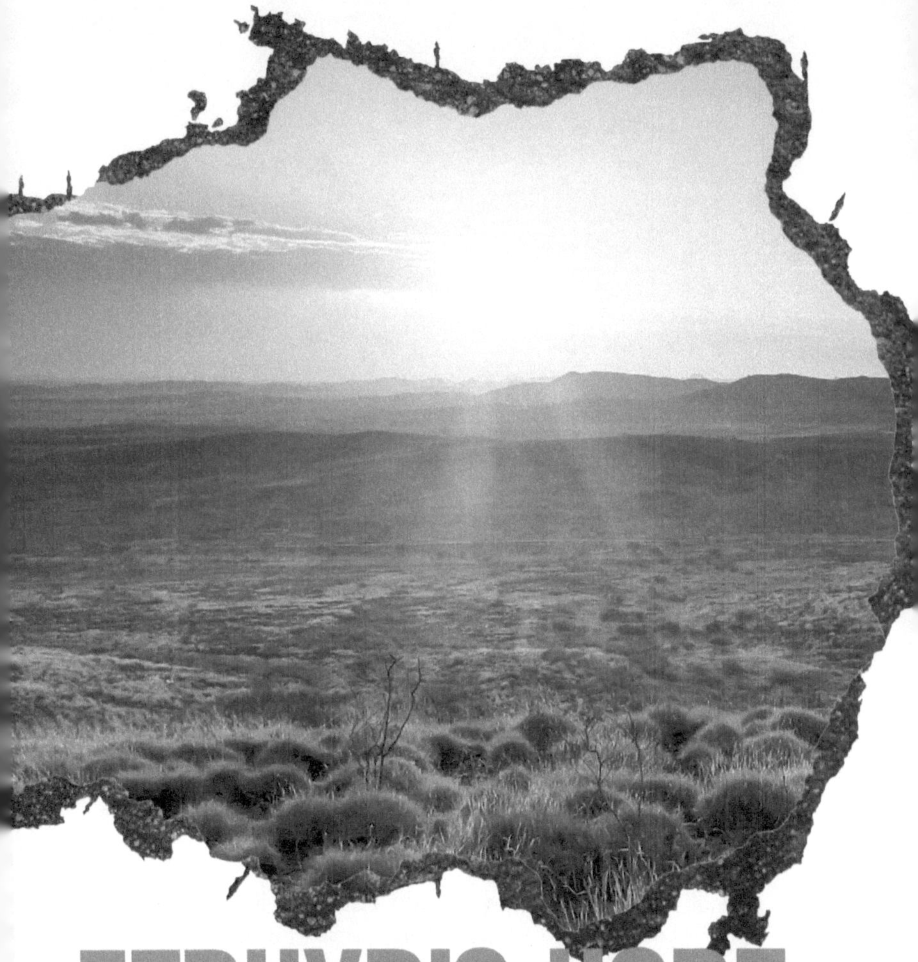

ZEPHYR'S HOPE

RYAN MATTHEWS

Layout and cover design by Ryan Matthews
Images used under license from Shutterstock.com.

Library of Congress Control Number: 2024904701

ISBN 979-8-9865388-9-1 (paperback)
ISBN 979-8-9901005-0-3 (hardcover)
ISBN 979-8-9901005-1-0 (ebook)

First Edition: May 2024

*No one is finally dead until the ripples they
cause in the world die away.*
—Terry Pratchett

CHAPTER 1: ARJUN

Staring at the starry expanse reflected on the slumbering ocean, I could almost believe life on Earth had returned to normal. The impressive horizonless view wasn't something I'd soon forget. Our vessel floated through time and space, distant from our home planet and its minuscule problems. Between Kolya's scientific observations and Francisco's vast knowledge of the seas, the voyage had been an educational experience. Yet something was missing. I longed for my companion, Ciro, and my brother, Hemant. Ciro would never again tread the earth, and my brother… well, I was unsure what to think about my twin. In recent weeks, it'd been impossible to determine whether his actions had been in his interests or mine. Our interactions had left me confused, a feeling I loathed. I couldn't decide which of Kolya's favored archaic idioms would best apply to my predicament. I was either blazing my own path or a ship lost at sea.

As the first hints of dawn revealed the lost horizon, I could make out the telltale marks of shore, looming in the distance. Under the flapping sails of the small fishing craft, we spent the next hour drifting towards a lonely shore that had passed ages without so much as a footprint. I'd made it to the final continent of my lengthy journey, an accomplishment that felt emptier than I expected. I tossed the aft spring line to our captain who stood perched on the crumbling concrete dock that had once been one of the Australian Territory's busiest ports. Under his broad hat, his weathered face held his typical stoic look. During my time aboard, I'd found the fisherman to be far warmer than his exterior let on. An expert at his craft, he eagerly passed his wisdom on to me like a father teaching his son.

His young twins had been the impetus behind his agreement to accompany us on such a perilous mission. If Kolya and I proved successful, the impoverished fisherman would be able to provide his family with a real future, one where humanity was no longer cowering underground or behind walls. He smiled up at me proudly as I tossed over the remaining lines. He'd carried out his unexpected duty with aplomb. Assuming the arrogant leader of Pod Bandung was a man of his word, Francisco would be promoted to boatmaster general upon his safe return—a much-deserved title for the seasoned fisherman.

With Francisco's initial step onto the dock after the long week of sailing, he'd done what no one was believed to have done in centuries— at least no one who'd lived to tell the tale. The three of us might have been the first people in the Australian Territory since humans had been eradicated from the expansive continent. It was unknown exactly how long it had taken the large, insect-like Arthropods to clear the region of humanity after their Outback landing in the mid-21st century. Within the first decade of their arrival, the United Territories of Earth realized the hopelessness of the situation and ordered the immediate global construction of the eleven underground bunker cities that contained humanity to this day.

The First Builders had begun construction for one such city in the southeast part of the territory, but Pod Wagga had never been finished due to its proximity to the alien hive. It had been overrun long before its completion. The Hive. Our destination. I'd traversed half the globe to reach the territory, having traveled all the way from Pod Horizonte in the Latin Territory. The reality of my whereabouts was slowly sinking in as the rising sun illuminated the jagged geometric formations shrouded in a lush green blanket that lined the coast. Somewhere deep under that vegetation were the remnants of our past civilization—a civilization that had crumbled like the dock our one-legged captain balanced on.

"Be a good lad and help me up, my boy," said Kolya, extending his hand and revealing the poorly tattooed theta—a mark of banishment that I'd yet to get used to.

Like me, the scientist was often misunderstood. His direct manner and poor hygiene had a tendency to put others off. He'd only joined us after our recovery at Pod Baghdad, much to my brother's dismay. The two had despised each other from the beginning with me forming the epicenter of their disputes. Once more on his feet, the portly man smiled at me through his mangy beard, revealing his browning teeth. Splitting from my friends to accompany Kolya had been the most difficult decision of my life. Hemant, of late, had perpetually wanted to hold me back. For my own protection, he would say. Kolya, on the other hand, was constantly driving me forward. When Kolya had put forth a peaceful alternative to our group's original mission to destroy every trace of Earth's invaders, I took it.

Kolya made his way down the wooden gangplank as it bowed slightly under his girth, singing its complaint with each step. His days of lazing around the boat stuffing himself with rations as Francisco and I manned the sails hadn't helped his physique. The man was already decades older than me. The last leg of our journey would be the most challenging one, but at least it wouldn't be fraught with attacks. He'd seen to that with his first successful communication with the Arthropod hierarchy—the Queens. After hatching the unusual scheme, Kolya had laced a powder moth with our pheromones and dispatched it to the Hive. Following in its wake, we hadn't been attacked the first time. Kolya had sensed the intelligence present in the creatures when so many others, including himself, had so easily dismissed it. Now our plans for peace negotiations were finally coming to fruition.

"I'll be honest," said Francisco, coiling a hemp rope in his rough hands. "I'll miss having you around, Arjun. If you ever make your way back to Pod Bandung, we'll share a glass of Yadira's homemade *arak*. Fair warning, it's stout enough to make this old sailor wince."

"Thank you," I replied. "I would be honored."

He cracked a subtle smile. He was a man of as few words as myself and enjoyable company. Thinking back to the surprise on Kolya's face when he had learned Francisco spoke United made me grin as we unloaded the rest of our supplies onto what was left of the cracked platform.

"Thanks for the passage, friend," said Kolya, slapping Francisco on the shoulder. "I guess we owe you Rudolfo's passphrase. You kept your end of the bargain and delivered us safely."

"*Ne plus ultra,*" I said.

"No more beyond," said Francisco. "An apt choice."

"You understand Latin?" Kolya asked, incredulous.

"Never take someone for simple because they speak simply," said the fisherman.

Kolya shook his head, muttering as per usual as his greasy hair slapped back and forth.

"Let's hope my return trip is as uneventful as the journey down here," said Francisco.

"I don't foresee that as an issue," I said, to which he arched an eyebrow. "I've taken the liberty of urinating on your deck for the past two days. My pheromones should offer you some protection until they wear off. I apologize for any smell."

The man let out a deep, raspy chuckle. "Fishermen tolerate a great many undesirable smells. I welcome the odor if it means a safe return to my wife and children. I wish you two well on your journey to the Hive. May your negotiations bring about the peace we all long for."

With that, he climbed onto the boat, retracted the gangplank, and weighed anchor. With the sun directly overhead, Kolya and I stared after him until his boat disappeared up the inlet and beyond the horizon. Compared to the sticky humidity of Bandung, the climate of the northern Australian Territory where we'd landed was quite pleasant. Even with the sun beaming down, the temperature was comfortable. Kolya was sweating, but then again, he was perpetually sweating. With a rub of my forehead, my fingers came back dry, feeling only the ample scar tissue from the burns I'd sustained from an exploding pill bug a lifetime ago. It wasn't very often I saw my reflection, but I still wasn't used to seeing the light swathes of pinkish skin running through my normally copper face. Omar called it battle scars. Krista called it warpaint. I called it the price of doing business.

"I suppose we should get a move on," Kolya said, turning. "By my reckoning, we have a month of walking ahead of us."

"At least he was able to get us far enough downriver, so we didn't have to make our way through that dilapidated city. That would've likely hampered our progress."

He lumbered over to a large boulder next to the bank and dropped his rucksack in the tall grass. Stretching the olive-drab canvas open, he pulled out a tattered old book and his brass compass from the bag.

"It's interesting how such antiquated items have become so invaluable during our expedition," he said. "Thanks to you bringing down the antenna bug network with those spores, my compass can now provide us with proper directions."

"It was my idea to use the spores, but I couldn't have done it without the help of the others," I reminded him. "We discovered them together."

Kolya was perpetually blind to the contributions my friends had made to get us as far as we had come. He believed that I was the sole reason for their progress, an incorrect assumption. I never would've left the others behind in Bhopal if I thought otherwise. They had their mission to find and destroy the Hive. Our goal was to reach it first, making peace with the creatures and removing the need for extermination. Since the Arthropods had done nothing to slow our progress and we had a significant head start, I had little doubt we'd beat my friends to the Hive.

"You don't give yourself enough credit, my boy," he said, flashing a brief smile. "Either way, without the aerials' electromagnetic interference, the thing works. Let's see… Hold this open."

I spread my hand over the crisp pages of the antique tome, its moisture-damaged pages feeling as though they might crumble at any moment. Kolya had the atlas open to the Australian Territory circa the late twentieth century, long before the UTE had incorporated the continent.

"I've spent hours pouring over this map by lamplight in the ship's hold. I can't find a better route than this," he said, stabbing at a road labeled "Stuart Highway" with a dirty fingernail. "I have no idea as to its condition or how it has changed since this atlas was printed, but it would lead us straight to the source. By my reckoning, the road should be a few kilometers to our east."

"I can think of no better option," I said, "Unless you can saddle a powder moth-like in one of your recollections."

"Arjun, my boy," he said, avoiding eye contact. "That tale may have been a bit… exaggerated. The point is valid though. I believe one can ride the dusters given the right conditions—"

"Let's start walking then," I said, already moving east.

Over the trees that had retaken the cityscape, I could still make out the few remaining towers off in the distance of what was at one time a prosperous port city. We called it Win City after the half of the city's original name that hadn't rubbed off the map's worn pages. We easily found a small paved path leading away from the river and inland. It was cracked and overgrown, but easier to traverse than the densely packed forest that had reclaimed the river bank in humanity's absence. At first glance, everywhere I turned was minimally different from the numerous jungles I'd traveled. On closer inspection, through the lush greenery were the eerie reminders of a past age. A stone cave or a crumbling warehouse? A natural arbor or a disintegrating playground? A twisted trunk or an honored statue? Musings cluttered my brain as the kilometers passed beneath my boots until I heard a crunch beneath my feet.

"What is it?" asked my companion, taking advantage of the pause to sit and catch his breath.

I reached down to pick up the glass I'd broken. Its colorful pigments flashed in the sunlight.

"It would appear to be some sort of an advertisement," I said, turning the piece over in my hand, careful to avoid its sharp edges.

I kneeled down and carefully pulled the tangled vines and leaf litter off of the pane until the image was revealed. A young man was smiling standing on some sort of board hovering over water. Nothing supporting its weight. I took in a breath.

"Before the Landing, humans possessed devices that today we can only dream of. I often stay awake at night lamenting what was lost when all of their technology succumbed to the inverts' potent electromagnetic field. It was, without a doubt, humanity's biggest setback since the destruction of the library at Alexandria," Kolya said, shaking his head in dismay. "You know, I thought I would feel relief finally free of the others and the Arthropods, but this place makes me deeply uncomfortable. An evil hand is at play."

"Evil?" I asked. "We have come all this way to make peace with the Arthropods. To what evil are you referring?"

"A gut feeling, then."

Despite being fearsomely logical, the former scientist refused to apply his scientific reasoning to his faith. When faced with harsh reality and the cruelties of nature, all he saw was humanity's fallen nature. His loyalty to his orthodox religion had led him to almost murder Marie, one of the companions we'd left behind who had been nothing short of loyal to our cause. She'd resorted to less-than-desirable methods to stay alive on Earth's hostile surface, and as a result, Kolya had never seen her as anything but the spawn of darkness. Arthropods aside, the world was still full of danger. Even something as simple as the glass I'd broken could spell death on the surface. Whether it was evil or not was irrelevant to my survival. I replaced the glass where it belonged and continued ahead. After a while, I could make out a wide expanse where nature had been slower to reclaim.

"That must be your highway up ahead," I said, nodding towards the clearing.

"Ha! Four centuries hasn't been enough to completely swallow our presence. One day we will be as strong as we were. Stronger, even!"

"I wonder how long it will take for us to regain our strength."

Kolya shook his head, not even venturing a guess. I had taken no more than a step or two forward when I froze. Something wasn't right and now I could sense it too. With intense training came fierce intuition. It was to that I attributed my survival. Kolya spun around as the native insects grew quiet. A subtle vibration reverberated through my body, rising through my soles. I turned south, squinting as I stared down the length of the highway, and saw a trail of reddish dust blotting out the blue of the sky. Drawing my razor net, I positioned myself for the first threat we'd faced since Kolya had sent our message. He turned to glare at me.

"We are here for peace," he said through clenched teeth.

When I didn't twitch, his eyes darted to my net—my weapon.

"Trust me," he said.

I collapsed the net, slinging it back around my shoulders where it stayed when not in use. The sound and vibration grew louder and louder as the mangled, rotting vehicles that lined the roadway in the distance spun up into the air before crashing down to the side, the vines anchoring them popping like gunfire. My hands were shaking, and the sweat that had eluded me earlier now poured from my brow. It took all of my willpower to ignore my sense of self-preservation screaming at me to fight or flee. The last remaining vehicle spun out of the way and across the intersection. I choked on the dust that saturated the air as I waited for the breeze to brush it away. Maybe Kolya had been right. What I saw ahead, now that *was* evil.

CHAPTER 2: DARREN

2042

"Thank you, Mr. Szalinski," I whispered into the headset before setting the earpiece back into its cradle.

"You got a call from Szalinski?!" said my cubicle mate, jerking off his headphones. "Nice!"

I shut my eyes in exasperation. *Well, I thought I was being clever.* Now that Stepan knew about it, it would be all over the office before lunch. I looked out the floor-to-ceiling window across the hall. It was a gorgeous day. Maybe I should run down to Marta's empanada cart over on Kearsley to escape the back-slapping. Call it an early lunch. Don't get me wrong, I was thrilled to get a call from the firm's owner, but that didn't mean I wanted the world to know about it. I glanced at Stepan's desk and saw his strange, hyper-ergonomic chair, swiveling empty. *Geeze.*

"Congrats on the award, Darren!" said Dom, leaning on the cubicle wall. "I hope this doesn't mean you'll be trying to leave Flint for some hotshot gig on Madison."

I chuckled. *So much for keeping a secret.* "I'm not going anywhere, Dom. You know I'm happy here."

"Good, because I hate to lose someone who can make ceiling

fan packaging interesting enough to win a territorial award! Speaking of interesting, here's the packet for Bridget's Boudoir. She had her guy do a VR shoot out in a field, and she wants you to make the holo ad look like an indoor runway scene."

"Dear God," I said. "Because *that* makes sense. I wonder how many pile-ups she caused on 54 having a bunch of scantily-clad models posing out in that field."

The art director let out a belly laugh. "I never thought about that. I'll have to see if I can get invited to her next shoot... for *research*," he said making air quotes.

I turned my attention back to Bridget's packet, reading through the brief as I listened to Dom's continued chuckles. *God, this woman is nuts.* They'll revoke my award when they see this ad shining on the nearest kiosk.

"Well, let's see what we have to work with," I mumbled, pulling up the server on my semi-circular screen.

Just as Dom said, the model footage was outdoors, and of all things, on one of Michigan's few sunny days. *How in the world am I going to make them look natural in an indoor setting?* I longed for the day I got to tell this particular client, "No." I'd love to see the look on her pouty face when she didn't get her way. I'd need to win a few more awards for that. Szalinski wouldn't risk sacrificing such an influential client just because she had outrageous demands.

I pulled up my inbox and shot an email to my favorite photog, telling him about Bridget's nonsense and asking him to stage an indoor runway shoot with enough lights to make it bright as daytime. With that done, I sent an email to the intern to clip all of the models out. She'd love that. Serves her right for drinking all my fair-trade coffee. *Don't think I don't know, Tera.*

I began carefully organizing my files and information for the ad while I turned up my favorite podcast, *Debunk Everything*. When I'd paused it to take Szalinski's phone call, the hosts were about to reveal to another cult leader that they had been plants, documenting the whole time. After a few minutes, I heard a ruckus and paused the audio long enough to listen, but whatever it was had faded, so I resumed my work. The podcast wrapped up, and I turned to Stepan.

"So, dude, this time they were in this sun-worshiping cult and they—" I began, but again greeted by Stepan's empty chair, a common site this morning.

Must have gone for coffee. I picked up my cup, swirling the cold quarter inch of coffee and silt that had escaped the filter. *I could use a fresh cup. Maybe I'll hide my coffee in a better spot when I'm done.* Making my way to the break room, I couldn't help but notice that all the cubicles were eerily vacant. No one was at their desk. Oddly enough, phones weren't ringing either. *Did I miss the rapture?* I thought jokingly. Agnostic humor at its finest.

"Alright, this is weird," I said, speeding up slightly.

When I rounded the corner, I found everyone. The entire floor of about forty people was packed into a room that comfortably held fifteen at best, glued to the news feed on the wall panel.

"What's happening?" I asked Nina, who shushed me.

On any other day, I'd be offended by this pasty white woman with dyed bouffant hair shushing a black man, but today, I ignored it. I looked for Stepan and found him in the corner, so dumbfounded that he wasn't eating. For Stepan, not eating meant something was really out of whack. The sandy-haired skater perpetually had something going down his gullet, yet never gained a kilo.

"What's happening, man?"

"Dude, don't you ever check your phone?!" he said in a shocked whisper. "Look!"

I looked at the screen expecting to see that a war had broken out or something. Surely not a mass shooting. It had been years since we had implemented the UTE's mandated arms restrictions, dramatically reducing worldwide gun violence. The crawl read, "Meteorite Lands in Outback," and the newscaster was going over what few details were known.

"Okay…" I said, earning me a few stink-eyes. "So another rock hit Earth. That happens all the time."

"Another rock?" said Stepan, "They never saw it coming! All the satellites and whatnot in orbit and no one saw it until it started breaching the atmosphere."

"Okay, but isn't space bigger than we can track?"

"That's just it, man. They've gone back over the data. The thing was invisible to tracking."

"That *is* strange, but there's still a lot we don't know about space. Maybe it's made of some new element the periodic table doesn't account for."

"That's not all that's weird though. Look at it," Stepan said, pointing.

It was hard to judge the scale, but compared to the news tilt-rotors buzzing around it, the meteorite on screen was sticking several hundred feet out of the ground. For the first time, it hit me, a meteorite that size would've had disastrous ramifications for the planet. I turned and looked wide-eyed at Stepan.

"Yeah. Now he gets it," he said. "They think it slowed down."

"Slowed down?" I muttered to myself. A pit opened in my stomach. If I'd learned anything from *Debunk Everything*, it was that most occurrences had a rational explanation, but I shuddered to think of any rational explanations that applied to why an object of such mass would slow down before crashing into Earth. I swore under my breath.

Markos, one of the managing partners, stood on a chair at the front of the lounge by the vending fridges as Nina muted the sound.

"I recognize this is a… peculiar event," he began. "As you know, I'm a family man."

Sure are, Especially if you count the mistresses and unclaimed kids.

"It's at times like these I prefer to be at home with my loved ones. I think it's only fair to offer you the same. With it being Friday, everyone take the rest of the day off. We'll just make it a long weekend. See you all on Monday."

What normally would've been an announcement received with glee, was met with stoic faces as everyone filed out of the cramped lounge and made their way back to their desks. I was more than happy to leave Bridget stewing for a few days. I grabbed my satchel, throwing the strap over my shoulder, still sore from the game of pick-up football the night before. It was time I started remembering I wasn't as young as I used to be. Stepan followed me quietly out of the building and down to the sidewalk.

"Stay safe," I told him, as he unfolded his bike.

He nodded absentmindedly. "I think I'll get a drink at O'Rourke's and watch the news over there. Kitty's not due back from her modeling session in Detroit until tomorrow night anyway."

"I'm glad she's not in Antwerp this time," I said. "With the flights canceled, who knows when she'd get to come home."

"Right?" he said, far from his usual self.

"If you get tired of day drinking, swing by the house. Patricia is off-shift. We'd be more than happy to feed you."

"Thanks, Darren. I might take you up on that."

With a slap on the back, he was off, zipping through the masses bustling their way home. I was glad I worked for a company relaxed enough to let us go. I couldn't imagine trying to focus on work when something so unusual was unfolding, even if it was all the way in the Australian Territory.

•••••••••

The trip home on the light rail was quiet as if everyone was afraid to acknowledge what was happening out loud. Everyone was wondering about the same thing—aliens. Could this be the first time we would meet extraterrestrials? We had scientific stations on Luna and Mars, but for all intents and purposes, we were still amateurs when it came to matters of the cosmos. Even scouring the stars with organizations like SETI, we'd yet to come across any sign of life.

I took the stairs up to our apartment, moving quickly past Mrs. Grimethorpe's door. If she caught me in the stairwell, I'd be here until Monday. My keys were turning in the deadbolt when I heard her voice.

"Darren, is that you?"

I quickly closed the door as if I hadn't heard and flung my keys into the brass seashell by the door. *Whew! That was close.* I could hear her houseshoes padding around on the stoop, debating on whether to knock or not. Patricia came around the corner with a cup of coffee in her hand, still bleary-eyed from her all-night stint at the observatory. Her hair was frizzy from running her hands repeatedly through it, a bad habit she had when staring at a computer screen for hours on end. I put a finger over my mouth until I heard Mrs. Grimethorpe's door click shut.

"You can't blame her. She has no one to talk to since her husband died," she said. "There's a full pot in the kitchen if you want some coffee."

"I know," I said, feeling guilty for dodging the woman. "I expected you to be asleep."

"I turned on the screen to fall asleep and saw the news. With my mind racing, I knew it was a lost cause. I sent the new *au pair* from the company home. Ugh, why did Reine have to graduate?" she said, sighing. "Alex is in his room playing peacefully if you want to see him."

I gave her a kiss on the cheek and went to see my son. He was rolling a semi-truck around with a doll perched on top. His close-cropped hair was getting long. We both could use a trip to the barber.

"She's riding to the beach to get a tan," said the six-year-old.

"Okay then," I said, laughing and picking him up.

"Are you home early?" he asked,

"Yeah. My boss decided to let us have a long weekend."

"Is this the one who likes the ladies?"

"Who told you that?!" I asked, grinning.

"I have ears, dad. You and Mommy aren't as good at whispering as you think."

I let out a deep laugh as Patricia rounded the corner with a steaming mug of black coffee in her hand.

"Thanks, babe."

"You're welcome," she whispered.

"See! You guys are doing it right now, and I can hear yooooou."

"Mommy wasn't trying to hide anything," I said.

"Good. Now you wanna tell me why you're really home?" said Alex.

I looked at my wife who shrugged. "You're such an astute kid."

"I don't know what astute means, but I'm smart."

"Close enough. You sure are," I said, pulling the globe down from his dresser. "Well, a meteorite landed in the Australian Territory. Here."

Alex rolled his eyes. "I know where it is, Dad. And we're here, in the American Territory."

"Exactly."

"So why were you sent home for a big rock?"

I heard Patricia chuckle as she leaned against the door frame, watching the Gestapo-like interrogation by a six-year-old from the comfort of her PJs.

"It's a strange situation, Alexander."

"I don't like it when you call me Alexander."

"Why not?"

"It means things are getting serious," he said, pouting.

"I don't know what it means, honestly. This rock is different in a number of ways. I think everyone is playing it safe until we know more."

"Will you promise me that you won't keep any secrets from me?"

I looked at my wife who nodded subtly.

"I promise."

With Alex entertained by his toys, I curled up on the couch with Patricia as we watched the wall screen on mute. Each of the territories was dispatching science teams to the rock. Apparently, there was some semi-secret base right near Alice Springs where it landed. They would be the first team on site and organize the others.

"I've got a bad feeling about this," said Patricia, using the cliche quote from my favorite old movie.

For the second time that day, a pit formed in my stomach. My wife had a crazy sense of intuition that made even my skeptical mind wonder about the supernatural.

"Hopefully, it's just a rock," I said, not even believing my own words.

CHAPTER 3: HUCK

"That's what we do with a drunken sailor.
That's what we do with a drunken sailor.
That's what we do with a drunken sailor.
Early in the—"

"**W**ait! Did you guys hear that?" I slurred, interrupting our shanty as I tried to blink away the stupor.

The room swirled as I sat up too quickly. The salty air whipped in through the round opening, cooling the rescue buoy's interior and making it slightly less claustrophobic with its eleven occupants. We'd passed days in the tight confines of the floating metal bastille somewhere in the Indian Ocean, hoping to the universe that the emergency beacon I'd activated still worked. It hadn't taken long for us to discover among the stores of distilled water were several bottles of some dark, aged liquor and vacuum-sealed pouches of tobacco. With the heavy mood and little else to do, it was only natural that we spent a fair amount of our captivity drinking.

"I don't hear a thing," slurred Krista. "*Way hay and up she rises—*"

"*Shh!*" said Omar.

She gave him a dirty look as he removed the long-stemmed pipe from his lips, listening intently. We'd all been neatly trimmed when we'd departed Pod Bhopal, which now felt like ages ago. In the weeks since, the guys had grown scraggly beards. Omar's normally buzzed head now sported several thick inches of growth.

He eyed the hatch with his dark brown eyes, all signs of intoxication vanishing. *There it is again! A voice!* Omar sprung towards the ladder, the thin metal flexing under his large frame as he climbed to the deck, skipping rungs with excitement.

I glanced at Fen, a risky proposition since I'd knocked her unconscious to silence her screams. After losing our entire thousand-troop battalion and our one-of-a-kind transport ship, losing her boyfriend, Mego, had proven more than she could bear. I could still hear the wails as her compact body flailed with surprising force against Omar, attracting the same ocean creature that had killed our comrades and sank our ship. With little other choice, I'd used our lifeboat's paddle to hit her upside the head. Despite saving our lives, the questionable action had made me an outcast for days. With the discovery of the alcohol, feelings had been expressed and forgiveness dealt out from all but Fen. Her eyes narrowed as she returned my gaze. I may have been our group's leader before we'd entered the militaristic Pod Bhopal, but inside, she'd been our squad leader. Since our departure, we'd split the burden of leadership. That task would prove difficult if our relationship didn't improve quickly.

"Oh my god!" Omar yelled back down through the hatch, more excited than ever. "It's a ship! They're yelling and waiving! We're rescued!"

"Thank the universe!" said Leisel, who'd never more than sipped the hooch.

"What I wouldn't give for a hot shower and to pee in private," said Ariadne.

The pipe practically fell from Hemant's lips and he scurried up the ladder behind Omar. Like Omar, his muscular frame challenged the ladder's welds. Everyone rose, anxiously waiting for a chance to clutter the buoy's tiny deck. We'd spent far too long crammed into the minuscule space to be concerned about danger. With so many people in the tight confines, privacy had been non-existent. I had never been so excited about the prospect of being alone again. That and eating food that didn't constipate the hell out of me.

"Need a hand?" I asked Roque, who had managed to stand with Ondo's help.

"Thanks, man," he said, hobbling over to a handhold. "I'll wait here for now. You can hoist me up in a minute. If they start coming aboard, I doubt there'll be enough room for a cripple up there."

"Stow that nonsense, Roq," said Ondo. "You know I hate that slur. With some decent medical care, you'll be back up and running in no time."

During our haste to flee the drill barnacle nauplii that had swarmed our ship, Roque had mangled his leg. On our first day on board the buoy, Marie and Ariadne, the ones in our group with the most medical expertise, had guided Omar in setting it. Roque's screams had been gut-wrenching. I shivered thinking back to those little creatures pouring over the deck leaving little more than the bones of our fellow soldiers in their wake. Whoever had initially claimed that the Arthropods stuck to land was full of crap, and the army that had accompanied us had perished for it. I was beginning to think Hemant's fear of the open ocean wasn't as irrational as I'd suspected. *And we still have leagues of it before we reach the Australian Territory.* I shook my head as I pushed the thought out of my inebriated mind.

I allowed everyone else to climb the ladder until only Roque, Ariadne, and I remained. She lingered, clasping my hand before following the others. Even after days without hygiene or grooming, her wavy hair and emerald eyes still captivated me like nothing else. I couldn't believe how lucky I was to be with her. I felt the room sway, partially due to the liquor's effect on my equilibrium and partially due to the redistribution of weight as the others plodded around on deck. As she climbed, I couldn't help but stare at the bomb. That loathsome hunk of metal was a fundamental part of our mission. We'd been tasked with lugging the thing as far behind enemy lines as a person could go. I couldn't so much as glance at it without dwelling on just how many people had died to get it this far. If I counted Pod Baghdad… Part of me wanted to roll it of into the ocean and never think about it again. Ariadne's booted foot vanished through the opening. With a final nod to Roque, I ascended the ladder to the crowded deck above.

As I emerged, a strange sound drew my eyes up instead of towards the ship coming alongside the buoy. High overhead, gray and white birds circled. Birds. Real, live birds.

"Look!" I shouted, pointing.

Leisel craned her neck and started laughing with joy. I looked at Ariadne whose eyes brimmed with tears. Attention was torn between our saviors and the rare life soaring above our heads. Birds were a sight few of us had beheld.

"Hail, buoy!" shouted someone on the ship's deck.

"Hail, schooner!" responded Omar in turn.

Krista began jumping up and down. I couldn't put into words how excited I was to see human beings again. Aside from Marie, who was perpetually unfazed by anything, none of us had slept well, always fearing another attack by either the breachers, what we'd taken to calling the drill barnacles, or the sea locust that had broken the back of our ship like a dry branch. If the spine back, the most formidable opponent we'd faced on land, had a sea fairing cousin, the sea locust would be it.

Tearing my eyes away from the swirling in the sky, I saw the boat for the first time. My heart soared. I hadn't realized just how much seeing our rescuers would affect me. The wind-powered schooner, as Omar had called it, was a long wooden vessel, far smaller than Madan's metal-hulled monstrosity that had carried our battalion until the attack by the sea locust and breachers. I found it quite disturbing that the two had orchestrated the attack together. Back in my home city, Pod Horizonte, it'd been hammered into us that the Arthropods were big, dumb bugs. Only the hypothesized Queens possessed any real intelligence. What we'd seen through the course of our travels showed anything but. The inverts were ruthless and conniving. If not for the fact that we played a role in their food supply, they would have eradicated us long ago.

As the ship's ebony hull came within arm's reach, Hemant and Omar gathered the lines and lashed them to the yellow buoy's railing. One of the birds alighted on the buoy's tower and promptly pooped on its rusting metal supports, splashing into my hair. I jumped back, hastily flinging the thick, white goo from my already greasy head as everyone laughed.

"Serves you right," said Fen, unsmiling.

"That's good luck!" yelled a coppery-skinned man, the sheen of his sweat glistening in the sunlight.

"It doesn't smell like good luck," I yelled back to the man, rinsing my hands in the ocean.

Several more of the crew, all similarly tanned, leaned over the ship's wooden railing, chuckling as they lowered a rope ladder down to the buoy's deck. Two of the men clamored down to meet us, leaving no extra space whatsoever.

"You must be the ones everyone's calling Memo's Misfits," the first man said, grinning from ear to ear. "People thought you were dead when we lost contact with General Madan. I knew you were alive though. They're saying you guys can't be killed. Egad, where are my manners? I'm Banyu, captain of the *Semeru*."

"Thank you for rescuing us, Captain," said Ariadne.

"I may be captain, but call me Om Banyu. Crew is family, and I see no reason for you to be any different. I apologize it took so long to retrieve you. The emergency receiver isn't checked daily. A young ensign happened by the display on Pod Bandung's bridge and nearly had a heart attack. Fool started screaming, 'Thank the Maker. Thank the Maker.' We were dispatched immediately, but we didn't know which buoy you were in, so we were in the process of checking every one from here to the Asian Territory's coast. I'll tell you, there are too many damn buoys. I can't decide if I want to smack or hug whoever came up with the damn-fool contraptions."

"Hug. Most definitely hug," said Hemant, beaming. "I'm so ready to be off this tin can."

"Then I will stall you no more," said Banyu. "You are welcome aboard the *Semeru*. As soon as you're ready, we'll make way for Pod Bandung."

"Give us a minute to retrieve our things," I said. "We have an injured man still inside and the weapon we are taking to the Hive."

"Allow me to ask, will this weapon pose a threat to any member of my crew?" Banyu asked.

"We've carried it from the Latin Territory without incident," I said. "I believe it to be safe."

"I will take you at your word and allow it on my ship," he said. "If you will gather your supplies, we can be back in Bandung in a matter of days."

"Jafar, my first mate, will help you with your injured friend," Banyu said, snapping his fingers.

"It's really not necessary," I said. "We fabricated a sling to hoist him to the deck for fresh air—"

"Jafar will help you," Banyu repeated, whether not hearing us or ignoring us, I was unsure.

With a boom eerily reminiscent of the sea locust's impact on the *Spearhead*, Jafar landed on the buoy's deck behind me. I turned to see a towering man with a mustache curled over his lengthy beard and skin as dark as the boat that carried him. I let out an audible gasp seeing this man who dwarfed Ondo. Around his head was a tightly wrapped turban.

"He's a Sikh," said Trivia, barely containing her excitement.

The foreboding man revealed a wide grin and threw back his head as he howled in laughter, his hand never dropping from the hilt of the ornate dagger tucked within a sash at his waste.

"You are correct, my young friend," Jafar said.

"I have so many questions!" Trivia said, her freckled face beaming at the prospect of new knowledge.

"Let us have them answered once we are on board. As for the moment, lead me to your companion."

Trivia nodded so emphatically that I thought her head would shake loose from her shoulders. Within moments, Roque was on the deck of the *Semeru*, comfortably reclined as Jafar climbed the rope later holding the bomb with one hand. Ondo's eyes, which were normally recessed in his girthy head, nearly bulged out at Jafar's strength.

"Are you guys seeing this?" he muttered.

Ondo was easily the largest and strongest among our entire team since he'd joined our ranks, a title that had been previously split between Hemant and Omar. The fact he was impressed said it all. I climbed back down to the buoy and helped pass the remaining articles to my friends on board. With everything loaded, I dropped down inside the buoy once more to verify that we'd collected everything. I caught a glimpse of myself in the mirror, edges rusty from exposure to the salty air. It was permanently mounted to the garish yellow metal wall that matched the exterior. Our journey had taken a physical toll on everyone. We'd lost what little fat we had, along with our innocence, in favor of scars and muscle. Though far thinner than Omar's beard, so many days without shaving helped conceal my facial scars. I still had trouble focusing my gaze on the long marks that would forever haunt my face, a parting gift from a mantis wraith. Ariadne vowed she saw right past them, but I never could. I still cringed sometimes when she'd kiss my cheek, reminding me of my haunting battle with the Huntress.

God, the Demented. With any luck, we were past their ilk. Hopefully not even the vile, twisted humans who survived on human flesh and Arthropod hemolymph could survive anywhere near the creature's Hive. Once we defeated the inverts, *if* we defeated them, we would face the ethical quandary of what to do with the Demented. Even as departed from human beings as they were, ridding the world of them still had all the earmarks of genocide. *Maybe there is some way to turn them back,* I thought, staring at Marie. At least the ones not too far gone.

CHAPTER 4: ARIADNE

I rested my arms on the lacquered wooden railing lining the deck of the *Semeru*. The dark, polished wood would've undoubtedly burned my arms if not for the cool ocean breeze. Krista and Leisel joined me, watching the buoy that had saved our lives recede into the distance. I couldn't help but look past it to the imaginary spot where the last survivors of the *Spearhead*, aside from us, had perished. The liquor's effects had faded, leaving me to face the raw emotions of our experience head-on—and with an unrelenting headache.

"They just vaporized. Everything happened so fast," said Leisel, her curly blond hair pulled back tight behind her head, matted from days without care. "They didn't feel anything, right?"

"I like to think so," said Fen, surprising us from behind.

We stood awkwardly for a moment before she put us at ease. Her hard Asian features had a habit of making her difficult to gauge. Since the loss of her boyfriend and the incident with Huck, her mood had been unpredictable. This morning, I saw nothing but sincerity in those deep brown eyes of hers.

"Don't feel like you have to hold your tongues around me," she said, reading my mind. "I was crazy about Mego, but neither of us had any illusions about how dangerous our lives would be among Bhopal's Clunkies. When we joined your quest, we knew that would only add to it. We resolved long ago to live every day as though it could be our last."

"I'm so sorry, Fen," I said. "For you and Roque both. I've lost numerous people I've been close to over the last few months but never a lover. I couldn't imagine losing Huck now that I have him."

Fen's gracious acceptance of my condolences vanished at the mention of Huck. I couldn't expect anything else. He probably saved us with his actions, but the fact remained that he had hit her in her moment of desperation. I'd even had a hard time looking past it.

"Speaking of Roque, I'm going to go see if he needs anything," said Fen, already walking away. "I'm sure he's missing TomTom."

"Is it normal to feel guilty for surviving when the rest of the battalion died?" asked Leisel. "What makes us so special?"

Krista harrumphed. "Yeah, guilt and even resentment are normal. I've felt both more times than I'd care to admit since leaving Horizonte. You can only watch everyone around you die so many times before you start to get jaded. I believe in our mission, so I redirect all of those feelings toward seeing it through. If I'm going to survive, I have to make my survival count, you know?"

Leisel nodded, soaking in Krista's every word. Because Leisel had joined us on our escape from Pod Kano, she hadn't seen quite as much action as we had. Nor had she had the level of training we'd had. That being said, any given week outside of the relative safety of the underground pod cities, we saw more violence than any person should be exposed to in a lifetime. All the Arthropods did was take and take. It was all they had done since they landed almost four hundred years ago. I still couldn't fathom a life completely free of fear.

The sail fabric snapped in the wind above my head, and I chuckled to myself. Back before the Arthropod Landing, humanity was at the peak of its existence. I'd learned from my studies that the world was far from perfect, but humans were in the best and most advanced state they had ever been in. Now, centuries later, instead of being leagues further, we are dependent on thousand-year-old technology. My arms were engulfed by shadow, pulling me away from my thoughts.

"Am I interrupting anything?" Jafar asked, blocking out the sun as he leaned on the railing.

I shook my head. I swear I heard the wood creak in protest under his immense musculature. I shifted my gaze back and forth between him and Krista. Their dark skin was all that they had in common. He was easily several times her size and something told me he was far more lethal than she was.

"Would you be so kind as to regale me with your journey?" he asked, bearing his teeth. "I would very much like to hear it for myself. There are many rumors surrounding 'Memo's Misfits.' I would like to know what is truth and what is exaggeration, especially in regard to Kano."

Pod Kano. The very thought made my skin crawl. It was only through the sacrifice of others' lives that we managed to escape. Why anyone would want to know more about that place was beyond me. Jafar must have seen the hesitation in my eyes.

"It was the pod of my birth," he said. "I and a few others managed to find our way here. I am the only remaining survivor, but I still have loved ones back in the pod. I would like to know how they fare."

"It's pretty dismal," said Leisel, who'd managed to survive in Kano her entire life, hidden away from many of the pod's dangers. "A kindly woman kept me and another safe in the Horticulture District, but many others weren't so fortunate. Even our friend Hemant was forced to do some unthinkable things during his tenure with Zabu's militia."

The woman, Miranda, had been one of the people sacrificed to make our escape possible. She was the kindest-natured soul, as best as they come. Her protection of Leisel and the simple-minded Cesar had prevented them both from being devoured by the insatiable corruption of the city. Thanks to Miranda's involvement with the Resistance, we were able to destroy the pod's primary drug manufacturing facility, weakening Zabu's iron grip on its populace. I like to think we had left Kano's citizens in slightly better conditions than we found them.

Jafar shook his head sullenly. "I must confess, I was hoping conditions had improved. It pains me to say it, but not a day goes by without me wishing for Zabu's death."

"That isn't something you should feel guilty about," said Krista. "The man is a monster. He kills and maims just for the sick pleasure of it."

Jafar withdrew into his mind before changing the subject. "Tell me about the rest of your journey."

"How much do you want to hear," I asked.

"Everything, if it pleases you."

"For a hot bath and a fresh meal, I'd describe my first kiss," said Omar.

•••••••

Several days later, we came within sight of Bandung's looming shipyard walls, bleached white by the unrelenting sun. Mouth agape, I stared at their sheer size. I'd never seen anything in my life so large outside of a pod. Our journey had been a pleasant one, unplagued by the sea locust or drill barnacles thanks to the boat's quiet nature and the Arthropods' defunct surveillance network. As the days passed, we had fascinated Jafar with our journey. The other crew members, Om Banyu included, listened intently when not on duty.

We told them of our survival of Release Day from Pod Horizonte; our travel across the Latin Territory with the original Misfits and their leader, Mueller; our first encounter with the twisted Demented; and our ocean voyage across the Atlantic to the Saharan Territory with Captain Lolade. Mesmerized, they listened as we shared our journey with the local transporters, Yanus and Taha; finding ourselves on opposite political sides in Pod Kano and our subsequent escape; our encounter with the Demented Huntress and the mantis wraiths; and our near-miraculous flight out in humanity's only known airplane. On the last day of our travels to Bandung, we concluded with our recovery in Baghdad; the plane crash on the way to Bhopal; our run-in with Proctor Evans and his miscreants; the moment when Arjun and Kolya split from us; how Madan co-opted our mission for his own; and how our entire battalion had died on the ship, leaving us stranded in the buoy. Not once did we leave out a single detail of the companions who had perished alongside us. With our long-winded tale complete, many of the sea-hardened sailors had wept with us. Each one having lost as much as we had.

In exchange, the crew had thoroughly shared their knowledge of the sea and Arthropods they'd encountered with us. Trivia, our resident expert, drank in every word. The sea locust and its minions had been creatures of near myth for longer than we'd been alive. Apparently, the two had a reputation for working together. The men referred to the sea locust as the Kraken, based on sailor's legends dating back long before the Arthropod Landing, when boats like the *Semeru* were commonplace. The drill barnacles they referred to as the spawn, though I thought our nickname of borers was more appropriate given the fact that the smaller creatures had no relation to the larger one. Aside from us, there were no reliable accounts of Kraken-encounter survivors. The few tales that existed were exaggerated beyond measure. Ironically, the truth was nearly as unbelievable.

We still knew very little about the creature aside from the fact that it was clawed, attracted to noise, and could move with a speed that a metal-clad ship couldn't slow. Stories of its attraction to noise had permeated Bandung, a pod known for its shipbuilding and restoration. It was due to these tales that their focus had largely switched to fabricating the antiquated nearly silent wooden sailing ships in lieu of restoring military vessels left behind by our surface-dwelling predecessors. If there was any good news, it was the fact that the rumors led you to believe that there were very few of the terrifying species.

"It's unreal, isn't it?" I asked Marie, who'd appeared at my side.

The intriguing woman stood emotionless, staring at the massive white walls of the city as we drew closer and closer. The boat bobbed and weaved in a strange pattern as it headed towards the main gate, flanked by what appeared to be two guard towers. The unusual woman had joined us after our capture by Proctor Evans. She had been one of the few good-natured people in the village willing to stand up to the bastard and help us escape his dastardly plans. I shuddered to think what would've happened had she not saved us. The woman was still a mystery. Her pale, tattooed face, partially hidden within her cowl, revealed little about her thoughts. She was unpredictable and lethal but loyal to us and our cause. Omar would never completely trust her, but I couldn't imagine going on without her.

"I have seen nothing like it in my life," she said as a loud clang permeated the air.

Ahead, Banyu was waving to the tower, and they had begun parting the looming gates. I watched as they swung open on rails barely visible beneath the tide lapping the barnacle-covered walls of the shipyard.

"I don't understand. I thought all the pods were the same," said Hemant. "If Arjun were here, he could—"

Hemant stopped mid-sentence, his voice catching. Trivia put a hand on his arm, comforting him. Her voluminous red hair was tied back in her usual double braids, cascading down her back. The two had been growing increasingly fond of each other since we'd been thrown in the brig for circumventing General Madan's plans in favor of our original mission. As an elite member of Bhopal's special forces, the Clunkies, she had sacrificed everything to help us. During our time in the buoy, they'd been regularly sneaking up to the deck alone. The two made a cute couple. I was glad they were taking advantage of our precious time alive. In a way, she'd taken Arjun's place as our font of information, though she could never replace him.

"What you're seeing *is* unique," said Trivia. "The actual pod is further inland, linked by an underground tunnel. The shipyard was built on the water for obvious reasons and has to be open air because of the size of the vessels."

"Ariadne, take a look at this," said Huck, leaning over the railing, eyes focused downward.

I walked barefoot across the wooden deck, worn smooth from years of foot traffic to where he was standing. The deck was hot under my feet. Like the rest of the crew, we'd removed our boots once on board, our bare feet gripping the wet wood far better than the pod's standard-issue boots' treads. I felt naked without them, but having my feet out for so long, I felt a new reluctance to don the footwear again. Huck pointed downward as I reached him.

I followed his finger to the undulating water, lapping at the sides of the traditionally built vessel, and saw nothing at first. I continued staring at the water until I saw it. Not in the water, but far below it.

"A city!" I exclaimed loud enough to draw attention from the others.

With interest peaked, the others ripped their eyes away from the shipyard long enough to see what I was going on about. Jafar laughed from deep within his barrel chest.

"You've found the old city, I see," he said. "Now it is nothing more than a home to the fishes."

"But how—" began Krista.

"I don't know all the details, but well before the Arthropod attack, the waters slowly rose forth from the seas, consuming entire cities. Some died. Those who survived moved inland. It was the largest problem humanity faced before—"

"Before them," finished Trivia, pointing at a swarm of inverts flying directly towards us.

CHAPTER 5: HEMANT

"**D**amn inverts," I mumbled, springing towards the weapon rack where my war hammer waited anxiously for action.

The stupid bugs hadn't bothered us on our trip from the buoy, the quiet boat somehow avoiding the attention of the Kraken and its friends, the breachers. Now within sight of land, we were exposed to the plethora of invert life that dwelled there. As I neared the rack, Jafar's massive hand slapped onto my chest, halting me in my tracks.

"Fear not, my friend," he said. "Watch."

I turned back, stepping forward to see past the billowing sails. I grew more nervous as the inverts closed the distance, now identifiable as hook beetles—a slow, but no less lethal—opponent. *Damn things figured out who we are.* The stupid inverts had a hankering for killing us. I felt dangerously exposed without the heft of my hammer in my hand, regardless of how the situation would unfold. Just when I was ready to shove past Jafar's bulk, I saw a flight of arrows hurtling toward the incoming group from Bandung's shipyard towers. The cloud dispersed as the arrows toppled their ranks. Deterred, what was left of them made a big loop away from the yard and headed back towards the safety of land. *No, they haven't recognized us yet. They would've sent everything they had.*

"You'll find the shipyard's defenses more than adequate. Our archers train from the moment they can hold a bow. They can hold off most smaller attacks. For the more vicious attacks, we have miniguns, but we must conserve ammunition," said Banyu, waiving his thanks to the guard now visible in the nearest tower. As the *Semeru* passed the threshold of the city, he boomed, "Welcome to Pod Bandung!"

My eyes brimmed with tears as I thought of Arjun. I knew he'd made it at least this far with his miserable excuse for a friend—that bastard Kolya. We'd been so close until a few misplaced words turned his manipulated mind against me. I wondered if we'd ever rebuild our relationship. We'd grown up training side-by-side back in Horizonte, which at the time, separated children from their parents and siblings. When I'd first met Arjun, I knew he was my fraternal twin, no question about it. Some things transcend understanding. Since that moment, we'd been inseparable. Arjun was… special. He was fiendishly smart, far more than I ever would be, and a fearsome warrior, but he struggled with the simplest social interactions. I'd taken him under my wing, and together we had proven to be a fantastic team. We owed our survival to his wisdom and keen observations. I felt Trivia's silken hand slip into mine. She could be such a hardened warrior and still manage to be feminine off the battlefield.

"Thinking about your brother again?" she asked, not really a question.

I nodded. "He was here. I wish he still was. Maybe I could talk to him."

She shook her head. "I never knew Researcher Kolya, but if he's as manipulative as you make him out to be, nothing you could've said would've helped him see reason. He has to discover it for himself."

"That conniving weasel hit him at his weakest point. If Arjun was like others, he would've never been—"

"You cherish him *because* he's not like others."

"You're right," I said, unable to tear away from her eyes, bluer and deeper than the surrounding ocean.

"We'll catch up with him. Then you and Marie can duke it out over who gets to eviscerate him," she said with the cutest, slightly devious, smile.

I laughed heartily. Kolya had angered the wrong people. Even if he was the smartest person on Earth, he'd stupidly pissed off the planet's most lethal one. Nothing sent shivers down my spine more than our companion, Marie. When she transitioned into assassin mode, death lingered like a static charge in the air. I was driven by passion—she was driven by a vengeful rage. She would stop at nothing until the coward who'd nearly poisoned her was convulsing on the ground, bleeding out from the throat.

"I still don't understand," I said, shaking my head. "Memo tasked us to blow the Hive to smithereens. With that done, we'd finally have the upper hand! The plan was far from foolproof, but we were dedicated. Then, that asshole lead him off on some idiotic idea to negotiate for peace. Peace! With those bastards? It'll never happen!"

I felt Ariadne's calming touch on my shoulder and turned to find the crew staring at me. We were approaching the dock, passing through vessels new and old in various states of construction and restoration. What would normally be awe-inspiring was overshadowed by deep-seated anger.

"Sorry," I said.

"You have nothing to apologize for," said Captain Banyu. "There's not a person here who would disagree with you. Your passion is what instills us with faith in you and your comrades. I don't just mean the crew of the *Semeru*, I mean everyone. You've dragged a potentially war-ending weapon from the deserts of the Saharan Territory almost within sight of the Australian Territory. You allowed hope to bloom where it previously could find no fertile soil."

I nodded, appreciating the support. "Don't get me wrong, I want to blow the inverts clear off our planet, but my top priority is to rescue my brother."

"Destiny has a way of aligning our interests," said Marie, receiving a grunt of confirmation from Jafar.

"I will do everything in my power to aid you in your quest," said Banyu. "Even if that means twisting De León's weak arm behind his back until he agrees."

The crew chuckled, drawing my attention away from Arjun. When I faced the city, it was as if a veil parted. For the first time, I observed my surroundings. My jaw nearly hit the deck as I whirled, taking in the scene. As the vessel pulled into the slip, men on the ground attempted to throw docking ropes to me, but I was so awe-inspired that they fell uselessly at my feet. Ignoring their yells, I made my way between the chaos of the crew making final preparations for shore to stand at the center of the deck under the main mast, spinning to take in the open-air city.

With a thud the gates closed, sealing in the tall white walls that encircled the shipyard. Reaching towards the heavens, the walls blended in with the clouds to the point where you couldn't tell where the walls ended and the sky began. They weren't without their blemishes. The centuries of exposure to the elements, particularly saltwater, had been harsh. Crews dotted the walls doing the never-ending work of scraping rust, patching holes, and repainting.

My breath disappeared at the sight of so many vessels bobbing up and down as the tide that had drifted in with us disturbed the sealed harbor's tranquility. I'd never seen so many pre-Landing artifacts. Here they were, being restored for humanity's use. And so many people! I'd never seen so many outside of a pod, living and working in relative safety.

"It's a head trip, isn't it?" said Banyu, resting a weathered hand on my shoulder.

I nodded, speechless.

"We're different here," he began. "We are not fighters like you or your comrades in Bhopal. Everyone is an integral cog in the survival machine. We put ourselves at risk to bring back salvageable vessels found and reported by the transporters. Maybe we'll get lucky one day and find another plane!"

Ondo gave an uncomfortable laugh. "After what Hemant told me, I can't say I'm in a hurry to ride on one. I don't think he is either."

Banyu loosed a deep laugh, slapping each of us on the back. I forced a chuckle at the sentiment. Some transporters had been lucky enough to come across a museum near Pyramid City a few decades ago. The plane was brought to Pod Baghdad where it was painstakingly restored by Engineer Hera and christened the *Sekhmet*. Without her, Samson, and the rest of the crew, we would've died in the desert. The familiar tug of loss weighed on my heart thinking about the continually growing list of people who had given their lives for this mission. Om Banyu could read the look on my face.

"Dwelling on the past will only hamper your future," said the wizened sailor. "Your mission lies ahead and so should your thoughts."

A leathery-skinned man approached the vessel with a clipboard tucked under his arm. A wide hat hid his face until he craned his head up to greet us.

"Captain Banyu," he said, "How did you fair?"

"Quite well, Boatmaster Francisco!" Banyu replied. "We've rescued them. As suspected, they are Memo's Misfits."

"Fantastic," said the boatmaster. "I'll review your manifest as soon as we get our guests squared away. While you're in port, I'll have a radio installed on your vessel. Now, which one of you is Hemant?"

Until this point, I'd been helping the men move a handful of used supply crates towards the gangplank, halfway listening to the unfolding dialog, but at the mention of my name, my head swiveled so fast I thought it would wrench off.

"I'm Hemant," I said. "How do you know my name?"

"I bear news of your brother, Arjun. He—"

"Make way! Make way for your Prime Minister, the honorable Rodolfo De León," shouted a man of comically small stature compared to the stout dock hands surrounding him.

"Wait! What about my brother?" I yelled.

"There will be plenty of time for idle chit-chat later, my boy," said the small man, his thin draping mustache and beard waving on the ocean breeze.

My eyes sprang to Francisco's face, who nodded before I lost sight of him among the bustle of bodies. At that moment, every other thought evaporated like the morning mist. All I could think about was what the boatmaster had been about to tell me. *Arjun.* I had to know what had occurred since we'd parted ways. We hadn't left each other's company on friendly terms, but I was desperate to locate him. I'd never be able to bear my reflection again if something happened to him. It'd be like losing half of my soul. The second I was free, I would tear the city apart to find this Francisco.

Behind the frail man was a portly gentleman with a bright red sash, holding a runt of a dog. A highly-maintained goatee encircled his thin-lipped mouth. By the manner in which he carried himself, I judged the man had an arrogance that would rival Yanus, the now-deceased pompous leader of the Saharan transporters. Even as much as I'd hated that man, his screams as he was carted off by the mud raptors still haunted my dreams. That was no way for anyone to die.

"Welcome! Welcome, my friends, to Pod Bandung!" the pretentious man said as the little dog yapped from his clutches. "I'm Prime Minister Rodolfo De León. I've found the rumors of your travels nothing short of enthralling. As long as you remain inside my humble city, you will be my honored guests."

"Umm… Thank you," said Huck running his hands through his thick black hair nervously.

Since leaving Pod Horizonte, we'd run into all sorts of leaders spanning the range from kind and helpful to menacing and dangerous. Rudolfo seemed friendly enough, but his kindness felt ingenuine. Though we were typically anxious to rest, resupply, and be on our way as soon as possible, our departure was always subject to the moods of the pod hierarchy.

"You must be weary from your troublesome journey," said the minister, beckoning a group of men carrying a plush sedan chair who lowered it so that he could climb aboard. "Advisor Zimo will show you to your lodging. You will join me for a welcome dinner tonight. Formal dress. You must be tired of those rags."

With that, the man was carted off through the sea of dock workers. His polished, pristine litter couldn't have looked more out of place among the working-class surroundings. I looked at Huck, eyebrow arched. The detachment of the prime ministers from reality never ceased to amaze me.

"You heard the minister, please follow me," said the willowy Zimo in a nasal voice, turning to walk away.

"Our friend is injured," I said, gesturing to Roque, causing Zimo to turn. "He broke his leg and needs medical treatment."

A look of exasperation quickly passed over Zimo's face before he responded. With a double clap, two members of his retinue darted over to Roque's stretcher and carried him off without a word. Fen made a move to accompany him, but Zimo stood in her path.

"The minister wishes *all* of you to attend dinner. Your friend will receive the necessary care and join you there," said Zimo, his voice becoming whinier. "Now, we've lost enough time as it is. Follow me."

We grabbed our belongings and the mission-crucial bomb. With thanks, we bid adieu to Captain Banyu and his crew who'd saved us from that tiny hole in the Indian Ocean. I caught myself hoping I would get to see them again.

"Is it just me, or is this guy super annoying?" I whispered to Ariadne as we walked.

"It's not just you," she said, cracking a thin smile.

"I've never seen anything like this place," said Ondo.

"It's something else," I said, still mesmerized by the sights.

Passing through crowded city streets under the open sky was an eerie sensation. The port city's interior was scattered with small shack-like homes built one atop of another, all protected by weapon emplacements on the looming walls. Sporadically placed throughout the city were small concrete shelters partially recessed into the ground, presumably for large-scale attacks. In the direction we headed, a guard tower stretched high into the sky.

"I knew about this place, but I never had any idea it looked like this," said Omar. "There are enough ships here to supply the world's transporters."

"With the sea locust out there, do you really think any of these ships stand a chance?" asked Krista, voicing the concern on all of our minds. "Maybe before but now?"

Ahead, nestled between what looked like warehouses, a cavernous tunnel appeared to sprout from the surrounding landscape. Zimo led us inside and day transitioned into the familiar green glow of fluorescent lights that I'd grown up under. *This must lead to the pod proper.* Zimo ushered us towards a small open tram on one of the lengths of track that seemed to stretch on infinitely down the tunnel. There was no sign of De León, but Roque was being strapped in a few cars ahead. Workers ending their shift filed into the cramped cars at the rear as Zimo led us to more spacious, comfortable seating up front. Marie climbed on trepidatiously.

"This is new," said Fen, as Ondo climbed on board, his giant frame lurching the entire car.

"Hey, you think there are any more of those Kraken things?" I asked Trivia.

She shrugged, turning to take in the last bit of natural light before we disappeared underground. "It's a struggle to separate fact from fiction, but sightings have spiked in recent decades. Reports have mainly been from the southeastern quadrant of the globe, which aligns with our experience. As much as I like to believe we've left behind the only one, I find that hard to believe. It's not like there are many attack survivors to interview."

I shuddered at the thought of their being more than one of these beasts. As the tram lurched forward with a whine from its electric motors, I couldn't help but dwell on the fact that to reach the Australian Territory we still had to cross a wide swath of open ocean—a swath that no one returned from.

CHAPTER 6: KOLYA

When the reddish dust finally settled from the air, it revealed the monstrosities that had torn through the long-abandoned vehicles littering the old highway to reach Arjun and me. Half of what I beheld came as no surprise. Mere meters ahead of us were two multipedes, their spiky, bulbous bodies extending out behind them until they vanished in their dusty wake. Instead of attacking as they tended to do, the pedes stood with their feet planted, rippling as if they were catching their breath. What I was wholly unprepared for was not the arrival of the pedes, but the vile creatures mounted atop of them. *Demented.* A vile word that sent chills down the spine of anyone with sense. A corrupt race of humans, a Demented's mind was severely twisted from consuming the hemolymph of the inverts. I took a deep breath, glancing at my young companion.

The Arthropods had made it clear that we were protected, and had made no effort to attack us on our journey to the Australian Territory. That courtesy in no way extended to the savages lingering ahead of me. I regretted forcing Arjun to put away his razor net. I slowly let my hand fall to the pommel of my sword but froze when the Demented on the left let out an animalistic grunt as he made eye contact. I examined the creature. Once human, the male was almost unrecognizable as the same species, having mutilated his body as they were wont to do. His visible skin was painted in old scars and fresh rudimentary stitches. He wore an outfit of leather from a source I'd rather not dwell on, since most of Earth's larger animals had been wiped out by the Arthropods. I withdrew the hand from my sword and the creature responded with a slow nod.

The second was once a female. She dismounted, throwing her reigns onto the pede's back and menacingly sauntered towards us. Similar in appearance to others, her body boasted metal and wood implants that made my skin crawl. Her flesh was as angry as her face. The scientist in me wondered what the life expectancy for these… *things* was given the prevalence of open wounds and poor hygiene. The woman got so close, I could smell the stench of her rancid flesh. *Not long,* I mused. She pulled out a leather canteen and took several long draughts from it, the viscous black liquid ran down her chin and onto her scarred breast, just visible under her leather vest. *Perhaps the hemolymph somehow prolongs life, Sveta,* I thought, addressing my deceased research assistant who acted as my conscience. I recalled Marie using the same dark liquid to help Leisel recover. The woman was hardly better than the Demented as far as I was concerned, using the creatures' hemolymph for her trade—and worse, communing with spirits! I regretted that Marie hadn't died at the edge of my poison-laced blade.

The female offered me the canteen, making a guttural sound that could be construed as friendly. I stole a glance at Arjun. There was no way in hell I was drinking that sludge. I shook my head and politely added, "No, thank you," hoping somewhere deep within her mind she understood some United English. The woman shrugged as she and her companion both laughed. Her haunting chuckle stood my hair on end. The woman gestured us to the backs of the multipedes to a smooth spot where the spikes had been ground flush with the carapace.

"I believe they are offering us a ride," said Arjun, relaxing nearly imperceptibly.

To our surprise, the woman nodded.

"Will you take us to the Hive?" I asked.

The woman's head cocked like one of the confused stray dogs that subsisted on the meager scraps of Pod Baghdad.

"The Hive," I said, making gestures with my hands imitating the images of the early Arthropod mounds that had been photographed so many centuries ago. That had been well before all the local humans were killed, or perhaps, turned into Demented.

The man barked something to the woman, who turned to me and nodded. She growled the first thing that sounded vaguely word-like, "Rafdo."

I nodded, wishing Arjun's friend Ciro was with us to provide his linguistic opinion. Based on what Arjun had told me, with enough time, the boy possessed enough talent that he could likely hack their language and be conversational by the time we reached the Hive.

"You think *rafdo* means hive?" I asked.

"It would make sense," said Arjun, reluctantly making his way to the relatively tame Arthropod and slinging the strap of his rucksack over a blunted spike in a similar fashion to the Demented.

Our sun-darkened guide climbed back onto her mount and stared at me, her oily skin harshly reflecting the light. I took a deep breath and followed their example, walking to the second pede and throwing my stuff on top. *I cannot believe I'm about to ride this thing steered by a Demented warrior. God help me.* I struggled to sling my right leg over the pede's rotund body, repeatedly sliding off of its smooth chitinous exoskeleton. The Demented howled their guttural laughs before the male of the pair eventually climbed down to help me. With unbelievable strength for what appeared to be a disease-ravaged body, he nearly threw me onto the creature before returning to his seat.

He barked what sounded like a question that I could only interpret as "Ready?" I nodded, hoping it was the correct response, and the creatures turned in such a tight circle that I thought their segmented bodies would crack at the seams. The creatures had barreled towards us, so I expected the same speed on the return trip but was mistaken. With the road clear, the pair took on what felt like a leisurely pace, but it still must have been nearing 100 kilometers per hour. If this was their casual pace, I couldn't fathom the top speed of the multi-legged inverts. I was appreciative of the body in front of me deflecting the wind, but the smell wafting back reeked of rot and decay. *Sveta, are these creatures even fully alive?* I caught myself wondering if the hemolymph had some parasitic quality allowing it to take over the host's body. I shivered, concerned about the small amount several of us inadvertently consumed in Evans' camp.

As the multipedes devoured the kilometers, I was taken aback by the landscape. What had begun as verdant, rolling hills transitioned into increasingly smaller plants and flatter, drier land. What in the morning had started as a band of bright green stretching into the horizon had now faded to a melange of browns and tans, broken up by the shrubbery indicative of a more arid climate. As the day wore on, I realized the sky was once again teeming with menacing life. Since Arjun had taken out the inverts' antenna bug network, which not only bathed the Earth in an electromagnetic field but also served as the Queens' eyes and ears, the sky had been clear for the first time in centuries. However, this close to the Arthropods' Hive, we were surrounded by roving patrols of every type of flying invert: stinging mud raptors, flesh-rending hook beetles, head-munching split wings, and poisonous powder moths. Each was supremely lethal in its own right should the inverts decide to turn against us. With their air superiority, it was no wonder human survival here had been impossible. Our guides took it in stride, oblivious to the constant threat. *Could their vile drink act as a mind-control agent or are they too stupid to know better?* I needed to discuss my theories with Arjun when I had a chance.

Like a train, we chugged along through what would've been lunch and dinner until the sky took on the indicative hues of dusk. Shortly before all traces of sunlight vanished, I noticed unnatural changes in the landscape. As we ventured inland, large sculpted earthen mounds of reddish dirt sprouted from the arid terrain. What had begun as a scattered few now lined the horizon from one end to the other. Each intricate mound was several meters wide at the base and reached as high into the sky as their bases would allow. Each entrance of the chimney-like structures hinted that the mounds' internal complexity was more than their exterior let on. As night grew darker, I could hear the chilling screeches and whoops coming from inside the towering mounds, distorted by the tubes into a gut-wrenching trumpeting. Unless my eyes were tricking me, the mounds emitted clouds of inverts like smoke, pluming from the tops. I felt a pit open in my stomach. *God help us.* There was no way in hell we would've lived following the other group's plan. They were as good as dead.

I'd never been quite so unsettled, dwelling on how many of the creatures lurked beyond my field of vision. My head pounded from the day's heat and lack of water. Regretfully, I'd placed my pack too far back, and I had endured the climate and motion on an empty stomach. By the time we pulled to a stop, my lips felt as though they would crack if I spoke. I drained my canteen, feeling the tepid water run down through my beard as I chugged. No sooner than I'd finished, I pulled out my flask a took a swig of the hooch inside. *Not exactly hydrating, but I'm beyond caring.*

"Careful, Kolya," said Arjun, waddling over, obviously as achy as I was from the long trip. "It won't do you any good if you vomit it back up."

I nodded. Ever the pragmatist. "I guess we're eating our rations. I can't imagine that we want to eat whatever this pair has in their knapsacks. Not that I have much appetite after what we saw today. This is not a friendly place," I said, searching for the inverts I knew were there but couldn't see. I felt disconcerted staying out so long after dark, exposed without a bivvy masking my presence. "I don't know how the others expect to beat them with brute force."

"That's why I chose to follow you and leave my brother. Without significant changes, I believe their plan to be suicidal. I hope they have the sense to turn back before they are killed," said Arjun. "At our current rate, we'll likely be at the Hive in a matter of days, not weeks, as previously thought. I can't begin to imagine what this parley with the Queens will be like."

"There's no way to properly prepare for such a momentous, yet mysterious, occurrence. We truly know nothing of these creatures, but I suppose that's part of the thrill. We have so much to learn. Their intelligence may not be apparent at first glance, but they obviously have more knowledge of space travel than our predecessors. Perhaps they are even the dominant species in this arm of the galaxy. How else can you explain their presence?"

"I can't," said Arjun, shaking his head. The boy never liked questions he didn't have an answer to. "I hope they provide us with some insight, though I'm unsure of a reliable method of communication. The fact that they bear so many similarities to Earth's native insects leads me to believe life *must* evolve in similar ways on other planets. That could mean there are more humanoids out there. More viable planets. Perhaps humanity isn't as close to extinction as we believe."

"Unless the Arthropods have wiped them all out," I said, "but let's hope otherwise."

I started to fish out a ration bar from my pack when the male approached me. He slapped his chest and growled, "Neesh."

"Is that your name?" I asked.

He cocked his head as the female had done earlier. The manish creature made eye contact, but I struggled to match his red-eyed gaze. I repeated his gesture, slapping my chest, and said, "Kolya."

The man nodded with enthusiasm, growling an attempt at my name, "Kohla." He pointed at the woman, "Jigna."

I nodded, pleased with our rudimentary communication. Arjun approached and introduced himself.

"Arjun," he said.

"Arjna," our guides growled in tandem.

"Well, we know their names," said Arjun. "It's a start."

Neesh barked some foreign instructions, pointing at some large logs, then pointed at a natural depression in the earth. Then he pointed at some brush, then again at the depression. Then mimed what I presumed to be fire.

"I understand," I said, nodding. "Apparently our ambassadorial status doesn't preclude manual labor."

I couldn't decide whether it felt more ridiculous or shameful to speak with such a corrupted being. These beings, however, were a means to an end. With their help, we'd reach the Hive where I could begin my negotiations with the Arthropod Queens. Neesh and Jigna patted the pedes, which then wandered off into the woods to presumably hunt for their own dinner. Our Demented guides disappeared in the other direction, leaving Arjun and me alone to arrange the campsite.

Above our heads, formations of inverts circled on their sweeping patrols of the continent, visible in the dim moonlight by the stars they occluded. We were far into "enemy" territory, yet somehow protected ambassadors of the human race, however scant million of us remained between the pod cities and clusters of Survivors. Maybe throw in a few hundred thousand Demented for good measure since I suppose they are still technically human. If I could establish a peaceful coexistence with the Arthropods, the first thing I would ask of them is for the eradication of their kind. The Earth didn't need to give evil any more of a foothold, especially in such a crucial time as our reconstruction.

Arjun and I quietly arranged a small campsite and had a fire roaring by the time our friends returned with something in tow. The local eucalyptus burned hot and fast, giving off a pleasant aroma and driving away the mosquitos as the night grew cool. Neesh pulled the canvas-wrapped load to the fireside and uncovered it. I nearly leapt out of my skin. Inside the bundle was a writhing juvenile cave grub. I had no doubts as to the purpose of its presence.

"I don't care what they think," I said. "I refuse to eat that!"

"May I remind you that eating the meat is harmless, provided it's properly drained," said Arjun.

"I don't care if they drain it, roast it, and slather it with garlic butter, I'm not eating it!"

"Suit yourself," said Arjun.

Neesh and Jigna proceeded to cut apart the grub while it squealed its protests as they ate clump after clump of its gooey raw flesh dripping with the invert's thick black hemolymph. I looked at Arjun, whose coppery skin had paled.

"On second thought," he said, "I will stick to rations this evening."

CHAPTER 7: DARREN

I sat at my desk, mindlessly shuffling images around the artboard for some restaurant's new holo menu. Promoting the establishment's new food specials seemed so unimportant with everything that was unfolding in the Outback. It'd been six weeks since the rock, dubbed AS-42, had crashed into the Earth. According to the news feeds, the object's impact should've caused a mass extinction event. They brought expert after expert, but no one had an explanation for the odd physics. Over the weeks, enough amateur footage had been collected to determine just how large the space rock was. Even slowing, it had still hit the ground with enough force to bury three-quarters of itself into the ground. Every time I closed my eyes, I was haunted by the visible kilometer-tall monolith surrounded by its relatively small crater in the reddish clay of the Australian Territory. And I wasn't alone. Overall, our office-wide productivity had dropped by over half.

For all the discussion about it, we still knew next to nothing. The first thing the United Territories government did was set up a fifteen-kilometer perimeter. Not even the field scientists that had been flown to Pine Gap, the nearby base, were allowed near the thing. All studies were being conducted from outside the perimeter with the most sophisticated tools the UTE had at their disposal, half of which had pronounceable names. Every time they'd mention one, Patricia would explain what it was before the talking head could. Leaning my head back, I palmed my eyes, trying for the umpteenth time to regain my focus.

"This is a bunch of crap, man," said Stepan, flinging his light pen onto the desk. "How the hell are we supposed to work like this? I've never seen you unable to concentrate."

"Yeah. I keep telling myself it's only a stupid rock, but not a fiber of my being seems to believe that."

"I'm right there with you. We need to get out of here. Extended lunch at O'Rourke's?"

"Again? If we keep this up, we're going to get fussed at."

"Look around," said Stepan, arms gesturing widely. "No one will miss us."

I spun around. From our joint cubicle, not a single person was at their desk.

"Alright, but I'm not having more than one drink," I said. "I'm already having enough trouble focusing."

"That's me boy!" said Stepan in a terrible Irish accent.

"Use that at O'Rourke's, and I bet they'll kick your ass."

"Spoilsport."

In a matter of minutes, we'd walked the distance to the pub. It was nice to escape the claustrophobic confines of the office and get some fresh air. I closed my eyes for a few seconds of the walk, taking in the singing birds, the regular passes of the light rail, the clicking of bike chains, and the occasional whine of an electric car. I felt a hand slap my chest and my eyes sprung open.

"Dude! You almost walked out into the freaking street," said Stepan. "Are you sure you need to drink at all?"

"Sorry, man," I said. "I've got a lot on my mind. Patricia's been working crazy long hours. Even when she's at home, she's constantly getting phone calls. I can't seem to escape all of this."

"That's why I'm dragging you out of the office for a pint of stout. That is unless you wanted something a little different. I always have some gummies stashed in my drawer."

"No, thanks," I said, forcing a chuckle.

The perpetual stoner might be able to work high, but one of the many things I had learned in my university classes was that all THC was good for was making me lazy and giggly. Not to mention, the last thing I needed to be right now was more paranoid.

"By the way, Tricia sounded great on the radio the other day," he said, holding open the bar door for me.

I smiled at his use of Tricia. My wife hated when people shortened her name, but for some reason, Stepan was one of the few who could get away with it, even in her company. I'll give it to him, the man had a way with people. The moment I walked into O'Rourke's, the tension in my shoulders dissipated. There was something about this place that relaxed me. The dim lighting and malty odors made me feel as though I could finally let go of my worries. I was thankful I had a buddy like Stepan to drag me out when I needed it.

"The usual, guys," said Tina, the host.

I nodded and we followed her back to the corner of the bar where we liked to hide out. Stepan's eyes never drifted from Tina's ass. When she turned to head back to her station, she caught his gaze and smiled. He was faithful to his long-time girlfriend, but that had never meant he'd stopped admiring the scenery. With his boyish good looks and laid-back charm, he'd never had to work hard for feminine company. Me, on the other hand, I was glad to be out of the dating circuit and in a stable relationship that I intended to keep for the rest of my life. I heard the drone of the news and turned to my left where the bartender had clicked the wall screen on for a patron.

"Dammit," said Stepan through a mouthful of bar nuts and throwing up his hands. "We can't escape it anywhere. I'll ask him to turn it down."

I shook my head and pulled him back down. "It's fine. It's that dude's right."

The bartender brought out two dark beers with thick heads and I downed mine faster than expected, not taking the time I normally would to relish the thick, velvety chocolate flavor.

"Alright," said Stepan. "What's up? I've known you long enough that when I see you drain a pint, you're not okay."

I took a deep breath. "They called Patricia last night. They want her out at the site."

"The site? As in *that* sight?" he said, pointing towards the glowing screen.

I nodded, then let my head droop. "It makes sense. She's an expert in her field. Like you said, she's a great science communicator."

"But she's an astrophysicist. I know her opinions are important, but with all the VR tech we have, does she even need to physically be there?"

"For one, she said there's nothing like having your hands on a specimen," I waited for Stepan's usual wisecrack, but he let the opportunity pass. "Two, she's not just an astrophysicist, she's an exobiologist."

"Whoa, whoa, whoa. Tricia never told me that," he said, surprised.

"She doesn't exactly advertise it," I said. "The field is still in its infancy, even being around for as long as it has. There's still so much resistance to life on other celestial bodies. Neither the base on Luna nor Mars have found so much as a hint of life yet."

"But the fact they are flying her out there says something, right? They are thinking the same thing we all are."

"I'm trying not to read too much into this, Step. The UTE is bringing in people from all over the globe, experts in every remotely-related field. All we know at this point, Patricia included, is that the rock has the same elements as Earth and that it has some residual radioactivity from space. Aside from the fact it avoided our radar and slowed down, it's a big dumb rock."

"Darren," he said, grabbing my shoulders, "It avoided our radar and slowed down. What about that says big dumb rock to you?"

"Hey! Hey! Somethin's happ'ning," slurred the drunk absorbed in the feed.

I turned back to Stepan, who was already rising. We made our way over to the large panel covering the wall behind the bar.

"…reports of low-magnitude earthquakes emanating from the meteorite. On-site seismologists believe the tremors are aftershocks from the meteorite's initial impact. Stay tuned to our non-stop coverage as we look into this new phenomenon."

Stepan was right. I couldn't keep lying to myself. The problem was if I stopped convincing myself that it was just a rock, then I had to consider what it might actually be. I stared at the rotor-wing footage playing on loop of the craggy, menacing rock. I couldn't bear the thought of Patricia being closer to that thing, whatever it was.

"You look like you need another pint," said Stepan.

"No," I said, shaking my head. "I need to go home to my family."

•••••••

"You're home early," Patricia said, wrapping her arm around me and squishing Alexander between us.

The living room of our apartment was littered with neatly folded clothes as my wife packed for her flight to the Australian Territory. She set my son down and continued pondering what articles to carry with her in the limited space provided on the supersonic transport.

"I realized this morning that I wanted to spend as much time with you as possible before you go. I took off the rest of the day and tomorrow," I said.

"Honey, I've been on field missions before," she said, smiling.

"I know, but this one feels different."

She wrapped both arms around me again, this time sans child, and looked deep into my eyes. God, she was gorgeous. How a graphic artist like me managed to score such a fiercely intelligent and ravishingly beautiful woman like this was beyond me.

"It's just another field assignment," she said. "I'm sure there's a logical explanation for everyone's fears. And if you're worried about the quakes, they said not one of them had been above a magnitude of three. This is pretty exciting for me. This is a chance to study something that has been careening through space. Maybe, just maybe, there's some trace life form on it from the unknown."

"That 'trace life form' is what I'm worried about," I said, resting my forehead against hers. "I don't want you coming down with flesh-devouring space fungus."

Patricia laughed melodiously.

"My biggest concerns are our local life contaminating the meteorite, not the other way around," she said, still giggling.

"Regardless, please be careful."

"Of course," she said, rubbing Alex on the head.

"How long before I see you again?" he asked.

"My flight leaves Detroit at 8:00 am, and since your dad took off work, you guys can accompany me to the airport. Let's see, a five-hour subsonic to LA, a short layover, then a six-hour supersonic to

Sydney… I'll VR you tonight from my hotel. I don't fly out to Pine Gap immediately. You can stay up a few minutes later than normal."

"Yippee!" Alex screamed.

It was my turn to laugh. "I might have to use late bedtimes as negotiation tactics while you're gone."

Patricia rolled her eyes. "Don't let him stay up too late. And you guys don't spend the entire time mainlining pepperoni pizza and apple juice."

"I was planning on mixing in Asian food every other day."

She punched me playfully in the arm.

"If it makes you feel better, you can call and check up on us every night," I said.

"I'm going to try to call you daily, but I can't promise that it will happen," she said. "Communications will be undoubtedly monitored. I haven't been completely read in, but I'm sure some things haven't been released to the public. It's possible—"

I kissed her so long that I heard groans of complaint from Alexander.

"We'll be fine. Call when you can, okay?"

Patricia rocked back in a mild romantic stupor. *Maybe that's how I got her.*

"Yes, sir," she said, giggling, then leaning over to whisper, "Help me get Alex fed and in bed, and I'll leave you with something to remember me by."

"Yes, ma'am!" I said, maybe a little too enthusiastically.

••••••••

The next morning, we woke up early to accompany Patricia on the train to the terminal. Alex wasn't near as cranky as I suspected he might be thanks to his early bedtime. I glanced over at my wife, admiring her bathed in the light of the sunrise, drifting in through the window. She caught me staring and smiled sheepishly back, tucking her hair behind her ear. We made silly faces at each other for most of the ride, feeling like carefree adolescents again after the night before.

When we arrived at the airport, the mood was different from normal. Air traffic had been reinstated since the emergency worldwide ban, but flights were limited to those of necessity. With the proliferation of high-quality VR over the last few decades, the need for travel has been drastically reduced. Usually, the terminal was a mix of business and pleasure seekers going about their travels, but today the mood was more somber. I couldn't make out any discernible tourists, and there appeared to be a heavy presence of the Territorial Guard.

When we arrived at Patricia's terminal, a suited gentleman stood waiting with a sign reading "Dr. Taggert."

"That's me," Patricia said. "I didn't know I'd be getting an official escort."

"You are worthy of one, Doctor," I said, kissing her on the cheek.

She grabbed my head and planted a lingering kiss on my lips. "I love you," she said.

"I love you, too," I said, blinking back the tears.

I helped her load her bags onto the cart her escort, Grayson, had provided. Apparently, the man would be escorting her all the way to Pine Gap where he would act as her assistant. As Grayson adjusted her bags, I couldn't help but notice the firearm in the shoulder holster under his arm.

"How dangerous is this situation?" I asked.

"It's just a precaution, I'm sure," she whispered. "They told me on the phone that they are having some trouble with alien junkies and religious fanatics trying to sneak out to the rock. One of the researchers was hospitalized after an assault."

"Why didn't you tell me any of this?" I asked.

"I didn't want to worry you, Darren," she said, gesturing. "I have an armed guard. I'll be fine. I promise."

"That's not something you can promise."

"Well, I will do everything in my power to stay safe so that I can return home to my boys."

"That's better. I love you."

"I love you too, honey," she said, then picking up Alexander. "And I love you too!"

She swung him around as he cackled with glee.

"Dr. Taggert, it's time," said Grayson.

She nodded, setting Alex down. "I'll talk to you tonight."

She blew us each a kiss and vanished with her escort through the double doors of the terminal.

CHAPTER 8: HUCK

As the narrow, vibrating tram sped through the tunnel towards Pod Bandung proper, I couldn't help but feel claustrophobic. The tunnel was wide enough to accommodate multiple tracks for people and cargo, but we'd spent so much time on the surface that being underground felt so unnatural. Humans were meant to live on the surface. It was our rightful place. I remembered the gulls that flew above the buoy, the first birds aside from farmed poultry I'd seen in my life. I couldn't imagine them having to remain underground, though I did chuckle at the prospect of them flying around the central shaft pooping on the workers toiling away below.

"What's so funny?" asked Ariadne, slipping her hand into mine.

"Nothing," I replied. "I was just imagining birds in the pods."

She smiled, revealing her dimples. *Man, she's cute.* "The prime minister seems friendly enough."

"I suppose that's a word for it," said Omar, adjusting his long naginata to be more comfortable. "I recognize ass-kissing when I see it."

"What could he gain from befriending us?" asked Leisel, struggling to keep her hair out of her face in the breeze generated by the tram's speed.

"Considering his arrogance, I'm sure he would find a way to play it to his advantage," said Fen.

The rest of the trip passed in silence, hypnotizing me with its repetition of aged white tiles and fluorescent lights. Eventually, I could distinguish a glow ahead. It wasn't daylight, but enough to tell that a destination was close. As the car began to slow, I hopped up and sat next to Hemant, who'd stared ponderously at the floor the entire journey, his wide shoulders slumped as his hand rested on the nuclear device he'd lugged halfway across the planet.

"Thinking about Arjun?" I asked.

"When am I not?" he smirked. "I keep asking myself if there's anything I could've done differently."

"You know there's not. You were being a big brother. Maybe a little over-protective, but who wouldn't be in this madness? Kolya's the only one to blame. He poisoned your brother's thoughts and turned him against you. We'll catch up with them, rescue Arjun, and blow the Hive to smithereens. Then you'll have a lifetime to reconcile with him while Kolya rots behind bars."

"You know Marie nor I have any intention of letting him walk out of the Australian Territory alive," he said, staring at me with eyes full of hatred.

"I don't think killing him is the right answer," I said, "but I wouldn't stand in your or Marie's way. He deserves a fair trial, but I'm reluctant to take his life."

"You heard Madan," Hemant said, raising his voice. "He literally permitted you to mete out battlefield justice. I didn't love the guy, but he died with honor. He considered your judgment adequate to sentence Kolya to death! Is that not enough?"

I felt hurt, but I tried not to show it. I hated seeing Hemant like this.

Zimo stood and braced himself against the tram's railing as it pulled to a stop, purposefully ignoring the conversation. "I would like to officially welcome you to Pod Bandung," he said as the tram entered the pod.

I was awestruck as we emerged from the tunnel. Every pod we'd been inside had been constructed near identically, but with the addition of the subterranean tunnel, an entire level in Bhopal was a depot. But that wasn't what had taken my breath away. It was the 360-degree mural that covered the walls of the entire area.

"It's beautiful," said Ariadne, who shared my fondness for art.

"You like it?" asked Zimo. "Minister Rudolfo has always been a patron of the arts. He commissioned our best painters to do what you see here. You will find this city to be far less drab than the others you've visited. I dare say that the inhabitants of Pod Bandung are the happiest on Earth."

"That's a big claim," mumbled Krista.

"Is that music?" asked Ondo.

Everyone froze, all listening intently. Sure enough, soft music played through the speakers of the pod-wide address system.

"These sounds… they are incredible," said Marie. "I've never heard anything so pleasant."

"Oh my God! Are you tearing up?" asked Omar.

Marie's hand fell to her dagger and even the unmovable Omar looked intimidated. As a survivor, she'd seen things that I couldn't begin to imagine. She was nothing short of lethal, not completely trusted, and almost impossible to read. Crying though… that was new.

"But how?" asked Ariadne, climbing out of the low tram.

"Originally, the transporters discovered a set of vinyl records inside a trawler's hold. We were lucky that the previous captain had a penchant for the ancient media. Rudolfo has prized them. Since then, he's put out rewards for anything new to add to his growing collection. He plays it non-stop through the simulated day. I believe this one is Gliere."

"That's so cool!" said Trivia, jerking Hemant up. "It makes me want to twirl around. Imagine, Hemant, to be able to make those sounds!"

We all laughed as this comically small girl flung around Hemant's muscular bulk with ease, moving in time to the instrumental music. The pair couldn't have looked more different, large-framed Hemant with his darker Bhopali features and petite Trivia with her pale, freckled skin. The feelings between them were undeniable. Trivia, with her vast knowledge of, well… everything, reminded us all of Hemant's missing twin.

"If you will accompany me, I will show you all to your apartments," said Zimo.

"Just a minute, Zimo," said Ariadne, making her way to the muraled wall. "I want to check this out."

"*Advisor* Zimo," the man corrected, though everyone had stopped listening.

We joined Ariadne at the foot of the painting, just in time to hear her gasp.

"Umm… this is not what I expected," she said.

I gazed up at the mural, for the first time analyzing it as opposed to appreciating its general beauty. It only took me a second to find what had captured her attention. "It's all Rudolfo," I said, easily recognizing the man.

"Look, here he is fighting the Arthropods with a sword," said Krista, running her hand on the smooth surface. "What's that falling in the background."

"Holy crap," said Omar. "That's the invert's aerial network."

"You mean the one you guys took down before we met?" asked Trivia.

"Yeah," said Hemant, dumbfounded.

I spun around the room, taking in the revisionist history that surrounded me. At the epicenter of each notable event of the last few decades was Rudolfo. He'd painted himself as the hero.

"Dear God!" said Krista, exasperated. "Can't we ever just go to a pod that's normal?"

"We've spent too long underground," said Ariadne, putting her palm on her forehead. "Everything is twisted. Humanity needs a massive reset."

"All the more reason to carry out our duty," said Fen.

"Excuse me," yelled Zimo from the tram. "Please allow me to escort you to your rooms now."

"I guess we need to get moving before he throws a hissy fit," I whispered as Ariadne chuckled.

Rodolfo probably liked the guy because he was a pandering wimp. The advisor would probably kiss Rudolfo's feet if asked.

"Surely no one believes this, right?" asked Leisel.

"Considering the things we've seen… I'm not making any assumptions," I said.

Zimo wordlessly led us to our apartments, which were the nicer ones on the higher levels of the hundred-story pod. By this point, we were used to special treatment—at least initially. There was always some discovery we'd make that would shed light on the extent of corruption in the pod. As I shared a look with Hemant, I was sure that we were both wondering when that curtain would fall this time.

"Please make yourselves at home," said Zimo. "You have several hours to get some rest, after which our master seamstress will oversee the final preparations for your dinner garments."

"Dinner garments?" Hemant asked, once Zimo was out of earshot.

I shrugged. I was done trying to understand the rigmarole that each prime minister set up for their guests. Each of us split off into our rooms. It had been days since any of us had rested on land, and all I could think of was a soft, motionless bed. The second the door was closed, Ariadne had her arms draped around me, hugging me tightly.

"Everything okay?" I asked.

"Yeah," she said, looking up into my eyes. "I'm just waiting for everything to go downhill, and I want to enjoy this moment before it does."

"They let us keep our weapons. Hell, Hemant and Trivia have a freaking nuclear bomb in their quarters. If the worst thing about Rudolfo is that he wants to suck up to us so he can play hero, I don't give a crap. I know who the real heroes are," I said, pulling Ariadne in for a lengthy kiss.

••••••••

I was leaning against the narrow island that divided the kitchenette from the living area watching the coffee percolate when there was a soft knock at the door. I stuck my head in the bedroom and woke Ariadne, closing the door behind me before I opened the hatch. A small Asian woman stood there, clothed in a dark wool-like fabric that came up high on her neck. Her graying hair was pulled back in a tight bun.

"My name is Xin Yi. I am here to fit you and Elite Ariadne with your garments for this evening."

"Please, come in," I said, as Ariadne joined me in the living area, pulling her hair back into a ponytail.

Xin Yi beckoned in two other ladies. One looked Asian like her, the other more Saharan. Each wheeled in a large rack of ornate clothes, filling the cramped space. Like our quarters, not a thing on the rack looked new, but all were beautiful and came in myriad different colors. Silently, she stared at us with her hand on her chin for an uncomfortably long time before selecting an outfit for each of us. She held a flowing green dress with fabric draped diagonally across it next to Ariadne's face.

"Yes," she said. "This brings out the emerald in your eyes."

She handed the dress to the Saharan woman who began taking Ariadne's measurements for the alterations and the two disappeared into the bedroom for fitting. The older woman repeated the process with me but grew noticeably more agitated with each outfit she rejected.

"*Aiyah!*" she said. "None of these match your spirit."

I let a chuckle escape.

"You laugh, but an incorrect choice will make you look silly and unnatural. The right one, however, will make you feel like you are floating. Every eye will be focused on you."

"I'm not sure I want that much attention," I said.

"You already have it. It's my job to make you look the part. Even for that windbag."

I could hear Ariadne's chuckle from the adjacent room through the thin wall panels.

"Auntie, you say too much," said the Asian woman taking my measurements.

"I'm too old to care what I say," she replied. "And as long as I make outfits flatter his ever-growing figure, he will tolerate my quips."

"What about that one," I said, pointing at a black outfit with a pinch of green similar to Ariadne's dress.

"I don't think so," she said. "That belonged to the prime minister's father. I don't know that it would have the desired effect."

"Can we try it?"

"The older I get, the more stubborn you young ones become. *Aiyah*, but don't say I didn't warn you."

She held the outfit up next to me and there was an audible gasp.

"That's the one, Auntie," said the Saharan woman, coming back into the room with Ariadne.

Then it was my turn to gasp. Ariadne practically glowed with radiant beauty. In a matter of minutes, the woman had teased out Ariadne's hair and applied the faintest makeup, no doubt reserved for only the most special occasions. On her roughest days, I thought Ariadne was beautiful, but today, she didn't seem of this Earth. From her ears dangled two subtle white teardrop pearls.

"You look… incredible," I said.

"Thanks," she said, her cheeks growing rosy as she tucked a stray curl behind her ear. "I'd still feel more comfortable in a jumpsuit fighting inverts than wearing this getup to a fancy dinner."

"You'll find the aristocracy to be just as treacherous," said Xin Yi, swatting my arm. "What are you waiting for? Go put on your suit so you don't look like her cart puller."

"Yes ma'am!"

CHAPTER 9: ARIADNE

I waited in the common room designated for our apartments, examining the pleasant abstract landscape that covered the aging walls. The image, no doubt, had been painted to provide a calming effect, but I couldn't help but think it straddled the razor-thin line between promoting hope and causing depression. I turned towards Huck, who sat next to me on the bench, arm wrapped around me. I'd love him regardless of how he looked, but groomed, clean, and nicely dressed—he looked incredible. I knew he was self-conscious of his injuries, but with the stubble he'd taken to keeping, his scars were barely noticeable, not that they bothered me in the first place. I looked down at my own injury, wondering how long it would take me to learn to paint again with fewer digits. With our destination set for the Hive, creative endeavors were the least of my worries at the moment. At least I had a hand, unlike Krista. I learned to cope, still able to draw and shoot my bow with lethal accuracy. Huck saw me staring down and took my hand, kissing where my fingers used to be.

"I love you," we said at the same time and smiled.

"You guys are too cute for your own good," said Trivia.

"You two don't look bad yourself!" I said, standing.

Where Huck and I wore green, Trivia and Hemant wore similar ensembles, but orange. Hemant looked dashing in his black suit with an orange handkerchief and tie. He kept fidgeting, tugging at the tighter parts of the outfit.

"Why couldn't we just wear clean jumpsuits?" he said. "It's not like we're known socialites."

"He's treating us with the respect he thinks we're owed," said Leisel, in a dress of gold that hovered above the floor.

I remembered Remi had compared Leisel to a goddess. If only she was alive to see her now, looking like she'd just stepped down from Olympus. Remi was yet another person who'd given their lives for our mission. She'd been such a good friend when I needed one most.

"Roque!" yelled Fen, emerging from her room and into the corridor.

After hugging him, she took control of Roque's wheelchair from the attendant and dismissed him, pushing Roque down the hall to where we were gathering.

"It's good to see you smiling, man," said Hemant.

"It's nice to feel like smiling. It might have something to do with the pain medication they gave me. For the first time in days, nothing hurts."

"What's the prognosis?" asked Trivia.

Roque's smile faded as his shoulders slumped. "This will have to be where we part ways. They told me…" Roque began, fighting back tears, "They told me that my bones are shattered. I'll never be able to walk normally again."

The room filled with gasps. Hemant slammed his fist into the wall in frustration as I ran to hug Roque. I couldn't help but think about the recouping, what the people were now called in Pod Horizonte who couldn't perform normal duties, living off basic rations and the generosity of others. I knew our friend Memo was making many positive changes. I hoped for Roque's sake that other pods would follow his example.

"Don't worry guys," he said, as Krista and Omar approached. "The medic who treated me said they have a fantastic rehabilitation program here as well as several jobs in which legs aren't as needed."

"Are you okay with that?" asked Fen, beginning to tear up. "You've spent so long training. Can you… Can you be happy, sitting in a chair behind a desk?"

Roque pulled her down into his lap, a move that if most men had tried would have gotten their asses kicked. "I'll be fine. I spent all of that time training to help destroy the inverts and destroy them I did. Hell, I contributed to the mission that's going to save the world!"

We all laughed, hoping he was right.

"And he's alive," said Krista, her thin, cream-colored dress perfectly complimenting her rich skin tone. "That's more than too many can say."

"Where's Ondo and Marie?" I asked.

In answer to my question, I heard pleading coming from the rooms as Marie stormed out into the corridor, Xin Yi's Saharan helper chasing after her with an armful of sashes.

"I will wear no such items!" she said to Huck, ignoring the woman's pleas.

Marie still wore the red-hooded, wide-sleeved outfit we'd found her in, albeit cleaner. In a way, I couldn't imagine seeing her in anything else. Surprisingly, it looked informal and formal at the same time.

"It's fine," Huck said to the tailor.

"But the minister… her prefers to be the only one in red during an event."

"The minister can get the hell over it," said Omar.

"As you wish, Elite," she said, bowing and backing down the corridor.

I gave a questioning look at Marie but was ignored. "What about Ondo?"

"I'll go check on him," said Hemant.

A few moments passed as we hung out and examined each other's outfits. It was good to know that none of us felt comfortable in such ornate apparel. We were soldiers and meant for the battlefield, not well-to-do parties held by aristocracy that had never set foot outside of a pod. Hemant eventually returned with a bashful Ondo, dressed in his jumpsuit.

"Now that's not fair," said Krista, half joking. "If Ondo gets to wear his jumpsuit, why do I have to wear all of this getup?"

Ondo took a breath and said something.

"What was that?" asked Huck. "I couldn't hear."

"Nothing will fit," he repeated, louder.

Omar began to laugh hysterically as everyone gave him the side eye. "What? The guy is too muscular for any normal clothes to fit. Dude, that's a freaking badge of honor!"

Ondo perked up, a grin slowly crossing his face. "Yeah, I guess you're right."

Before long, everyone was laughing, save for Marie. On the few occasions Marie laughed, it was terrifying. It was nice to feel safe, even if the moment never lasted. This is what kept us going, reminding me of just how much we needed each other. Like all good things, it came to an end when whiny Zimo came along and spoiled our fun.

••••••••

Dinner was served in a room I'd never seen before, so high up in the pod Nucleus that the meal was partially lit by the waning light of the sun shining through the portholes in the ceiling. Pod Nuclei were reserved for the administration and not a place the average resident was allowed, even the high-level trainees. That being said, we'd spent a fair amount of time as guests of prime ministers in the various Nuclei. This space was new. No spaces in a crowded pod were useless and what little space there was was utilized to the max. A dining hall of this size was pointless for numerous reasons. I couldn't help but wonder what more important things had been pushed from the space. Like the parts of the pod we'd seen, a mural lined the walls here as well, though depicting a massive battle between human and Arthropod. There was no sign of Rudolfo himself, but every human warrior bore a striking resemblance to the man.

"I don't think I can eat in here," said Krista, turning away from the violence-clad walls.

"Why would anyone want to eat in a room with this much death?" I asked.

"Because they've never lost a companion in battle, much less feared for their lives," said Huck.

I heard a throat clearing and turned to see Rudolfo had just arrived with Zimo in tow. Huck swallowed loudly next to me. Unless the prime minister was deaf, he'd heard Huck. For a split second, I saw anger on his face, quickly replaced by joy.

"Welcome, my friends," he said, petting the snub-nosed dog under his arm with a bejeweled hand. It is good to see you in more fitting attire. Xin Yi never ceases to amaze. Please, I know you are tired from your journey, sit."

Rudolfo clapped and several drably-dressed residents began to place drinks in front of each of us. I glanced at Huck and wondered if the meal reminded him as much as it did me of our first breakfast with that tyrant, Ndulue Zabu. I pulled out an antique, ornately carved wooden chair so beautiful that I was reluctant to sit on it. It must have been centuries old even before the Arthropod Landing. Rudolfo saw me admiring.

"My historians believe it to be over six hundred years old. It was found near Pod Munich. You wouldn't believe the amount of raw copper I had to trade to acquire it. If you look at this pattern here, you can see that—"

"Oh my god! Is that red wine?" asked Omar.

"It is!" Rudolfo said, having forgotten all about the chair. "You must have an educated palette. Please try it."

We all took a sip. I'd never been much of a drinker and what little was available in Horizonte was hooch, a hard liquor brewed by the laborers. I had drank more in that stupid buoy than I had in my entire life. I took a swallow of the wine, prepared for the acrid taste of hooch, but was pleasantly surprised. It still tasted alcoholic, but in a way that I was drawn to drink more. To savor more, parsing out each flavor.

"Wow!" said Krista. "This is incredible. I'm afraid to be alone with this stuff."

Rudolfo laughed heartedly. "Even here, it's an extremely scarce luxury. We only make a few crates a year. The land portion of the shipyard also serves as my personal farm. Most of our food is grown aquaponically below, but it's only fit for peasants."

At this, the woman placing my plate in front of me made eye contact. Was that envy—or anger? She quickly dropped her gaze and mumbled an apology. I stared wide-eyed at the plate in front of me. There was a large portion of meat bathed in a green sauce with decorated bones sticking straight up. At its side was a pile of blanched carrots, cucumber, and peppers covered in a beige sauce. It looked delicious. I reached for my utensils, my mouth watering, all tiredness forgotten. Huck reached over and put his hand on mine to stop me. Everything was dead quiet.

"Oh Great Maker," Rudolfo wailed loudly. I looked around the table, the few that were religious had bowed their heads and shut their eyes as the rest of us stared awkwardly at each other. "Why must the Arthropods continue to torment us? Why must we continue to live a life of desperation and deprivation?" Roque rolled his eyes at me. *Like Rudolfo's life is either.* He continued to drone on and on, lamenting his privileged life and humbly proclaiming his sacrifices. At one point Trivia stifled a giggle and got such a cold look from Zimo that she bit her lip to keep from snickering. Marie silently spun her wicked dagger, boring a tiny hole into the priceless tabletop. Ondo and Leisel, who had started absorbed and respectful in the prayer now were glancing out of the corners of their eyes, wondering if and when Rudolfo's whining would end. "Endow these young people before me with success so that we may once again have the dominion we deserve. Amen."

"Amen," everyone passionately said in unison, as if saying, "Thank the universe that's over."

"I'll be surprised if the food is still warm," whispered Fen into my ear.

Once the prime minister picked up his silver utensils, we took the cue to follow. My knife practically fell through the soft meat. The table was silent as we ate. Until this point, the best food I'd ever tasted was the first time out of Pod Horizonte when Kurt had prepared fresh river-fish sashimi. Up until that point, we'd been living off of the bland, nutritionally lacking food grown in the pods that had few fresh resources to add to the cycle. Kurt had introduced us to the wide variety of fresh food sources that were ubiquitous on the surface in addition to teaching us how to obtain it. I began to cry.

"What's wrong?" asked Huck.

"I was just wishing Kurt could taste this," I said, sobbing. "It's so good."

Aside from Omar, who rarely showed any emotion, anyone who'd known Kurt was tearing up.

"Who is this Kurt?" asked Rudolfo. "Since he is so important to you, I must invite him to my table. Zimo?"

"He's dead," said Omar. "Died back in the Latin Territory when we were bombed by a bunch of dusters. Something you'd know nothing about."

That look of anger passed across De León's face again, and just like before, was quickly replaced by a false veneer. "I apologize if I have caused you anguish, Mistress Ariadne," said the minister. "Master Huck, I fear I have caused your coterie distress. I'm sure you are tired. Please take your leave and rest. Tomorrow with more level heads we will discuss our plans to go to the Australian Territory."

"Our plans, sir?" asked Zimo, nearly spitting his drink.

"Rudolfo De León can't desert his people in their hour of need. I will accompany these youths to the creature's Hive and return victorious, a hero in my own right!"

Hemant, Huck, and I traded looks. *Here we go again.*

CHAPTER 10: HEMANT

My ears must be playing tricks on me. Surely this blowhard doesn't think he's going to accompany us to the Hive. Rudolfo doesn't look like he'd last a day without pampering, much less outside of the city walls. Judging by his soft hands, I doubted whether he'd even held a weapon aside from the silver knife he was using to cut his dinner.

"Surely you need me to stay here and run things in your absence," said Advisor Zimo.

"Nonsense. I need you to tend to my needs during the travel," Rudolfo said, slapping Zimo on the back. "It'll be great to be back out in the wild again."

"Sir, you've never—"

The prime minister's idiotic little dog started barking.

"See, even Lord Ransford agrees!"

Zimo's pleas faded as we made our way down the corridor. I was having to hustle to keep up with Fen, pushing Roque at a breakneck speed. The second we were out of earshot, everyone started talking in a jumbled mass of confusion.

"I'm not dying defending his ass."

"Who does he think he is?"

"He wants to go with *us?*"

"Why does everyone do this?"

"Can he even fight?"

"Like hell he is."

"Quiet!" said Huck. "I don't like it any more than you do, but we need his cooperation to get to the Australian Territory. Om Banyu is willing to take us, but he can't just leave on a whim. What's the harm in taking him?"

"Huck, man, we were looking at the same guy, right?" I asked. "I'd bet a month of ration points he's never set foot outside these walls. I mean, did you see his hands? Those are the hands of someone who's delegated everything and done nothing. I bet if you told him he had to eat lizard for dinner, he'd pass out."

Omar nodded, chuckling. "With that extra girth around his middle, I doubt he could run very far. He'll be picked off by a hook beetle before he takes three steps from the boat."

"That might happen," said Huck, "but I feel a responsibility for everyone, including him."

"In his case, you might need to let that go," said Krista. "He *did* invite himself."

"Maybe he can learn. Like I did," said Leisel.

"You didn't have just us, you had Trainer Gempo," I said, walking backward to face the others. "Rumor was he was a badass back in the day. Christ, he made you practice in the dark. Can you imagine Rudolfo in the dark? 'Zimo, Zimo, hold my light. I can't see the invert about to eat me!'"

Everyone started laughing, then immediately stopped. I backed up into someone and almost fell. I ungracefully turned to see two guards, each dressed in jumpsuits not too different from our own, but modified to resemble old castle guards. *What is it with this guy's fetish for the sixteenth century?*

"I remind you that you are guests of His Eminence and should respect him as such," said the guard on the right.

The guards looked beefy, each bearing the scars and tattoos indicative of their surface survival. Surely they felt the same about the asshole that ruled this place, not that they'd be allowed to show it.

"Our apologies," said Huck.

"This part of the Nucleus is off-limits to unescorted residents. You will follow us to the nearest exit, where you will immediately depart for your rooms, do I make myself clear?"

"Yes, sir," said Huck.

We followed the duo to one of the catwalks that extended across the central shaft to the nearby market district. They stood silently watching us from the Nucleus. Trivia lightly squeezed my hand in an attempt to distract me from the heights as we crossed the span.

"Hey, Ariadne," I said. "You remember how we first met?"

"How could I forget?" she asked, laughing. "You and Huck barreled me down on a catwalk just like this. Outrunning guards with those stolen tapes."

"Those stolen tapes saved our lives," said Huck. "I don't know what we would've done without Guilherme and Arjun."

"We would've died," I said honestly.

After the grand major had heard us plotting to steal the tapes, he would've had every right to turn us in, but instead, he'd helped us along. It was his mission that we still carried out and the reason we were called Memo's Misfits.

"Don't forget me," said Omar. "I helped you guys hide."

"Instead of betraying us," added Krista.

"Well I didn't, did I? Despite what Carvalho wanted."

Most of this wasn't news to Trivia and the others who'd joined us more recently. Days trekking through woods and crossing oceans gives you plenty of time for chit-chat. Thankfully, talking wasn't typically enough of a vibration to attract the inverts. Friendship was one of the few things that made surface life bearable. That and Arjun.

We finally arrived at our apartments and parted ways. The couples each shared a place. Ondo and Roque shared a room, having known each other far longer than the rest of us. Fen and Leisel bunked together too, but mainly because they both kept to themselves. And no surprise, Marie slept alone. I couldn't help but wonder if that was what she wanted or if no one wanted to share a room with her. *Probably both.* With as much time as we'd had to share stories, the woman was still a complete mystery to me. At our door, Trivia pulled me down to her level and kissed me.

"Go find Francisco," she said. "I know you've been thinking about it all day."

I hesitated, slow to leave the comfort of her arms. I couldn't take my eyes off of her contagious smile. The one that warmed me inside out like a summer sunrise.

"Go," she said, smacking me on the butt. "I'll be here when you get back."

"You know… I'm in love with you," I said.

"I'm in love with you too, Hemant. Now get out of here."

I backed away a few paces, smiling at her like a child who'd just received a caramel, before eventually turning and practically skipping to the elevator.

••••••••

I took the electric tram out to the shipyards, nearly empty save for a few workers heading home. I supposed that some residents lived in the pod and worked in the yards and vice versa. The ability to live and work on the surface here under the city's protection was unique. Of the eight pods remaining, most of the two-million-odd residents lived exclusively underground, except when they participated in the barbaric event known as Release Day.

Each pod had its own variations of Release Day, all of which were at their root some form of population control. The fact of the matter was that underground space was limited. Fact or not, there had to be better ways than training the youth in combat and survival before booting them out among the inverts and saying, "Hope you make it!" Before it had been corrupted, I suppose the original intent made some sense. Instead of simply euthanizing the old or weak, they've viewed the opportunity as a chance to take down some of the enemy. The problem was our enemy was infinite. That's why our mission to the Hive was so important. It would be a blow that would finally give us the foothold we needed to change the war's direction.

Our journey had only served to highlight the corruption running rampant among the pods. The cities' elite always managed to maintain a luxurious lifestyle while less well-to-do residents struggled. It was people like that who'd been the strongest proponents of Release Day. "It's tradition," they would cry anytime it was questioned. *As if that meant it was free from scrutiny.* Despite the fact I hated the man, Kolya had pointed out something we'd all missed. The reason the inverts hadn't simply wiped us out was because we were a major part of their food supply. The pods acted as giant food dispensers, releasing fresh meat at regular intervals. I felt my eyes grow moist. It's part of why I was so mad at Arjun for listening to that snake. There could be no peace with a species that considered us nothing more than food. They had to go. They had to!

The tram came to a stop at the end of its run as the driver said something about disembarking. I wiped the tears on my sleeve and walked out of the tunnel. Night had fallen, but unlike the orange glow of the sodium lamps that signified night in the pod, the shipyards were bathed in a warm yellow light coming from electric lamps hung from each building, giving the place an old-world feel that I only recognized from pictures. I could almost sense why Rudolfo was drawn to whatever past age he was. It was a quaint, simple time, though far from peaceful. I didn't remember a ton from history, not seeing it valuable to surface survival, but I remembered that they hadn't eradicated most diseases. Hell, they didn't even know to wash their hands. I guess looking back on it, you could appreciate the advantages and too easily forget the drawbacks.

Under the night sky, the village took on a different life. Still humid, the workers, having returned from their shipbuilding, walked the streets in relative safety with their families thanks to the pod's stout defenses. I passed a restaurant where people ate off of wooden tables set atop barrels, the smell of fish filling my nostrils. I hadn't eaten as much as I would've liked at the prime minister's dinner once Ariadne had broken down. Even now, as my stomach growled, I didn't want to stop. I only wanted to find Boatmaster Francisco, but I didn't even know where to begin searching. I rounded a corner and saw what had to be a drinking establishment, another wooden construction with what appeared to be a house atop it. A voluptuous woman leaned against the rail out front, fanning herself in the evening heat.

"Hi, um, excuse me," I began.

She grabbed my collar and tugged me closer. "You're a handsome one. What'll it be?"

My eyes grew wide and I jerked back a few steps. "Not that," I said, stumbling over my words. I felt my cheeks burning.

She laughed, brandishing a hand. "It's not often I find someone with their innocence still intact. I'm Sofia. Since you aren't interested in the obvious, what *are* you looking for? A drink, perhaps."

"No, ma'am. I was looking for a man."

"Oh!" she said.

"No! Not like that!" I backpedaled ferociously, my face on fire now.

Sofia laughed all the harder. "You are an interesting young man.

What's your name?"

"Hemant," I said, rubbing my face with my hands. "I can fight inverts all day, but can't talk to a pro—" I caught myself.

"It's okay, you can say it. Prostitute, madame, woman of ill repute. That last one's my favorite. I have no shame from my job. It puts food on the table. The universe blessed me with good looks, so I aim to use them while I have them. So, tell me Hemant, what man are you looking for?"

"I'm searching for Boatmaster Francisco. He has information about my brother."

"That, my dear, I can help you with. Walk straight down towards the docks. When you reach the water make a left and walk until you see a row of houses that extend out over the water. His is the last in that row."

"Thank you, Sofia."

"Anytime, Hemant," she kissed me on the cheek.

There went my cheeks again. I smiled politely and left her company, thankful she'd been so willing to help, however awkward the conversation had been. I followed her instructions and found myself walking out on the pier where Francisco's house was located. The neighborhood was hardly more than shacks but each couldn't have been better maintained. They were clean, well-constructed, and inviting. These people lived in poverty but still had pride. I was surprised that someone as high-ranking as a boatmaster lived here. I knocked on the door. After a few moments, a small-statured woman answered.

"Yes?" She said, timidly.

"Hi. My name's Hemant. I'm looking for Boatmaster Francisco. I understand he has information about my brother, Arjun."

The woman gave a polite smile and opened the door for me to enter. She was pretty, but a hard life had aged her prematurely. The house was even smaller on the inside, from the look of things, two rooms. I didn't expect opulence from a position that would always be working-class, but I expected more than this modest dwelling.

"Hemant," said Francisco from the floor with his kids, who appeared to be twins. In the faint glow, he looked even more weathered than he had in the sunlight. "It's good to finally meet you. Help me up, if you would be so kind."

For the first time, I noticed he only had one leg. I pulled him up to a nearby wooden chair, letting him down gently.

"Ah, that's better. It's getting harder and harder to play down on the floor," he said, laughing quietly.

"Who are you?" asked one of the twins.

"He's a guest in our house," said Francisco's wife, turning to me. "My name is Yadira. These are our children, Tio and Tia. Would you like some tea?"

"Yes, if it's not too much trouble."

She nodded and left Francisco and me to talk, though there couldn't be much privacy in such a small space. I kept looking around the place. It was quite small but felt more homey than even the nicest apartments I'd stayed in. There was a warmth to it, not from the heat of the region but an emotional warmth that put me at ease.

"Not what you expected, is it?"

"To be honest, no."

"I was a simple fisherman before my promotion. A promotion I owe to your brother, I might add. Rudolfo never would've agreed to my terms if he thought I'd survive," he said, chuckling. "There's still some spunk in this old body."

"How did my brother help you with the promotion?" I desperately wanted to ask about Arjun, but this man seemed to do everything in his own time.

"When Rudolfo learned about their… unusual idea to travel to the Australian Territory, he knew I was the only one crazy enough to do so. He thought he could rid himself of them and me in one fell swoop. I took advantage of his assumptions and agreed to do it for the promotion. Here I am, Boatmaster."

"So why stay here?" I asked, gesturing around the room.

"This is where I've lived my life. Where Yadira and I had our children. I'm friends with all of my neighbors. I have everything I need. Why bother leaving that?"

"No, you're right."

"Are you here to play with us?" asked Tia.

I laughed. "I don't know that I've ever really played."

Tia examined me with a foreign look from under her bowl-cut hair. Yadira brought Francisco and me small bowls of fresh tea, ushering the kids away from us. I nodded my thanks.

"It saddens me how our children are forced to grow up so fast. That's why I agreed to carry your brother and his friend across the sea. I'm willing to sacrifice almost anything so that my children can live the life they were meant to."

"How is my brother? Tell me he's okay."

"He was when I left him."

An invisible weight I didn't know I was carrying fell from my shoulders. My body flooded with relief, bringing back the tears. I tried to hide, taking the opportunity to taste the tea.

"Have no shame here, Hemant. There are few things more important than family, especially for an old codger like me."

I nodded, unable to speak. Yadira brought some crackers and dried fish, setting it down in front of us. Her fingers were nearly as callused as her husband's. This family was no stranger to hard work.

"I greatly enjoyed my time with Arjun," he said as I nibbled on a cracker. "He was a quick learner. Mastered basic sailing far faster than I ever did. You'll probably think this is silly, but in a matter of days, he started to feel like a son to me."

I smiled, happy at the thought. "Arjun and I never had a father. Not that we knew. Pod Horizonte was like that. They thought it was better for everyone."

"That's a shame. No one should have to be without family. The day we forget that is the day we lose what makes us human. If that happens, the Arthropods will have won."

"Then we can't let that happen. I have to find my brother."

"And I have faith you will."

CHAPTER 11: KOLYA

When Jigna and Neesh disappeared in the morning, I half expected them to return with another screaming cave grub for breakfast. The remnants of the prior evening's meal were gone, drag marks the only sign of its existence. I shuddered to think how close I'd been to whatever terrifying invert had carried it away during the night. I mindlessly poked a stick at the twinkling orange embers of the fire. *Can we make peace with a species so inherently violent? What would living harmoniously with these creatures look like?* We were a long way from answers to questions like that. Once we brokered peace, then we could iron out the minutia. Perhaps they could occupy a dedicated continent, leaving us to the others. Relatively speaking, it wasn't that long ago in Earth's history when indigenous people lived amongst the predators of the wild. Sure the occasional person disappeared, but for the most part, they prospered. Still, the whole idea was an intellectual leap. Individual Arthropods might be stupid, but they were far more dangerous than the occasional leopard with a taste for humans. Considering how the inverts' actions were influenced by the Arthropod hierarchy, we would have to reexamine their intelligence.

A rustle in the bushes announced the return of our guides, waking Arjun. They clutched tightly wrapped bundles. My stomach growled with desire for something more than a ration bar, but I didn't have high hopes given their unusual tastes. When they unfurled their cargo at my feet, I was pleasantly surprised by objects that resembled what I considered food. On the ground were small, speckled eggs and wrinkled brown fruits whose stems bore beautiful purple flowers.

I laughed aloud and gave him a thumbs up, hoping the gesture was a positive one among the foreign culture. "Neesh, you old dog! You were holding out on us. Food like this we can eat!"

Neesh and Jigna began barking with excitement, bouncing up and down. Jigna picked up a nearby rock, cracking it cleanly into layers and flopping a flat piece down onto the smoldering coals. Once the stone was hot, she cracked all the eggs onto it, scraping them around until we had a scramble. Next to the eggs, she removed the fruit from its vine and warmed them whole. While I questioned her hygiene, ravenous hunger won out. With the food prepared, we devoured it wordlessly. The eggs had a mild fishy taste, which under normal circumstances I would've found unappetizing. The fruit had a tomato-like texture, but a taste more like a spicy raisin. It complemented the eggs nicely. When I'd eaten my fill, I leaned back against a rock, satisfied for the first time in a while.

"A fine meal," I said, patting my stomach. "I imagine I'll be sick of it by the time we leave this god-forsaken territory, but for now, I'm quite content. What do you think that fruit was, Arjun?"

"Something from the nightshade family, I believe, though I'd need to consult with Ariadne for proper identification. I was hoping it was one of the benign varieties, otherwise, we'd be in no shape to continue."

"Well, my boy, I'm glad you didn't share your concerns. I might not have eaten them with such gusto had I been worried about their effects on my mind."

Arjun gave one of his rare chuckles. "I'm grateful that we didn't have to watch them eat another grub," he said, pausing. "It's interesting to me. They have some sort of symbiotic relationship with the Arthropods, yet, they consume them. Do you think that relationship works both ways? Do you think they would expect it to continue after peace has been established?"

"Those are deep thoughts for a morning without coffee," I said, laughing. "But valid nonetheless. Perhaps I should've brought two flasks. One for alcohol and one for caffeine."

The pair of Demented watched our exchange curiously. Once our food had adequate time to settle, we loaded our gear onto the multipedes. When I thought no one was looking, I walked to the beast's face, having never seen one so close. Cute wouldn't have been the first word I'd use to describe it. The creature had bulbous golden compound eyes protruding from its caramel carapace. I found their lack of pupils disconcerting, not knowing where the pede's gaze rested. From their face sprouted two antennae, the same shade of brown as their face. Below rested the stinking maw I'd personally seen devour many a human, idly clicking away. As I walked the length of the beast, I couldn't help but think of how many people had been impaled on the beast's golden spikes. I shook off the feeling of chill, even here on the desert morning, and reached for my canteen. *Empty, dammit.*

"We need water," I said to Jigna, tapping the empty canister against the pede's chitinous exoskeleton.

Jigna proffered her canteen, which still resounded with liquid. I shook my head emphatically to which she shrugged. Neesh watched the exchange and approached, pointing off the road.

"How far?" I asked.

Neesh cocked his head. Arjun took over, patiently making a gesture in regard to the sun. Neesh seemed to understand and responded in kind. Neesh held up two fingers, close together.

"It must be close," said Arjun.

I saw little other choice than marching through the woods, but agreed. According to the books I'd read, the Outback was home to some of the world's most dangerous creatures *before* the Arthropods invaded. It wouldn't do me any good to make it this far and perish from a venomous bite. With Neesh's help, we made our way through the trees, pushing branches and shrubs aside, scratching my legs up in the process.

"Fascinating!" said Arjun.

I glanced up from my feet and noticed that the trees had taken on a significantly more tropical appearance. "What the…"

Neesh and Jigna led us on for a few meters more before the forest opened up into a natural spring. The water was clear and beautiful—an oasis trapped by time.

"What? How?" I asked.

"It must be ground-fed," said Arjun.

Jigna barked instructions, pointing from his canteen to the lake.

"I guess it's potable," I said, leaning down. I could instantly feel the heat steaming off of the water. "A hot spring! I'll be damned."

Just then, a yell scared me out of my wits followed by what I supposed passed for a Demented's laugh as Neesh sprinted naked between us and jumped into the pool, splashing everyone. I was hot, stinky, and miserable, and it had been eons since I'd bathed.

"What the hell," I said, removing my shirt.

Before I had stripped down to my underclothes, Jigna was nude in the water alongside her friend. I did my best to avert my eyes as Arjun and I lowered ourselves into the water. *God does this feel good.*

"Oh, I needed this," I said aloud as I leaned against the stony bank and closed my eyes.

●●●●●●●●

After the necessary bath, I reluctantly remounted the beast for another day's ride across the Australian Territory's famed expanse, desperately wishing that there would be hot springs dotting our way to the Hive. *Maybe this trip wouldn't be so miserable after all, Sveta.*

Around lunch, we pulled a few kilometers off what was left of the crumbled highway and parked the multipedes next to an ephemeral lake. Judging by its appearance, we'd caught the water level at a good time, only about a quarter below its full capacity.

"Not bad, my friend," I said, slapping Neesh on the back. "You know how to pick them."

The man grunted and returned the slap so hard that I fell to one knee. Arjun cocked an eyebrow as if to say, "What did you expect?"

While our guides chowed away on something I'd rather ignore, Arjun and I cooked the fish we'd caught and skewered from the lake. After such a long time hiding every trace of our existence, it was downright pleasant to traverse the surface, nearly free of worry as we cooked, traveled, and slept. With the meal complete, we set forth, pleasing our antsy companions.

The further inland we went, the darker the sky became with our nemeses. Inverts patrolled the skies, each species flocking with its own. I caught myself wondering if the nearly invisible mashi were swirling around up there too. Those tiny little bugs could whittle a human to bone in seconds, moving at a near bullet-like velocity. All it would take was one of the measly critters through the heart or brain and you were a goner. *How the hell did anyone survive long enough to build the pods?* If nothing else, you had to admire the Arthropods' lethality.

Arjun had been more quiet than usual after parting with Francisco, the wizened sailor who'd carried us down here. I didn't have high hopes that he'd return to Pod Bandung unscathed, but I hoped the man made it back. He'd been as good of an escort as any, not expecting me to carry the burden of my passage, though Arjun had done it willing enough. If a man couldn't operate his own boat, I didn't see why I should be bothered to help him.

"A penny for your thoughts," I said to Arjun over the quiet repetition of the multipedes' numerous feet thumping along the ancient roadbed.

"I was trying to wrap my mind around the Demented's relationship with the Arthropods," he said, without breaking eye contact with the horizon.

"And what conclusion have you come to?"

"Every time we've encountered Demented, they've been very animalistic, often not thinking for themselves. I suspect they might be drones. Perhaps even slaved to the Hive in some fashion. It's something I never would've considered before we met Neesh and Jigna."

"Hmm," I said, scratching at my beard and coming back with sweat-covered fingers which I wiped on my shirt. "This is a thought I have been considering as well. But what about the Huntress that you described? The one that nearly killed your friend, Huck?"

"I've considered her too. I think she was more like a leader of sorts. If my hypothesis is correct, they have some degree of autonomy. Look at our friends. They can function independently of the Hive. Maybe it's more like a compulsion rather than—"

"A zombie," I said, finishing his sentence. "I think your idea is spot on. It wouldn't be the first example of a parasite controlling its host. As we continue, let us look for proof of your conclusion. However, be sure not to preclude other ideas in the process."

Arjun nodded. It was nice to be working with someone of equal intelligence as my own, not having to hold their hand through every realization or having to develop background knowledge so that I could plead my simple case. Like me, Arjun was a scientist at heart.

As we rode further into the Outback, the terrain became more and more repetitive. The ground was a sea of red ground from one end of the horizon to the other, broken up by sporadic pale green brush and the increasingly larger Arthropod mounds. As the sky turned as orange as the earth, we pulled to a stop at what had once been a major intersection. It was all I could do to keep my eyes open, continually nodding off, trying my best not to impale myself on the needle-sharp spike in front of me. The road was littered with disintegrating vehicles from humanity's past age, more than we'd seen in days. Despite the prolific rusting shells, the small town hadn't been a bustling one. The buildings had long since turned to rubble, but a nearby reservoir held enough water to see us through the remainder of our trip to the Hive. *God, Sveta, I can't believe I'm going to see it tomorrow. We will be the first humans to lay eyes on it—perhaps ever.*

"Arjun, we have our choice of shelter," I said, looking towards the east. "I could use it, too. I was about to fall asleep sitting up."

I heard no response and turned to see Arjun gaping at something over my shoulder. I turned, unsure of what to expect. Behind me, I'd failed to notice a pair of the largest invert mounds I'd seen to date. The towers we'd seen had gradually transitioned from meters in diameter and tens of meters in height to tens of meters in diameter and as much as fifty meters tall. As I craned my neck, I beheld a pair of towers that nearly eclipsed the sun. The twins had to be a staggering hundred meters in height!

"Dear God," I whispered.

"I would have thought it physically impossible," said Arjun, visibly astounded as the Demented set up camp at their base as though nothing was new.

"Our definition of intelligence needs a revamp," I said. "This is… This is nothing short of an engineering marvel."

The mounds by all logic should've collapsed under their own weight. The area's high clay-sand ratio had substantial limitations, which the towers should've far exceeded. I'm sure the Arthropods added their saliva like glue, but even that couldn't explain the sheer size of the towers.

"I have more questions than answers," said Arjun.

"The time will come, my boy. The time will come."

•••••••

After repeating the previous day's breakfast, we pulled out, still unable to peel our eyes from the massive structures that partially occluded the sky. Our route took us closer to the edge of their sloping bases, but in the interest of self-preservation, I refused to go closer than we had to. Something about their construction put me ill at ease as if they could topple at any moment.

"The others' mission is doomed to failure," said Arjun after a speechless morning.

I agreed, but wanted to hear his conclusion. "How so?"

"Everything our mission was based on was that there was a central Hive. *One* central Hive. These creatures seemed to have a nodular existence. I believe that even if my companions were able to successfully detonate their device in the primary structure, these others wouldn't cease to exist. Bee colonies can create new queens simply by altering their food. What's to say that it wouldn't be the same with the Arthropods?"

"That, my boy, is why I am on this quest for peace. Your friends thought it stupid, but it is the only viable alternative."

"Thus far you've proven correct," he said. "Even in regards to my brother."

"I couldn't bear to watch you held back. This way, you will live to your true potential, and hopefully save Earth in the process."

With any luck, we will bring in this new era of peace with us at the helm, I thought, a sinister smile crossing my face. For once, maybe Earth could have someone competent in charge, not someone placed by nepotism or wealth, but by intellect! Of course, peace couldn't exist without sacrifice. My gaze lingered on the two guides who'd carried us across the ocean of dust before my mind went to the runts following us with Dieter's bomb. *Whatever it takes,* I thought. *Whatever it takes.*

CHAPTER 12: DARREN

Patricia had only been gone for three days, but already it felt like I was trapped in some sort of time dilation. I drifted through work each day in a daze before picking up Alexander from Mrs. Grimethorpe's, who'd kindly offered to watch my son in my wife's absence. It was a wonder I could make it to work on time. Escaping the woman's conversation took half the morning, regardless of how many subtle hints I dropped about being late for work. What could I say? The woman was watching my son for free in return for my company. I had no right to complain. Her apartment, brimming with a lifetime of porcelain knick-knacks, never struck me as a place for a young child. The older woman never seemed to mind, even when he inevitably broke a piece from her collection. She would calmly carry on with the stiff upper lip the European Territory was known for, saying that the item had served its purpose. When I picked up Alex after another day of mindless work, she handed me a warm casserole to accompany him.

"You are too kind, Mrs. Grimethorpe," I said, thankful I didn't have to eat another pizza.

I could cook if I had to, but my dishes paled in comparison to Patricia's. I'd never had a mother's cooking to compare hers to, but my father did well to microwave dinner. We'd subsisted on frozen meals my entire childhood, and I had the stretch marks (though no longer the weight) to prove it. One day, he never came home. I was a latch-key kid, so I went on as usual, accustomed to him pulling long shifts at the department. It was only when an officer showed up that I knew something was wrong. My father hadn't died doing anything heroic like saving orphans from a burning building but had instead been killed outside of a convenience store picking up a few cigars—his one vice. Murdered for the forty-odd bucks found in his wallet. His case was still open when the United Territories of Earth had been formed, but it had been forgotten like so many others in the local law enforcement's transition into the Territorial Guard.

Being sixteen, I'd only spent two years in Detroit's foster care system, but that was enough. I maintained a straight-A average despite less-than-ideal living circumstances and was accepted to Wayne State on a full scholarship. It was there that I met Patricia as an undergrad. We'd dated through her grad work until we eventually wed. When she'd received the offer to be the lead scientist at the newly constructed, state-of-the-art Longway Observatory in Flint, she hadn't even hesitated. She'd been a little unnerved when she'd found part of her role to be community engagement, but she'd grown into it. She was as passionate when talking to kids in the planetarium as she was behind the optics of the state's largest telescopic array. It was long hours, essentially working two jobs in one, but she loved it. Somehow she managed to do that and publish papers in exobiology and astrophysics, all the while being a great mother and wife.

"When mom gets back, we need to do something really special for her," I said to Alex as I unlocked the door of our apartment.

The place felt empty without her.

"When's mommy coming back?" he asked.

"I don't know, bud. That rock is a big deal. She may be down there for a while."

"Is it such a big deal that she can't call us?"

I collapsed into my favorite chair and picked up my son. "Remember what she said. She didn't know how often they'd let her talk, but she was going to try to call us when she could."

Alex nodded, then scooted off my lap to go play in his room. With Mrs. Grimethorpe available, I hadn't bothered to use the new *au pair*. Not to mention, it felt a little strange having another woman around the apartment while my wife was gone.

I made my way to the kitchen and began warming up the casserole. Poppy seed chicken. Awesome! Today, I was spicing it up with mint chocolate ice cream I'd brought home for dessert. I was pulling the pan out of the oven when the wall screen rang. I looked over to see it was an unfamiliar number with an Australian prefix.

"Alex, it's mom!" I said, darting to the screen to accept the call.

"Hey, guys!" she said, doing her best to mask her obvious exhaustion.

Behind her was the black canvas fabric of a tent and a table scattered with scientific instruments. Her hair was in a high ponytail, and she was sweating like crazy.

"Mommy you look hot," Alex said.

"Mommy *is* hot, baby," she said. "I don't know whose bright idea it was to use black tents in the desert. This is my research station and home for the next few months."

"Few months?" I asked, arching an eyebrow.

"Unfortunately for you guys, yeah. I'm thrilled to be here though. I mean… this is my life's work. Everything that was previously theoretical is right here in front of me. Well, a handful of kilometers away. Site admin has a plan of attack. This week, robots. Next week, humans. They're starting us pretty far out, letting us move inward a few kilometers a day. The real research isn't going to start until the week after that."

"Wow," I said. "You do your thing, and we'll make do, but we already miss you. I'm pretty sure Alex is going to be tired of my cooking before too long."

Alex made a show of wrinkling his nose before telling her all about his day at Mrs. Grimethorpe's. God, a few days with the woman and the kid was already becoming long-winded like her.

"That's great, baby," she said. "Hey, can you give Daddy and me a minute?"

"I thought you said you wouldn't keep any secrets," he said.

"We want to talk about lovey-dovey stuff," she said.

"Ew, gross. I'll be in my room if you need me."

"What's up?" I asked when he was gone.

"I think we are going to have to bend our promise a little bit for his sake," she said.

"Okay," I said, drawing out the word.

"Whatever's going on here is not normal. Not in any sense we understand. The seismic activity coming off '42 is still low magnitude, but it's almost constant. The seismologists have buried a bunch of seismographs around the perimeter. The epicenter of every quake is the rock, but there's no fault activity."

"Granted, I don't know much about tremors, but that doesn't sound natural."

"I don't think it is."

"Then what *do* you think it is?" I asked, wary of the answer.

"Alex is out of the room, right?" she asked.

I looked around to verify and nodded.

"What I'm about to tell you is personal speculation. It's a gray area of our non-disclosure agreement," she said, taking a deep breath. "I think something is alive inside the meteorite. Maybe it's a gigantic egg, maybe some planetary seed, perhaps even some sort of ship. Hell, I don't know," she said, sighing as she massaged her forehead.

"Knowing that, I don't suppose you'd pack up and come home, would you?"

"You know if you asked me to, I would."

"I won't do that to you. I can tell, the mother in you is skeptical, but the scientist in you is excited. This has the potential to be the pinnacle of your career. I can see the holo scroll now," I said, waving my hand across imaginary text in the air. "Dr. Patricia Taggert Confirms Alien Life."

My hand grew cold with anxiety. What could be so exciting was also absolutely terrifying.

"Extraterrestrial life," she corrected.

I forced a laugh. "Fine. Go find ET," I said. "Just update me as best as you can, okay?"

"Of course. I love you."

"I love you, too."

••••••••

Patricia called a few times over the next week, but then it was silence for the first week of the scientific outings. I watched the news as much as I could stomach, but with little information released to the press, I knew about as much as they did. The earthquakes were radiating further out, but their intensity wasn't any stronger. Now that there was a little data, the real speculation began. There was so much unfiltered nonsense floating around the feeds. Since the Media Bias Act was enacted in 2025, at least there was a banner scrolling across the screen when the newscasters went into opinion mode. The mysterious rock had probably been the longest-running news cycle since the sea-level rise displaced the entire population of Bangladesh.

"It's so freaking weird," said Stepan, his arms crossed over his chest as we topped off our coffee in the breakroom.

"Anything specifically?" I asked.

"Think about it. A rock from outer space slows down and lands, intentionally not killing everything on the planet. Then, it begins to vibrate, shaking the ground further and further out. What if something's digging underground, man?"

"Oh, Stepan," Nina said, "Do you really think so?"

I rolled my eyes, not even bothering to suggest otherwise as she all but ran from the room. Nina would believe anything anyone told her, then spread it like wildfire. Maybe that's why the universe had given her red hair, so you could see the inferno coming and escape.

"Patricia's out there, you know?" I said, rhetorically. "I really don't need something else keeping me up at night."

"Would you do me a favor?"

I shrugged.

"I know the world's geniuses are gathered out there, but maybe they haven't thought about it. Sometimes the eggheads get so caught up in data, they forget to look at the obvious. Would you at least mention my idea to her?"

"I don't guess it'd hurt, but I haven't heard from her in days. I don't think they like them talking too much."

"Maybe it's because they know the truth would cause a panic," said Stepan.

"Well, if there are burrowing aliens out there, it would," I said.

• • • • • • • •

That night, as I was throwing together a taco salad and nursing a Guinness, I was relieved when I saw Patricia's field number come up on the screen. Alex heard it and had Patricia's face up on the wall before I made it into the room. I could see bags under her eyes and worry etched across her face. Despite it being morning there, she obviously hadn't slept. We talked politely in front of Alex, before once again, ushering him off to his room. I never lied to Alexander, but I left some of the more worrisome parts of our conversation out.

"I know, lovey-dovey stuff," he said, walking to his room with his hands buried in his pockets.

"What's going on in the land down under?" I said, attempting humor with the cliche phrase and my horrendous Aussie accent.

Patricia gave a polite laugh. "The robots didn't tell us anything we didn't already know. Our line-of-sight instruments are pretty damn good."

Uh-oh. When my wife turned to vulgar language, something was up.

"And the scientist trips?"

"The closest we've gone is three kilometers. Today, we're going all the way. They are busing us into the three-K boundary, then we're footing the remainder. If readouts are all good, we should have hands on the rock today. Gloved, of course."

"Is that why you aren't sleeping, excitement?"

"That noticeable, huh?"

I nodded.

"I'm concerned. I never thought I'd say this about science, but we're moving too fast. Without knowing the cause of the tremors, I'm reluctant to walk right over the areas where they've been happening. They've been using ground-penetrating radar the whole time and assure us the surface is solid as deep as their gear can indicate."

I took a deep breath, trying to put on a good face. "You always hear about researchers on the verge of discovery getting antsy. Hopefully, that's all there is to it. Just promise you will be careful. No unnecessary risks."

"No unnecessary risks," she repeated.

"By the way, Stepan insisted I tell you something. I think it's dumb, but I promised. He wanted me to tell you he thinks the underground tremors could be tunneling aliens."

Patricia's response wasn't what I expected. She went a little pale and her eyes began to move nervously.

"Patricia?" I asked, my hands as cold as ice.

My wife turned to her side. "Grayson, can I have a moment alone? I vouch for his confidentiality."

"As you wish, Doc," his voice said off-camera.

"Has he been there the whole time?" I asked.

She nodded. "Every call."

"Now those comments the other day are awkward."

"Relax," she said. "He couldn't be more understanding or professional. Technically, you aren't supposed to know that we're under surveillance. He had to listen to another scientist have phone sex the other day, so I imagine your comments were nothing of note."

I shuddered. "That scientist must have not given a rat's ass who was listening to him."

For the first time, Patricia laughed. "It's actually a lesbian couple. She's an incredible botanist, and I love hanging out with her."

I couldn't help but snicker myself. "There are a lot of guys who'd like watching a video chat like that."

"Not if you've seen Noni," she said. "She's a great pal but far from a looker."

In the distraction, I'd almost forgotten her reaction. "So why was it that you dismissed your little eavesdropper?"

"Darren, I… Well, some…" she paused. "Darren, some of the scientists think the same thing."

"So, what? You're still going to go out there?" I could feel my cheeks flushing.

"They pushed for more safety regulations and a slower, more methodical study. Hell, one even pushed for military presence."

"So what happened?"

"It was all denied," she said. "Several packed up and left. Very few of the scientists are required to be here. This is a mostly voluntary operation."

"What about you? You just said things were moving too fast. Are you going to pack up too?"

"Darren, believe me, I thought about it. This is the discovery of a lifetime. You know I'm not in it for the fame and glory, but this is everything I've worked so hard for. It has the potential to legitimize my field, to prove we aren't alone in the universe."

"Since I've had you in my life, I've never felt alone in the universe."

She smiled in a way that nearly melted me. "I will be careful, my love. The first hint of danger, I'll be on the supersonic for LA, deal?"

"Deal," I said. "And for the record, exobiology has always been a legitimate field. Go and make your discoveries, but after all this, I want to see you on the cover of some of these magazines that are always around the apartment."

Patricia teared up in a mix of exhaustion and happiness. I brought Alex back in and we said our goodbyes. The only thing I was confident about was that the world was about to change. The question was: Would it be for the better or the worse?

CHAPTER 13: HUCK

Ariadne and I lingered in our temporary quarters, savoring the slow morning, knowing soon our lives would once again be in constant peril. Even having had a cup of coffee, I'd almost dozed off when heard a clink at the hatch. I rose as Ariadne stretched.

"What is it?" she asked.

I made my way to the door and opened the mail slot. I was surprised to see not only paper but nice, new paper. With such limited resources, most pods had over-recycled their materials to the point of degradation. Items like paper were used over and over. It had taken me months to accumulate enough paper to stitch together my sketchbook, much of it bearing its previous life on the reverse side. *It's been ages since I've drawn so much as a tree.* So focused on survival, I didn't spend a lot of time thinking, "Oh, I should sketch this plant."

"It's an embossed invitation," I said. "Clearly from Rudolfo. I don't know who else could afford to waste materials like this. He's inviting me to his office to discuss our 'imminent departure.'"

Ariadne sat up, alert. "Well, I knew it had to end. I just didn't expect it so soon."

"We do have a planet to save," I said. "Do you think I should bring Fen? Since Bhopal, she's kind of been our leader too."

"I think you should, but I don't envy your conversation to invite her."

"We've got to patch this rift up. It poses a risk to all of us."

Ariadne came over, draping her arms around my neck as if we were about to dance to the prime minister's omnipresent music.

"I know you'll make the right decision, whatever that is."

I kissed her, lingering as long as possible. "I love you."

"I love you."

With a deep breath and some reluctance, I left our apartment and went to knock on Fen and Leisel's door. Fen opened the door in the middle of laughing at something Leisel had said, stopping cold the second she saw me. I held up the invitation.

"We've been summoned to a meeting."

"Give me a minute," she said, slamming the hatch in my face.

I waited patiently, wondering how much of the time was Fen intentionally stalling. Finally, the door opened. Fen was dressed in her Clunkie jumpsuit. The solid gray material with the piping of the Bhopali Elites. Even though I wore the same jumpsuit and carried the same title, she'd donned her old military facade. At that moment, it was as though we were on two different planets. She took off down the corridor, headed towards the Nucleus. I had to hustle to match her pace. It was the first time the two of us had been alone since the incident.

"Fen, slow down."

Nothing.

"Fen!"

"If I don't, are you going to wallop me upside the head again?"

That hurt. "I said I'm sorry."

She spun so fast that I almost ran into her. "Sorry doesn't make it okay! I was distraught! I had just watched someone I loved die in front of me and instead of comforting me, you knocked me unconscious!"

Our route forced us through the floor's busy market district to reach the Nucleus. The upper-level residents were gawking, likely collecting material for fresh gossip. I tried my best to ignore them.

"I'm sorry, okay?!" I yelled. "I made a split-second decision to save our lives! Was it a great one? No! But it was a spur of the moment! You know as well as I do that if you take the time to think, you die! I only did it to save our lives! I'm sorry I had to hit you, but I did what I had to! What would you have done?!"

"I… I…," she stammered, tears cascading down her cheeks. I could almost see the steam as her voice fell to a whisper. "I don't know, okay?! Are you happy?! I don't know what I would've done."

"No. I'm not happy about that," I said. "I won't be happy until we've smoothed things over. You're my friend, Fen. So was Mego. Ever since that day, I've wanted nothing more than to comfort you and tell you I'm sorry about Mego. When you shut me out, it made his loss that much worse. I care about you, and I'm sorry. For everything."

Fen lost her rigidity. For a moment, I thought she was going to collapse down to the floor. That would give the uppers something to talk about. The same group that people were putting their hope in to save the world couldn't even cope with their emotions. Catching me off-guard, she leaned towards me, hands against my chest, her body racking with sobs. I put my arms around her until her crying subsided.

"I miss him so much," she said. "We knew we would die but knowing and experiencing are two different things. Does it get any easier?"

"Not really." I'd never lost someone quite so close to me, but the list of friends who'd died was extensive. The thought of losing Ariadne was unbearable. "I use it as fuel to see this mission through.

Honor what they died for by ending this god-forsaken war. I'll be surprised if, by the end of this, we're not all suffering from the Shock so badly that we can't dress ourselves."

Fen harrumphed. "You're probably right." She stood, collected herself, and looked me in the eyes. "I don't like what you did, but I forgive you."

"Thank you," I said, relieved. "If you ever have to return the favor, I'll be more understanding."

She laughed. It was good to have her back. Fen might have been physically small, but she made up for it in grit. I pitied whoever thought she would be an easy target. Under that black, tightly braided hair and pale face, was a hardened warrior at her peak fitness. I'd only thought I was fit until we had joined Sigma Squad's ranks in Bhopal, where she'd been our lieutenant. We'd lost so much between Pod Bhopal and Pod Bandung, but we'd emerged harder, stronger, more resilient, and more resolved.

"Let's go see what the fuss is about," she said.

•••••••

We must have been an interesting pair when we arrived at Prime Minister Rudolfo's office. Fen's eyes were still puffy, and I wasn't exactly chipper. If the minister or his advisor noticed, neither said anything.

"Welcome, Elites Huck and Fen," he began. "I have to confess, I didn't expect both of you to be joining me. Zimo, please prepare an additional tea."

"As you wish, milord."

I resisted the urge to roll my eyes. Lord Ransford was napping on a wide red pillow in the corner of the room, his spot bathed in sunlight from a porthole in the ceiling. The damn dog had a better life than ninety percent of the pod's inhabitants.

De León's office was decorated just how I'd imagined for someone so preoccupied with appearances. Everything that wasn't vintage was designed to look so. I couldn't quite wrap my mind around the disparity between the pampered minister and the weathered dock hands that kept the pod's industry running smoothly. Through a complex system of barter, each pod's specialization was how Earth's remaining humans had survived our over-extended underground existence.

Zimo proffered a fine cup of tea to Fen that matched my own. The gold-swirled porcelain had to be hundreds of years old. I was almost afraid to pick it up, not knowing how the minister would react if I happened to break it. I couldn't fathom how a man could live like this outside fighting for his life with nothing less than a gold-filigreed hilt wrapped around a painstakingly hand-engraved blade.

"So," he said, imposing his girth on his antique wooden desk. "I was under the impression you were the leader of your friends. How does Elite Fen play into this?"

"When Memo, err… Prime Minister Leal, gave us our mission, and he put me in charge. That worked pretty well until we became cadets in Pod Bhopal. There, Fen was our superior officer. Since then, we've kind of been sharing the responsibility. Umm… milord."

"I see," he said, stroking his goatee. "I think of myself as open-minded. I see no harm in a woman helping a man with his leadership duties."

Fen tensed. I gently placed a few fingers on her knee to prevent her from saying something that could threaten our passage south.

"Prime Minister, Fen is my equal in leadership. Whatever her command, I support wholeheartedly and the reverse is also true."

The minister shrugged. "Well, I suppose it has worked thus far. Well, from here on in, I will assume responsibility for this role."

"With all due respect… milord," said Fen through clenched teeth. This time there was no stopping her. "Every time a prime minister has meddled with Leal's mission, it's turned out to be a disaster. Every. Single. Time. Hell, I watched General Madan's…" Fen's voice broke slightly. She paused, taking a deep breath. "I watched General Madan's entire battalion die at sea because they didn't trust Leal's plan."

"Oh, um, well… dying at sea wouldn't be best for… my people. You see, my people, they depend on me. And the loss of the *Spearhead*, most unfortunate too. That was some of our best work. The last of the larger ships. We spent decades sourcing the material for that one." Rudolfo sighed deeply. "Well, if our survival depends on it, let's hear more about Leal's plan, shall we?"

For the next several hours, we carefully explained the details of Memo's plan. The minister was slow to understand and reluctant to concede to our judgment, but in the end, we prevailed. Captain Banyu would carry us, the minister and his entourage, and Dieter's weapon to the Australian Territory. It would be a small infiltration force, as designed, that would hopefully escape the notice of the Arthropods until it was too late. I wasn't looking forward to our new untrained participants, but one step at a time.

"How soon do you think we can leave, Prime Minister?" I asked.

"It'll take at least a day, perhaps two, to allocate provisions and prepare the pod to run in my absence. Why don't we say the day after tomorrow?"

I looked at Fen, who gave me an approving look. "That's acceptable, milord," I said. *God this ego-stroking is getting old.*

I heard the tea service rattle as Zimo struggled to gently set down the teapot. "Sssir," he stammered. "The day after tomorrow? Is that soon really necessary?"

"I think we've delayed our new friends long enough. The day after tomorrow it is!"

●●●●●●●●

When Fen and I arrived back at the common room, everyone was up and growing restless. On our return, Ariadne smiled the moment she could tell the chemistry between Fen and me had improved. We had grown unbelievably close as we experienced the elation, peril, and loss that you couldn't escape on the surface. As a result, when there was infighting, it negatively impacted the group dynamic, not something anyone wanted in a survival scenario. Maybe it was my imagination, but everyone seemed relieved.

"So, what's the verdict, you two?" asked Omar, cleaning out from under his nails with the tip of his dagger as he was wont to do.

"We sail the day after tomorrow," said Fen to cheers.

It was funny that with all of the dangers the outside posed, we were all so excited to face them. There wasn't a single one of us who wanted to linger longer than we had to. Every single one of us longed to see this war's end.

"And Rudolfo?" asked Krista. "I don't suppose he's staying behind."

I shook my head. "No luck. He's adamant about coming. Him, Zimo, and Lord Ransford."

"The little animal? He brings it for food, right?" said Marie.

Everyone grew quiet until she flashed her brilliant white teeth. *A joke.* Everyone laughed uncomfortably, still unsure even after all this time how to respond to her unusual sense of humor. I didn't care for the dog any more than the rest, but deep down, I sincerely hoped Marie had truly been joking.

"I could stand to relax another day or two," said Hemant, putting his arms behind his head and leaning back into Trivia's lap.

"Like hell!" yelled Fen, startling me. "You lazy bums haven't so much as stretched since we've been stuck in that buoy. Everyone up! We're going on a run through the tunnel!"

"The forty-kilometer tunnel?" asked Ondo. "That one?"

"Is there any other?" Fen said, already heading towards the elevator.

"Surely we're not going to run the whole thing, right?" asked Leisel.

"I liked her better when she was mad at you," said Hemant, shaking his head.

Ariadne and I took off down the hall after everyone. There was no denying we needed to regain our physique, which had been at its peak mere weeks before. If Fen was planning to do it in two days, it was going to suck. At least she was back to her old self. Maybe she was exactly the type of person we needed to help keep us alive. I smiled to myself.

"I guess I'll just stay here," I heard Roque say, his voice already fading.

CHAPTER 14: ARIADNE

It turned out that not even the highly motivated Fen could run eighty kilometers without stopping after our buoy-driven hiatus. After a good stretch, Huck and I had chugged along after her for hours as others dropped off one by one. We made it so far, we could see the faint light of the shipyards ahead. After so much downtime, we just couldn't make it the full forty-odd klicks. I collapsed on the gravely path that ran alongside the trams, my chest heaving from over-exertion. Huck remained standing, hands on top of his head, gasping for breath as he winced.

"When… on the surface… have we ever… run this far?" he asked.

"Never," I replied. "Fen's just… trying to… keep us fit."

"Speaking of which…"

"You guys giving up?" asked Fen, running by with Omar, already on her return trip.

"Hell, yes!" Huck yelled after her, getting a few laughs from dock workers passing by on the tram.

I kept an eye on the two of them as they ran maybe a hundred more meters and stopped, slowly walking back to us, catching their breath. By the time they'd arrived, I could breathe normally, but my legs felt like jelly.

"Wimps," said Omar.

"Whatever," said Fen. "You were maybe four or five steps away from giving up yourself. I recognize the signs."

"I guess the only one of us still in great shape is Marie," I said. "She passed us a while before you did."

"That freak is inhuman," said Omar. "You remember her in that last round of Tenner. If that war game had been for real, she would've killed every damn one of them before they'd known what hit them."

"She kind of terrifies me," said Fen.

"Which is why I'm happy she's on our side," said Huck, the one who'd brought her into our ranks after she'd saved Leisel's life. "I wouldn't want to go into the Hive without her."

"That's great and all, but can we go pick up the others and get something to eat?" asked Omar. "My breakfast was gone more than an hour ago. I might have eaten better if I'd known we were running a freaking marathon."

"Fine," said Fen. "Maybe we can run the full eighty tomorrow."

Our three heads swiveled to her. "I'm kidding of course. Just a fast-paced 10K."

I groaned, but we needed to stay fit. We still had about ten more days on a boat where we'd have almost no space to run, though I had no doubts that Fen would find some exercise for us. We hopped on a mostly-vacant tram, and Huck asked the driver if he'd mind picking up our friends. The other passengers didn't mind the frequent stops. The people of Bandung had been so kind and friendly. I got the impression they'd be that way whether we were "heroes" or not. We picked up Hemant, Trivia, Krista, Leisel, and Ondo. *Still not a sign of Marie.* When the train finally pulled into the station, there she was, waiting patiently on the central shaft's railing. One foot was flicking impatiently back and forth, not the least concerned about the 100-story drop behind her.

"There's no way," Hemant whispered.

"Did you run the whole way?" I asked, already sure of the answer.

"Wasn't that the point?" she said, smiling as relaxed as if she'd taken the tram to the shipyards and back.

Omar muttered something about hemolymph behind me, but I ignored it. Marie had been a healer in Proctor Evans' village of Survivors. Since she'd joined us, she'd doubled my knowledge of medicinal plants. Though I'd always favor my medkit, knowing what plants were helpful had saved our lives more than once. Her long-term survival on the surface without the protection of the pods was a testament to her abilities. What we'd experienced in Evans' village had been terrifying, and some of that fear still spilled over into our perceptions of Marie. She'd admitted having used the Arthropods' hemolymph, the substance that slowly turned people into the Demented. Because of that fact, we valued her presence, but we never trusted her as completely as Huck did.

"Chit-chat is great and all, but can we please go get something to eat?" asked Hemant.

Marie hopped off the railing with cat-like grace and tailed us to the elevator. Turning my back on her still sent shivers down my spine.

•••••••••

With lunch finished, Huck and I made our way back to our room. As tired as we were after the run, we found some extra energy to devote to each other. Afterward, I laid with the cool sheet partially covering me, my back exposed to the recirculated air blowing through the cracked vent in the ceiling. Huck laid behind me, stroking his finger softly along my back, tracing each scar that

I'd accumulated from our travels. Try as hard as I might, I couldn't suppress the jerk and inevitable giggle when the sensation tickled.

"I'm beginning to think you enjoy doing that," I said.

"There's nothing about you I don't enjoy," he said, kissing my back ever so gently.

I rolled over to face him, planting a lingering kiss on his lips as I held his scarred face tightly against mine.

"I want to spend the rest of my life in your arms," I said when I finally came up for air.

"I wouldn't have it any other way," he said, climbing on top of me and resting his warm body against mine.

"Too tired to finish Fen's run, but not too tired for this?" I asked, arching an eyebrow as I wrapped my arms around his back.

"I may have some energy left yet."

•••••••

Hours later, we emerged from our apartment, grinning like little kids who'd been given sweets, playfully hugging and fondling each other all the way to dinner. Wanting something with no frills, we headed down to the mid-levels where that type of food was ubiquitous. We found a little stall off the beaten path where patrons were sitting cross-legged on floor cushions, laughing warmly as they scooped a divine-smelling dish into their mouths with their hands.

The aging concrete walls were draped with tattered, ornate rugs making the place feel more like someone's home than a restaurant. We dropped to the floor at a vacant table and ordered whatever it was that seemed to be the house special. Moments later, it wasn't our waiter who returned, but the restaurant's owner.

"Good evening, friends. My name is Darsh. I know it's not much to look at, but this is my humble establishment. Whatever you desire, it's on the house, made fresh by me."

"Thank you, Darsh," said Huck. "We'd love to pay you. It's the least we can do."

"You have done so much for us already, I can't take your—"

"Darsh, they said they want to pay you. Don't argue with them," said a beautiful Bhopali woman who came to his side, wrapping her delicate arm through his muscular one. "Forgive my husband. He's generous to a fault. He'd give away every meal if he could, giving no thought to his family."

Darsh shrugged. "She's right. I can't help but give what I have."

"He just has a habit of forgetting that what he has is a result of *paying* patrons," Amira said, teasing him.

"We want to pay you," I said. "Ration points won't do us any good on the surface."

"He will take your money," said Amira, "and treat you to food worth every point."

"Amira, bring them some chai with a dollop of cream. Can't you see they are thirsty? Then *paya* soup, and *poha*, and *shahi tukda*, and—"

"I think that will be more than enough Darsh," said Huck, laughing. "We still want to be able to walk tomorrow."

Darsh returned the laugh. "I'm sorry. I get carried away when I'm excited. I will bring you my best but not so much you can't walk."

Despite the nutritional limitations, Darsh had somehow managed to squeeze every bit of flavor from the few ingredients on hand, making the same foods that every other restaurant offered taste exquisite. It was no wonder the place never emptied. Not only did we eat until we'd almost entered a food coma, but we hung out with Darsh and Amira around a hookah for hours after they'd lowered the roll-down door. Like so many vendors we'd met around the world, they took the utmost pride in serving their clientele.

"If you ever find yourselves back in Bandung, you will always have a place at one of my tables," said Darsh, pulling the chain that raised the door to let us out.

As Huck shook hands with Darsh, Amira gave me a big hug, filling my nostrils with the pleasant aroma of shisha and clove. "You take good care of that one," she whispered. "He's a keeper."

My cheeks glowed bright enough that I was certain they'd illuminate the dim corridor. With one last wave, we left their shop and meandered our way towards the central shaft to take the elevators back up to our apartments.

"What a couple, eh?" said Huck, groaning as he massaged his bloated belly. "I don't think I'll need to eat until we reach the Australian Territory."

"Knowing you, you'll be out-eating Hemant at breakfast. I bet he—"

The words froze in my mouth. At the end of the corridor was a wide-shouldered Asian man blocking the path, not looking too friendly at all.

"Why don't we head the other way?" said Huck.

"I think that's the best idea you've had all night."

We spun on our heels just in time to see two others emerge from the opposite end, closing us in. My eyes darted to Darsh's door as I debated on shouting for help. Reading my mind, Huck shook his head.

"We can handle this," he whispered. "There's no reason to endanger them."

We waited on edge as the three men closed the distance. What had to have been seconds trickled by like hours.

"Hey, guys," said Huck. "You having a good evening?"

Not what I would've started with, but I'll give him credit for trying.

"We have a problem," said the bearded Asian we'd seen first, likely their leader.

Huck and I backed imperceptibly towards the wall so that we could keep an eye on both parties, readying our stance. We each carried daggers, but our primary weapons were back in our rooms. It was a good thing we never went completely unarmed.

"What problem is that, gentlemen?" asked Huck.

"You," said one of the others, sneering with a wide, yellow smile.

"Umm… Okay," said Huck. "How are we a problem?"

"You're sticking your noses where they don't belong, going off to the Hive like you are," said the guy with a scar across his left eye. "We heard what happened at Baghdad when you left. It didn't work out too well for the rezzies there, now did it?"

I started to speak, but Huck shook his head. He was trying to keep all the attention on himself, allowing me to go unnoticed. He was betting that these guys wouldn't think I was as lethal as he was. My hand subtly dropped to my dagger.

"We're trying to end the war, guys," Huck said, attempting to de-escalate the situation.

"You'll fail like all the others, but not before you get us all killed," said the leader. "We're here to put a stop to that."

"How do you propose to do that, gentlemen?"

"The only way we know how," said Yellow Teeth. "We're going to hang you and your friends on the outside of the shipyard walls, with your blood spilling from your throats so that the inverts know you're dead and leave us the hell alone."

"You know I can't let that happen," said Huck. "We're highly trained. Not one of us will let you hurt the others."

The leader scoffed. "You think we weren't candidates? I served my time! Came from Wuhan, I did. Killed all matter of inverts along the way, including ripping the legs off an eight. Don't speak to me like I'm a bloody matriarch."

"My apologies, gentlemen, but rest assured, we will walk out of Pod Bandung unscathed and continue our mission. There's nothing I'm going to let you do to stop that."

"See, that's where you're mistaken," said Scar, who sprinted towards me, drawing a blade as he did so.

I waited until the last instant to jump out of the way, planning to let him run into the wall and maybe knock himself unconscious, but with superhuman speed, he jumped after me before I had a chance to draw my weapon. As I sped down the corridor, I couldn't outrun this guy who easily had fifty kilos on me. *What the— Dust.* The realization hit me like a ton of bricks. No, that was my assailant who hit me like a ton of bricks.

When my chin impacted the hard concrete floor, I saw nothing but stars. Every particle of air was driven from my lungs, which burned like hell. The bastard jerked my arms behind me, stressing every joint, making me scream in agony. Huck had to be fairing better. I felt the heat of breath on my cheek, the man's stench stung my eyes.

"You're a pretty lass, aren't you," he whispered. "It'd be a shame to throw you over the wall immediately."

I fought against his restraint, but fueled by Dust, it was as fruitless as trying to bend iron with my bare hands. The familiar dissociation of the Shock began to set in, but I forced it out of my mind. *Not today.* I flung my leg up and kicked him in the back of the head, throwing him just enough off-balanced that I squeezed out from under him. The brutes' leader had Huck against the wall, Huck's weapon against his throat.

"You'll stop right there, missy," he said as Yellow Teeth grabbed me by my collar.

Scar stood and slapped me with the back of his hand across the face. "Stupid bitch."

"That's a good girl," said the leader. "We're going to head to the tram. Just friends out for an evening stroll, eh?"

The trio began to lead us down the hall. I had no intention of willingly marching with this man to my death, but before I could come up with a plan, I felt my captor go limp. Yellow Teeth spun when he heard his friend's body collapse, but before he could react, a butcher's knife sprouted from his neck. He clutched his throat, gurgling as he fell to the ground. The leader's knife went tight against Huck's neck, drawing blood.

"Drop it," he said to someone behind me. "I'll have his blood pooling before your knife touches me."

I heard the clatter of steel raining onto the hard surface. Just before the leader could speak again, he staggered back and collapsed.

"That'll teach you to mess with *my* patrons," said Amira, withdrawing a fillet knife from the man's side.

I ran to Huck, hugging him tightly as Amira checked his neck.

"It's nothing more than a scratch," she said. "Come inside, we'll get you cleaned up."

I turned to see Darsh staring at his bloody hands. "I swore I'd never kill again," he whispered.

"You saved our lives," I said, putting my hand on his shoulder, "maybe even the lives of our friends."

Darsh nodded blankly. I wouldn't be able to remove his guilt, but maybe I'd lightened it.

"The world can't be rid of that crap fast enough," said Amira, taking Darsh's wet hand and leading him inside. "All the more reason to get yourselves to the Hive. If the inverts are destroyed, so are their pheromones."

Amira slipped some money to a neighbor to dispose of the bodies, before taking care of Huck's wound and my bruises. "Are you sure I can't walk you back?" she asked.

"I can't imagine that we'd be attacked again," I said. "Short of more Dust-crazed scum, we should be able to defend ourselves."

"I'm so proud of the way you hold yourself against your enemies, Ariadne. You are a woman of great strength."

"Thank you," I said, staring worriedly at her husband.

"I'll take care of him," she said, resting her hand on my forearm. "He's always struggled with death. He's the only person I know to offer a prayer over each Arthropod that died by his hands."

"I've only felt saddened by the death of one type of Arthropod," said Huck, undoubtedly thinking about the innocent striders we'd been forced to kill.

"Is there anything we can do to show you our gratitude?"

Amira nodded, before leading us out of earshot. "Go to the Hive and kill every one of those bastards."

CHAPTER 15: HEMANT

Over breakfast, Huck and Ariadne spilled the details of their attack the night before. It was still crazy to me that there were people in the world who had become so apathetic that they no longer cared about reclaiming our planet. Regardless of how it felt otherwise, we were at war, and collateral damage was an inevitable part of ending it.

If we thought the attack would hamper Fen's desire for training, we were wrong. She wore our asses out. After a brief stretch, she'd led us on what she referred to as an easy 10K, but the speed she maintained was nothing of the sort. Afterwards, we made our way to the weight-training rooms. Judging from the constant stares, we had already gained notoriety around the pod. When Fen asked if we could use the room for a few hours, they'd canceled the day's schedule, giving us free rein of the entire space. I had no desire to be treated as some hero, but it was nice to get whatever we needed. After a lengthy workout, I was beat. As Omar spotted me on my last rep, I let the weights fall back on the rack, sweat pouring off of me in the humid space.

"You think Lieutenant Pain will let us rest yet?" I asked, scoffing.

"Doubt it," said Omar. "We haven't done anything with our legs yet. Once the girls get done, we can swap."

"Ugh," I said, dropping back to the bench. "Why the hell can't running count for legs?"

Everything was already sore. Maybe I'd pushed too hard. We had been pretty lazy the past few weeks. Even having been at our peak, as the old saying goes, "You don't use it, you lose it." For some reason, it reminded me of that bastard Kolya. He was always a fan of old anecdotes. I shut my eyes and massaged them, wishing away the soreness and fatigue. Trivia snuck over and jumped on top of me, straddling me across the bench and knocking the wind from me.

"You have to have sharper reflexes than that if you're going to survive!" she said, laughing.

I leaned forward and wrapped my arms around her. "I'll show you reflexes!" I said, tickling her until she giggled like mad.

"I'm out," said Omar, heading towards Krista.

Trivia moved off me and onto the adjacent bench, leaning back against the corroded metal wall. Like nearly everywhere else, the pod's skilled workforce constantly fought a losing battle against the elements. Corrosion, oxidation, degredation… There were only so many times that you could repair or recycle something before it was worthless. And humanity had far outstayed our welcome in the subterranean pods. They were only meant to last until a solution was found. Little did the United Territories of Earth know how long that would take—or that the biggest threat to humanity's long-term survival would be a blend of entropy, corruption, and apathy.

"You nervous?" asked Trivia.

"I'd be a fool if I wasn't," I said. "I've had a pit in my stomach all day. Not that it ever really goes away. I worry about Arjun. Wonder if he's okay. I feel like he is, but I need to see him. Touch his face."

Trivia grabbed my hand, clenching it tightly. "We'll find him. I can't wait to get to know him better. Our time together was almost non-existent since Kolya dragged him off as soon as I'd met him."

"Kolya didn't drag him anywhere. He wormed his way into Arjun's mind and twisted his thoughts. I sincerely hope he's seen the man for what he is," I said. "I can't wait for you two to hit it off. You'll spend all your time talking about things that go well over my head. Remind me again why you love a big, dumb oaf like me?"

"Just like Arjun does. I love you for who you are, not what you can do."

I squeezed her hand as Jafar's huge frame squeezed through the hatch to enter the weight room.

"Elite Huck, the presence of your team is requested at the farms," he said.

"You get off lucky this time," said Fen.

"I swear she's a masochist," I whispered.

Jafar laughed. "You will not think it luck when you see the work ahead. We have much harvesting and loading before we sail tomorrow."

The entire room groaned. It made sense though. If we were part of the crew, we helped with every aspect of the voyage, including the preparation.

"Come on," said Trivia, jumping to her feet and jerking me up.

"Alright, alright," I said, chuckling. "I wish I had half of the energy you do."

•••••••••

Outside of the tunnels was blindingly bright after even a few hours underground. I held my hand over my face waiting patiently for my eyes to adjust. By the time I could see, Jafar was already quite a ways ahead as we hurried to catch up. Even in the heat, he still wore his black and crimson cloak and turban. I would never understand why people like Marie and Jafar would rather bake themselves alive than change from their signature outfits. We followed him past several bunkers before Trivia couldn't help herself.

"Why are there so many bunkers?" she asked the giant.

Jafar flashed a grin of amusement. "Do you recall what Om Banyu told you about the defenses?"

"Archers and miniguns, right?" I said.

"Yes, but there isn't always enough warning, and occasionally, the inverts like to overwhelm our defenses. In the tower," he said, pointing towards the tallest edifice in the shipyard which sprouted from what looked to be a factory, "there's an old hand-crank air-raid siren from the Second World War. When you hear that, you best find yourself cover—fast."

"I knew this open area was too good to be true," said Huck. "No one can truly live on the surface while the inverts haunt our planet."

"A fact I hope you change, my friends."

We walked under the shadow of the tower, which was tall enough to see over the fortress walls encompassing the city. The shade from the wide construction was more than welcome in the intense heat of the day. I squinted, trying to examine the tower's uppermost story, which appeared to be a large lookout platform. The view must be insane. I looked at Trivia, bouncing along beside me. *I wonder if I can take her up there before we leave.* Show her something pleasant before we're surrounded once more by death and destruction. I dry swallowed. That tower was *really* high. Maybe I can brave my fears… for her.

We arrived at the farms, which took up a large portion of the exterior land and included the berm built over the factory below. Sure enough, there was Rudolfo's vineyard, wasting a lot of arable land. Dotted across the field were workers, mostly female, carefully tending to the plants. I immediately recognized some of the crops, like cassava and coconut, we'd not only come across but depended on for food during our travels. We'd spent much of our journey in tropical climates, so it made sense that what was cultivated here was familiar native flora.

"Most of our stores are harvested," Jafar announced, pointing to several large crates. "But there has been a potato shortage. They are only just now ready. As a large portion of our diet at sea, we will need two crates. The harvesting is labor intensive and rests on your shoulders. Two crates, by sundown. The rest of the crates must be loaded onto the ship. No one rides for free."

I don't see Rudolfo or Zimo out here helping, so apparently they do.

"Figures," said Krista. "Fen wears us out, and then we have to work our asses off."

"It's for all of our good," said Fen, pushing Roque's wheelchair along.

"Are you afraid of a little work?" asked Marie. "When your survival depends on what you grow, you get very comfortable with it." She picked up a pitchfork and went to work, gently poking the ground.

Jafar cocked an eyebrow, then said something indiscernible to the nearest worker and departed. The older, chestnut-skinned woman approached us and did a subtle bow. Like so many of the above-ground workers, her skin was weathered from all the time under the blazing sun.

"Your friend knows what she's doing," she said, smiling. "I am Greenskeeper Diah. I will show you the technique for pulling the potatoes from the earth. It looks as though I don't have to demonstrate."

Marie had already pulled a bundle of small potatoes from the ground, dusted them off, and was carrying them to the crate.

"Follow your friend's example. Take a pitchfork, and carefully stick it in the dirt. You want to loosen the ground's hold on the potatoes, not damage them. Once they are free, use your hands. They are your greatest tool in the garden."

It occurred to me that I'd never done anything like this before. I knew what was involved with growing. Every pod did it, but most pod food was grown aquaponically or with minerally-depleted soil. None of it was as nutritious as what was grown in real ground, under the warmth of the sun and soaking afternoon rain.

Ariadne and Leisel dived right in, both having spent ample time working in the gardens of Pod Kano while I'd been… tangled in pod politics. I owed my life to these people. They'd risked everything to save me from that dark period of my life that I wanted nothing more than to forget. Thanks to them, I'd lived long enough to meet Trivia. Hopefully long enough to save my brother.

"How long have you been working the fields, Greenskeeper?" asked Leisel.

"All my life," she said. "Please call me Diah."

"Me too," she said.

A look of momentary surprise flashed across the greenskeeper's face. "Forgive my boldness, but you don't look it."

"I worked underground," she said, showing Diah her hands, calloused from years of working in the gardens. It was an odd juxtaposition. In every other respect, she didn't look like she'd worked a day in her life. "Kano's gardens were nothing like this. This is… beautiful. I dreamed of working in a garden like this."

"Maybe not this hot though," said Ariadne, wiping dirt across her sweaty forehead with the back of her hand.

Diah chuckled melodiously. "You get used to it."

Despite the heat, the ground was cool. I found the anxiety I'd had about the upcoming day slowly subsiding. I thought back to the lake I'd fallen in love with back in the Latin Territory. Maybe one day I could build a cabin there. Grow my own food. Maybe even Trivia would like to live there with me. I smiled at her, laughing when I noticed all of the dirt and hair matted to her face. We'd known each other such a short time, and already, I couldn't imagine living without her. She saw me laughing and flung a clod of dirt at me.

"Goober," she said, returning to work.

Man, I am crazy about this woman.

"If you don't mind me asking, I've noticed most of the population here looks to be the same ethnicity," said Ondo. "Most of the pods I've been to are more…"

"Diverse?" finished Diah. "Yes. Bandung is not an easy city to reach, so we don't have quite the numbers of the others. Most people born here stay here."

"How is that?" asked Roque, perking up under the sunlight. "When Release Day comes, do they not have any interest in other pods? Other jobs?"

Diah shook her head. "We've never suffered from overpopulation to the extent of other pods. Release Day has never been a necessity here. The majority of the residents chose to work in the shipyards like the generations before them, supplying the global transporters with their vessels."

"How is overpopulation not a problem?" asked Omar.

"The shipyards are a very dangerous place to work. Over the course of a year, as many are lost to the Arthropods here as in your Release Days."

"Oh," I said, letting it sink in. "Aren't you afraid to work up here?"

"Aren't you afraid to go to the Hive?" she asked, smirking.

"A little, but the end goal is more important."

"Exactly. When it's my time, it's my time. No sense in losing sleep over it."

"A greenskeeper and a guru," said Omar.

"It seems to come with the job," said Ariadne as Leisel agreed.

We toiled away for several hours, finishing around dusk but well before dark. After lugging the crates to a grateful Captain Banyu, we were free of duties for our last night in the city. As we hopped into the tram, I half-expected Fen to announce a midnight run or some nonsense, but she was content to leave us on our own recognizance.

Exhausted, Trivia and I begged away from the others, anxious for a few moments alone. Now knowing that not every resident was excited about our mission, I made sure to stay on my guard. We strolled down level by level, relishing the solace until we discovered a hole-in-the-wall establishment named Lombok where several off-duty dockworkers were eating after the day's toil. When we entered, everyone looked in our direction. At first, I thought it was due to our fame, but as quickly as they returned to eating, I supposed not. Here we were nothing more than outsiders. I ordered *rendang* and Trivia, something called *pempek*. Neither of us had eaten either dish before, but they were amazing. The locals knew how to properly spice their food. The fact that some of their food was actually fresh, as opposed to what I'd grown up with, made a huge difference. When it came time to pay, our tab had already been covered. The server wouldn't say who paid and no one so much as made eye contact.

"Thank them for us," I said as we departed towards the central shaft.

Standing on the edge of the vast chasm dimmed for the night, the faint lights of the Nucleus twinkled like stars, a cosmos just beyond our reach. Below glowed the faint purple hues of the nuclear reactors keeping the pod running. For the first time, I appreciated the city for what it was: a living organism. The Arthropods may have taken away our technology, but they couldn't take our spirit. We were survivors. It was that resiliency that kept my faith in humanity.

"What?" asked Trivia, smiling.

"I have an idea."

I grabbed her and took off at a steady pace, laughing together like fools. I didn't stop until we reached the base of the tower in the shipyard. It was probably a silly thing to do, each of us armed with only our daggers, but I was head-over-heels in love. When we arrived at the base of the stairs, two guards blocked our path.

"I'm sorry, Elites," said one of the pair. "This area is off-limits without explicit permission from Rudolfo."

"We're here for Lord Ransford," I said. "We need to pick up his…"

"Pillow," said Trivia, remembering how Huck had described the prime minister's office.

"Yeah, his pillow."

The guard looked at the other and shrugged. "Be quick about it."

Once we were a flight up, I whispered, "I can't believe that worked."

"Everyone knows the minister will do anything for his little dog," she said, stifling a laugh. "Now that we've snuck in here, what's this crazy idea of yours?"

We reached the balcony and nearly tumbled out across the floor, silly and lovestruck.

"What are you two doing here?" asked the guard on watch. "You can't be in here!"

"We're here to relieve you for your break," I said. "We'll keep watch until you return."

The guard gave me a questioning look but left anyway. I guess our reputation had its benefits. Finally alone, I looked out over the edge and instantly grew nauseous.

"Whoa there, Hemant. You okay?"

"Yeah. Just questioning this decision."

"Well, you must have had a good reason to bring me up here given your fear."

I pointed her towards the view as I looked away from it.

"My god, it's beautiful," she said, gasping.

"Not as beautiful as you," I said, facing away from the long distance down.

Cheesy, but true. In the distance the ocean lapped against the walls, the sea breeze played with her hair, her eyes twinkled in the moonlight.

"If we survive all of this, would you live with me?" I asked.

She blushed and laughed it off, taking it more light-hearted than I'd intended.

"I mean it. If we survive this, I want to spend the rest of my life with you."

She smiled, suppressing worry. "Hemant, we haven't known each other very long. What if you find something about me you don't like? What if I find out something about you I don't like?"

"I've told you everything. About the killing, the Dust, Arjun. There's nothing more to say aside from 'I love you.' Which I want to say to you over and over again as long as I live. However long that may be. I want to live by a lake, grow food, have little kids—"

Trivia had my head in her hands and her lips pressed tightly against mine before I knew what was happening. She was crying when she finally pulled away.

"Yes!" she said, nodding, as I pulled her close. "But if you die on me, I'll be pissed."

"That's fair," I said, wiping the tear from her cheek with my thumb. "Now that I know life with you, I don't think I could live it without you. Though eventually, you'll have to tell me your real name."

Her eyes took on a distant look.

"What is it?"

"We need to sound that alarm."

CHAPTER 16: KOLYA

Despite the lack of need for them, Arjun and I still slept in our bivvies. The inverts' heat-seeking abilities were no longer a concern, but they insulated against the frigid Outback nights. Sadly, they did little to make the rough terrain more comfortable. We may have been safe, but a sound night's sleep proved impossible. No sooner would I nod off than the towers would spew their living contents into the sky with high-pitched screeches and the bass thrum of wings. Friendly or not, the sounds were quite disorienting and deeply unnerving. Even if Arjun's friends made it this far, they would likely run with fear, soiling their pants as they did.

When morning finally broke, our guides had disappeared from the makeshift camp. We'd been encouraging the vegetarian breakfasts, but eventually, their fallen nature prevailed. Neesh and Jigna returned with a creature that could only be described as an unripe banana with legs. Arjun looked at me with disappointment. Though repetitive, we had been hoping for more fruit and eggs. Without delay, our host ripped the flailing legs of the screeching nymph, splitting its abdomen with excitement and ripping out bits, consuming the morsels raw. It was too much for my companion, who rushed to a bush to regurgitate what little fluids remained in his stomach.

"Couldn't take it anymore?" I asked on his return, proffering a small handkerchief.

"It's not just the act, but the type of nymph," he said, extending his hand towards the flayed corpse. "That's a spine back."

"Oh-ho! That explains your reaction."

The Nightmare was the single most vicious invert that Arjun and his companions had encountered. Omar had dealt the death blow on both occasions they'd come across the spine backs, demonstrating nothing more than his ability to take credit for the kill. Though his contributions were rarely acknowledged, Arjun was often the one responsible for their battlefield successes. Arjun had said after the first creature was slain, its body burst with offspring which scattered into the woods. If one of these creatures was formidable, I could scarcely imagine hundreds of them. For a creature so feared even among the Arthropods, these two Demented had had no qualms about dispatching its young.

"Our friends seem to have no fear," I mused.

"There must be some mutually beneficial relationship that we have yet to discover."

"Arjna. Kolha," grunted Neesh, pointing south.

"I guess it is time," I said, with one last glance up at the monstrous twin mounds.

We mounted our pedes and hit the trail. Barely an hour out of town, we stumbled upon the most fascinating rock formation—gigantic boulders stacked atop boulders. The red limestone spheres appeared less like a natural occurrence but rather objects sculpted by God's own hands. I yelled, motioning for Neesh to stop so that we could inspect the site, but with a bark, my request was declined. I turned in my seat forlornly, watching the marble-like stones recede in the distance. One of the few sights of interest in the mostly barren expanse and we couldn't take the time to appreciate it. I guess nature's beauty wasn't something the Demented valued. *They are nothing more than animals, my dear. Animals that had no place in humanity's future.*

With each kilometer we traveled inland, the architecture of the Arthropods had become more astounding. I was anxious and nervous about seeing the actual Hive. It must be a least triple the size of the towers we were leaving in our dusty wake. *No, that wouldn't be possible. The twins alone are a feat of engineering.* I figured that the Hive must be an extensive underground construction, perhaps with a tower of its own, but mostly below ground level where there would be more structure. Like an anthill, the little evidence on the surface barely hinted at the labyrinth below. Within moments, equally large mounds were visible on the horizon, already larger than the twins. *It can't be, Sveta. The waves of heat emanating from the ground are distorting the perspective. That must be the case.* But the more mounds I saw, the more I doubted my hypothesis. They *were* getting bigger. Aside from the unchanging red dirt, dehydrated brown grass, and short pale-green trees, the only shift in the landscape was the size and frequency of the Arthropods' earthen constructions.

"Why didn't we see mounds like these in the other territories?" asked Arjun.

"I don't know," I said, stroking my beard. "They were relatively small on the edge of the continent. Perhaps 400 years hasn't been enough to expand this aspect of their existence. With their food supply limited, they can only grow so fast."

"These mounds bear a striking similarity to our pods, perhaps each with their own lesser queen," he said. "Based on what Ciro and I discovered, while they can reproduce outside of the Australian Territory, the majority of their reproduction occurs here in the safety of their nests."

I nodded, processing his words as we rode on. I'd grown tolerant to the smell of Neesh drifting back from in front of me, but every time the breeze wafted it strongly, I had to suppress the urge to vomit. The oppressive heat did nothing beneficial for the putrid odor that plagued his flesh. The term "zombie" flitted across my imagination, and I wondered to what extent this host, assuming we were correct, could operate after its death. The thought made me shudder. I was almost certain that this beast of a human couldn't be alive without that alien sludge surging through his body.

Arjun's guide's slender black body was poorly covered by her leathery attire. Even though it had been too long since I'd enjoyed the company of a woman, the condition of her body held no attraction. Reduced to their most primal instincts, I would bet all my ration points that the pair's relations more closely resembled assault than love or passion. When I rolled my eyes, I couldn't help but notice the mesmerizing sky.

"Would you look at those clouds," I said as the sun peaked high above our heads "It almost gives the impression that we are heading for a jagged mountain range."

"It does give that effect, doesn't it? For all the evolution the human mind has experienced, it still struggles with optical illusions," he said. "From what I've read, there is a preponderance of large hills near what used to be Alice Springs where we are destined, but I doubt they could be misconstrued as mountains."

"Was that a joke, my boy?"

Arjun had the faintest hint of a smirk.

I chuckled. The boy had just as much depth to him as anyone else, likely more. You just had to be sharp enough to catch it. I munched on my mid-day ration bar from my mount, which I'd timed for when a crosswind kept Neesh's smell at bay. The first day had nearly beaten the nerves in my buttocks to a pulp, but after the initial soreness dispersed, I found the cross-country excursion to be downright pleasant. The multipedes undulating motion had a rocking sensation that by the end of each day could nearly lull me to sleep. With none of the scenery changing aside from the mounds and exhaustion nipping at my heels, staying awake on our third day proved challenging.

"Kolya?"

"Yes?"

"Those cloud formations… they haven't changed."

I followed his gaze into the distance. Sure enough, they hadn't. I'd been ignoring the sky, lost in my head as I struggled to stay awake. The realization impacted me like charging multipede to the chest. They *were* mountains!

"That can't be. Minor faultlines span the continent, even the occasional volcano, but nowhere near enough tectonic activity to produce a mountain range of that scale, at least not in the periods we're discussing."

"There's only one other possibility," said Arjun.

"No," I said, lost for all other words.

"Think about all the seismic activity recorded from Pine Gap after the Landing. The Arthropods have had centuries to accomplish their work."

"But mountains, Arjun? if we can see them from this far away, do you realize how large they would have to be?"

He thought for a moment, his mathematical genius calculating faster than my mind could even fathom.

"If you account for distance traveled, atmospheric refraction, and the curvature of the Earth, I'd estimate the tallest one to be between eight and ten thousand meters. That's as accurate as I can be without more precise measurements."

"Arjun, do you realize what you are saying?"

He looked at me, patiently awaiting my simplistic response.

"The Hive is the size of Everest."

•••••••

The largest peak grew in size as we traversed the compacted earth leading to its widely-sloped base. The closer we were, the more excited our Demented guides became. *"Rafdo, rafdo,"* they chanted incessantly with increasing enthusiasm the more the structure loomed on the horizon. *The Hive, Sveta. My God is it huge.* A mountain, far larger than I'd ever imagined. Though not a volcano, its spawn spewed forth into the sky like ash and rock, partially occluding the sun like a hurricane whose eye centered above the peak. The sheer size of the structure… for all intents and purposes, it should be physically impossible. As we approached, the sky grew darker, more ominous. In the artificial twilight, the terrain assumed the dark gray hues of the Arthropods' excrement that caked the landscape. A deep vibration saturated the air, unnerving me to my core. This was a place of evil. For the first time, I second-guessed my desire for peace.

Towards what I could only assume to be the beginnings of dusk, we passed through the first ring of towers, each one significantly taller than the pair under which we'd spent the previous night. As the minutes crept by, our guides took us progressively deeper and deeper into what I could only describe as enemy territory. Each sequential ring of towers was larger than the last, further defying all I knew of physical law. Arjun stared with such wide eyes that I thought his eyes would leap from their orbits. As the clouds of beasts swarmed high above, I wanted nothing more than to find a small hole and cower. Protected as I was, I could not have been more terrified.

What hubris Memo had that he thought he could destroy this! I thought of Dieter and Guilherme's puny collaboration—the now inert chemo-nuclear weapon that Arjun's companions now lugged far behind us. Even had I not sabotaged the weapon, I doubted its effectiveness. Placed dead center, deep within the mountain of this scale, not even it could destroy enough of the Arthropods to vanquish them from our planet. *No, peace is our only chance of survival.* I suppressed the fear ravaging my body and forced myself to sit up straighter as we traversed the final ring through an earthen tunnel. *This is it. This is what I've worked so hard to achieve.*

Night fell prematurely as we traveled underground. The cavernous space had to be hundreds of meters long, illuminated only by some sort of photoluminescent worms. *Glass worms!* I spun towards Arjun, whose lips had curled in a sneer. It must have taken substantial self-control to restrain from lashing out against the species that had killed his beloved. The most passionate I'd ever beheld my companion was when he'd sliced one of the shinies into halves in a fit of rage. At the moment, the only emotion I felt was gratitude for their greenish hue lighting our otherwise dim path. Between me and their glowing bodies, I could faintly make out the nearly imperceptible distortion of mantis wraiths. The invisible creatures were perhaps the most lethal of the invaders, with razor-sharp appendages, stayed only by our ambassadorial status.

When we emerged from the final ring's tunnel, we descended into a basin surrounding the base of the Hive. Scattered all over its exterior were humongous tunnels burrowed deep into the mountain forming a maze from which nothing could escape. The creatures' nest had been built on such a scale that from this proximity, its face appeared flat—a sheer wall shooting up from the ground at an impossible angle. A deep bass trumpeting reverberated from within, echoed by all the beasts. The cacophonous tone shocked my ears and nearly stopped my heart. It shook the land, raining down loose dirt and rock from the surrounding towers, heralding our arrival. In an unexpected move, Arjun took my hand and squeezed it tightly. In all my time with the boy, I'd never known him to seek touch from anyone but his lost lover or his twin brother.

"My God," I said, staring up at the swarms above that had halted to hover in mid-air.

Neesh and Jigna gracefully slid down from their mounts, falling to the ground to prostrate themselves before us as though we were royalty. Every pair of compound eyes faced us. Uncertain of how to proceed, I simply slid down and waited next to the multipede as Arjun copied my example. In my many years of dedicated study of the Arthropods, I'd never come across anything like this. No human had. Ahead, I spotted movement from the entrance. Like back in the desert, a glass worm was trundled out on a bed of polies. I rubbed Arjun's shoulder soothingly, knowing a repeat of his violent outburst would spell our demise. He nodded subtly.

The shiny halted in front of us. The strange creature had been the only method of communication thus far aside from the pheromonal message I'd dispatched with the powder moth an eternity ago. As rudimentary as the method had been, it had seen us safely here, where I had no doubt we were the first human presence in ages. The glass worm raised to its full height, spreading itself wide, and its light show began. The crude message was far more simple than before but even more exciting. Two green lights moved toward a red, vaguely triangular object. *Us. The Hive.* The dots moved within the triangle, led by other red dots. Then the red dots fell back, and the triangle disappeared. Purple dots blinked into existence in a circle surrounding the two green dots. *The Queens!* I almost jumped with joy. The image winked out as I nodded profusely.

"Yes," I said, nodding, unsure if the creature could understand. "We go. Meet Queens," I said, gesturing.

The glass worm mimicked my nod, forming an arm-like appendage, and repeated my gesture. Then the invertebrate made a buzzing along the edge of human hearing. Two four-person teams of Demented emerged from the tunnel bearing empty wooden litters, each warrior as scarred and raw-fleshed as our guides. They lowered the chairs, poofing the dust in front of us, and I noticed that attached to each arm was a bowl of fresh fruit.

"Should we proceed?" asked Arjun, hands shaking.

I took a deep breath. "We're way past turning back," I said, smiling.

We sat, and the Demented hoisted us up to their shoulders. All the Arthropods jolted back to life, trumpeting their approval as we were carried towards the dark maw that would lead us deep into the Hive to meet the Queens.

CHAPTER 17: DARREN

2042

It took ages to fall asleep, knowing with each passing hour, Patricia was closer to the anomaly in the middle of the Outback. My last thought before I finally succumbed to sleep was sympathy for the people of Alice Springs, whose city had been decimated by the impact of the rock nearby. Luckily, there had only been a handful of deaths, but the town had been evacuated with no prospect of return. I couldn't image what it was like to have your entire life upended like that.

"What the…" I muttered, half awake. "Finally get to sleep and someone's calling."

I stumbled across the bedroom to the wall screen and hit the icon for audio-only. No one needed to see what I slept in. I was too groggy to even bother to see who was calling.

"Darren," said Stepan. "Are you there?"

"Dude, do you have any idea what time it is?" I asked. "Please tell me you don't need a pickup from another mushroom party. I had so much trouble getting—"

"Darren! Shut up and listen," he said.

Aside from running his mouth too much, Stepan was perpetually chill. His telling me to shut up was so far out of character that I was instantly alert and listening.

"Alright, you've got my attention."

"I'm pretty sure you don't know then," he said, taking a deep breath.

"Darren, there was some sort of cave-in at the meteorite. It's all over the feeds. Dude, I don't know how to tell you this, but they said the science teams… most of them are missing."

My heart plummeted through time and space. *Patricia.* I minimized the call and activated a silent news feed. The crawl on the bottom told me everything I needed to know. "Catastrophic collapse near meteorite. Scores of scientists missing."

"Oh my God. Oh my God," I repeated.

"Is there any chance she was back at Pine Gap? The collapse only extended a few kilometers out from the rock. Everyone there is fine, but shaken up."

I shook my head in a gesture Stepan couldn't see. "She… she was scheduled to go out to the site today. She told me she was hoping to have her hands on the rock. Oh god…"

"We'll be over there in a few," he said. "See if you can reach Pine Gap in the meantime."

"Okay," was all I managed to say, the the call ended.

I threw on a robe and called Patricia's temporary number. I expected every scientist there to have family desperately trying to reach them and didn't expect the call to go through. I was surprised when it was answered immediately by Grayson.

"Grayson, it's Darren," I said, seeing his suited figure on the screen.

"I thought you might call, Mr. Taggert," he said. "I was hoping for more information before I contacted you."

"Patricia?"

He shook his head slowly. "I'm sorry, Mr. Tag— Darren, but she's one of the ones missing. I was watching the closed-circuit feeds. The dirt… It just opened under their feet. The few instruments that weren't destroyed on impact registered forces unsurvivable to humans."

I shook my head, "But she could be alive. You're still going to look for them, right?"

"Eventually, but they have to make sure the area is safe, otherwise we risk losing even more people. We've called in the Territorial Guard. They are experienced in search and rescue operations."

"And how long will that take?!" I asked, raising my voice.

"I don't know. I'm sorry. There are over three hundred personnel missing. I assure you, this is a top priority for every agency involved."

"What can I do?" I asked, beginning to hyperventilate.

"Dad?" asked Alexander, rubbing his eyes.

"Oh, son," I said.

"Mr. Taggert, I'll leave you two. You can reach me at this line any time. I'll do my best to keep you updated."

I nodded slowly, and Grayson cut the feed. Hugging Alex helped slow my rapid breathing.

"Something's happened to Mommy," I said. "I don't know what yet, but we have to be strong, for her, okay?"

Alexander's lower lip began to quiver, but he did his best to remain calm, perhaps more so than I had. I heard a knock at the door.

"That must be Stepan," I said, dabbing my eyes with my sleeve.

"Is it alright if I turn on the news?" he asked as I closed the door behind them. "I hope you don't mind Kitty coming. She thought you might want a hand with Alex."

I nodded in response to both as Kitty took Alex by the hand and walked with him down the hallway, asking about his toy collection.

"Any word?"

"I talked to her escort. He verified that she's missing. He said it's unlikely that anyone survived the fall."

"Oh God, Darren," he said. "I'm so sorry."

"I can't give up hope yet. They're setting up a search and rescue operation, but he said the progress will be slow. They are trying to avoid a repeat incident."

"Makes sense, but it's not easy to sit around waiting."

"You think I should fly out there? To the Outback, I mean."

"Darren, that's not rational. Even if you did, there's no way they'd let you get anywhere near the place. Not to mention, you've got Alex to think of."

"You're right. I thought I'd ask," I said, listening to the news. For the first time, I saw the images from a circling rotor-wing, and a pit, not unlike the one on the screen, formed in my stomach. The meteorite stood as erect as ever, slightly more of it revealed than before. Holes below ground level were now visible in the rock's structure, giving merit to Stepan's no-longer-crazy idea. The ground had formed a gargantuan crater-like basin, far larger than the initial crater had been. From the vast distance, all I could make out in the darkness were jagged rocks and lingering clouds of dust. "No one could've survived that."

"You just said you weren't giving up, man," said Stepan.

"Look for yourself," I said, raising my voice. "If I fell off the Renaissance Center, you wouldn't be telling Patricia not to give up!"

"Darren," he said softly, "why don't you have a seat?"

I took a deep breath and collapsed on the couch, sobbing. "People always say they can feel when their loved ones are still alive. I don't feel anything but pain. She's gone, Step."

"If that's the case, she died doing what she believed in."

•••••••

Forty-eight hours passed before I heard from Grayson again. Search and rescue had finally established it was safe enough to rappel down into the abyss. News had confirmed multiple times, they didn't expect to find anyone alive. As much as it pained me, I had begun to reconcile myself to my wife being gone. Alexander had taken the news in stride, staying strong, just as I had asked. At night, we sleep together, often falling asleep crying. I felt as though my heart was a cracked vase, never to be mended. Mrs. Grimethorpe had continued to be amazing, taking Alex in during the day. As a retired teacher, she'd counseled countless students throughout her tenure. Today, she was demonstrating the relief that can be found in baking. For the first time in a while, I smiled. I could imagine Alex covered from head to toe in flour, handing me a cookie with cat hairs sticking out of it.

I sipped the black coffee from Patricia's favorite mug, took a deep breath to quell the anxiety in my bosom, and readied myself to watch the live search and rescue. The firm had told me to take as much time as I needed. Not everyone was lucky enough to work for such an understanding company. Patricia and I had never been wealthy, she wasn't "that type" of doctor, but we had enough in savings to last for a few months. *Especially with one less mouth to feed,* I thought, choking back a sob.

On the wall screen, the rotor wings were circling significantly closer to the crater's edge. The newscaster was saying something about the photog team not going closer to avoid showing gruesome footage. I pushed the thought of Patricia's mangled corpse from my mind. I would always remember her as the radiant soul that she was and nothing less.

The first few hours were boring and repetitive. I learned nothing new from the footage of ropes hanging off into the gaping hole. Finally, on the ground, I could see noticeable movement.

Something was happening, though the details hadn't reached the pair at the news desk.

"Viewers, it appears that there have been new findings by the S&R team at the AS-42 site. Those of you sensitive to graphic information might wish to change the feed at this time."

I sat on the edge of my couch, anxious to learn anything about the demise of my wife.

"What the Territorial Guard found in the crater is perhaps the most troubling information we've received yet. After hours of searching, they have found blood, but no bodies. I repeat: They have found no bodies."

What the hell? Three hundred scientists didn't simply vanish. *I get it, maybe fifty unaccounted for, but all of them?* I was standing now.

"We're going live on the ground with Pamela Johnson, who's with the head of the search and rescue battalion and director of research at Pine Gap. Pamela?"

"Thanks, Dean," said the curly-haired reporter. "I'm here with Colonel Dennis Scott of the Northern Region's Search and Rescue Battalion and Pine Gap Research Director Matt Foster. Colonel Scott, would you share with us what you've discovered?"

The pair looked like neither had slept since the incident. Scott had the typical build you'd expect from his duties, similar to the firefighter build of my father. Foster was an older gentleman but appeared in excellent shape, aside from the invisible weight he carried on his shoulders.

"I'll be honest, Pamela, it's the damnedest thing I've ever seen in my eighteen years of service," he said, placing a hand over his mouth in exasperation. "It's like someone already came in and removed the bodies."

"Would you mind explaining that, Colonel," said Pamela, just as surprised by the revelation as I was.

"Sure, yeah," he said. "When something like this happens, there's rubble everywhere. Not to offend, but it's not a pretty sight.

Don't get me wrong, there was quite a bit of blood down there, but not a body to be found." He paused. "There were trails, Pamela. Trails that led into caverns in the rock. When we realized what had occurred, I immediately withdrew my teams to the safe zone."

Stepan's digging comments echoed in my ears. *No. This can't be happening.* I couldn't imagine some alien carnivore taking away my Patricia. As far-fetched as the idea was, someone or something had taken my wife's body. I seethed with anger. Pamela was at a loss for words, staring into the camera, while I was sure the production assistants were screaming in her ear. Dr. Foster didn't seem as surprised, more resigned, if anything. He had the presence of mind to start talking on his own.

"Pamela," he began. "Our initial research indicated there were cavities in the meteorite, but our scans led us to believe they were empty. In light of the discoveries by Colonel Scott and his team, I have recommended that the region's Territorial Guard be deployed to secure the perimeter and neutralize any potential adversaries that may be in the area."

Pamela finally refocused, and asked, "Dr. Foster, are you saying what I think you are saying?"

"I'm saying our findings indicate the possibility of hostile life inside the meteorite."

"There you have it," stuttered Pamela, visibly shaken and voice trembling. "Back to you, Dean."

The view switched back to the studio, but before Dean spoke, you could hear Pamela screaming, "Get me the hell out of here!" followed by a barrage of terrified language before the audio tech cut her microphone.

Aliens? Patricia's studies had always been so… theoretical. I refused to believe that we were alone in the universe, but hostile forces on Earth in my lifetime? I never thought it would happen. My body was wrought with chaotic emotions. I didn't know whether to be distraught, furious, or panicked. If there was any hope that Patricia was alive, it was gone.

"My wife is gone," I said to the empty room.

I hoped to the universe she was dead long before whatever it was dragged her off. I went to the kitchen for another cup of coffee but never made it. I fell to the floor in racking sobs, my entire body shaking, as I called my wife's name knowing she would never again respond.

CHAPTER 18: HUCK

At first, we didn't hear the alarms. We were lounging in the common room at the end of the apartment corridor, as far from the central shaft as you could get. We'd been laughing hysterically as Omar did an impression of Rudolfo, using an old shawl he'd found on the ground somewhere. Fen suddenly leaned forward and froze, listening intently. Like flipping a switch, every one of us went into survival mode. Thundering footsteps resounded from the shaft, nearly drowning out the wails of alarm cascading down through the pod's interior.

"Something's happening," I said, jumping up. "I'm getting my gear!"

Fen made to push Roque, but he waved her off. "Go! I'll be fine."

She looked reluctant to leave but trusted his judgment. Like well-oiled machine, we sprinted to our apartments, grabbing our weapons and donning the light armor that covered our jumpsuits. I didn't care what the emergency was, I wasn't showing up unprepared. I hefted the fine Wuhan-made blade in my hand as Ariadne strapped on her last set of plates.

Grabbing our packs, we rushed out of our apartment and met the others in the hallway. Each of us prepared as though we were leaving immediately. Together, we sprinted down the corridor before Krista pulled us to a halt.

"Wait!" she yelled. "We have to get Hemant and Trivia's stuff!"

"On it," responded Omar, grabbing Ondo.

Aside from Hemant, they were the strongest of our team. It would be no struggle for them to carry the extra weight. A moment later, they emerged, and Omar threw me Ondo's bag, strapping on Trivia's.

Before I could ask what was happening, Ondo ducked out of the hatch with Hemant's bag and the attached nuclear weapon we'd lugged halfway around the world. *Oh, I'd nearly forgotten about that.* Cumbersome as it was Ondo carried the load with ease. We resumed our sprint and immediately noticed everyone running was able-bodied residents, all carrying weapons.

"What's going on?" I yelled over the screaming alarms, the emergency strobes nearly blinding me.

"An aerial attack is overwhelming our defenses," yelled a man back.

"This alarm is summoning every able-bodied person to defend the shipyard," said a woman armed with a stout pipe.

"Does this happen often?" I yelled.

"Not like this," said the man, deep worry in his eyes.

Everyone was running towards the various stairwells, tucked away at the end of each district. None of the pod's staircases could singularly handle this volume of people but spread out between them, maybe we could avoid the potential traffic jam.

"This is taking too long!" yelled Ariadne over the din. "By the time we get there, the attack might be over and maybe not in our favor."

The tram normally took about an hour to run the length of the 40-kilometer tunnel. Not exactly ideal reinforcements for what would inevitably be a fast-paced battle.

"The trams can go twice as fast as they normally do in emergencies," said the man, already breathing heavily as he took the dusty, lesser-used steps two and three at a time. "Regardless, we have to defend the yard. Everyone here is a fighter first. By the way, I'm Sven."

"Evelyn," said the woman.

"I'm—"

"Huck," Sven said, smiling. "We know who you are. Everyone does."

"What about the bunkers?!" yelled Krista. "Can't everyone just hide until it's over?"

"The bunkers are made for waiting until a raid peters out," said Evelyn. "If we're hearing this alarm, it's no harrying raid. They are trying to do serious damage."

We piled out of the stairwell and made for the rapidly filling tram. Ariadne and I traded a knowing look. *They know we're here.* We climbed aboard, the tram more loaded than I'd ever seen it, and the driver strained its motors to speed us toward the shipyard. The wind whipped my face, as Ariadne hurriedly braided her hair. I hoped to the universe that Hemant and Trivia were okay.

The screams reached us well before we breached the tunnel's end. The tram emerged into pure chaos. We'd always done less fighting at night when the creatures had the upper hand, choosing instead to camp in our camouflaging bivvies. In this instance, there was no choice. The inverts were growing bolder by the day, risking their human food supply for our group's destruction. If having every invert on the planet after me wasn't so terrifying, I'd take their fear as a compliment.

"Drive them off!" shouted Rudolfo from an enclosed bunker on the hillside near the tunnel's mouth. "Kill them all!"

I couldn't see the minister through the thin slits in the concrete emplacement, but I recognized his whiny voice anywhere. I bet his dog was in there with him, cowering just like he was. I turned to see Sven and Evelyn rushing into battle, axe and pipe raised. Sven's long blond hair trailed after him.

"Once more unto the breach?" I asked Ariadne as I dove into the fracas.

Men and women ran alongside me, yelling battle cries as they slashed at the flying inverts landing among us. Hooks, raptors, and chompers were everywhere I turned! I'd slash fruitlessly at one, while another attacked from behind. For every one I took down, another would appear in its place trying to cleave off my head or rip me apart. *This is madness!*

I heard a scream and watched a mud raptor pick up a soldier, carrying him off into the night sky. His companion tried to shoot him but missed his opportunity for the mercy killing. I shuddered to think what would happen to him. Another raptor picked up Evelyn, who'd been fighting at my side. *Not Ariadne, thank the universe.* I felt instant guilt. She was just as important to someone else. Ariadne loosed an arrow, taking her in the heart. The raptor, deprived of its fresh meal, dropped her into the harbor's dark water with a splash. My eyes burned with tears of anger. I *hated* these creatures.

"Get it off me! Get it off!"

I turned to see a soldier with a chomper about to devour his head and sliced it in half before it could finish the job. It was too late. The man flopped to the ground, clutching the back of his neck, bleeding out from around his severed spine at an alarming speed. *Damn it! If only I'd been faster!* Another split wing was bearing down on Ariadne, who was firing arrow after arrow into a hook beetle's compound eye, trying without success to bring it down. I swung just before the chomper made contact, separating its head from its thorax. Its still-throbbing tail instinctively continued spitting out encapsulated larva onto the ground. I stomped them with zeal, using my boot to grind them into oblivion. I'd barely survived my encounter with those bloody parasites, still feeling phantom itches from time to time.

"Behind!" said a wide-eyed woman, armed with a sledgehammer.

I turned to see three men, running towards me as fast as their bodies could move. In an instant, their bodies were riddled with holes, spraying a fine mist of their blood everywhere before they fell to the ground in mangled mounds of flesh.

"Mashi!" I screamed. "Mashi!"

The hauntingly small inverts dove around like zipping bullets, decimating anything in their path. Worse than the miniguns on the ramparts, the mashi could change direction on a whim, barely affected by inertia. In my pack was a blanket that could protect me, but I couldn't fight wearing it. I took a deep breath and pushed on without it. *Universe protect me.* Hemant heard my screams, and he and Trivia barreled towards me, daggers out. Measly weapons, but better than nothing.

"Drop!" I screamed.

They each fell to the ground, narrowly missing a swarm of the infinitesimal inverts. Once they'd passed, Hemant leapt to his feet.

"Damn bugs!" yelled Hemant. "Tell me you have my war hammer!"

"And my bow!" said Trivia.

"They're out here somewhere!" I yelled over the din. "Find Omar and Ondo!"

They sprinted off, back to back as they swung their daggers. Omar distantly bellowed his war cry, leading the pair in his direction. I turned to face my next enemy just as an explosion nearly rattled the teeth from my skull. *Pill bugs! God, could this get any worse?* That means powder moths are up there too!

"Masks up!" I yelled. "Cover your face!"

Ariadne heard my cries and passed the message on as more polies detonated in the distance. I threw on the mask I'd stolen from the Dust farm. Thankfully, the air was only minimally hazing. The dusters were sticking close to the water. *Of course! They're bombing the boats!*

"Defend the boats!" I yelled, pushing towards the harbor.

In the distance, wooden houses burned. Homes, belongings, lives… Trivia ran up behind me, bow at the ready, and started firing on the dusters. They were hard to see, but thanks to the flames, their beige underbellies were lit. The creatures' slow flight worked to our advantage, making them an easy target for the experienced archers. In a matter of minutes, the bulk of them were down, but most of the damage was done. The last of the metal-hulled boats were half sunk in the shallow harbor, their bows and sterns sticking out of the water at unnatural angles like the gravestones they were. All over the harbor, the wooden vessels that had proven so valuable were burning.

"They're falling back!" someone yelled, amid cheers.

At what cost?

I turned and was filled with relief when I saw Ariadne running towards me. Together, we surveyed the damage. The ocean breeze quickly cleared the air of the dusters' toxic poison, allowing the moonlight and flames to reveal the extent of the damage. So many of the smaller buildings were ruins, either piles of rubble or burning embers. Bodies littered the ground, human and invert alike, as their blood and hemolymph pooled on the ground. Miraculously, the tower and factory remained standing. The walls had missing chunks and gaping cracks but were mostly intact.

"Let's find the others!" said Ariadne. "I need to know they're okay."

We ran toward the tunnel mouth where people were gathering. As I covered the distance, I had to continuously jump over corpses, many incomplete. Tears of rage as hot as the harbor fires burned my eyes. The villagers had banded together, making a bucket line from the harbor, attempting to save every vessel and home they could. *The others will have to wait.* I slowed and joined in the line. Trivia and Ariadne, no longer sensing me behind them turned and added themselves to the group's ranks. For what felt like hours, we passed bucket after bucket. I reeked of smoke, sweat, and blood. Eventually, the buckets slowed. We'd halted the fire's advance but had only saved a quarter of the wooden dwellings.

The group gradually dispersed, giving their thanks, and we headed back towards the tunnel to find our friends. As the dawn light crested the walls and illuminated the tower, it shown like a beacon of hope after the long night of despair. I wanted nothing more than to run, but I had nothing left after everything we'd done. The three of us walked silently through the field of corpses. Ariadne's lip quivered, but she held her tears at bay. I looked up at the sound of hurried footsteps. *Sven!*

"Huck! Come with me!" he said, dried blood caked the blond locks to his face.

I took off after him, somehow finding the energy because of his sense of urgency. I was completely unprepared for the sight that greeted me. The tunnel to the pod had completely collapsed. Men were working to clear the rubble, but it would take days if not weeks. I thought it had been the emergency that I'd been summoned for, but Sven stopped and directed me towards a much smaller pile of rubble. My feet froze in their tracks. Leaning against the rubble was Leisel, a broken piece of hook beetle leg sticking out of her stomach.

"She asked specifically for you," said Sven. "Huck, I'm sorry, but she doesn't have long."

I walked to her side and kneeled, taking her hand.

"Huck," she said, spurting blood from her lips.

"Shh. Don't speak."

She gave a gargley chuckle. "It… doesn't matter."

I gently pushed the hair out of her face, my tears streaming down to the ground. Leisel and I had been so close before Ariadne and I had gotten together. Though no longer romantic, we'd remained close friends. Leisel was the most gentle soul I'd ever met, never having allowed the adversity of Pod Kano or the surface to change her innocent outlook and pure demeanor. Trainer Gempo had taught her to be a fearsome warrior, but off the battlefield, she'd always retained her meek personality. I glanced down at her wound. The invert's leg was the only thing keeping her from bleeding out.

"I asked for you—" She coughed up more blood. "I wanted to—" My heart was breaking, watching her struggle for breath. "I never stopped… loving you."

Her muscles relaxed in my hand and I gently lowered her head down onto the rubble beneath her, carefully closing her eyes and kissing her on the forehead. I rocked back onto my haunches, balling my fists in anger as the tears soaked the front of my jumpsuit.

"She couldn't have died more honorably, Elite Huck," said Sven, resting his iron hand on my shoulder. "She fought by my side through the entire battle, tirelessly slaying as many of the enemy as I did but with a grace you couldn't imagine. Never in all my years have I beheld anything like her. We shall sing of her prowess and beauty for ages to come."

I looked up into his blue eyes, also brimming with tears. "Thank you, Sven. Nothing would mean more to me."

CHAPTER 19: ARIADNE

By the time Huck rose everyone was gathered behind him for the most part uninjured. I hated losing Leisel, but her last words had stung. I knew she still had feelings for him. Hell, everyone did. I'd felt guilty when Huck had chosen me over her, and I felt guilty at the twinge of jealousy now. I waited until last to pay my respects, approaching and kneeling by her side only when everyone else's attention was occupied.

"I'm sorry, Leisel," I whispered. "No matter what anyone says, I have always felt like I stole Huck from you." I continued after a deep breath. "I wish… I could never let go of Huck, but I wish things had worked out differently." I squeezed her cooling hand and sobbed. "You were the kindest person I ever met. If it wasn't for you, we never would've helped all of those people in Kano. My life is richer because I knew you, but I can't help but wonder if you'd have been better off without knowing me. I hope you and Cesar have the peace you deserve. I love you."

"Of course she was better having known you," said Huck, rubbing my shoulder. "I didn't mean to eavesdrop. I came to comfort you."

I rested my head against his firm hand as the tears cascaded down my cheeks, mixing with the rain that had begun to fall. As I stood, the morning shower washed away the effluence from the all-night battle, helping give the people of Pod Bandung the fresh start they needed. We stood silently around Leisel's body until Prime Minister Rudolfo interrupted our vigil, having left the safety of the bunker only when no threat remained. *Not exactly the hero you were painted to be, as if I had any doubts.* Zimo trailed on the minister's heels. Behind them, two men carried Dieter's weapon. I was relieved that it had survived undamaged.

"We've endured such loss today, but we will rebuild!" he said, rain drizzling off of his cap. People barely acknowledged him. "First order of business, find a functioning ship so that we can remove all these bodies before the tropical heat gets to them. Secondly, Memo's mission *must* get underway."

"Are you mad?" said Omar, all patience exhausted. "These are your citizens, not just *bodies.* Treat them with some bloody respect!"

The minister's feathers ruffled, but he let the disrespect slide. Angry, drenched in blood and hemolymph, and with a gash across his thigh, Omar wasn't someone you wanted to trifle with.

"Prime Minister, if I may…" interrupted Boatmaster Francisco. "Everyone is exhausted and many are injured. I believe some slack is in order. Elite Omar, the minister is right about one thing. Your mission is of paramount importance. Captain Banyu, is your ship intact?"

"She floats, but there's extensive damage. The supplies seem to be intact."

"Can the damage be repaired underway?"

Om Banyu considered the idea for a moment, himself bloodied and sooty from the battle. "I'll make it work."

"Prime Minister," said Francisco, "You were planning on accompanying the team to the Hive, correct?"

"I was. As the leader—"

"Then I suggest we prioritize your departure. I will remain behind and see to burials and tunnel clearing, assuming you have no objections, Elite Huck."

Huck looked for confirmation from each of us before continuing. None of us were excited about the minister's choice to tag along, but we'd make do. "It does. Om Banyu, with your permission, I'd like for us to bury Leisel at sea."

"Of course," said the captain.

"I'll have a team man the gates immediately," said Francisco. "I wish you luck on your voyage, Prime Minister."

"But… What…" Rudolfo stammered.

"The pod is in good hands, Minister," said Om Banyu, practically shoving the rotund man along. "Let's get a move on. We have a lot to do before we can get underway."

●●●●●●●●

By early afternoon, the *Semeru* pulled out of the harbor. I felt horrible leaving without saying goodbye to Roque in person, but we'd left notes for when the tunnel was reopened. In a way, we'd lost two people in one day. It would've been impossible for Roque to continue with us, his injury far too severe. Greenskeeper Diah had offered to take him into her home, one of the few still standing in the yard. Roque had been excited at the prospect of helping in the gardens. Once his leg was healed, he'd agreed to assume the role of advanced combat trainer. No one would make a better instructor.

While we made the essential repairs to get us seaworthy, the sky traded rain for sun. There were still numerous smaller repairs that would need attention at sea. As it was, half of the railing was still missing on the port side, but the torn sail, broken boom, and burned wood on the stern had been replaced by pilfering the wreckage in the harbor.

As we drifted towards the gates, the damage became all the more apparent. The shipyard was in shambles, only the debris blocking our path had been removed. Months of work lay ahead and a fraction of the labor force was available to do it with. The people of the city had been unbelievably generous with their time and their goods, but many had given everything for our cause—even their lives. As always, we left a wake of destruction. *All the more reason we had to succeed. If we couldn't... would anyone?*

"It's not our fault," said Huck, putting his hand over mine as shipyard gates closed behind us with a rumble. "The inverts can sense their demise and are lashing out as a last resort."

"I know, but that doesn't make me feel any better," I said, voice cracking. "A lot of people died last night. Leisel…"

"It's like we've talked about before, we *have* to make it count."

We silently watched the city recede into the distance, letting the gentle rocking and cool ocean breeze soothe our raw emotions.

"We're ready," said Jafar.

I nodded, following his looming shadow. On the starboard side, Leisel's body had been enshrouded on a hinged plank, ready to be commended to the sea. The crew, now including Rudolfo and Zimo, gathered around. Om Banyu motioned for me to proceed.

"I met Leisel in the horticulture district of Pod Kano. From the first moment, her kind nature was undeniable. She had devoted her life to caring for Cesar, a simple man who she loved like a brother. Despite the evil scourge she and the Resistance had battled against, Leisel had not only thrived but bloomed, becoming the woman we had the privilege to know. With dedication and training, she became the awe-inspiring warrior that saved so many lives last night." I paused to keep my voice from breaking. "She never lost what made her Leisel—her beautiful, radiant soul. She will be forever missed. May she rest in peace."

"May she rest in peace," the crew repeated.

Huck, Hemant, and I—the three who'd known her the longest—tilted the plank up and let her body fall into the ocean, disappearing beneath the waves.

"She deserved a better death," I said, sobbing.

Huck held me close as Hemant patted me on the back.

"I like to think she'll become a mermaid," said Krista, taking my hand. "Forever swimming the seas at her leisure, that gorgeous hair of hers drifting behind her."

I laughed. "I could see it. Leisel the mermaid."

For the rest of the day, Om Banyu left us to our mourning, the crew of the *Semeru* doing the majority of the labor. I sat wordlessly on the forecastle, hugging my knees tightly to my chest. As kind as Banyu was, the downtime wouldn't last. Everyone on the boat had a role. Well, everyone except the minister and his advisor. They'd commandeered the captain's cabin, leaving Om Banyu to sleep with his first mate, Jafar. They'd disappeared in there the moment the funeral had ended and no one had seen them since.

Eventually, night fell and Huck came to drag me down to our berths, which were nothing more than hammocks strung between posts among heavily snoring sailors. Needless to say, I wasn't in a hurry to leave the fresh night air. We sat quietly, mesmerized by the starry expanse to the music of the lapping waves.

"In moments like these—the ones where for the briefest few seconds I'm safe and comfortable, surrounded by beauty and friends—I can forget that anything is wrong in the world," I said. "*This* is what keeps me going. *This* is the world I want to leave for those behind us."

Huck kissed me on the forehead. "I can think of no better gift for humanity."

●●●●●●●●

Three days into the voyage, the routine felt second nature. We didn't help with the critical aspects of sailing, but we danced a delicate ballet to accomplish our duties without interfering with theirs. With the best eyesight on board, Marie spent most of her time atop of the mast, standing on the tiny perch and keeping an eye out for anything threatening our passage. My greatest enemy was the harsh sun. When possible, I would prioritize my tasks based on the location of the shade cast by the rippling sails above. Below deck during the days was stifling, even with the portholes open. Today's chore was painting the repaired deck railing with Krista. Black and brown, like everything else on the boat. The work was almost complete when Jafar burst from the pilot house, beaming.

"My friends," he boomed. "I bear news!"

Everyone welcomed the respite and gathered around. He still wore his token turban but had shed his dark cloak in the immense heat. His bare muscle-bound chest beaded with sweat, soaking the sash around his waist.

"Zabu has fallen!"

I cheered with joy as did Hemant and Huck, forgetting about the paintbrush still in my hand and splattering Ondo, who stood at my side. He laughed, taking it in stride as the crew rejoiced and laughed. By now everyone had heard our stories about the horrors we'd faced under the corrupt dictator's reign.

Rudolfo turned to Zimo, who was fanning himself dramatically, and whispered, "I don't understand what the excitement is about. I never found Ndulue to be that objectionable."

I reluctantly bit my tongue, but I couldn't hide my eye roll.

"Do you know what happened?" Huck asked once the excitement had subsided.

"Boatmaster Francisco spoke directly to Pod Kano's new prime minister. The Resistance led the people to revolt. Zabu was overthrown by the day's end! He was to be publicly executed the following morning, but the coward killed himself before the gallows were even erected."

"I wish Leisel could've known," I whispered to Huck.

"Hopefully she does," he said, smiling and kissing the crown of my head.

"There is more," said Jafar. "Their new minister wanted to thank Memo's Misfits for your contribution to the Resistance. Without your destruction of the Dust facility, motivating the people would've been impossible."

"I'm glad to know it counted for something," said Huck. "A lot of people died to bring that wretched place down."

Zabu hadn't been an idiot. Knowing the people wouldn't stand for outright tyranny, he'd used Dust to enslave large portions of the population through addiction, forcing them to endure and commit atrocities no one in their right mind would consider. Even Hemant hadn't been immune.

"At least when we eradicate the inverts, addiction will fade with them," said Krista.

Jafar sighed. "No, sister. Addiction has haunted man since the beginning of time. Earth was far from perfect before the Arthropods arrived. But perhaps you can give people a reason to live instead of escape."

Everyone resumed their work with newfound gusto, leaving Huck and me by ourselves in the middle of the deck.

"It's not just destruction that we leave behind," he said. "Think about what we did for Horizonte, and now for Kano. There are places we left better than we found them. Let's just hope we can do the same for Earth."

"You heard Jafar," I said. "There will always be something. Some war. Some drug. Some catastrophe. What if we save humanity, and it just finds another way to endanger itself?"

"We can't think like that. Humanity has survived for ages, always adapting, always growing, always learning. It had its ups and downs, sure, but it always strove to improve. Remember what we learned in class? They had the technology to do things we can only dream of! Before the inverts, they were in the longest age of peace ever. Lifespans were at an all-time high and starvation was at an all-time low. Without a doubt, we'll have growing pains, but the point is that people will be alive to have those pains."

"What about you and me, Huck? What are we going to do after all of this?"

"Aside from spending my life with you, I haven't given it much thought," he said, ruffling the back of his hair. "I've been so focused on survival. There can only be an after if we survive the before."

"What do you want?" I asked. "You said when you lived in the pod, you were always dreaming of the outdoors. What did you imagine? Did you want to live in a cabin by a lake and pop out kiddos like Hemant and Trivia?"

Huck roared with laughter, pulling me out of the way of the deckhands adjusting the sail. "I'm happy for them. I hope we can give them the future they envision. Me… love the mountains. I want a place where I can meander through the woods without a care in the world."

"I'd like that, but I don't think you'd be completely satisfied," I said. "I can see Hemant living in the middle of nowhere. You, however, are different."

"How so?"

"You thrive around people. You may have been thrown into leadership reluctantly, but you've grown into the role. It suits you. There's going to be a great need for leaders once this is over. Think about how many surface colonies there will be."

Huck mulled it over. "Maybe you're right. How about a colony near mountains?"

"See, now you're thinking."

"What about you? Do you want kids? What does Ariadne want?"

"I think I want kids, but right now I can't imagine bringing one into a world where a single Arthropod lives," I said as Huck agreed. "I'd like to do something like Marie, living in your mountain colony and serving the people's medical needs."

"Preferably without the cannibalism," Huck interrupted.

"Yes, without the cannibalism," I said, playfully smacking him. "Maybe paint if I have free time. Do you think we could have an art room? Something with big windows?"

"I'll give you anything you want," he said, kissing the top of my head. "But all I really need is a future with you."

"I love you."

"I love you, too."

We stood there for another minute embraced before Jafar started scowling.

"I know. I know. That sail's not going to mend itself," said Huck, then whispering, "They never told me heroes would have to sew."

CHAPTER 20: HEMANT

"**C**an I see you in the pilot house?" Captain Banyu said to Huck. "You're welcome as well, Hemant."

Huck set down his needle and thread as I returned my mop to its bucket. We followed the wizened man into the pilot house, situated above the captain's cabin, which had been absconded by Rudolfo. The captain thankfully avoided our titles. Constantly being called Elite this and Elite that got old quick, despite the hard work we'd put into earning the rank. Honestly, the distinction only served to widen the gap between the crew and us, as if we were some indestructible heroes. We were just as human as the rest of the crew and younger too. Many of these sailors had survived on the surface longer than we had been alive. Just because we'd graduated from a program didn't make us better than even the lowest-ranking man on the ship.

"Should I get Fen?" asked Huck.

Fen and Ariadne were below, helping the ship's eccentric cook, Ernst, prepare lunch. At first I'd thought kitchen duty would be better than scrubbing decks, but every night they returned to the berths soaked in sweat on the verge of collapse. At least on deck, I got fresh air and sunshine when it wasn't raining.

"No need," said Om Banyu. "You won't be making any decisions. This is informational. You and Hemant can relay it to your friends later."

We entered the pilot house where Jafar, Rudolfo, and Zimo were waiting. The windows were open, the salty air keeping the space's temperature bearable. The prime minister refused to wear anything but his archaic outfits at the expense of his comfort. Even Zimo tugged at his high collar, his wispy long mustache adhered to his face by sweat.

"About time, Captain Banyu," said Rudolfo. "Any longer and I'd miss my lunch."

Om Banyu ignored the comment and led us to the large map table centered in the cramped room. Despite being surrounded by windows, the middle of the room was dim. Above it was a single light bulb, powered by a small wind turbine on the mast. The captain caught me eyeballing the dangling bulb.

"Just because we were on a traditional vessel doesn't mean I'm using a lantern," he said, smirking.

On the way to Bandung, Banyu had said that before the Arthropods, most sailing had been done by computers guided by satellites in space. I'd almost laughed at how far-fetched the notion was, but it was the truth. None of that mattered to Banyu. With a compass, map, and sextant, he could carry us anywhere on Earth. According to him, anyone who couldn't had no business commanding a boat.

The decaying map showed a chain of pale green islands on a light-blue background, with lines plotting our journey to the Australian Territory. Instead of being labeled "Indonesian Region, Asian Territory," as I would have expected, the map read *Republik Indonesia.*

"This is from before the United Territories of Earth was formed!" I said.

"Sharp eyes," said the captain, pointing at a tiny pin, shaped like a ship. "This is us. For the last seven days, we've been loosely following the coast of this island chain, not straying close enough to attract attention. I'm sure you are tired of hearing this, but your taking down the antenna bug network has completely changed ocean navigation. Not to mention, we can finally talk to the pod from sea."

"Yes, and…" said Rudolfo, motioning impatiently for Banyu to continue.

I didn't know what he was so anxious to return to. Every time I saw him outside of "his" cabin, he was sitting on his laurels, chatting away with Zimo as everyone buzzed around him. He had a sword, but it had yet to leave its scabbard. Zimo had brought a spear onto the boat, but given the man's timid nature I couldn't imagine him being useful with it.

"For the most part, we've been heading east, but to hit the Australian Territory, we'll be turning south. This will present two problems. One, unless we go way the hell out, we're going to rub shoulders with some coastlines, which means we run the risk of being seen."

"I thought the entire reason we were taking a wooden boat was that it didn't attract the Arthropods," Zimo whined.

"It's *less* likely to attract the sea-faring inverts, who hunt mostly by vibration, though it's far from undetectable. From land, the *Semeru* is no less visible than any metal-hulled ship."

Zimo paled.

Did he think this trip would be a pleasure cruise? "What's the second problem?" I asked.

"The Arthropods have shown that they can still communicate across vast distances, even without their eyes in the sky. If we're seen when we cut through these islands," said the captain, tapping a deeply tanned finger on the channel we were entering. "It's going to leave us exposed for a 600-kilometer stretch of open ocean."

"Oh," said Huck.

"But that's extremely unlikely, right?" asked Rudolfo.

"That depends on a fair amount on luck, *milord*," said the captain, filling the last word with disdain.

•••••••

By the time the first coast came into view, word had spread across the ship about the perilous passage. Even the loudest-mouthed sailors were as quiet as Wuhanian monks who'd taken vows of silence. Our safety rested on the crew's years of experience and its captain. Every member of the crew had survived long enough for their skin to have a tanned-leather appearance, boding well of their skill.

Save for the sails that still snapped in the wind, anything that could make noise had been tied down. Anything powered had been shut off. It was unnerving to be in such potential danger and yet have my war hammer tucked away, lashed to the deck at my side. Everyone except for Banyu and Jafar sat against the railing but still carried their daggers. Banyu wasn't dumb. He knew we'd need the ability to quickly access our weapons if everything went to hell. The reflective surfaces on the boat were already covered in matte black paint. The crew lowered dark fabric over the windows of all but the front of the pilot house. Anything to reduce our visibility.

I sat as motionless as I could, occasionally glancing at the others but unable to speak. Knowing that sound could carry great distances over the calm water, Om Banyu had ordered for silence to limit any chance of exposure. Trivia tugged at my sleeve and pointed towards a landmass. *The second island.* It was the channel between the two that we were trying to squeeze through. Each island, pushing us towards the other and just inside the horizon. Another few kilometers and the curvature of the Earth would've kept us hidden safely away from both.

I squirmed, growing increasingly uncomfortable as time ticked by, earning me a scowl from Jafar. *Fine! I'll sit still, but it's not going to help much if we get attacked and my ass is conked out.* Trivia rubbed my hand comfortingly. *We'll get through this, like everything else,* I reminded myself. I leaned my head back against the scalding railing and squinted at the sun beaming down. There was no respite from the baking sun here. I let my eyes drift closed. I couldn't sleep under the circumstances, but I could rest. There was no sense in worrying.

After a few minutes, I heard a soft tapping. I looked around and saw Jafar, still leaning against the mast, looking pissed. Zimo was making the noise, his face bloodless with fright. With everyone's attention, he began frantically pointing towards the east. I followed his finger, but couldn't see anything. I looked at Trivia to see if she'd identified it. Her eyes scanned back and forth over the sky, then grew wide. She turned my head and pointed. I could barely see… *Mashi!* A cloud of them. I made a move for my bag, but Jafar reached down and stopped me with his iron grip. He pointed up, then motioned to be still.

The swarm was flying right over us, from one island to the other. For whatever reason, they hadn't noticed us. *That's all we need. The dart beaks boring holes through us and our hull.* Everyone froze. Out of the corner of my eye, I could see Banyu in the pilot house not so much as twitching a finger. The tiny-bodied mashi harmlessly passed over us, casting the faintest shadow from their sheer number. When they began to disappear in the sky, I let a sigh of relief escape. We still had a while before we were out of sight of land, but at least the mashi had—

Someone screamed. I turned just in time to see Ondo leap up, clutching his neck as blood poured from the wound. Omar stood and stomped on something, slamming his foot down repeatedly onto the deck. A rogue mashi had found its way down to our boat! Ariadne and Marie jumped up to tend to Ondo, bringing him slowly down to the deck. Ondo cried in pain, his dark skin paling as he lost copious amounts of blood. I heard Marie mumble something about stitches.

"They are coming!" shouted Jafar, followed by a slew of vulgarities. "Cover yourselves!"

With little to no way to combat such a small threat, the only defense was the specially weaved, layered blankets that would deflect them or at the least, arrest their momentum. Fortunately, the ship was equipped with larger ones than we carried. Trivia and I unfurled one, covering ourselves and two other sailors, holding it tight against the deck and hoping someone would yell the all-clear. From under the blanket, we could hear muffled screams. Some sounded like Ondo, others sounded like the crew. All around, I could hear the zipping of the mashi storming the boat, feel the impacts on our cover. With each splintering sound, I could imagine coming out from under the blanket to a ramshackle schooner, incapable of carrying us further. I reached out for Trivia's trembling hand, surprised to see my normally fearless companion frightened.

"It'll be okay," I repeated until I finally heard Om Banyu's voice.

"We're clear of the mashi and those god-forsaken islands," he said, "though not without cost."

The four of us stood, letting the sawdust-covered blanket fall to the ground. Crew members still danced around, stomping on the injured dart beaks that littered the deck. The ship had seen better days, but it wasn't listing like the *Spearhead* had after its attack. No one was bailing water or rushing to the tiny dingies expected to carry us all. Every exposed wooden surface boasted myriad holes, straight through from one side to the other. Splinters covered the deck making it a nightmare for our bare feet. The decimated bodies of two crew members were being covered with a shroud, their bones stripped of more than half of their skin and muscle, pieces of which were splattered across the deck. I turned, stifling a gag. I started to go check on Ondo, but Trivia grabbed me by the arm, pulling me back to her. She'd stopped crying but was still shaking. I pulled her into a hug, kissing the top of her head.

"Claire," she said into my chest.

"What?" I asked.

"My name is Claire. Under that blanket and unable to fight, all I could think of was dying and you not ever knowing my real name. I hate it, but I wanted you to know it."

"It's the most beautiful name I could've imagined," perplexed as to why she'd disliked it.

"You really think so?"

"I do. I love you, Claire."

Trivia—Claire—buried her face in my chest.

"My best friend was killed by dart beaks when we were headed to Bhopal. She never stood a chance. I hid in a hole for days before I convinced myself to emerge. I don't like any of the Arthropods, but I have a special hatred for those little assholes."

"Well, I've got a list of inverts I have a special hatred for," I said, chuckling.

Claire laughed, her bright smile returning. "Do me a favor and keep the Claire thing to yourself, okay?"

"You got it, Claire."

She playfully punched my arm and we went to check on Ondo.

He was lying on the deck, breathing regular, but pallid. A large bandage covered his neck.

"I've never stitched someone in complete darkness," Marie was saying. "By candlelight, maybe, but not darkness."

"Will he be alright?" asked Trivia, falling to her knees, tears threatening to return. "I can't lose Ondo. He's like a brother."

"He's lost a lot of blood," said Ariadne. "If I can identify a willing donor with the same blood type, there's an excellent chance he'll recover. The mashi nicked his carotid artery, but we got it sealed in time."

"I'll do whatever it takes," said Trivia, rolling up her sleeve.

"After seeing the way he fought to protect the pod," added Captain Banyu, rolling up his as well, "so will anyone on this boat."

One by one, each crew member rolled up their sleeve, brandishing their arm as Ariadne prepared her test kits. Solidarity. That was how they survived.

CHAPTER 21: KOLYA

As if cheering us on, the Arthropods blared their spine-tingling chorus as our litters vanished into the light-swallowing depths of the Hive. *We are here, Sveta. We made it.* The change in air temperature was immediate, dropping from the sweltering desert heat to a moist, yet comfortable, one the moment we entered. As my eyes adjusted to the darkness, I could feel the faintest breeze tickling the hairs of my forearms.

"The tunnel must serve as ventilation," said Arjun.

"I was thinking the same thing," I replied.

Ahead, long greenish tubes lined the walls, casting a dim glow that barely illuminated the wide tunnel. *More glass worm larvae. Likely more for the benefit of us and the Demented than the Arthropods.* The inverts had proven remarkably similar to our Earthen insects and had keen eyesight in darkness, far superior to our own. Only the bivvies' camouflage and the exploitation of the neem trees had allowed humans to stand a chance at long-term survival on the surface.

A scuffling sound announced the closure of the entrance behind us as spring tongues, one of the more dexterous Arthropod species, sealed us in. I suppressed a surge of panic as the last of the moonlight winked out. *We're trapped,* I thought as the tingle of the breeze ceased.

"I believe it's a routine procedure in the evenings, Kolya," said Arjun, sensing my fear. "It retains the warmth during the cool nights. If I'm correct, they will reopen them in the morning."

Now that he'd mentioned it, the concept sounded familiar like something I'd read many years ago. Again, I was grateful to have Arjun's expertise and intelligence at my side. The spring tongues still left me discomfited, being one of the invert species that had nearly killed me. I could still feel the damaged muscle in my back from when they'd stretched me like a medieval prisoner on a dungeon rack. I was surprised to see them in the heat of the desert, being a marsh-dwelling creature. The Hive had many secrets we had yet to unearth, an unexpected haven for the toadies being only the first of them.

I examined the slug-like glass worm on its litter ahead, differentiated from the ones on the wall by its later stage of life. When not engaging its luminescent cells, the creature was so transparent that it was like trying to focus on an oil slick in a puddle. However, unlike the mantis wraiths, the fine airs covering its body gave it a gray-tinged halo, preventing it from ever truly vanishing like their brethren. The invisible wraiths were nightmarishly lethal, usually leaving you dead before you knew you were being stalked. It was only through sheer chance that Arjun and his friends had survived their subterranean encounter with the stalkers back in the Saharan Territory. It was hard enough to see the visible inverts in the dim tunnel. I couldn't imagine trying to battle invisible ones. Trainer Gempo, notorious in Pod Baghdad, was renowned for making his students train in the darkness for precisely this reason. I doubted I could survive in a place like this if not for our protection. I had been a fearsome warrior once, but age had taken its toll.

The ride meandered through tunnel after tunnel and interchange after interchange, ascending steep hills and descending sheer drops, leaving me without the slightest clue about our location. I ran through several mental exercises to keep me distracted from the incomprehensible amount of earth that towered above me. Anyone with severe claustrophobia would've struggled in the subterranean pods, but being this deep inside of an alien-constructed dirt and secretion mound would give even those with the strongest constitution pause.

"How much longer do you think this will take?" I asked, forcing myself to take a slow breath.

Arjun shrugged. "At our present speed, a few hours."

"I know you've never been much for talking, but I would appreciate the distraction at the moment."

Arjun thought for a few seconds before responding.

"How will we communicate with the Queens? The glass worms can serve as an interpreter of sorts, but I can't see how their limited ability would serve for complicated peace talks."

"You're correct," I said. "Everything the shinies have shown us has been rudimentary concepts at best. It's not as though we can use our pheromones again."

"This trip will prove pointless if we reach their hierarchy and can't establish a reliable method of communication."

"Arjun, everything we know about the Arthropods is based on their warriors and drones. It was only with hours of in-depth study that I theorized the Queens' existence. Those purple dots were confirmation of leadership. Short of seeing them with my own eyes, I can't imagine their capabilities. Perhaps they have evolved the ability to speak, though I doubt it. I don't believe that they would invite us this far if they didn't have a plan, though we should keep our minds open. It may be different from what we expect."

Arjun was silent, not content with my answer. In reality, there was no way to prepare for the first parley with an alien species. If nothing else, perhaps time and study would provide us with the means to do so. I dismissed any notion that it was a race. Arjun's companions would never make it this far. The Demented had served here successfully for untold years, presumably quartered within the Hive. Living underground again wasn't exactly appealing, but the thought of departing the Hive as humanity's primary intermediary with the Arthropods held a certain luster.

The further we traveled, the more moist the air became, filling my nostrils with a mildewy odor. We entered a cavernous larvae-lit space where toadies clung to the walls, busily harvesting chunks of the meter-wide mushrooms so abundant that they shrouded the earthen walls. More of the same pale green glow emanated from among the fungus making the room feel nothing short of fantastical.

"It must be some species of *Termitomyces*," I said. "They *do* eat something other than animals! Arjun, do you have any idea what this means?"

"They may be able to survive without consuming animals," Arjun said with a look of excitement. "Without eating us."

His eyes were wide as he took in the sight, twisting his torso in his seat to examine the cavern from every angle. Across the space's floor, Demented gathered the dropping chunks of fungus into large woven baskets, carrying them on their backs beyond our sight into the various dark tunnels that branched off the room. It was no wonder they had survived all the attempts to destroy them. Like the pods served us, the Hive provided the Arthropods with a self-contained ecosystem, capable of sustaining their way of life for decades, perhaps even centuries, to come.

The creatures had demonstrated their resistance to radiation when the UTE had resorted to nuclear weapons not too long after their arrival. According to the documentation I'd read of the incident, all it accomplished was destroying part of the meteorite and the inverts caught in the blast, but little more. Arjun's companions' plan was predicated on reaching the inner sanctum and detonating the device there, obliterating their holy of holies and hierarchy and decimating the core of their reproduction. The more I saw, the more asinine their mission became.

As it turned out, the fungal farm was one of many. It made perfect sense. To build and maintain a colony the size of Everest, the Arthropods would need an equivalent workforce—a workforce that required copious amounts of food. Outside of the Hive, inverts subsisted on humans and animals, both of which they'd nearly hunted to extinction. Ironically, Release Day had saved us. Had the world pods not regularly released food in the form of humans, the inverts would've likely breached the pods and consumed their contents long ago. It was a morbid way to think about it, but the Arthropods were like any other creature, prizing their survival above all others.

Our Demented guides marched on as the path we followed spiraled downwards, deeper into the alien nest. Moisture and warmth increased as the heavy air assumed a fetid odor. I wrinkled my nose, wondering about the source of the smell. I yelled at Jigna, who was marching in front of the pack. He fell back between Arjun's litter and mine.

"What is that smell?" I asked, pointing at my nose.

Jigna barked back something incomprehensible and held out his hands as if holding a rugby ball. I nodded as if understanding and Jigna returned to Neesh, who I'd finally decided must be the equivalent of his girlfriend. No pairing born of such evil could be condoned in the eyes of God.

"What did you make of that, my friend?"

"I don't know. The way he was holding his arms… It reminded me of…"

"Go on, boy. Spit it out."

"Babies."

I shuddered. *Babies.* Well, we knew that the Hive was a major source of reproduction. Did the Queens trust us to the extent that they would let us see their nursery? We'd come as ambassadors, but they had no guarantee that we were unarmed.

"I'm surprised that they would let us see such a sight."

Arjun looked at me, perplexed. "Why not? We're surrounded by such a force that if we breathed in a threatening manner, they would tear us apart."

"But how do they know we aren't carrying a bomb?"

Again, perplexed. "You of all people should know that insects can see into the radioactive spectrum. Their other senses can detect all manner of chemical traces that we couldn't achieve with another million years of evolution. It's not out of the realm of possibilities that they can pass on experiences from one generation to the next. I surmise that they would be able to detect a threat long before it entered their home.

"That's why I brought you, my boy. You see things that this old man has long forgotten," I chuckled, an odd sound in such a desolate place.

Arjun redirected his attention forward. *Perpetually a voice of reason, my dear Sveta. That he is.* Ahead, I could see a faint glow, but unlike the fungal farms, the blue-tinted glow emanated from another species of fungus that stretched out into the tunnel. When we reached the opening, the cavern was similar in circumference to the farms, but the sight made a pit form in my stomach. The room was a seemingly infinite vertical shaft, overwhelming me with vertigo as I stared up the shaft and down over the edge. I rocked back in my litter seat with such force that my Demented bearers had to compensate to keep me from toppling. I broke out in a cold sweat even after the swaying had subsided.

"This is unlike anything I was prepared for," said Arjun.

I gasped, awe overpowering the unpleasant aroma.

With the threat of toppling passed, I examined the room with a more balanced mind. As far as I could see were hexagonal capsules nestled in the walls, inside each a developing writhing creature illuminated by fungus. The wide ramp, covered in an endless line of mindlessly marching Demented, spiraled down into the abyss before vanishing from sight. Surrounding our escorts as we continued our downward journey were worker Arthropods tending to the young. *The nursery must be stratified by species.* Everywhere I looked, adult hook beetles hovered up from the depths, tending to the capsules by regurgitating a milky-white substance, tidying up the mud constructions, and placing egg-like objects into vacant chambers before floating back down into the pit. Mud raptors and split wings flew up into the heights, presumably to tend to their own.

"There must be millions of Arthropod young here," I said.

"This is exactly why we never stood a chance in a war of attrition," said Arjun. "Peace or eradication. Those are our only two options. Though, frankly, I don't see any chance of successful eradication."

"Then peace it must be."

As we traveled deeper into the earth, the sizes, shapes, and orientations of the capsules changed to accommodate the various species' needs, but curiously, I saw no polies. It dawned on me shortly thereafter. Keeping such a volatile creature in close proximity to the others could prove catastrophic. Depending on how many there were, a cascading explosion in the right place could bring the Hive down on itself.

After hours of traversing the spiral, we reached the bottom of the nursery chamber and saw the source of the milky substance. Across the floor were multiple ponds, each filled with various shades of an opalescent fluid being excreted by small groups of each species. Demented stood with long paddles, stirring each earthen vat. From large openings converging on the area, endless lines of like inverts emerged, carrying fresh eggs up the chamber.

I pointed towards the openings. "Correct me if I'm wrong," I said. "The fungus fuels the workers as they go about their routines, tend to the young, and generate this jelly."

"It's all quite practical," said Arjun. "They are too busy to hunt. This implies that they can survive on the fungus alone—at least for a time. It *is* more closely related to animal than plant."

"Unless they are getting meat from somewhere unknown to us."

"Let's hope not. With their numbers, I don't know how we could ever hope to keep them fed and give humanity any chance of long-term success."

This is where Arjun's shortsightedness tended to emerge. Peace meant sacrifices on both sides. Sacrifices that couldn't be limited by a narrow concept of morality. If the Arthropods could survive solely on fungus, I couldn't help but think that they would have already done so. There would have to be trade-offs. I wanted nothing more than to offer them the Demented as food, being hardly better than animals, but they already had a place in the Hive hierarchy, making it a tough sell. I would strive to reach a symbiotic relationship with the Arthropods. Perhaps humans could farm pigs at such a rate to satiate the inverts' ravenous hunger. Perhaps the inverts could, in turn, limit their populations. *There are always the weakest of us, Sveta— the unabled, the failed ones, the most criminal laborers—but they are too few. When I emerge from this as a world leader, I will have to make decisions. Tough decisions, my dear. Decisions that ensure not only humanity's survival but the best of humanity's survival.*

CHAPTER 22: DARREN

2042

It didn't take long for the implications of Dr. Foster's words to incite worldwide panic. Around the planet, everyone was coming to terms with the prospect of aliens. The capitalists monetized the ordeal, the religious proclaimed the apocalypse, the fanatics pushed for contact, but the regular working stiffs just wanted to be with their families. I'd lost the love of my life. My son had lost his mother. I was thankful Patricia's dad had preceded his daughter in death. Her mom was in assisted living, with no recollection of her entire life. Both were a blessing in their own way. The news was now showering the world with opinion rather than fact as the Australian Territorial Guard secured the 1,200-kilometer area.

No one was allowed to enter the controlled zone. Dr. Foster maintained his position as the leader of the science side of the containment, but Colonel Scott had been replaced by someone far more militaristic, General Maddox. Last I'd heard, the zone had complete air and ground support and the various government heads were batting around the idea of wrapping the meteorite in a giant plastic bubble to limit further threats, whether lifeforms or contaminants. Dr. Foster had renounced the idea as impossible on the scale suggested. So far, there had been no activity from the rock. The ground disturbances had stopped. Things were eerily quiet.

After a week of setting up the containment, I got an unexpected call from Grayson.

"Hey, Darren. How are you holding up?" he asked.

I shrugged. "Learning how to cope without my right arm, I suppose."

"Look, man, I know you and I weren't ever close or anything, but I got to know your wife. She was a hell of a scientist and talked about her family constantly. She cared about you two more than anything else in the world."

"I know," I said, allowing myself a smile. "Thank you for telling me. I'm guessing that's not why you called."

"You're right. They're taking me off the project in the morning. Sending me back to the American Territory. Before I leave, I wanted to share with you what's not in the news. I feel like I owe you that."

"You don't owe me anything, Grayson. Don't tell me anything that would put your career in jeopardy."

"Nah, it's fine. It'll be all over the news in a day or two anyway. There are too many damn journalists running around to keep information contained. I was hoping to bring you back Patricia's body for a funeral, but I'm sure you are aware that it can't happen."

"I understand," I said. "We'll have a service for her soon. You'll have to send me your contact info so I can invite you."

"I'd appreciate that. I would."

"So what is it you wanted to tell me?"

"Yesterday, in a closed-door session here at the base, General Maddox decided to deploy a tactical squad with orders to enter and secure the meteorite. Mission launch is tomorrow. They've been ordered to shoot to kill."

"I figured that would happen eventually. Military always trumps science. I hope to the universe there's something left to study when it's all over."

"I thought you'd be more excited to see them vaporized."

"Believe me, I've thought about it. Some nights I'd like to blow the thing to kingdom come, but we don't know what's in there. Destroying whatever's inside without at least attempting diplomacy or capturing whatever's inside goes against everything Patricia stood for."

"I suppose you're right," he said. "Either way, it's out of my hands. Tomorrow, maybe the scientists will have a few new specimens on their tables. Those that are left anyway."

"Thanks, Grayson. For everything."

●●●●●●●●

"You should return to work, Darren," Mrs. Grimethorpe said as she dropped off Alex and another casserole for dinner. This time green bean with little fried onions on top. "Might take your mind off things." She gave me a motherly pat on my shoulder before returning to her apartment.

I nodded politely and thanked her again. She was right. Stepan had been saying the same thing, but I didn't want to return until I had Patricia's funeral, and I didn't want to have that until after I had some closure. Tonight, my time, was when the tactical team would be entering the rock. I planned to stay up late after tucking Alex in to watch it as I had the search and rescue. Most of the action wouldn't be televised, but I had to know what was inside. I could always sleep in tomorrow.

The non-stop coverage continued like it always did, with speculation from the same experts they'd been using throughout the process. I'd seen the deposit notification in my account from

Patricia's last media appearance. It was piddly, but every little bit helped. Her posting at Pine Gap had been a voluntary post, but a paid one. The managing agency of Pine Gap had already sent an email to all the families saying their loved one's salaries and hazard benefits would be paid out once the investigation was concluded. *As if the hazard money will put a dent in the loss.* I made my way to the kitchen and grabbed a cold Guinness, threw some *queso picante* in the microwave, and pulled a bag of stale tortilla chips from the cabinet.

When I returned to the living room, the reporter was interviewing Sergeant Tanner, the leader of the tactical team heading down to the rock. In the background, the team was loaded with standard projectile and optical weapons and even an explosive launcher of some sort. I was surprised that some team members carried non-lethal weapons. I saw what appeared to be a shock pole, net canon, and harpoons. *They're prepared for anything.* After an hour or so, the group was finally ready for their descent into the basin. As the footage alternated between ground and air, the team leapt backward off the craggy lip, rappelling into the depths.

The rotor wing hovered close enough that I could make out the troops crawling across the rubble like ants, quickly covering the kilometers bathed in the shadow of AS-42. The anchors grew quiet in anticipation, which under any other circumstances would've been a broadcast taboo. It was mid-morning in the Outback, but the cliff edges surrounding the crater shrouded the soldiers' approach in darkness. Anxiety overwhelmed my senses, filling me with dread. *What if they unleash something terrible?* Time trickled by as the team neared the primary cavern carved into the mysterious rock, just one among numerous smaller ones. The one chosen by General Maddox was around six meters in diameter judging by the the soldiers preparing to breech the object. Through the rotor-wing's telephoto lenses, I could make out the cryptic hand signals syncing their efforts. Without flourish, they disappeared inside. Five seconds. Ten seconds. Thirty seconds. For that two-minute eternity, the entirety of the human race was singularly focused.

"We have received reports that Team-1 has fallen out of radio contact," said the newscaster, unable to hide his concern. "It is believed to be interference from the meteorite, which was an expected possibility. Team-2 is being dispatched as we speak."

Team-2 followed in the footsteps of Team-1 as my drink and snacks went untouched. Another minute went by. Then soundless flashes brightly illuminated the opening. *Could that be weapons discharging?* The distance was too great for the microphones to pick up any ambient audio. *What are they shooting at?* Team-3 hustled across the expanse and vanished into the cavern. More flashes.

"Reports confirm that the tactical unit has engaged… hostiles," said the newscaster, taking a deep breath. "I apologize viewers, but at this time, our information is extremely limited. Be advised that the following live content is unpredictable and may be graphic."

I watched so intently that I had to remember to breathe. On-screen, Team-3 began sprinting from the meteorite, the high-definition broadcast clearly showing the terror etched on the hardcore soldiers' faces. *What the hell?* Another soldier backed out of the opening, his optical rifle elevated, blasting away at something inside. I realized I was standing directly in front of the wall screen as if the proximity would help me see better. Something large was looming in the shadows, filling the opening, only visible from the laser fire. Over the distance, the mic could barely pick up what sounded like high-pitch screeching. Suddenly, two bone-white appendages rocketed out from the opening, spearing the soldier through the chest before jerking his body inside.

"Holy Christ!" I yelled, then lowered my voice, realizing this was the last thing Alexander needed to wake and see.

"Oh my god!" said the female anchor, all professionalism forgotten. "What the hell was that thing?"

From the opening, pale spider-like creatures began to flood the basin, storming after Team-3. The soldiers were no match for the giant beasts' dexterity across the jagged rocks. They caught up with the unit in a blink and ripped their bodies apart on a live feed. *Oh god! That's what killed Patricia?! Holy hell! She was dead from the fall. She had to be. She was dead from the fall.* Finally, someone at the station summoned enough sense to turn the camera away from the carnage. The screen showed two dumbfounded anchors at their desks, one crying.

"We'll return after a short break," said the anchor, voice cracking.

"We're doing uninterrupted coverage, Dean," said a production assistant off-camera.

"Cut to a damn commercial!" he screamed.

The feed started playing an ad for men's cologne as the screen notified me of a call from Stepan.

"Yeah," I managed to say.

"You saw it too," he said, his face as bloodless as I imagined mine to be.

I could hear Kitty retching in the background.

"I'm so sorry, Darren," he said, struggling for words.

I nodded. "She was dead before those things found her. I know it."

"What are they going to do?" he asked as Kitty appeared next to him, wiping her mouth on a towel. The normally pale-skinned model was deathly white.

"They should blow the thing to hell, science be damned," I said. "I doubt Patricia would've—"

Stepan's call automatically minimized when the coverage returned to the newsroom.

"Viewers. The news coming from the AS-42 site is extremely disturbing," said Dean. "All three teams… have been horrifically killed by what Research Director Matt Foster has begun referring to as giant arthropods, a name based on their few known characteristics. All non-military personnel are being evacuated from the containment zone. At this time, the UTE president has authorized a tiered plan of attack to end the threat. Again, we must reiterate that viewer discretion is advised. We are going now to Pamela, who's on a rotor wing above the crater. Pamela?"

"Thanks, Dean," she said through compressed audio of a headset.

Unlike last time, Pamela's highly-maintained curly hair was pulled back into a tight ponytail as she struggled to hold herself together, her eyes wide with fear. She tucked her trembling hands between her legs as she spoke.

"We're circling over the crater now, the giant spiders are trying to climb over the edge, but the military vehicles are firing into them, pinning them down. If there's any good news today, it is that our weapons are very effective against them. The problem is their numbers. Arthropods are pouring from the meteorite in what seems to be an inexhaustible supply. The troops can hold them off, but not push them back. All available nearby guard battalions are being flown in, in addition to heavier armaments. They are expected to arrive—"

"Something is happening down there," yelled the heavy gunner at Pamela's side.

The camera panned down as a cluster of narrow, beetle-like arthropods emerged from the meteorite, comparable in size to the spiders. Once clear of the rock, they took flight. Pamela turned to the camera in shock, then to the pilot, "Get us the hell out of here!" The feed went to a three-up shot with Pamela, the female anchor, and some expert who began to spout hypotheses about the new species.

"Now there are two of them?" said Stepan, who I'd forgotten was there. "I'm all for protecting nature, but I'm starting to agree with you about blowing the thing to hell."

"Patricia said she had a bad feeling about this," I said. "I just wish she'd listened to her instincts. Maybe she'd still be—"

On-screen, Pamela was panicking. The expert disappeared and the feed went to a side-by-side of her and the anchor.

"Pamela, what's happening?"

"The beetles are coming after the rotor-wings. They've already… Oh god! They've already destroyed one," she said, sobbing as the gunner next to her opened fire on an unseen assailant. "They're filling the skies. Help me!"

Pamela screamed, pleading with the viewers for aid that was powerless to help. The camera tumbled, revealing only the metal-clad deck of the crew bay. The audio filled with curses and screams followed by rending metal and ripping flesh. A spray of blood slathered the deck in red—then static. When the camera returned to the desk, both anchors were visibly shaken. The woman was sobbing and unable to speak. Dean's voice was barely strong enough to send the broadcast to another unplanned commercial.

What am I going to tell Alexander?

CHAPTER 23: HUCK

"**P**ut your backs into it," shouted First Mate Jafar. "I still feel the burrs beneath my tender feet!"

"How does it feel to have Jafar's blood in you?" I whispered to Ondo, who sat watching us from atop a crate.

Ondo rolled with laughter. "Maybe that's why I'm so grouchy lately."

It'd been two days since Ondo's near-death experience. His upbeat mood had returned with his color within the first 24 hours of his transfusion. Today was the first day Ariadne had let him stray from Zimo's pallet. Neither Zimo nor Rudolfo were thrilled with the arrangements, but Om Banyu hadn't budged on the issue. Jafar had turned out to be what Ariadne called a "universal donor." It was a shame he wouldn't come with us into the Australian Territory where the threat of blood loss would be high.

Over Ondo's bed rest, we'd finished repairs to the ship. A fair amount of it had been cosmetic, but there was some structural damage that needed more permanent fixes than what we could do at sea. Banyu said that it'd need a few weeks of restoration once it returned to port, but the *Semeru* would see us safely to our destination. Hemant, Omar, and I had made a putty from the clean wood fragments and had been using it to patch the holes while the crew managed the sails around us. No matter how smooth we sanded each surface, it was never enough for the first mate. I glanced up and saw his smile vanish. I think Jafar actually enjoyed our presence, though he would never admit it. He was having too much fun putting us to work.

We'd performed a sea burial for the two fallen crew, Dante and Chavo. Despite even Jafar's level of cleaning, the deck was permanently stained with their blood, tattooed into the wood by the tiny inverts.

"A fine job you've done bringing the ship back to its former glory," said Rudolfo, taking his morning stroll around the deck.

It was about the only time the man left his appropriated cabin. Zimo followed him around like a puppy, while the actual puppy dozed in the prime minister's arms. Rudolfo would pace, tugging periodically on ropes to inspect their knots—of which he knew nothing about. Zimo would follow, mimicking the minister. It would've been comical had the man not been the leader of one of the last human cities on the planet.

"Great work as always, Captain Banyu," he said. "Keep it up and there will be a fine reward for you on our return."

Zimo scratched something into the worn, wood-clad notebook that never left his hands.

"The only reward I want from that man is to rid us of his presence," said Jafar, once Rudolfo had shut the door to his private cabin.

Om Banyu shared a look of agreement, but wisely kept any opinions on the matter to himself, then turned to us.

"I think you've done enough repairs for now," he said. "Ernst and your friends are preparing the rambutan for lunch before it spoils. Why don't you three grab the rods and see if you can catch a marlin."

"Any suggestions on how we do that?" asked Omar after the captain left.

"Squid, boy," said the gnarled sailor next to me. Wen, I think his name was. "Use the nets. Marlin love the boogers."

"Thanks," I said.

Hemant and I grabbed the net out of its crate and went to the stern. After stretching it between the three of us, we sloppily hurled it out into the water, narrowly missing it catching on the rudder.

"You bind up that rudder, Banyu will have our asses for lunch," said Omar.

My face reddened. I had no idea what I was doing, but you learn through experience, right? We'd had extensive training in the pod, but no program could prepare us for everything. I'd learned a ton on my journey, but no matter how much I learned, there was always more. We let the net drift down below the wake, waiting a few minutes, then began pulling it up.

"It's heavy!" yelled Hemant. "We must have done something right."

As we pulled, we carefully avoided the rudder. We had it halfway up when I saw it. Down in the bottom among the single squid and few silver fish was a drill barnacle. My stomach leapt into my throat.

"Is that what I think it is?" asked Hemant.

I swallowed. "I'm pretty sure it is."

"Don't bring that damn thing up here!" said Hemant.

"Don't let it go!" shouted Omar. "Are you crazy?"

"Tie off the net," I said, already wrapping my rope around the ship's railing.

Once the net was secure, I looked over the edge. This was the first time I'd seen a breacher so close. It was like something out of a nightmare. Its empty eye stared up towards us. From one end, a beak snapped open and shut, revealing tentacle-like objects inside. On its opposite end was a barbed stalk, perfect for piercing hulls.

"But how did it know where we were? The mashi?" asked Hemant.

"Maybe not," said Omar. "Maybe the ocean is full of these things."

"When have you ever seen just one invert?" asked Hemant. "Even the Nightmare had buddies."

"We have to tell Banyu!" I said, sprinting towards the pilot house.

Inside I found Jafar manning the helm.

"Where's Om Banyu?!"

"The galley. Why?"

Without answering, I took off down the hatch, heading below deck as Jafar yelled "Why?" after me. When I thundered into the muggy space, every head swiveled up. Ariadne and Trivia's hair clung to their faces as they peeled mounds of rambutan, revealing their white interiors.

"What's your hurry?" Ernst laughed. "Belly button scraping your spine?"

"What? I— Nevermind. Om Banyu, we netted a drill barnacle!"

"Care to run that by me again?" he asked.

"We captured a drill barnacle. It's suspended above the water in a net."

Om Banyu moved with impressive speed past me up the ladder. Ariadne and Trivia jumped over the counter and followed as Ernst returned to his work, singing the same shanty he always did.

By the time I reached the stern, half the crew was there waiting, each arguing about either what it meant or what to do.

"Quiet!" yelled Banyu, silencing everyone. "Trivia. Tell me everything you know about these creatures. Fact, not fantasy."

"Umm…" She blushed, from the praise and the pressure. "They bore through hulls, causing rapid leaks. They have rudimentary eyesight." She took a shaky breath, "Their offspring can flay an entire crew in minutes…"

I thought back to what had happened to the hands on board the *Spearhead*. The mess their offspring, the nauplii, made of most of our Clunkie comrades made me shudder. I was still haunted by all the bodies, missing what made them look human. Trivia continued to spout off every fact she could dredge up."

"And I don't think they ever travel alone," she finished.

The captain was silent for a moment. "Huck, Fen. I want your team on watch. Shout if you see anything remotely resembling one of those damn things anywhere near my hull. Jafar, break out the harpoons."

•••••••••

Through the calm afternoon, we waited, a perimeter of harpoons stationed at every point around the deck. My legs and arms were beginning to ache from the stance and the weight of the barbed pole. The weapon felt like an old friend in my hands, bearing such similarity to the spears I'd used in training. What posed the largest threat was a wandering mind. A feeling of *déjà vu* came over me, reminiscent of cruising through dense fog, anticipating an attack.

With Ondo on my left and Krista on my right, there was nothing to do but stare at the undulating waves, searching for any sign of the enemy. All day it had been nothing. Ernst had kindly brought us the rambutans and cassava bread that were meant to accompany our lunch, but without anything to go with it, I was starving. I started thinking about living in an idyllic village on a surface free of Arthropods. *Could I really lead?* It seemed like something Omar would be better at, having been groomed to be a leader by his nefarious father before he'd died.

"Stay sharp, man," said Ondo.

I realized my upheld harpoon had drooped significantly.

"Sorry," I said. "I'm having trouble staying focused."

"Me too," said Krista. "And this harpoon isn't getting any lighter."

"I get it. I do," said Ondo, "but we don't have enough people to run the boat and keep watch. Besides, we're the Elites here."

"The crew is nothing to smirk at," I said. "They've survived out here a long time without our help."

"True," said Krista, "but they also didn't have us attracting every nasty critter to their whereabouts."

"She's got a point," said Ondo. "Think about what they did to the *Spearhead*. What they did to our friends. *That's* what keeps me alert."

I hefted my harpoon back to its ready position and refocused on the white-capped water.

"What made you decide to become a Clunkie?" Krista asked Ondo, without lifting her eyes from the water.

"Aside from my size, you mean?" said Ondo, chuckling. "Everyone always assumed I'd be one. I guess I just became a self-fulfilling prophecy. I'm big. I'm strong. I'm quick, despite my size. Why not?"

"That training kicked my ass," I said. "'Why not?' wouldn't have seen me through it. I would've given up if that was my only reasoning. Surely you had something more motivating."

"Can't sneak anything past you, can I?" he said, sighing. "You know what my nickname was when I arrived at Bhopal?"

Krista and I shook our heads.

"Crybaby," he said. "That's why I reverted back to Ondo as soon as I proved myself worthy."

"You're a gentle giant," I said, "but I can't see any reason you'd be called Crybaby."

"That's because you didn't see me when I arrived. Madan almost kicked me out the first minute. I was blubbering like a baby." Ondo looked distant.

"Why?" asked Krista.

"I guess I owe you the whole story. You've shared yours. Believe it or not, I came to Pod Bhopal from Pod Pittsburgh."

"That's where Ariadne and I were headed before Release Day," said Krista, pausing. "Well, before we joined Huck."

"That's a hell of a hike," I said. "I can't see how a crybaby could make it that far."

"I failed my siblings," said Ondo, rubbing tears away with his free hand. "Back in Pittsburgh, I was an orphan. Me and a bunch of other scabs survived on the margins of society, stealing food to survive. I was their leader. They looked up to me. Eventually, security found the den where we were holed up. It was a nasty, mildew-ridden place. A place no one would want. Well, until they found out we were using it. It was cleaned up and retrofitted, but not for us. Those heartless bastards put us out on the thoroughfare."

"That's awful," said Krista. "Where did you go?"

"There was nowhere to go. The prime minister was hellbent on clearing out all the scabs. The asshole put us on the list for the next Release Day, even though we were too young and untrained."

"Untrained?!" I asked.

"Pittsburgh was all about lineages. If you didn't have a notable family, you were nothing. You've been to enough pods to see how the upper crust lives. Now imagine a pod completely organized by caste. Your lineage dictated where you belonged in society."

"And those without lineage were at the bottom," said Krista.

"Bingo. No benefits. No rations. No training," he said, no longer bothering to hide the tears. "For the few months leading up to our Release Day, they put us with this old broad, Cassandra. Everybody called her Mama Cass because of these songs she used to sing. God,

I loved that woman. She was the closest thing to a mother I ever had. Made us pray *every night* before our meager excuse for dinner. It was the first time I ever considered there was something bigger than us. I got to where I kind of liked talking to him, though I've never figured out why he let humanity be wiped out."

I patted Ondo on the back. "Is she still alive?"

"I like to think so, but she was old when we fell into her lap. I doubt I'll ever see her again."

"I'm sorry," said Krista.

Ondo shrugged it off. "I'm used to disappointment."

"So how do you go from self-sufficient orphan to crybaby?" I asked.

"So on our Release Day, my siblings and I—not biological, that's just what we considered each other—were expelled from the pod with the normal heats. I was the oldest at fifteen, but the youngest among us was eight, Huck!"

Tears poured down Ondo's cheeks as he turned to us and lowered the tip of his harpoon to the deck.

"Almost every single one of them died. I held the top half of one of my brothers as he took his last breath. I watched one of my younger sisters eaten alive! Not a night goes by without reliving the nightmarish death of each of my siblings. The last of them fell before I got as far as Munich. I'm the only one of my family still alive. That's why I was bawling like a baby when I reached Pod Bhopal. Everything hit me all at once."

Krista leaned her harpoon against the railing and went to comfort Ondo.

"You asked why I became a Clunkie. It wasn't to fight the inverts. It was to return to my home and free the scabs. They deserve a better life than that. Hell, maybe I dreamed about taking out the prime minister too. Then I learned about Memo's Misfits. *You* showed me there was something bigger than my personal vendetta. When I met you, I decided my future was going forward, not back. Taking out the Hive will give the scabs the chance at life they deserve."

"God, Ondo," I said. "If only I'd known."

"You've done more than you realized, Huck. You helped me let go of something that would've eaten me from the inside as surely as the inverts."

I hugged him, barely able to wrap my arms around his muscular girth. When I let go, I turned to see everyone on deck watching. A schooner wasn't a large boat and Ondo's emotion-fraught story had captured everyone's attention. Even Rudolfo was vaguely interested. I was curious what he thought about Ondo's desire to kill a prime minister.

"I'm sorry for your losses, Ondo," said Om Banyu. "For what it's worth, I think you're doing the right thing by your siblings."

"Here, here," yelled one of the crew.

"Now, it's time everyone got back to—"

The boat lurched to the side as several impacts shook the hull, sliding me a good several centimeters across the deck. *The moment we weren't keeping watch!*

"The bastards have been playing with us the whole time," said Omar.

CHAPTER 24: ARIADNE

From the first impact, there was no doubt as to the cause. Ondo's breakdown instantly dissipated as he hefted his harpoon and looked over the side.

"Breachers on the port side!" he yelled, leaning over and trying to stab at them.

Most of the crew made for the port side to help rid the ship of its unwelcome parasites.

"Defend the starboard!" I yelled.

Half the crew turned and rushed over to help. The breachers hadn't attached themselves to my side yet. Maybe we could successfully defend it and prevent them from doing so. I scanned the water until I saw them. They were lining up, preparing to charge in sync.

"Not my boat," yelled Jafar, hurling himself over the edge.

I had a moment of panic as he fell towards the water, but then the line he'd tied around his waist caught. He was standing on the side of the ship a meter or so above the water. The drill barnacles reared back to charge. When they did, Marie, Hemant, and I launched our harpoons as Jafar stabbed at them from above.

I'd misjudged. My harpoon sailed right past my target, vanishing beneath the waves. The impact shook the deck beneath my feet. As I hastily began reeling the rope back in, I saw that Jafar was brandishing his harpoon, a speared breacher bleeding down the barbed pole. Hemant had missed and was pulling in his rope, but Marie had nailed her target dead center. Jafar was futilely poking at the breachers below the water line.

"They're too deep!" Huck yelled from the port side.

Jafar grunted his assent and began hauling himself back up the side. "We must deal with them from inside."

"Jafar, take Ariadne, Trivia, Marie, and Jorge," yelled the Captain. "Get those leaks sealed!"

Om Banyu began barking instructions to the rest of the crew as I sliced the rope off of my harpoon and ran down the ladder after Jafar and the others. When we thundered into the galley where Ernst was screaming, hacking unsuccessfully at a strange brown appendage sticking through the wall with a cleaver.

"Get away! Get away!" he yelled, scoring a minor hit.

The appendage began squirting hemolymph everywhere, its movements becoming even more erratic.

"Ew!" he cried, indignant. "Not my apron!"

Ernst charged, slicing off half of the appendage. The drill barnacle let loose a piercing wail that carried through the water and the hull. In a retaliatory strike, it smacked Ernst in the chest and flung him into the wall, knocking him unconscious. I gave a passing look at Marie. *At least he's not in the way.* The creature went limp.

"Watch out for the peduncles!" shouted Trivia.

"The what?" I asked.

"The stalky bit!"

"You don't have to tell me twice!" I said, watching water begin to leach through the gap. "What do we do?!"

Jafar shoved open the hatch to the hold and began hurling

crates to the side. "Where are they?!" Then finally, "Ahh." He ran back into the room with several wooden pins and a mallet nearly as large as his head. "I will order Ernst's ass for breakfast when he wakes, piling his goods on top of my pegs! It will go nicely with a side of eggs!"

He rushed over to the limp peduncle in the wall, lined up a peg, and drove it home, through the creature's dead body, splattering him with the black goo. The leak slowed to a trickle. With a few more hits, it had stopped completely.

"Five to go!" he yelled, wiping the dark fluid from his face with a bare hand. "Each of you, take one. Kill it however you can. I will handle the leaks!"

Jafar charged off to deal with one himself. I ran towards the next one, dodging its flails. At least it didn't have eyes on this side. I drove my harpoon into it. It wailed, but continued to thrash, breaking the handle in the process. *The hell with this!* I pulled the dagger from my belt and climbed up the side of the hull and swung down with all of my might. I sliced the stalk clean off the creature, drenching the wood with hemolymph.

Jafar finished driving the peg into the second hole and rushed to take care of mine. "Help the others!"

Marie had just finished off hers, so I ran to Jorge, who was struggling to dodge the peduncle.

"I can't hit it!" he yelled, repeatedly lifting his rapier. "I can't anticipate its movements!"

"Just swing, dammit!" I yelled.

Jorge swung down and missed, losing his balance and falling towards the writhing peduncle. I expected him to be thrown back like Ernst, but instead, the tip of the breacher's stalk hit Jorge's chest dead center. For a moment, they each froze.

"Jorge, take my hand!" I yelled, my arm extended towards the trapped sailor.

He turned to face me, just as the peduncle exploded through his back in an eruption of blood and bone.

"No!" I screamed, as his body went limp.

Marie appeared out of nowhere and sliced the thing to ribbons before Jafar pegged the last hole shut.

"It was my fault!" I cried. "I told him to swing! When he missed…"

Marie crouched, lifting my chin until I faced her. Those dark, captivating eyes barely visible under her cowl were almost hypnotic.

"His death is not yours to carry," said Marie, icily calm.

She released my chin with the slightest caress and headed for the ship's ladder. I sniffled as I wiped my tears and stood.

"She's right, you know?" said Trivia. "Blame Jorge's inexperience. Blame the Arthropods. Whatever you do, don't blame yourself."

I nodded as she put her arm around me and led me towards the deck. Right as I put my hand on the railing, I heard it. The sound that sent chills through my bones rivaling only that of the Nightmare. The sea locust. I pushed all thoughts of self-pity from my mind and raced toward the deck, nearly running into Huck.

"Are you okay?" he asked.

I nodded. "I'll tell you later. If there is a later."

Before he could respond, Om Banyu yelled, "Lights out! Everyone freeze!"

The ship went dead silent. The only sounds were the inescapable creaks, pops, and splashes as we barely perceptibly rocked from side to side, lit only by moonlight. Everyone's eyes darted to everyone else's, waiting to hear the next wail of what the sailors referred to as the Kraken. The second wail didn't disappoint, sounding closer than the last. With any luck, the creature had lost us.

"What do you know about the Kraken?" Banyu asked Trivia in a barely audible whisper.

"It destroyed the *Spearhead* with a single blow, and that was a metal-hulled ship."

The captain acknowledged her and thought for a moment, stroking the stubble on his chin, nearly as loud as his whisper. "Are you aware of any vulnerabilities?"

"It packs its power into a short burst—"

A closer wail. Huck slipped his ice-cold hand into mine. Everyone was getting antsy.

"Meaning?"

"It probably stops close to line itself up with its target before it strikes. That would be our only chance if it found us," she whispered. "I think."

"We don't have anything else to go on, do we? Weak points?"

"We just don't know enough about it," said Trivia, exasperated. "Most carapaced Arthropods have a weak underside, but I don't think anyone wants to get into the water with that thing. It hit the *Spearhead* near the surface. If someone crazy enough could get on top of it, they might be able to drive a harpoon down through its head."

Om Banyu's head swung towards Marie. With a nod of assent, she strapped a harpoon to her back and began silently climbing the ropes to the highest yardarm of the main sail.

"I know she's drunk hemolymph and tattooed her face, but not even she can be that nuts, right?" whispered Hemant.

I shrugged. I'd seen the mysterious woman do unimaginably crazy things, each of which had kept us alive. With her almost superhuman abilities and catlike reflexes, if anyone could mount a sea locust, it would be her.

Another wail sounded so close that it hurt my ears and vibrated my chest. I couldn't have squeezed Huck's hand tighter. Normally unshakable, Omar's face shown with fear. Hemant was breathing hard, ready for a fight. Fen's eyes burned with rage after what the creature had done to our battalion and Mego. My fingers itched for my bow, which lay in a corner a few meters away, where I'd left it while watching for the drill barnacles. At least Huck wore his sword and Hemant held his warhammer. *A light! Who the hell turned on a light?* Rudolfo came barging out of Banyu's cabin, Zimo, as always, on his heels.

"Who turned off all the lights?!" the minister boomed, Lord Ransford yapping in his arms. "I woke from my evening respite in utter darkness! Why are you all just standing there? Someone see to the lights!"

"Shut up!" said Krista through clenched teeth.

"I will not be shushed, especially not by you, *girl*. May I remind you that you are a guest—"

The sea locust roared as it breached the surface off our starboard, before slinking back underwater.

Om Banyu grabbed the trembling Rudolfo by the lapels and flung him into the wall as Zimo stared on, wide-eyed. "You miserable sack of crap! You may have just killed us all!"

All pretense of stealth dropped. Banyu began shouting orders for everyone to arm themselves. I ran and grabbed my bow. I didn't know what use it could be, but I felt naked without it. I joined Trivia on the side and nocked an arrow. If it was going to charge, I'd make it look like a pincushion first.

"Huck," said Banyu. "I want your team and the weapon in a dingy, now!"

"But—"

"But nothing. I didn't carry you all this way to see you die off the coast of your destination! Go!"

"But—"

"GO!"

"Perhaps I should join—" the minister began, but the scowl he got from Banyu and Jafar sent him cowering.

I fought back tears, knowing the sacrifice they were committing to. Hemant and Omar ran below to get the bomb as Krista and

I rushed to the port side and lowered a lifeboat into the water. Within moments, it was loaded with everyone save for Marie and was paddling softly away from the *Semeru*.

"Let's kill this bastard and give them the chance they deserve!" yelled the captain to cheers. "If there are any survivors, take to the lifeboats and head due south!

No sooner than we'd cleared the bow, I saw the ripple across the ocean's surface as the Kraken emerged from the depths to charge its target. It was like watching our companions die all over again. I wanted so badly to turn away, but I couldn't. I put a hand over my mouth to hold back the choking sobs racking my body. Huck stopped paddling and held me.

"Look!" whispered Fen.

I could barely make out a dark shape swinging over the water, then caught a flash of red flipping through the air.

"Marie!" I whispered excitedly.

With perfect finesse, she landed softly amidst the ripples. In one fluid motion, as she stood she raised her harpoon and drove it deep into the creature's head. The wail that rent the night air sent goosebumps down my body—the single most horrifying sound I'd heard in my life. The calm water frothed as the sea locust whipped back and forth, writhing in the throes of death, Marie no longer visible. After seconds that drifted by like ages, the beast arched its back, let loose a final wail, and then was still. Boisterous cheers echoed over the water.

"They survived!" I yelled.

"As long as there was only one of those bastards!" said Fen.

As quickly as Huck and Omar could paddle, we headed back to the boat. Banyu and Jafar helped us on board and got the lifeboat reseated. Elation thickened the air. We'd yet again stared death in the face and come away unscathed.

I could make out the beast's carcass, floating in the water near the boat, slowly listing. As death consumed it, its carapace lost its red hue, reverting to a putrid grayish tan. The head took up the first third of its body, followed by a long segmented tail. Extending from the front below the creature's dead eye stalks were sharp-edged, club-like appendages—ideal for smashing hulls and slicing prey.

"It's messed up, isn't it?" said Krista. "That nature would create something so ideal for destruction."

"Yeah," I replied. "But nature isn't sentimental. That's a human convention."

"Well Marie put it in its place," said Omar, wrapping his arms around Krista, "I guess I owe her congratulations. Where is that woman?"

I searched for her, but there was no sign of her pale face or red cloak anywhere.

"Where's Marie?" Huck asked Banyu.

"She never returned," he said. "Jafar is searching with the scope, but he's yet to see any sign. I'm afraid she's gone."

"No," Huck said, almost breathlessly. "I thought she'd outlive all of us."

I led him to a nearby crate and helped him to a seat.

"She saved my life, more times than I can count," he said, tearing up. "She was… well… Marie, but she was my friend. I owe her more than I can ever repay."

"You know what she would say if she heard you right now?"

Huck shook his head.

"She'd laugh in that beautiful, chilling voice of hers and say, 'You are a fool.'"

Huck cracked a smile. "You're right. She wasn't one for tolerating any moping. Or any emotions, really. She was a strange one, but that's what made her so special."

"It's a shame," said Omar. "I was just starting to like her too."

CHAPTER 25: HEMANT

We didn't have time to mourn Marie. Though Captain Banyu had always tried to avoid night sailing, we had to escape the area before the Kraken's decomposition attracted more inverts. As the crew manned the sails, we resumed our watch, but everyone's attention was on Banyu.

"Your carelessness nearly killed everyone aboard!" he yelled, centimeters from Rudolfo's face. "Marie might be alive right now if not for your ineptitude!"

"You will not talk to me in that—" said the minister.

"On my ship, I'll talk to you how I damn well please. I've had my fill of your cowardice and arrogance. You have no business being outside of a pod, much less leading it. You are *nothing* like the man you imagine yourself to be. You are a shame! When we return, you *will* voluntarily resign your post, effective immediately. Is that understood? Let every person here serve as witness."

"I... I...," Rudolfo stammered. He panned the faces of the crew, searching desperately for sympathy but found none. His head fell for a moment before he faced Captain Banyu. "As you wish, Captain."

Rudolfo untied the red sash that stretched diagonally across his chest. One by one, he unpinned the medallions which emblazoned his breast, handing them to his advisor. He even removed the gemmed collar from Lord Ransford. Zimo placed his hand on Rudolfo's shoulder, but he shrugged it off. Before us wasn't the leader who'd presented himself with the air of nobility and poise, but rather a sad, defeated, oddly dressed man with a spoiled pet.

"I always wanted to emulate the great leaders of the past. Perhaps I never possessed the ability to become one myself," he said with resignation. "Advisor Zimo, please formally note my agreement to Captain Banyu's terms. As my last official act, I would like to name Boatmaster General Francisco as my successor. He is an honest, hard-working gentleman from a long line of humble Bandung residents. As a man of the people, he will hold the office with dignity. In his place, I would like to name you boatmaster general, Om Banyu. I will vacate your cabin immediately."

Silently, he, Zimo, and Ransford headed towards the captain's cabin. I didn't like the guy any more than anyone else, but strangely, I felt sorry for him. I didn't know his story. I had no idea if he'd ever seen battle or how he'd achieved such a high position. Regardless, he would be returning to Pod Bandung in disgrace, likely eking out a meager existence in solitude.

"It's what he deserves," said Fen, coldly. "I have no respect for a leader unproven in battle."

I made noises of agreement. It was too easy for a leader to send people to die when they'd never faced death themselves. His murals had been exaggerated, and in at least one instance, a bold-faced lie, but had there been no truth to any of it? What a farce. Maybe Fen was right and disgrace was what he deserved.

After the drama had concluded, it was easy to focus on guard duty. I wanted to be alone with my thoughts and grief. I'd never completely trusted Marie, but she'd been invaluable on our journey.

I'd miss her dessicatingly dry humor and fierce prowess as a warrior, especially as we entered the infamous Australian Territory.

As time drifted by like the waters below, my eyes grew heavier and heavier. Once we were a few hours out from the scene, Om Banyu ordered the sails lowered for the remainder of the night. Except for the next watch, everyone went below to squeeze in a few hours of much-needed sleep before we arrived at the coast of the most dangerous place on the planet.

········

Sunlight was glaring through the porthole and shining through my eyelid, interrupting my last few minutes of shut-eye. I pried my crusty eyes open. *That's far brighter than the light of dawn.* I'd slept in. Huck and Omar laid next to me, their hammocks rocking slowly with the motion of the ocean. I climbed down, trying not to disturb the others. Omar's eyes sprung open. *A light sleeper, that one.* Huck took a little more effort.

"What time is it?" Huck asked groggily.

"Mid-morning, I'd guess," I said.

"I suppose they figured we needed more sleep," said Omar, rubbing the rheum from his eyes. "The crew will be sailing back in relative safety compared to the voyage down, whereas we will be tromping through the Outback under a sky crowded with inverts."

"When you put it that way, it makes me less excited about making landfall," I said. "And I despise being out on the water. Thank the universe for Ernst's stock of ginger."

"How's the oddball doing?" asked Omar.

"Ariadne said he has a concussion and a few bruised ribs, but he'll be fine," said Huck, looking towards her empty hammock. "I bet she's down there helping him now."

"Speaking of which, I could go for some breakfast," I said.

"This is our last chance for a decent meal. Then it's back to random fruit and reptiles. Joy."

We made for the galley, hoping we hadn't missed breakfast. Ernst was there as usual, ribs wrapped in tight cloth as he ordered the women around the kitchen.

"Anything left for us?" Huck asked.

"No empty bellies in my galley!" said Ernst, gesturing to himself with his thumb. "We're getting a start on lunch, but there are egg sandwiches on the counter for you. The girls insisted."

"You're amazing, Ernst," I said, greedily unwrapping my breakfast from the cheesecloth.

"I know," he said, smiling, "but so are your companions. If they weren't taken, I might have to steal them away from you."

Ariadne and Trivia laughed, used to his quirky sense of humor. Ernst had grown fond of the girls, but not in any romantic sense. That didn't stop him from joking around about it. God, did he make good food. Freshly harvested from the shipyard gardens, the *Semeru's* food stores under Ernst's talent had been some of the best we'd eaten. It wasn't refined or elegant, but always filling and delicious.

"Man," I said, mouth full of eggs and tomato. "You sure you don't want to come with us?"

"Ha!" said Ernst. "Even healed, I would pass. I served my time marching through jungles eating grubs. My job now is to fill your little bellies so you can go be big heroes."

"With food like this, I'll conquer the planet," said Omar. "Any chance you could pack us—"

Rudolfo walked into the galley, bags under his eyes from what must have been a deplorable night's sleep. Zimo was just behind, looking much the same. Both wore the standard-issue citizen clothes, making our gray elite jumpsuits feel more formal by comparison. The soon-to-be-former prime minister looked defeated. His normally trimmed goatee was unkempt and surrounded by a day's stubble and his shoulder-length black hair was uncombed from the night before, loosely pulled back in a ponytail.

"Care if I join you?" he asked.

I shrugged. *My, how the mighty have fallen.*

The pair took seats at the galley bar next to us. Omar grabbed two sandwiches from the pile and passed them down. Rudolfo looked at the meal as though it was foreign, but eventually, hunger won over and he began eating.

"This is humble food, but it's as good as anything my chef prepared for me in the pod," said Rudolfo.

"Thank you, mil— sir," said Ernst.

"Call me Rudolfo. I'm not worthy of any title."

It was clear that Zimo had placed his value on being the advisor to the prime minister. Though connected to the office, not the man, he seemed just as deflated as Rudolfo. I thought about asking what his plans were but dismissed the question as inappropriate. Omar had no such reservations.

"You going to serve Francisco, Zimo?" asked Omar.

Zimo was taken aback at first but responded. "No, I don't believe so. I've spent my life serving… Rudolfo," he said, speaking informally with great difficulty. "I tire of politics. I believe I will help in the gardens if they will have me. I have always enjoyed growing things and I certainly don't have the build for a warrior or builder."

"There are few more noble pursuits," said Ernst.

"What about you, Rudy?" asked Omar.

Rudolfo raised an eyebrow at the nickname, but let it be. "I've never had to think about it. I've been groomed to be a leader, like my father before me. The generational grooming, ironically, removed us further and further from the masses. My destiny was always to lead, so I've never considered alternatives."

"You clearly have a fondness for humanity's history," said Trivia, dusting flour off of her hands. "Have you given any thought to being a scholar? With the world free of Arthropods, we'll need teams of historians to collect and catalog Earth's history, at least what we can piece together. Humanity needs to know our past. So much has been forgotten."

"You are wise beyond your years, young one. Perhaps I will," said the minister.

"Land ho!" Jafar shouted, loud enough for everyone on the boat to hear.

I crammed the last two bites into my mouth and charged up the ladder. Everyone in the galley close on my heels. When I reached the deck, I joined the crew looking from the bow. There it was—the Australian Territory. The most danger-ridden, invert-infested territory on Earth. The place we'd worked so hard to reach. The destination so many had given their lives for.

"We're here," said Huck.

••••••••

"City or country?" asked Om Banyu as the coastline came clearly into view.

Directly ahead was a long-forgotten port city of Darwin, a once booming metropolis now nothing more than a quiet tombstone for its fallen. Aside from Arjun and Kolya, no one might have set foot into this territory since it had been abandoned centuries ago. Boatmaster Francisco had referred to it as Win City, a name based on his time-worn map, but it had to be one and the same. I pondered the captain's question. Both options were equally dangerous. In the city we would have cover, but so would they. The inverse was the case in the countryside.

"City, unless Fen has any objections," said Huck. "Maybe at some point, we'll pick up Arjun's trail."

"Doesn't matter to me," said Fen. "If we're entering hell, it doesn't matter if we use the front or back door."

"City, then," said Banyu, spinning the helm towards Darwin. "Francisco dropped them off upriver, but if what you say is true, the pair had protections that we don't. I have to consider the safety of my crew. I'm dropping you off and wishing you luck, and then I'm pointing my bow back towards Bandung."

"I understand," said Huck. "We've put you guys in jeopardy long enough."

After being dismissed, I went below to ready my pack and suit up. After spending most of our ocean journey barefoot and unarmored, I wasn't excited to put it back on.

"I'll be thrilled if the day ever comes when I never have to wear armor again," I said.

Trivia laughed. "Like that'll be in our lifetimes! Even after we blow the Hive, we'll still have zillions of inverts to eradicate from the surface. This is only the beginning of the end."

"*Ugh,*" I moaned. "Why do you have to go and be all realistic?"

"Because I'm the rational one, remember?" she said, pulling me in for a kiss.

"Alright, alright," said Fen. "Get all of your fondling out of the way before we set foot on land. After that, I'm not tolerating any of it. Distractions like that will get us killed. That includes you too, Huck."

"What?" he said, shrugging. "We weren't doing anything."

"No, but you will," she said, flashing the briefest smile.

Fen's mood had been hard to gauge since Mego's death, but she was starting to revert to her old friendly self. She was still as hard-edged as ever but with our best interests at heart. She'd never been a stealthy assassin quite like Marie, but she was an invert-killing machine in her own right that I was glad to have at my back. I finished packing and Ondo helped me lug the heavy bomb to the deck.

"I will flood with relief when that thing is off our boat," said Jafar. "I haven't forgotten the atrocities humans committed with such weapons before the treaties. Humans shouldn't have toyed with the atom."

"This weapon is how we are going to take down the Arthropods," I reminded him.

"Let us hope that it will be the last one ever used."

"As far as I know, it's the only one in existence," said Ariadne. "But you know, if it wasn't for harnessing the atom, the pods wouldn't exist. They've only lasted as long as they have as a result of their nuclear reactors."

Jafar grunted in consternation and turned to fuss at a crew member.

"He's got a point," said Trivia. "I hope that when we return the reins to humanity, we don't take the responsibility lightly. We've screwed up a lot in the past."

"Humans have always learned the hard way, though I would prefer if it wasn't under the threat of annihilation, from ourselves or others," said Rudolfo. "My role may be changing, but my support hasn't. I wish you and your companions the best of luck. It is *your* legacy that should be preserved in the murals. Perhaps that can be my legacy. To encourage the new minister to cover my arrogance with something more fitting."

"You know, you're alright, Rudolfo," I said as the *Semeru* pulled close to a rocky peninsula jutting out into the ocean.

"Umm… Thank you," he said.

"If it's all the same to you though," I said, "I'd prefer that the residents of Bandung won't be living underground long enough to repaint the murals.

Om Banyu vanished into the pilot house and returned with a small short-wave radio and battery pack, which he handed to Huck.

"Don't you need this?" he asked.

"I've already informed Pod Bandung of our arrival," said the captain. "You'll need it far more than I will. How else will we know to collect you once your mission is accomplished?"

"Thank you for everything, Om Banyu," I said.

"The pleasure is truly mine," he said.

We loaded our supplies and ourselves into the wooden dingy for our trip to shore, the crew all the while patting our backs and wishing us well. Jafar volunteered to row us to shore, and after a short trip, left us on a rocky outcropping of tan stone with our gear.

"May fortune favor you," he said, placing his hand over his heart before climbing back into the tiny boat dwarfed by his frame.

We stood watching forlornly as he paddled back to the ship. With a final wave, we were alone—in hell.

CHAPTER 26: KOLYA

To the side of the opalescent pools that supplied the growing Arthropods' nutritional needs, our weary Demented escorts lowered our litters to exchange crews. I'd lost all sense of time, but it had been hours since we'd entered the Hive. We'd traversed untold kilometers and no telling how much elevation. Our crews were worn by the exertion, mine more so than Arjun's. He was a wisp of a boy compared to me, decades his senior. Even my recent time on the surface hadn't managed to loosen the excess girth around my midsection. Before the new crew could take over, I leapt off of the litter's seat and crouched at the edge of a holding pond to study the shimmering liquid. Before I could react, an invisible blade was across my throat. I could sense the mantis wraith at my side, chittering menacingly.

"Kolya, back up slowly," urged my companion. "I don't think they like you that close."

"Yes," I said, nervously, afraid to swallow lest the razor edge slice my neck.

I slowly retreated and cautiously rose, gently dusting off my knees where I'd fallen to inspect the milky-white liquid, making sure to use the least aggressive motions. The floor of the space was scattered with nearly every conceivable species of invert and Demented. All focused on me, who'd made a huge *faux pas*.

"I'm sorry," I said, backing towards the litter, open hands raised.

The creatures resumed their normal routine, the mantis backing away into non-existence. *My God, Sveta, they're watching every move.* I wondered how long that wraith had been at my side, ready to cleave the head from my body at the slightest hint of danger.

"Behave yourself, Arjun," I said. "One wrong move…"

Arjun nodded, knowing that I was speaking as much to myself as him.

Our guides carried us into another dim tunnel illuminated by the glass worms and continued the wind downward. Shortly after the fear had subsided, I was bursting with excitement at the prospect of giving the Hive all the meticulous study it deserved. That oily, white goo would be one of the countless items on my list. I'd never heard of the substance in my many years of studying the invaders. Then again, no one had ever ventured as far as we had. We were the first uncorrupted human eyes to behold this place, and we'd barely scratched the surface. Once peace was established, perhaps I could bring in the best scientific minds from around the globe, carefully vetted and serving under my authority.

Even with all of the excitement, I hadn't realized how tired I'd become. My eyes grew heavier by the minute. We'd been riding all day long, and it had to have been getting close to midnight. Eventually, our litter crews took a branching tunnel which opened into a smaller, lamp-lit cavern with Demented guards flanking each of the wood and iron doors nestled into the walls. Soot stained the ceiling above where the oil lamps burned. A large brazier in the room's center took the cool edge off of the air, which had grown noticeably more frigid. Our escorts sat down the litters as Jigna and Neesh approached our sides. With a few barks and gestures, they pointed toward two of the rooms and mimicked sleeping.

"They must be sleeping accommodations," said Arjun, stifling a yawn with the back of his hand.

Our litter crews vanished, leaving us alone with a pair of guards and the two Demented who had accompanied us across the territory. They motioned good night and headed into one of the adjacent rooms. Within moments, from behind their closed door, wildly animalistic sounds pierced the air.

"I suppose they're making up for lost time," I said, snickering.

It struck me that they'd been too proper to do it around us. *How odd.* Arjun and I made our way to our doors, anxious to escape the primal love-making. No sooner than we'd entered, the guards outside started barking encouraging noises to their intertwined companions. I couldn't help but wonder what Demented spawn would look like. The thought made my blood run cold—a Demented child. I shuddered at the unpleasant thought and prayed to God that they were sterile.

"I doubt we'll be allowed to do any exploring," I said, anxious to shift the direction of my mind.

Arjun nodded his head in agreement. "Did you notice the scratching coming from the ceiling outside?"

I glanced up at the exposed rock ceiling of the antechamber and saw trickles of dust raining down. "The guards aren't the only thing watching over us."

"Kolya, would you mind if we shared a room?"

"Not at all, my friend. I wouldn't rest easy leaving you alone in such a foreign place."

I slid the iron bar into place, latching the door. The rudimentary device was exactly what I'd expected from the Demented. No inverts had constructed this portion of the Hive. This was the work of human hands. With as many of the twisted humans as we'd seen, they likely had their own barracks scattered throughout the mountain. Perhaps even nurseries. Another shudder. The room followed the same lack of attention to detail as the door. Two simply constructed pallets, a basin of questionably fresh water, a bowl of familiar fruit, and a lidded hole in the rear of the space were all there was in the spartan room. Candles lit the smoothed mud walls.

I eagerly devoured more than half of the fruit before I stopped myself. Arjun patiently ate one of the fruits, not savoring so much as consciously consuming every bite. Draining the last of my canteen, I used the basin to rinse my face and made use of the facilities while Arjun was kind enough to roam the room just beyond the door. As I was recapping the toilet, I could've sworn I saw a flash of movement in the darkness. I tried to dismiss the thought, knowing it would already be difficult to rest in this environment, despite the overwhelming exhaustion. Once we'd settled in bed and snuffed the candles, I couldn't stop dwelling on what we'd seen. Judging from Arjun's breathing, his mind was also churning too much for sleep.

"What's on your mind, my friend?" I asked.

"We're dealing with a species possibly more fit than ourselves," he said, referencing Herbert Spencer's definition of "fit."

"Meaning natural selection has identified its new leaders, and it's not us," I said.

"Do you think they have any reason to bargain with us?" asked Arjun. "They've spent the last four hundred years demonstrating their superiority. What do they have to gain?"

"They need us," I said. "Not only for food, but they use the Demented like slaves. Maybe that's something we can use to our advantage."

"I don't think that's a card we want to play."

"Why do you say that?"

"Did you pay attention to the Demented during our descent?" he asked. "Not Jigna and Neesh. For whatever reason, they're different. I mean the others."

I thought back to what I'd observed. "There was a certain mindless quality to them," I said.

"That's precisely what I mean. The travel has given me time to think about the parasite/host relationships we've discussed. The Arthropods must have some degree of control over the Demented's minds. As we've speculated, it has to be from consumption of hemolymph."

As if the drink wasn't vile enough. Several of us had unintentionally participated in a ceremony and consumed a small amount, but no one as much as that temptress Marie. If the creatures' blood could take possession of a Demented's mind, what would stop it from doing the same to her? I'd even caught her communing with the spirits. *Her "spirits" were nothing more than the Arthropod Queens.* It's of no importance now. If she turns on the others, that's less I have to worry about. Her judgment will come in due time.

"They are as much a part of the Hive as the Arthropods," I said. "You fear peace would entail becoming subservient to the inverts."

"Yes," answered Arjun.

"How would you broach peace?"

A lingering moment passed before Arjun gave a thoughtful answer.

"The only viable option isn't an enjoyable one. I believe humanity's age of supremacy has come to an end. Regardless of what we tell ourselves, it ended long ago. I believe that our only opportunity for survival ends with us being subservient to the Arthropods."

I'd thought along similar lines. What I didn't think Arjun had considered was that there could be those who benefit from the situation as much as suffer from it. I'd made up my mind long ago that I wouldn't be the latter.

"Humans would serve the inverts like the savage gods of old, generating offerings to provide for their safety," I said. "We provide the food or we become the food."

"I'm afraid so," said Arjun.

●●●●●●●●

A harsh rap at the door woke me from my slumber.

"I suppose it's too much to expect coffee," I said.

Arjun gave me a blank look.

I rolled my eyes. The boy could be so sharp and miss the most obvious sarcasm. Without waiting for permission, two Demented slaves entered bearing fresh trays of fruit, eggs, and water, then departed as quickly as they'd come. I rolled the egg around on the tray, trying to establish its origin.

"I think it's a boiled reptile egg, Kolya," said Arjun, taking a drink of the water without fear. "I believe it's safe."

"And the water?"

"Minerally, but aside from that, fresh. I'm nearing the point of dehydration, so it's an acceptable risk."

I took the water in my hand, examining it. It had the slightest cloudy appearance but otherwise was clear. I downed the vessel in one motion. It was cold and the most refreshing drink I'd tasted since we'd entered the desert. Maybe better than coffee. *Well... no.* I opened the door and motioned to the guard.

"More?" I asked, holding out the cup.

The guard disappeared, hopefully, to retrieve more water.

"I would caution you against drinking too much at once. The high mineral content might have undesired effects."

I nodded my thanks. If the water had been collected from deep underground as I suspected, the calcium content would be high, resulting in a laxative effect. Not something you want when you are already nearing dehydration.

Once we'd finished breakfast and a second cup of water, some Demented females collected our trays. The woman approaching me was far less mutilated than the others I'd seen. Aside from her discolored, bloodshot eyes, and her stitched leather garb she appeared almost normal. She bent deeply for my tray and I admired her sultry, sparsely-covered form. I wondered briefly how wild things could be with someone of her primal sensibilities.

"Kolya," said Arjun, obviously not for the first time. "They're waiting for us."

I shook my head to clear my mind, but the woman was already gone. *No, Sveta, I mustn't give into such temptation. The time will come when I can take what I want, but that time is not yet upon us.* If the Arthropods would back my leadership once we'd reached a peace accord, I would want for nothing—and wouldn't have to lower myself to such sinful debauchery. Heaven could never bless a union between a Demented and a human. It wasn't natural.

"Alright, my boy," I said, rising.

We exited our quarters into the large space where our litters awaited. The glass worm had returned with a similar message to the day before.

"Today, we will meet the Queens," I said, almost giddy.

We mounted our litters and resumed the spiraling march downward. The new cavern was far less trafficked than the previous spaces. The walls of the smaller passage were intricately carved with the unrepeating swirls that could only be found in nature. Unlike our native insects, these Queens had surpassed an animalistic desire for pure function and evolved to appreciate beauty. Everything about these creatures demonstrated that they were far more intelligent than anyone had initially suspected. Judging by the look on Arjun's face, he'd reached the same conclusion. The tunnel widened before it ended, leading us into a gargantuan circular room deep in the earth. We climbed down from our litters and aside from the glass worm, all other Demented and Arthropods departed. When I examined our surroundings, I almost forgot to breathe.

In the center of a room was a vacant dais, like a stunted stalagmite with an angled, bowl-like depression. Bordering the room were similar formations with varying shapes to accommodate differing bodies. Each of which sat in front of darkened alcoves in which something stirred. Arjun tugged at my sleeve, staring up with mouth agape. I followed his gaze and felt my mouth go dry. High above us was the bottom tip of the meteorite—the same meteorite that had crashed into the Earth so many years ago. The only thing interrupting its streamlined appearance was an alcove inside it. We were inside the Queens' royal chambers—their sanctum—and they were watching us. I was at an utter loss for words.

CHAPTER 27: DARREN

After Patricia's small memorial service, we headed back to my apartment. Not wanting to leave me alone, Stepan and Kitty had bought some finger foods from the nearby deli and brought them over.

"We have to consider the implications," said Stepan, raising his voice. "Aside from these… Arthropods, there's going to be panic, food shortages, looting and rioting… We've binged all the same end-of-the-world shows. You know what happens when people lose their cool."

"You think I haven't thought about that?" I asked, unbuttoning my dress shirt. "What am I going to do? Where would I go? I've got a kid for chrissakes!"

"Maybe it won't be as bad as you think, honey," said Kitty, bringing out the charcuterie board from the deli. "People are stronger than you give them credit for, not to mention every active service member has been deployed to—"

"Won't be as bad as I think?" asked Stepan. "Screen on. World Updates."

"Specify channel," the disembodied AI voice replied.

"Do I look like I give a damn? Play the news."

"Here is an option you might like," it responded, pulling up one of the numerous popular news feeds. It wasn't the one I preferred, but nowadays, they all repeated the same things.

"…at Kuyunba Conservation Reserve where they were being temporarily held until relocation. As of this moment, there are no confirmed survivors of the massacre."

Kitty's hand flew over her mouth as the anchor continued. The archive footage showed the fields of tents in the park where the evacuated residents of Alice Springs had lived. As I watched the people in the shot try their best to go about their lives, I couldn't think of anything except the fact that everyone in this footage was dead—all thirty-something thousand people.

"In response, thousands of concerned citizens are protesting in front of the UTE's Bureau of Affairs in Munich, demanding immediate action."

The camera panned sign after sign showing every possible opinion, frequently accompanied by vulgar language or specific threats. Almost every poster had the same general message: Kill the bastards. Stepan cycled to another channel.

"…overrunning others. Twenty-four shoppers were killed before they could make it through the entrance. This is just one of numerous cases of shopping hysteria occurring around the globe—"

"You see what I mean?" said Stepan, unusually riled. "We've got to go somewhere. Anywhere! I want to get the hell out of the city. There's too many damn people."

"Are we leaving too, Dad?" asked Alex, having just walked through the door, Mrs. Grimethorpe on his heels.

I turned to Stepan with a look of frustration.

"I'm sorry, man. I'm just worried about all of us."

"I know you're just trying to help," I sighed. "You're right. What's happening out there in the world is crazy and could potentially happen here, but again, where would we go?"

Mrs. Grimethorpe cleared her throat. "I have a little place. It's not much and it's out of the way, but maybe it could be a place we could all get away for a while and clear our heads. That is, if that's alright with you, Darren?"

I hadn't given much thought to leaving the city before Stepan had mentioned it, but I had spent sleepless nights worrying about Alex and my safety. Just a century ago, food and resources had to be rationed through a major war. *War, that's what this is.* I'd studied the history. War demanded sacrifices. I couldn't imagine standing in line for hours with a crying child to get a moldy half-loaf of bread and a liter of sour milk, much less during the colder months. Leaving the city… Maybe it was a better idea than I'd given him credit for.

"I think that's a terrific idea, Mrs. Grimethorpe," I said, conceding.

"Dorothy, please," she said. "If we are going to be living with each other for a bit, you may as well call me by my name."

I smiled. "What exactly did you have in mind, Dorothy?"

••••••••

Stepan and Dorothy had ganged up on me, but their plan had merit. Stepan and I would take a sabbatical from work, and we'd disappear into the woods until urban life calmed and the world adjusted to its new normal. They had some grand idea that we would grow our food, but if all else failed, Dorothy said there was a community grocery not too far down the road where the threat of a human stampede would be nonexistent.

First thing Monday morning, Stepan and I took the train into the city center and made our way to our office, each with a notice of sabbatical leave in hand. Normally these types of things were done well in advance, but with everything going on, I wasn't too worried about the firm's reaction. I'd been a dedicated worker for just over a decade, winning awards and recognition for the company on more than one occasion. Hell, the most time I'd ever taken off had been with Patricia's death.

The second I walked through the door, the environment felt different—oppressive. Coworkers were crying. Others looked upset enough to break something. Some just stared at the floor. Stepan and I traded looks before pushing through the cluster of people towards Mr. Szalinski as Nina passed me, bawling. She made eye contact as if to speak, but then buried her face in a handkerchief and nearly ran out of the door.

"Darren! How've you been? Alex still growing like a weed?" asked Szalinski.

"Um… We're fine," I said. "Look, Mr.—"

"Whatever you're going to say, let me say mine first," he said, raising his hand.

I nodded. Who was I to tell a managing partner what to do?

"It's good that you and Stepan are here together. It'll save me from having to repeat the same message. Look guys, you know times are difficult right now. We don't want to do this any more than you do, but for the good of the company, we are letting you guys go."

"You're what?!" asked Stepan, indignant.

Szalinski appeared highly uncomfortable. Judging by the room, this was the umpteenth time he'd delivered such undesirable news.

"We don't think given the current climate that people will be focused on trivial things like advertising. Myself and the other partners will stay, tending to a few select clients until things return to normal. The board believes we won't be able to generate the income necessary to pay you through this recession. We'll pay out severance and accumulated days, but for now, I'm afraid we have no choice but to cut you loose."

Stepan was about to become unhinged, but I rested a hand on his shoulder. "It'll be fine, Stepan. We'll manage."

"That's the spirit, son," said Szalinski, giving me a condescending pat on the back. "You have my word, when things return to normal, you'll each have a place here if you desire."

"Thank you, Mr. Szalinski," I said. "It's been an honor to work for you."

"The pleasure was mine."

"Can you believe that guy?" said Stepan once we were on our way back to the station. "He must have some nerve…"

"Step, you *do* realize he gave us almost exactly what we wanted, right?"

"Yeah, but he didn't know that. I mean, he just fired us!"

"I'm sorry, man. I've got a limited attention span and I can't waste any of it on being angry for someone inadvertently giving me what I want."

"When you put it that way… you're right. I've been worried about other people losing their cool and here I am losing mine. Thankfully I have your voice of wisdom." Stepan laughed, anger receding. "So what's next?"

"I need to pull Alex out of school."

"And after that?"

"I guess we need to buy some seeds."

"And chickens, right?

"Yes, Step. And chickens." I said, shaking my head, chuckling.

If only Patricia was around to know we were trying our hand at farming, she'd laugh herself silly. Part of me was thankful she wasn't around. I had the sinking feeling that the world was going to get a lot worse before it got better.

••••••••

"This is the place," said Mrs. Grimethorpe, climbing out of her vintage Range Rover.

Riding with her had been nothing short of terrifying. It was apparent from the first moments that maybe we shouldn't have let her drive. Her vision wasn't as good as she believed it was, nor were her reflexes.

"Thank god we made it alive," whispered Stepan, joking about Dorothy's driving abilities rather than actual threats like people were facing in the Outback.

Wow! I thought, taking in the place. Under different circumstances, the cabin's natural setting would've been idyllic. If not for the distance and lack of a caretaker, Dorothy could've made a killing off it as a short-term rental. The two-story building appeared plenty sturdy, but here and there was missing one of its moss-covered wooden shingles. One of the shutters was drooping low and a cracked window pane reflected in the sunlight, but nothing was irreparable. More than anything, it needed a good tidying up.

Kitty pulled Alex out of the decades-old gas-guzzler Dorothy refused to part with. Only because of its antique status was the petroleum-powered vehicle even allowed to be on the road. I could see the attraction to owning such a thing: ample space, direct travel, no waiting. With the world's burgeoning population, dedicated personal vehicles no longer made as much sense. *Not that it would ever stop some people.*

"Where are we?" I asked, popping my back which was aching after the long ride.

"The middle of nowhere, as requested," said Dorothy, pulling tools and supplies from the back.

Dorothy had always been the little old lady down the hall, perpetually wearing a knit sweater and reading glasses like some cliché grandmother, but here in jeans and a flannel shirt, was a different person.

"It doesn't look like much, but it's got a roof, rooms, and plenty of land for a garden. Stepan, dearie, there's a small coop out back for when your eggs hatch. I'm sure it needs repair unless you want a raccoon eating your chickens before you do."

"It'll be the first thing I fix," he said. "But how many times do I have to tell you guys, they're for eggs, not food."

"And how many times do I have to tell *you* that it'll be very difficult to maintain your vegetarian lifestyle out here," said Dorothy, smiling. "You may as well get used to the idea. You and Kitty could use some meat on your bones, in this case, quite literally."

"Can I go play, Dad?" asked Alex.

"Sure, bud. Just stay within sight of the cabin and avoid the ravine."

Alex ran off happily, dragging Kitty with him. *If anyone looked out of place in the woods…* She hadn't owned so much as a pair of off-road shoes before we'd gone to the store and bought everything we thought we'd need for our unknown-duration cabin adventure. Dorothy was right, there was more than enough cleared land for a sizable garden. Woods surrounded the location but stopped about thirty meters or so from the cabin. I knew little about fishing and even less about hunting, but there wasn't much Dorothy didn't seem knowledgeable about.

"Other than a thick layer of dust and a few mouse nests, the interior looks just like Winston and I left it," said Dorothy, dusting her hands. "And let the boy go to the ravine. When we moved here, my brothers and I left all of our friends behind. With little else to do, we spent most of our free time playing in the creek down there without getting into too much trouble." She laughed, shaking her head as she relived the memory. "We drank from it all the time, too. Even as a teacher, I rarely got sick. The microbes in the water must have had something to do with that."

I couldn't help but laugh as she winked. "At least we won't die of dehydration," I said as Stepan approached.

"We won't die out here as long as you are willing to learn and do a little hard work. It'll be a good experience for you both. Next thing you know, you'll be reluctant to return to your desks."

Out here in the solace of the woods, I could almost believe it.

Dorothy led us to a small shed. It took me and Stepan to tug the door open, which promptly broke under the excessive force. Inside, she handed us each a rake.

"Lesson number one: To have a successful garden, you need clear ground."

"I *do* know a thing or two about gardening, Dorothy," said Stepan.

"I don't think those are the edibles we'll need to survive, man," I added, chuckling.

"A little relaxation never hurt anyone," said Dorothy, winking at Stepan.

If nothing else, this little vacation should prove interesting. It might be beautiful and peaceful out here, but I hope Alex and I can go home before too long.

CHAPTER 28: HUCK

With a final wave to the crew of the *Semeru*, we watched as the last glimmer of civilization disappeared, anxious to return to its berth. I'd miss the friends who'd rescued us from that hole in the Indian Ocean and braved the trip to the Australian Territory with the Arthropods' most wanted. Om Banyu and his crew had faired better than the others we'd traveled alongside. Mueller had lost all but Otto from his transporter team. Samson, Hera, and the rest of the *Sekhmet's* flight crew had perished. Captain Banyu had somehow escaped our contagious bad luck having lost only one hand—Jorge.

"You know, I hope Rudolfo finds his way," said Ariadne. "It took staring death in the face to force him to see reality, but I believe he's a changed man."

"I hope he does too," I said, facing the city. "Fen, you care to share your plan?"

Fen nodded. "We're heading into the outskirts of the city, where the danger will be minimized. Huck and I believe it's the best compromise between cover and danger. I spent three days copying Banyu's map, but I don't know how much we'll need it. Darwin's major highway will take us straight to the Hive."

"You make a suicidal gauntlet sound like an evening stroll," said Ondo.

"They certainly won't let us 'stroll' to the Hive," said Hemant, changing to a posh upper-level accent. "Excuse me kind inverts, may we enter your abode so that we might blow you asunder?"

All but Fen let out a hearty laugh. "Joke all you want, but it doesn't get more serious than this. If they knew we were here, which I'm guessing they don't because we killed their sea-faring buddies, they'd be tearing the territory apart to slaughter us."

"She's right," said Omar. "This might be our only respite. When they figure out we are here… it's on."

"How the hell are we going to walk—What did you say, Omar? Fourteen hundred kilometers?— to the Hive on some roadbed?" asked Krista. "I don't remember a ton from our classes, but I *do* remember that this place is a desert. That means *no* cover. We sure as hell can't walk into a death trap without some protection."

"She's right, man," said Hemant. "Surely you guys have something more than this."

"I have a plan, but now I'm rethinking it," I said, rubbing the back of my head.

"Crap," said Omar, slinging a stick into the dirt. "What are we supposed to do, strut across the desert like we have a death wish?"

"It's a little late now to be rethinking it," said Ariadne. "What was it? Maybe some of it's salvageable."

"A wagon," I said. "I knew the vehicles here would be useless, so I thought we could build a wagon out of scrap. Something with cover, possibly our bivvies, and light enough that we could put our supplies and water on it and still pull it."

"That's not a terrible idea," said Krista. "Ondo could pull a tank."

"I'll help, but I'm not your bloody pack mule," said Ondo, smirking. "Though I suppose I'm hung like one."

"God," said Krista, rolling her eyes.

"I don't know about you, but I'm not in a hurry to cut up my bivvy," said Omar. "The thing's heat masking only holds up *because* it seals. Too bad we didn't keep the bivvies of our dead. We could practically cover the road from here to the Hive."

"I have Marie's medical supplies, but she never used a bivvy," said Ariadne. "I know she slept, but where and how was always a mystery to me."

"Granted, I thought Huck's idea would be more fleshed out, but there's merit to it," said Hemant. "Why don't we head into the city and see what we can find? We're resilient. I'm sure we'll figure out something."

"A wagon…" Omar said, shaking his head as he walked into the brush.

"It wouldn't hold up to attack, but it would be quiet," I said to Ariadne. "I thought it could be like the *Semeru*, running on natural power as opposed to a combustion engine."

"You still have to work on your confidence if you're going to be a leader," said Ariadne. "I think you could've sold it if you'd stood behind it."

"You think so?"

"It's not like anyone voiced a better idea. I know you and Fen share leadership, but maybe there should be more collaboration between you two."

"I agree," I said. "We're better, but we're not as tight as we used to be."

"That's something you both need to move past, especially when it has a direct effect on our survival," said Hemant.

"Fair point," I said, before Hemant thankfully changed the subject.

"Man, I'm starting to wish Banyu would've dropped us off closer to the city," he said, pulling out his dagger to hack at the branches Omar had missed. "Once this is over, I'll be okay if I never have to see a jungle again."

I couldn't help but chuckle at that. I couldn't imagine this being over. We'd spent our lives training to survive the trip to our chosen destination pod. We'd far exceeded that. At this point, we'd visited four different pods on our journey to the Hive—something unheard of. The hardest part still lay ahead. They'd given me a hard time for my lack of detailed planning, but how could any of us possibly plan for an incursion into the Hive? We didn't know what it would look like, how big it was, or even how well it was guarded. I didn't like going in unprepared, but this entire mission was uncharted territory, requiring a certain degree of improvisation.

"Want to know something depressing? It doesn't matter how far we've come if we die in sight of the Hive," I said, the thick blanket of decaying leaves squishing under my feet. "Humanity would be no better off than before."

"That's not true," said Trivia. "If you accomplish nothing else, you brought down the aerials and brought the people hope. That counts for something."

"Don't get all pessimistic on me now, Huck," said Ondo, already beading with sweat. "You know where my siblings would be if I'd thought like that? Junkies, slaves, dead. We won't get through this without a little optimism. When I met you, I couldn't believe you were the people everyone was talking about, but you proved me wrong. Just keep doing that. Prove everyone, including the inverts, wrong."

We had to prove them wrong. We *had* to succeed.

"Hey, up here!" yelled Omar.

I hastened my pace, no longer slicing through the branches, but careening through the jungle, not caring what scratched my body or tugged at my jumpsuit. When I reached him and Krista, he was standing on cracked pavement, staring at a sign.

"Dude," said Hemant breathing heavily, "We thought you were hurt or something."

"Sorry, no," he said, pointing.

For the first time, I examined the sign. Bright colors showed through where he'd scraped the centuries of gunk from it, the same gunk that had protected it. I couldn't decipher most of the text, but it was clearly a simplified map.

"This path is too small to be a road," he said. "Walking path maybe. Whatever it is, it leads into the city."

"It's awfully overgrown," said Krista. "We might be better off going straight."

"No," said Fen, pointing at where the green met the blue on the sign. "It'll take us along the coast. That's one less side for an attack."

"Agreed," I said. "We'll be surrounded soon enough. May as well take advantage of it when we can."

Krista and Omar continued clearing a path from the front as Hemant and Ondo watched the rear. I hadn't known what to expect, but I thought there'd be more Arthropods here. It was a vast landmass. Maybe not even they had the numbers to control every square inch of it.

The coastal route was breathtakingly beautiful, but I spent most of my time on edge anticipating an attack. The trees, which Trivia identified as mangroves, had roots that stretched into the water like hundreds of legs, biding their time until they could walk onto the land. When we stopped for lunch, I'd have to sketch one. With having just started, lunch would be hours away. A shame, because I was already beat.

"I know we didn't work out much on the boat, but I feel exhausted," I said, wiping sweat from my brow.

"I'm a little tired, but— Huck! You're pale!" Ariadne shouted. "Omar, hold!"

Ariadne helped me sit on a boulder and that's when she saw it—a blood midge. Right where the pack met my back. It had nestled in so inconspicuously that not even the people directly behind me noticed it.

"Got it," said Trivia, drawing her dagger and slicing its rostrum in one fluid motion.

The small invert, not much bigger than my canteen, fell to the ground squealing before Trivia put it out of its misery. I didn't have to encourage everyone to check themselves. We found three more, but no one had lost as much blood as I had. Thankfully, the midges didn't seem to run in the same groups as the larger, more aggressive inverts. It didn't mean they weren't dangerous. I struggled to stay focused with such a light head.

Ariadne poured water down my throat and forced me to eat a berry-flavored ration bar. Bland and dry as they were, they had the necessary vitamins and minerals to rapidly rebuild my blood supply. Some food scientists at Pod Pittsburgh knew the common problems people encountered on the surface. Though from my experience, most people lost blood far faster than it could be replenished.

"He needs rest," said Ariadne.

"We don't need to stop anywhere, but especially not in the open," said Omar.

"What do you suggest?" asked Ondo. "Look at him."

Omar rubbed his eyes with his thumb and forefinger and sighed. "Everything we've passed has been nothing but rubble, but there's an old building up there that may be stable. Maybe we can find a defensible spot to hide out in until tomorrow. Can he make it half a klick?"

"I can make it," I said. "Hemant?"

"Got you, man," he said, helping me to my feet.

Together we hobbled the remaining distance to the building. Sensing the need, my body quickly digested the bar and was begging for more by our arrival. Omar's chosen building was a short, blocky one, constructed with stout enough concrete that it had survived the years relatively well. I stared towards the formerly towering, now fractured structures that must have been part of a thriving downtown, the copious amounts of metal and glass doing little for their integrity.

"This'll work," I said, thrilled at the prospect of rest.

We kicked our way through what remained of the broken glass doors, taking advantage of the fact we had yet to be discovered. The sight that greeted me was wholly unexpected.

"Sweet!" said Trivia, grinning from ear to ear. "It's a museum! I could stay here forever!"

She grabbed Hemant and began dancing around, the broken glass and plastic of exhibits crunching under their feet. I sank to a pedestal nearby and reclined against the cool interior wall.

"Need anything?" asked Ariadne.

"Energy would be nice."

"I'm sure Trivia would share hers if she could."

At Ariadne's request for me to eat meat, Hemant and Ondo accompanied her into the woods to hunt. By the time they returned in the afternoon, I had completed my sketch of the mangrove trees and eaten enough ration bars that I'd regret it when they reached my intestines. Feeling safe deep within the building, we scavenged some wood from a jungle diorama and cooked the fish they'd caught, which was nearly the size of Fen. Trivia being who she was, quickly found the display on local wildlife and identified as a barramundi.

"I was glad I had Hemant and Ondo with me. It took all three of us to get that thing out of the water," said Ariadne as it rotated on our makeshift spit. "It was trapped in a natural pool when the tide went out. We didn't have to even use our tackle."

"We just had to get soaked," Hemant said, rotating himself in front of the fire. "You should've seen it! When Ondo first lifted it out, it smacked him in the face with its tail."

By the time the fish was cooked, we were laughing so hard that our sides hurt. The delicious fish had so much meat that we each ate our fill and dried some for later. Trivia, despite Hemant's warnings, had wandered deeper into the museum the second she'd finished her food. Before long, she came sprinting back.

"You have to see this!" she said, tugging on Hemant's arm.

Everyone followed her through the corridors until we reached a vast triangular room. The years hadn't been kind to its metal ceiling, but the holes illuminated the space with the waning light of day. From one end to the other were boats—or what was left of them. So many types and styles, all beautiful in their own right. I couldn't help but run my hand along one of them, wondering how long ago other hands did the same.

"You know," began Ariadne, "that you're not supposed to touch things in a museum, right?"

I was about to make a smart remark when a piece broke off in my hand. "That would have happened anyway."

We toured the numerous halls and rooms, taking in what we could of the historical, natural, and artistic exhibits. So many had been destroyed by time. Wild animals must have run rampant before the Arthropods hunted most of them to extinction. I could still find prints preserved in undisturbed corners. Water had leaked through the ceiling, taking its toll on many of the artifacts, sometimes even causing parts of the building to crush displays. It was sad to see what was lost but encouraging to see what had survived. I could've spent days with my sketchbook, documenting— Suddenly, there was an eruption of light and distorted sound.

"…are quadrupedal marsupials of the family—"

"I'm sorry, I didn't mean to," said Krista, backing away from the wall as the room returned to normal.

"What the hell was that?" asked Hemant. "What did you do?"

"I'm sorry," cried Krista. "It was an accident."

"We're not upset, Krista," I said. "What did you push?"

"I think I stepped on something. There!" she said, pointing to a pedal in the floor.

Ariadne made her way to the pedal and pushed it again.

"…are native to Australia. Living species are approximately one meter in length…"

Amazed, we stared at the life-size depiction of a man carved from light and telling us in an antiquated accent all about one of the Australian Territory's native creatures. As abruptly as it began, it stopped.

"No, keep it going," said Trivia.

Ariadne pushed on the pedal again and again, but nothing happened.

"I think we broke it," I said.

"That was… incredible," said Trivia, still in awe. "How did they…?"

"There's no telling how much knowledge and technology we've lost over the centuries," said Hemant. "I'm surprised as hell that it worked at all, but I'm glad it did."

As we progressed through the rest of the museum, we were careful to check every button we found. Sadly, not a single one worked like the one in the wildlife wing. It was disappointing until Ariadne discovered the museum's collection of art.

"It's unlike anything I've ever seen," she said, tearing up. "I always painted from things I'd seen or experienced, but this… it's like they painted what they felt, dismissing the rules in the process. Unbridled creativity. I… I love it."

I took her hand, equally enthralled, soaking in the abstraction in front of me. The ripped canvas looked as though a single touch would turn it to dust, but the faded image shown clearly.

"Come check this out," shouted Krista.

Reluctant to leave the painting, we followed the sound of her voice until we reached a large, darkly painted room, made darker by the rapidly approaching night. She was staring at what looked like a giant mound of dirt, partially destroyed by a ceiling support that had fallen untold years ago.

"I don't get it," said Omar.

"Look," she said, pointing at the description.

Although its plastic shroud hadn't protected it from water damage, the title was still visible.

"It's a model of a termite hive," I said, feeling a sudden chill despite the room's warmth as I beheld the towering object.

"Still don't get it," said Omar. "We aren't hunting termites."

"Look at the scale, Omar," said Krista.

He leaned in close and saw just how small the tunnels were relative to the hive and the implications set in.

"Ah merda."

CHAPTER 29: ARAIDNE

My night's sleep was a restless one, tossing and turning as my mind stirred up all kinds of nightmarish horrors that likely awaited us in the Hive—a dark, huge, terrifying edifice packed to the brim with killing machines. It was no wonder that I couldn't get any rest dwelling on that. I wasn't about to chicken out now, but from here on my mind could prove my greatest enemy.

Breakfast consisted of decent coffee and dried barramundi. After the rough night, I struggled to choke it down. Only half of us were well-rested, from either staying up late or plagued by similar disturbing thoughts after seeing the mound display. Trivia and Hemant had wandered the museum well into the night. Huck and I had passed most of the evening in the hall of animals. I watched while he sketched the skeletons that hadn't been ravaged by nature. So many of the creatures had been hunted by Earth's invaders to extinction, but seeing them—touching them—made them real in my mind.

We'd had history classes during our training, but they were pieced together from the references stashed in the pod during its hasty construction or found by transporters over the centuries.

Over time, many had been lost or deteriorated, their knowledge with them. Since I'd been on the surface, there had been so much new. So much to learn. The prospect of life after the Arthropods was starting to take shape, and within it held a future of exploration that made me nothing short of giddy.

Eventually, the time came to leave, as much as we all wanted to linger. The sky was rimmed with gray, the edge of a storm on the horizon when we reluctantly left the museum. Traveling through tropical areas and deserts, we were more than familiar with rain, but the storm stirred up heavy winds. Lightning crackled across the sky with claps of thunder that scared me out of my skin. The rain poured down in sheets, but we couldn't stop. The longer we stayed in one place, the more likely we'd be found.

"There's good news," yelled Omar over the gusts. "The storm should affect them too."

"Doesn't do us much good if we stumble on top of them," said Hemant, loud enough for only Huck and I to hear.

We headed east from the museum, hoping to stumble onto the highway that would take us deep into the Outback. Unlike the dense jungles of the other territories we'd passed through, here we crossed as many open swathes of deep red sand as we did lush patches of jungle. We pushed forward, slowed by the storm, but trudging forward regardless before finally reaching the road.

"This has to be it," yelled Fen, rain cascading down her face. "I'm not checking the map. If it gets damaged or lost, we're screwed!"

By the looks of things, the six-lane highway had been in the midst of an expansion when the Arthropods landed, the work never completed. From our understanding, life had continued relatively normally until the threat was truly realized. By then it was too late, the inverts' foothold to strong. It was all humanity could do to get the pods built, an effort that only saved a fraction of the world's population. And here, the continent where they had landed, their underground city had never been completed, overrun before the work was finished. Somewhere on the far side of the territory was a half-completed pod, an homage to the inverts' resilience. Save for the few locals with the means to escape, most of the territory's inhabitants had perished.

One by one, we hopped over the barricades and onto what remained of the road's cracked surface. Vegetation had encroached over the sides, swallowing the outermost lanes. Ancient vehicles littered the highway, trees and vines erupted through the pavement, consuming them. I'd given up on talking to Huck over the deluge. According to Arjun, voices might not be enough vibration to attract Arthropods, but I wasn't about to press my luck. We painstakingly made our way through the dilapidated transports, even passing the ghost-like shell of a high-speed train before pressing towards a goal that still lay weeks away. Without a vehicle, this would be a long hike.

There were plenty of vehicles on the road, making Huck's wagon idea all the more plausible. The issue at the moment was the water. The unmaintained drainage system couldn't keep up with the torrent that the barricades channel towards us. We pressed on, fighting against the current as we waded along. Rain soaked our jumpsuits and filled our boots, making the passage miserable. When I thought it couldn't be worse, the current knocked Fen on her back, smacking her head into the asphalt hard enough to make it bleed.

"We can't keep this up!" I yelled, wrapping an already saturated bandage around her head. A bolt of lightning shattered the sky, rattling my teeth. "We can't see! We can't hear! If anything—"

A giant bolt of lightning struck the tallest tree, exploding its bark in all directions and showering us in splinters. The broken mass of the tree steamed as the rain continued to pour.

"I'm done," said Hemant, turning towards one of the ruined buildings that lined the road. "If lightning does that to a damn tree, I don't want to know what it would do to me."

Not a soul argued, instead following him to the only nearby structure still with an intact roof. Anxious to be out of the rain, Hemant was moving so fast that it was hard to keep up with him. I sped up, nearly chasing him around the corner of the building. No sooner than I'd reached the corner, Hemant lurched back with astounding speed, landing on top of me.

"Wh—" was all I got out before he slapped his hand over my mouth.

With the other, he put a finger over his lips. Everyone froze in their tracks.

"What is it?" Huck mouthed.

Hemant mouthed something back, but I couldn't tell what it was. When Huck gestured his confusion, Hemant began drawing a repeating shape in the air—the number eight. *Bone Arachnids.* Rain drained down into my eyes. How could any of us fight in this? We clung to the wall of the building, which offered us no protection from the raging storm.

"How many?" I asked, leaning over to whisper in Hemant's ear.

He opened his hand, five fingers in the air.

Everyone was visibly dismayed. There were only eight of us. Two-to-one odds were challenging on the best of days, and we didn't even have those numbers. Bone arachnids predominately lived in dry areas. I had expected to see them further into the desert but not here and certainly not in a storm. There were so many things we still didn't know about these creatures, and here we were, heading towards their Hive.

The wind howled, blowing a rusty sheet of metal down the road in front of us. One hit would've incapacitated, if not killed, any of us. We *had* to find shelter, eights be damned. I jumped on the other side of Hemant and peered around the corner. There were five eights alright, marching away. I felt a smidge of relief before I realized what they were doing. *They are patrolling!* So many questions popped into my mind. How many patrols? How often did they pass? Was it like this everywhere? I leaned back against the concrete wall with my eyes closed, trying not to cry as a flood of doubt hit me. These guys were more organized here than we'd ever seen them. *How the hell are we going to get anywhere near their home?*

"Are they gone?" Huck whispered.

I peered around the corner in time to see them vanish around the corner. I nodded and led the others inside the building, through the debris, and up the stairs to the building's second floor. All the windows had long since shattered, but two windowless walls offered us some protection from the elements. We huddled in the corner, using each other for warmth as we shivered drenched to the bone but unable to light a fire.

•••••••••

The ominous clouds finally blew over our shelter around lunchtime. The sun emerged from hiding, slowly evaporating the water and saturating the air. Once the storm had abated, we wrung out our jumpsuits, but my boots still squished when I walked. On lengthy hikes, wet feet were asking for trouble. Once we reached safety, we'd have to take the time to dry them. During the downpour, I'd managed to time the eights' rotations. Their patterns were somewhat randomized, but they passed roughly every half-hour.

"Astounding," said Trivia when I shared my observations.

"You think they patrol the entire continent?" asked Krista.

"Why else would they patrol *here?*" I asked. "There's nothing special about Darwin aside from it being a coastal city. There hasn't been for centuries."

"They're probably just worried about the coast," said Ondo, adjusting his war hammer. "Just because they patrol here doesn't mean their patrols are as widespread further inland."

"At the very least, we should assume that they are," I said. "We were lucky on the other continents. They behaved like animals. Here, they are more… organized."

"Nothing about our journey has been lucky," said Omar. "We've lost countless friends and nearly died ourselves. What you're saying is here they're even more dangerous."

"I'm afraid so," I said.

"Great," said Krista. "I didn't think that was possible."

"Right now, we need to make some progress while we have a chance," said Fen. "By Ariadne's reckoning, we have less than a half-hour. Let's get moving."

Cautiously, we headed down the stairs and back out to the street, and from there, back onto the highway. We hadn't seen any inverts until we'd left the main road, so we were hoping their patrols were concentrated in the city. The crumbling barricades lining the road were over a meter tall and while they didn't look like they'd offer much protection, they helped shroud us from view. By unspoken agreement, if one person ducked, we'd all followed suit. After traveling and battling together as long as we had, it was second nature to operate like different parts of the same body.

About a kilometer down the road, we saw them—the aerial patrols. Not the aerial network Mathias, Arjun, and I took down in the Saharan Territory but roving bands of flying inverts operating in a distinct pattern in the skies. Omar spouted off a handful of obscenities, crouching until they flew out of view.

"We'll need to rethink our entire approach, Mr. Wagon," he said.

"Alright," said Huck. "The wagon was a dumb idea but harping on it doesn't help us. We need to figure out where to go from here. For now, we can hop from building to building."

"Too much risk, Huck," said Hemant. "The next patrol of eights may rotate in fifteen-minute intervals. Or an hour. Even if we did, what would we do outside of the city? They're covering the land and the sky. We can't traverse 1,400 kilometers like this. We'd never make it."

"Give me a minute," said Huck. "Fen, can I see your map?"

Fen unfolded the map, spreading it out on the hood of a derelict car while the others kept watch. I made my way around the vehicle, examining it closely as Huck and Fen debated on our next course of action. I felt a pit form in my stomach when I saw a dry-rotted infant seat in the back. The damn inverts didn't care whether their next meal was adult or child, sentient or oblivious. They'd wreaked havoc on our home world. The damage they'd done to our ecosystem was irreparable, but maybe in time, we'd settle into a new homeostasis. I hoped more animals had escaped extinction than were apparent.

I slung my bow over my shoulder and pulled my hair back into a ponytail, exposing my neck to some much-needed airflow. With eyes closed, I let the warmth of the sun reinvigorate me. My clothes were finally drying, and my boots were less soggy than before. I was about to head back to Huck when I saw the last thing I expected to see.

"*Eep!*" I gasped.

"What? What is it?" asked Huck, instantly at my side with sword raised.

Speechless, I pointed at the south side of the road.

"I don't get it," said Krista, looking over the barricade. "What'd you see?"

I doubted my sanity. *No freaking way.* We'd encountered pockets of survivors, protected by skill and flora, but here? Overrun by the enemy. The first territory to fall. Home of the Arthropod Landing. How could there be any humans here aside from Arjun, Kolya, and us? Blond hair, blue eyes, a gap-toothed grin—not a sign of Demented characteristics.

"A… boy!" I stammered.

Everyone spun in the direction I had been staring to find nothing there.

"The heat must be getting to her," said Omar.

"Are you sure?" asked Huck.

I nodded. "Right there. A kid. Grinning at me."

"There's no way," said Trivia, shaking her head. "Even with neem, this too harsh of an environment for human survival, not to mention everywhere we turn are more inverts."

I'd studied medicine long enough to be familiar with hallucinations and how real they could seem to those suffering from them. I'd been under constant stress for months, suffered from the Shock, watched numerous friends perish, and even inadvertently used pheromones. My mind had been through hell. Imagining a child running around the Australian Territory was the culmination of my stress.

"You're right," I said. "I'm seeing things."

"I'll massage you before bed," said Huck, kissing me on the forehead. "Have some of your valerian-root tea. Anything to help you get a good night's sleep. I love you."

"Thanks," I said. "Love you too."

Huck gave me a comforting squeeze and went back to examining the map with Fen. I went around the side of a crumbling truck to gather my thoughts. *He's right. I just need a good night's sleep.* Moments later, I heard a squeal. I ran out, arrow nocked and ready.

"What is it?" I asked.

Krista had her hands over her mouth, then slowly lowered them. "Either we're having the same hallucination, or there's a boy out there."

CHAPTER 30: HEMANT

I ran to the edge where Krista had seen the boy and craned my neck over the barricade just in time to catch a booted foot disappear into the vegetation-encrusted drainage ditch running beneath the road.

"Do we chase him?" I asked, resisting the urge to thunder after him.

Without answer, Ariadne vaulted over the rail and vanished into the darkness.

"Don't do anything stupid," I yelled, jumping after her.

The last thing we needed was this kid to lead us into an ambush. Doubtful considering his age, but stranger things had happened. Hell, we'd almost been eaten by other people. By now I was used to weird. The others clamored behind me as everyone gave chase. This could either end very well or very poorly. Ariadne had a good sense of judgment, but chasing a strange kid alone, here of all places, hadn't been her smartest move. Huck caught up with me as we raced along, snapping vines and splashing water from one end to the other.

"Ariadne!" he yelled. "Wait up!"

"Shh, man! We're already drawn enough attention to ourselves."

Ahead, Ariadne stormed out into the light on the opposite side of the road and continued chase. When we emerged in what must have been a residential area centuries ago, there was no sign of either.

"Dammit," yelled Huck, frantically searching for her in each direction.

What must have originally been wooden homes had long since rotted away, consumed by nature and time. Only fractured driveways and crumbling foundations indicated the purpose of the land. A scraping sound echoed from the north, and Huck took off just as Omar and the others emerged from the ditch.

"I'll follow Huck, you guys stay here," I said, already pursuing the sound.

"The hell with that!" said Fen, footfalls resounding behind me. "We're staying together!"

Fortunately for them, I wasn't difficult to keep up with, carrying the added weight of the weapon. Between my pack and the bomb, I was carrying upwards of fifty kilos, made heavier by the heat. I skidded around the corner after Huck to find another fractured stretch of pavement, identical to the first save for two patrolling multipedes glaring at us.

"Oh, crap," I said.

"Crap is right," said Krista, skidding to a stop next to me.

They stood stone still, staring us down as we stared right back at them. No sign of Ariadne. Steam wafted off of the broken asphalt in curls, like a wave about to break. I wrapped my fingers tightly around the haft of my war hammer and heard the drawing of blades from sheathes, the snap of arrows to bowstrings. Without warning, the pedes charged.

With the orchestration that comes from experience, we divided into two groups to intercept the spiny creatures. The pair split, each electing their target group. When the pede was meters in front of me, I spun to the side, lifting the hammer over my head and bringing it down through empty air, making contact with nothing but the street as it curled around my blow.

"It's gonna be like that, huh?" I yelled.

Ondo's blow connected, cracking into one of the beast's segments, but not enough to paralyze it. Instinctively, the creature swung in retaliation, sending Huck flying into a bush where he landed with a crack. With all the spikes covering a multipede, he was lucky to have not been impaled.

The pede made a chitin-popping turn, plowing towards us. I could hear the other team battling with their foe but couldn't spare so much as a glance. With forearm blades deployed, Fen timed the creature's approach. With perfect finesse, she spun out of the pede's way and drove her blade into the gap between its head and first segment. The beast wailed, pinching her blade and carrying her down the street as she screamed, unable to release the blades bound to her arms.

"Come get me!" screamed Ondo, pounding his hammer on the pavement to draw its attention, sending chunks of rock flying into the air. "You want some Ondo?! Come and take it!"

The pede turned, giving no thought to Fen's existence, and thundered back at us. She loosed gut-wrenching screams as the creature mercilessly slammed its spiny legs onto her compact body over and over. Trivia crouched at Ondo's side aiming an arrow, waiting for the perfect shot.

"Anytime," I said, as Huck began to stir behind me.

"Not yet," she whispered.

When I was about to scream, her arrow flew. I never saw it hit, but it disappeared into the beast's compound eye. It began to flail as it convulsed. The front half of its body arched up and slammed down repeatedly, dark hemolymph spraying from its face and slathering the road. The pede came down one final time and was still. The others cheered, having downed theirs at the same time.

"Fen!" yelled Huck, running wobbly towards her.

I sprinted to Fen's side, sliding the last few meters. She was gasping for breath. Nothing more than shredded muscle and tendons remained of her legs, her torso pierced beyond measure. Her blood flowed in rivulets, draining into the cracks running the length of the street. Trivia rested a hand on my shoulder and reached up to place mine atop hers. Though in a different squad, Ondo and Trivia had known Fen far longer than us, regularly doing inter-platoon training with or against her squad. *Does nothing matter to these ingrates?* Huck lifted her head, resting it on his thigh.

"This is it… isn't it?" she asked, between bloody coughs.

Huck nodded, brushing the hair out of her face. Even if her injury had occurred in a pod, she didn't stand a chance. The damage was far too severe. Anger seethed in my bosom as tears burned my eyes, watching the strongest of us die helplessly in front of me.

"Do you want morphine?" asked Omar, pulling his pack around.

"No," she said with a subtle shake of her head. "I want to embrace death… aware."

"You're the bravest person I know," I said, taking her hand which failed to grasp back.

She gave a weak smile and said, "My only regret… see you… kill the bastards."

Her head drooped and she was gone. Huck laid her gently back down as if he could still hurt her. I wanted to lash out at the dead pedes, grinding them into oblivion, but resisted. Anger and grief would come later. If we were going to bury her, we needed to do it fast. I was about to say so when I heard Krista's panicked voice.

"Guys," she said, frantic. "Guys!"

I spun toward her and stared where she was pointing. Headed for us was a cloud of inverts—hooks, chompers, dusters, and raptors. Word was out! The cloud must have been nearing a thousand strong.

"Leave her!" shouted Omar. "If we don't find cover, we're dead!"

"I'm not going anywhere without Ariadne!" yelled Huck on the verge of despair.

"I don't want to leave her any more than you, but we can't risk everything for her," he said. "The mission must come first!"

No one wanted to leave Ariadne behind. The thought made me want to puke.

"Find shelter!" yelled Huck. "I'll find her. If we're not together by morning, go on without me. See this through!"

I spared a second to grasp Huck's arm. "Good luck," I said.

"You too, Hemant."

Inside, I was screaming! It felt like having another brother torn apart from me, and right after I'd lost Fen! Those damn inverts were going to pay for every wrong, and I was keeping a tab. I turned to pursue Omar and the others, making for a culvert. The far end of the road appeared to be an industrial area. With any luck we could hole up in a stout building there. If one had lasted this long, hopefully, it could withstand a few hundred inverts.

"Huck! Hemant!" yelled a familiar voice.

I turned to see Ariadne, bounding out of the woods. *Thank God!*

"Ariadne!" yelled Huck, darting towards her. "Where have you—"

"No time," she said. "Come on."

I glanced at the cloud, at most a minute away. Whatever needed to happen, needed to happen fast! She sprinted through the woods as fast as she could move. Between the battle and the weight on my back, I struggled to keep up. Everyone passed me but Ondo, who stayed at my heels, shouting encouragement. Branches snapped into my face, scratching and tearing at my flesh. I tripped twice, but Ondo jerked me back to my feet each time. The buzzing of the inverts vibrated my mind. If they caught us, this mission was over!

When I couldn't run anymore, we emerged into a clearing. In the middle, the young boy was holding open a thick metal hatch inset into concrete, waving for us to join him. The whole experience was eerily similar to Release Day when Omar had beckoned us into a cavern, saving our lives. One by one, we plunged into the darkness. I leapt over the ledge and fell onto more concrete. The landing shot jolts of pain up my legs, but I was alive. Ondo was the last to jump, just as a hook beetle snapped its jaws above the opening, narrowly missing him. The inverts swarmed the entrance as Ondo slammed the hatch closed, ensnaring the head of a raptor. With a chitin-busting blow from his hammer, the smooshed remnants of the invert were still. The boy jumped up and swung a bar into place, locking it.

The sounds of a bunch of pissed-off bugs slamming fruitlessly into the thick iron hatch were muted by the thick concrete. The space echoed with our heaving breaths as we took measure of our surroundings and injuries, which were thankfully minor. The blond kid stood, staring at us without saying a word. His clothes were familiar but unlike anything I'd seen before. They were neither the jumpsuit of the pods nor were they the simple fabrics of the survivors. Who was this kid, and what the hell was he doing in the middle of the Australian Territory alone?

"Wait, where's Fen?" asked Ariadne.

While catching his breath, Huck filled Ariadne in on the attack and her death. She cried profusely but would save the real grieving for when we were safe.

"Thank you," I said, once I could breathe. "What's your name, kid?"

"Artim," he said. "It's a pleasure to make your acquaintance, sir. And I'm not a child. I turned thirteen during the last moon."

Omar and I passed a look between each other. *Who the hell is this kid?*

"Hello, Artim," said Ariadne, adopting his surprisingly formal speech as she wiped her eyes. "My name is Ariadne."

We each introduced ourselves, some just as formally, others not.

"Why were you alone on the surface, Artim?" asked Huck.

Artim looked down at his feet and kicked at the dusty floor. "Prior Jacobi prohibits me from doing so, but I'm an explorer. I take protection," he said, brandishing a dagger not much longer than his hand. "I've become quite adept at avoiding the dark ones."

"Prior Jacobi?" I asked.

"He's the leader of our colony."

"Your... colony?"

"Zephyr's Hope. Did you come to visit us? We've never had visitors."

"Never?" I asked, my senses suddenly aroused. "No one who looks like me, but smaller. A larger man with a bad smell?"

Artim cocked his head to the side. "No, sir. None as long as I've been alive. You may ask my father. It's possible that someone visited during his lifetime."

"No, this would've been recently," I said, deflated.

"Don't take it too hard, Hemant," said Ariadne. "It's fortuitous that he stumbled across us. The fact they didn't visit this colony doesn't mean they're not here."

"How many other people are there?" asked Artim, excitedly.

I looked at Ariadne for permission to proceed, then back to him. "What do you know about pod cities?"

We spent the next hour filling Artim in on the status of the world beyond his little bubble and our mission, of which he couldn't get enough. He had managed to live his life with virtually no knowledge of the outside world, piecing what little he knew from things he discovered during his perilous ventures on the surface. He finished the ration bar I'd given him and stood.

"I should return home. My parents will begin to worry soon."

"Would it be alright if we came with you?" asked Huck.

"I can't promise how you will be welcomed, but it would be my pleasure!" Artim said, beaming.

CHAPTER 31: KOLYA

Arjun and I couldn't take our eyes off the metallic surface of the ancient meteorite, stabbing down through the earth into the parabolic royal chamber carved from the deep Australian bedrock. I wanted to speak, but no words came forth. The only visible occupant, a glass worm, assumed its position at the foot of the dais. The familiar glowing dots reappeared and showed us the first detailed image we'd seen the creature display. On its chest was a vaguely human form in green, prostrate on the ground. I was reluctant to debase myself from the first moment in the Queens' presence, wanting to start the meeting off on equal footing. I glanced at Arjun who was already dropping to his knees. *Well, he's serious about being subservient.* After an eye-roll, I dropped to the smooth, dustless floor. As the shiny had illustrated, I placed my forehead on the ground, observing the room through my periphery.

The slightest tingling began to build in my forehead. The ground was vibrating, ever so slightly. As the seconds dragged on, the vibrations grew in intensity, ever so slowly. The Arthropods either had no perception of time or moved at a pace profoundly different from humans. After about twenty minutes, the loud noise drowned out all else but had yet to reach its crescendo. The buzzing vibrated all of my being with enough force that my nose began to run, yet I was afraid to move to wipe it. Mucus pooled on the ground as the intensity painfully increased to the point I thought blood would pour from my eyes. Then finally—silence.

I took a moment to collect myself as the phantom drone in my head subsided. Around me echoed the chitters of the various Queens as they left the safety of their alcoves, taking their places around the central dais. From my position, I could see little more than the tips of their legs as they clacked across the hard stone. It took all of my power to resist the urge to look around. When all traces of movement ceased, there was a new sound, not coming from our sides, but from above. Particles of dust drifted down on my head and neck, knocked loose by whatever was crawling high above us. Beads of perspiration formed on my head before running onto the floor. Every fiber of my being was pulled in a different direction, a mix of fear and awe. *Surely they wouldn't lure us this far to kill us, right dear?* All sound stopped.

"Riiise," hissed a voice so cold, so unpleasant, as though it emanated from Hell itself.

Remembering the life-threatening response at the food ponds, I rose as slowly as my old knees would allow. The nightmarish sight drained the blood from my face. Arjun stifled a gag. Everything around me ceased to exist for that brief moment, there was nothing but what lay ahead. Having drifted down on her wings from the meteorite above was the Queen of Queens, come to rest on her throne. She bore a striking resemblance to the mud raptors, but far larger than the largest females we'd seen on our journey. The creature was easily two stories tall, every square centimeter of her hardened carapace evolved for two purposes: lethality and reproduction. The source of terror was not simply the Queen of Queens, but also her slave and the source of the voice. Lashed upside down to her lower abdomen was a frail human body, barely alive and green with the signs of decaying flesh, not a sign of the Demented's corruption visible from the dead, cloudy eyes staring back at me. Sprouting from his head was the Queen of Queens' stinger—curled upward into its mind, controlling him like a puppet. Arjun retched on the floor, shaking like a tree in the wind. My blood ran glacially cold, more scared than I'd ever been in my life and regretting every decision that had led me here.

"Naaames?" scratched the voice.

I took a deep breath, the smell of Arjun's sick burning my nostrils. "Kolya," I stuttered, placing my hand on my chest. "Arjun," I said, gesturing to my rising companion.

"Caaall … Sammmraaajniii. Whyyy … heeere?" Her voice had an unusual cadence, taking effort to understand the simplistic language and unusual pronunciation.

"We seek peace," I said, proud that it hadn't sounded as shaky as before.

"Peeeace?"

The Queen of Queens—Samrajni—made a horrendous clicking as she waved her arms around the room. For the first time, I beheld the other occupants. Like the Queen of Queens, each species we'd run across was represented by a larger, more vividly-colored specimen built for breeding, but no less lethal. The room held familiar species like split wing and bone arachnid; less common ones like the desert borer (which I'd never seen above ground) and cave grub. And creatures of near legend—spine back and what could have only been an ice crawler. The only Queens not present were the ocean-dwelling species, but something told me they weren't far. The blood froze in my veins. The excitement of discovery that I had anticipated was replaced by the urge to flee to the far end of the Earth from these beasts. The Queens responded with a slew of noises from their varied mouth parts, their discussion leaving us in the dark.

"Kolya, I'm afraid," said Arjun shakily.

"Me as well," I replied, taking his hand.

"Nooo … Peeeace," said Samrajni through her gravelly-voiced host. "Onlyyy deathhh. Fooood. Reeeach skyyy."

Death? Why the hell bring us here? Reach sky. What the hell does that mean? Arjun and I spun to face each other, faces blank with fear as our deepest concerns were realized. The Hive was a tower to space. *They want to propagate the universe!* It would be centuries more before it could be done, but Jesus, we had to stop them. If not for us, then for any alien life that may be out there. How had I been so stupid to think I would come out of this as some leader of humanity?

"Is that possible?" whispered Arjun, shock across his normally placid face.

"With a base wide enough, it could theoretically breach the atmosphere," I replied. "They survived in space before. If they figured out a way to somehow launch themselves out of Earth's gravity, say with the pill bugs… Yes, I'm afraid it's possible."

"Oh my god."

"Neeeed … wisssdom," she added. "Giiifts."

Fear was instantly replaced by self-interest. "What knowledge? What gifts?"

Her Majesty let off a slew of foreign sounds and several Demented brought forth trays piled high with fresh food—meats, fruit, and vegetables. Following behind it was a tray of raw gems and precious metal ore—rubies and sapphires, gold and platinum! Last, a Demented-constructed cage rolled out, full of attractive men and women, not a soul Demented.

"Giiifts … fooor wisssdom."

"All of this?" I asked, forgetting all my doubt.

"Yesss," she said.

"Kolya, what are you doing?" whispered Arjun. "If peace isn't an option, we have to escape. I have to find my brother and destroy this place. Oh, god! Hemant was right. Hemant forgive me. What have I done?"

"Pull yourself together, boy!" I said, slapping sense into him. "She desires information. We will leave as wealthy men. If this is the last page of humanity's history, we will close the book as kings."

Arjun shook his head, betrayed by my words. "I want nothing save for my brother. I was a fool not to see it before. To not see *you* for what *you* were before."

Arjun moved to leave, but a Demented guard blocked his path.

"Whiiich … wiiiser?" she asked, waving a long appendage over the two of us.

I tracked the arm, desperately trying to avoid looking at the inverted near-corpse lashed to her body. What I could only assume was cerebral fluid trickled down the stinger as she controlled him directly through his brain. I looked over at Arjun and knew the Queen of Queens only needed one of us.

"It was fun while it lasted, my boy," I said, kneeling. "Great Queen of Queens, I am the wiser of the two of us!"

"Gooood," scratched the voice.

ARJUN

Kolya fell to his knees in front of Samrajni, turning his back on me without hesitation. He might be the smarter of us, but all regard for my well-being had vanished. *Has he ever cared for me?* I was a fool to have not seen his selfishness. I was nothing more than a means to an end. I had ignored my brother and followed Kolya blindly into the Hive. At that moment, all I wanted was to apologize to Hemant before my death.

For all of my interest in the Arthropods, when I panned the room, I felt only negativity—anger, fear, disgust. Everything that once fascinated me now repulsed me. The Queen of Queen's prisoners reached helplessly through the bars, pleading in languages I didn't understand for aid. *Where are they from? Are they bred here?* The thought strained my already taxed emotions. I had to help them, but I was powerless to help even myself.

Ignoring the lesser Queens around the room, I watched as four Demented flanked Kolya as he kneeled in front of his new monarch. I couldn't help but wonder what his god would think of such a quick betrayal. Kolya exuded excitement. For all his self-righteousness, he'd forsaken his friend and his god in the pursuit of earthly pleasures and potential power. I wish I possessed Omar's mastery of expletives to better express my feelings. I was often accused of lacking social awareness, but I no longer had any misapprehension in regards to Kolya.

"My wisdom is yours, my Queen," he said, giddily.

Samrajni was silent. The four Demented positioned around Kolya moved in, raising him to his feet and walking him in the direction of his rewards. My face burned with righteous anger.

"Oh… okay," he said, masking the quaver in his voice.

While he was being carried in the direction of the food, four other Demented moved to Samrajni and began removing the decaying stranger adhered to her abdomen. The Queen of Queens withdrew her stinger, severing the connection to her host's brain. The body blinked a few times, then went limp—lifeless. I hoped the man's consciousness had departed long before his body became enslaved. If we hadn't been forced to leave our weapons in our rooms, I would've used that moment to attack, suicidal or not. Samrajni had to be stopped before a single progeny made it out into the universe. Powerless, I stood my ground, clenching my fists so tightly that I was sure blood would drain down from my palms.

"Your Majesty, what's happening?" asked Kolya, uncertain.

I turned to see Kolya, now well past the platter of food, being laid out on a large elevated slab adjacent to Samrajni's dais. Unable to speak without her host, she advanced towards him, silent. Ropes appeared in the Demented's hands as they started lashing Kolya to the earthen slab. Foe or not, my adrenaline surged at his peril.

"Samrajni! I said I'd share my wisdom!" Kolya shouted, voice shaking as fear returned. "What are you doing? Your majesty?"

I made a move towards him, felt an iron-hard grip on my shoulder, and turned. I was surprised to see Neesh slowly shaking her head. I felt a hand on the opposite shoulder and knew without looking it was Jigna. Kolya's panicked shouts had devolved into screams, pleading for help from me—from anyone. I tugged at the hands restraining me but could do nothing to intervene. Something about the hemolymph afforded its consumers inhuman strength.

Samrajni's massive wasp-like frame came to a halt over Kolya, rotating so that her stinger was positioned above his head. *Her next host!* I wrenched from my captors' grip and made it about a meter before I was tackled to the ground. Neesh growled in my ear so close I smelled the decay on her breath, felt the heat of it on my cheek. Kolya continued to scream as I writhed on the ground crying.

"Let me help him! Let me help!"

My screams mixed with those of the captives in the cages, all equally terrified by the unfolding scene. The way Neesh had me pinned, I couldn't see Kolya directly, but I could see the shadows cast on the nearest wall. The Queen of Queens lowered her singer towards Kolya's head. When it was less than a meter away, I turned away, unable to watch. A warm sensation began at my groin as fear overwhelmed my senses. Tears stung my face as my former companion wailed in agony for what felt like hours, then went silent. Once I summoned enough courage to look back at the wall, the empty, flayed husk of Kolya's body was still and Samrajni was gone.

Neesh slowly loosened her grip before standing. I rose, whimpering, wiping the snot from my face. After another glance at Kolya's remains, I retched again. *He was never going to be the host. Her offer of rewards was nothing more than a lie.* That vile organism had vivisected his body from head to toe, somehow collecting her wisdom directly from his mind. This species, intelligent or not, wasn't trustworthy. I carefully made my way to his remains, fighting lightheadedness. The scene was gruesome. I could make out no resemblance to the man who'd accompanied me from Pod Baghdad. I collapsed by his bound hand and squeezed. The man was a miserable excuse for a friend, but he was worthy of life and a decent death.

After ages, I rose. The rewards had disappeared. The Queens had withdrawn into their alcoves. It was just Kolya's corpse, Jigna, Neesh, and myself. Neesh did something unexpected. She took my hand and the two led me back to my room. After looting Kolya's things, they nodded and departed. *They can only fight their nature so much.* I heard the clank of the lock on the bar. I was a prisoner. I reclined on the makeshift bed, staring at Kolya's empty one. For the first time since I'd left Pod Horizonte on Release Day, I would've welcomed death.

Chapter 32: Dorothy's Journal

It's been ages since I wrote in our cabin's journal. Running my hand across its worn leather cover and deckled pages is like reuniting with an old friend. When I pulled it off the mantle, it sent me into a coughing fit from all the dust it had accumulated. The cabin looks just as I remember it, but perhaps dirtier. Nothing a little elbow grease and a strong back can't fix. Good thing I have both with me. I haven't returned since Winston's death. Even though it was my girlhood home after my parents immigrated to what was then "The States," it didn't feel right coming alone after all the time Winston and I had spent here together. I invited Darren and his son, Alexander, and his friends Stepan and Kitty to stay here at the cabin with me until this alien nonsense blows over. What kind of a name is Kitty? She looks too beautiful to be out in the woods. Perhaps she's a sprite! She's adapting faster than I expected. Stepan is an unusual young man. He has lots of very strong opinions, but I think he'll fit in well. His passion for nature is invigorating. Darren knows nothing of gardening or anything outside the realm of urban life. I think it'll be a rough transition for him, but he's willing to do anything for his son. It's a shame what happened to Patricia. What is life aside from a cycle of death and birth? None of this seems real. Aliens. Who would've thought? My hand is hurting so. Arthritis, Dr. Menchin tells me. I'll suffer through tending to the garden. I'll die before I stop putting my hands in the dirt. I'll leave the writing to Darren. He has such beautiful penmanship.

— Dorothy Grimethorpe, 2043

Wow. The last place I thought I'd be is living in the woods, especially with Mrs. Grimethorpe, Dorothy rather. She couldn't be a more wonderful host. I say host, but most hosts don't make their guests work like she does. The cabin always smells delightful as Dorothy teaches us how to cook, smoke, and can the various foods we gather. You should've seen how funky Stepan's first batch of pickles looked! He was the only one of us brave enough to eat one. Let's just say that he's not in a hurry to eat another pickle. I can't believe a year has passed since Patricia's death. All hell has broken loose since that damn rock cracked open. Alex and I are fine. He's a thriving, precocious seven-year-old. He wants a dog, but that's not happening. To be honest, I'm tempted to let him have a lizard since they eat bugs. We're doing well to feed ourselves, having lugged in all the food and seeds we could pack into Dorothy's old Rover. It should be enough to last us until the garden is going strong and we can harvest our seeds. We're thankfully far from the action here, deep in the American Territory woods. There for a while, life continued as normal, but then things started changing. Shortages. Layoffs. Panic. Exactly as Stepan had predicted. Dorothy has a collection of books here, but I've lost my taste for the few science-fiction novels she has. It's less exciting when you're living it. After I lost my job (me and half the known world), I don't know what I would've done if Dorothy hadn't offered us sanctuary at her cabin. It's gorgeous out here. I'm still not used to all the insects, but they only bother us when we're away from the cabin. Winston grew a lot of bug-repelling plants out here to keep the mosquitoes at bay. What do you know? His doomsday prepping paid off. I think we have a lot of the tools we need to hole up here for as long as we need.

— Darren Taggert, 2043

*S*ometimes, I wish Patricia could see what's happening in the world, other times I couldn't be happier that she's missing it. I know she spent her life studying space and searching for signs of alien life, but I can't imagine this is what she wanted. It's bad. Real bad. I don't know where the hell the Arthropods came from, but they are like the worst of Earth's bugs, except gigantic and live to slaughter any human or animal that crosses their path. So far, the experts have identified four different species and believe there to be more. The hook beetles fly and rip all living things apart with their razor-sharp beak. The bone arachnids are a special type of asshole (I hope Dorothy doesn't mind language in her special book.), which envenom with their fangs or stinger unless they decide to slice their prey apart with their legs. The multipedes are like long, spined centipedes the length of a tractor-trailer that can bash anything apart. Lastly, the cuddly-in-appearance powder moths can clear a city of life in a matter of hours with their aerosolized poison. Not exactly happy stuff, is it? I know it's strange to think about, but I don't think we are going to be able to return to the city. Sometimes I think about my apartment and all the memories and sentimental possessions that I was unable to bring with me. What's worse is my recurring nightmare about Patricia returning and being unable to find us. When I wake in a cold sweat, I realize all over again that she never left the Australian Territory.

— Darren Taggert, 2044

All attempts at containing the Arthropods are failing. The Containment Zone (if you can still call it that) has grown to over six hundred kilometers in radius, engulfing most of the Outback. Pretty soon they will displace the population of Adelaide. About a million of its residents have fled, but not everyone can afford to leave their homes. In a matter of months, there's going to be a million refugees. And where are they going to go? Sydney? Please. Another few months and it will be overrun too. I'd take solace in the fact that the invertebrates fear the water, but there are enough islands in the South Pacific to hop to the Asian Territory. We're safe here in the woods, but for how long? The UTE finally wised up to the threat. After years of procrastinating, they decided to nuke the landing site. The explosion blew off the top of the meteorite, but within days, the "inverts" were visible from satellites. Living underground protects them from the blast and they seem to be resistant to radiation. Our weapons can easily kill them, but they multiply at a faster rate than they die. A few escape the Zone every day. Those are the ones that worry me most. On a brighter note, everyone, even myself, has become quite adept at living off-grid. Aside from the radio, we have minimized our contact with the outside world. Now that we've become fully self-sustaining, we hardly make trips to the local store anymore. The Rover has been acting up. I'm not sure we'd be able to get the parts to fix it anyway. Step and Kitty finally caved on being vegetarian. They took their first foray into the world of carnivores once winter hit. I'm glad too. It didn't matter how much she ate, Kitty couldn't seem to keep meat on her bones. They both already look healthier.

— Darren Taggert, 2045

The experts say judging from the original Pine Gap seismic readings and the new ones taken from across the Australian

Territory that the inverts are building a complex network of tunnels underground. Not even the global government has the manpower to build anything of sufficient size to retain them. As predicted, most of the major cities in the territory have fallen. A number escaped to other territories, but that doesn't make me feel better about all the dead. In a way, I feel like the ones who escaped only bought some time. I can't stop thinking about the cricket match in Brisbane. The city was doing its best to keep life normal for the residents who remained. With the Arthropods still pretty far from the city, people were still attending public events. Unbeknownst to anyone, the inverts had tunneled into the metropolis. They erupted from the ground and massacred everyone in the stadium—adults and children alike. Sixty-five thousand people, dead in an instant. With so little warning, the rest of the inhabitants were killed shortly thereafter. As if news couldn't get worse, electronics have stopped working anywhere near the Containment Zone (Why the hell are we still calling it that?). Some sort of electromagnetic interference. The scientists have reverted to analog technology. God, I would give anything to rewind time to before it crashed. If I had any idea what would happen, I would have barricaded Patricia in the apartment to stop her from going and called the damn UTE president myself to warn him. The news is lying about the whole thing being under control, I guess in an effort to keep panic down, but I still keep in touch with Grayson, stationed at the moment in Perth. He's telling me that we're not in control at all. Patricia was so excited about identifying extra-terrestrial life, but I never thought to ask her, what if it's hostile?

— Darren Taggert, 2045

I'm sure Grayson is dead. Everyone at the Perth Science Station is history. Hell, the majority of the Australian Territory's population is history. In the four years since the Arthropod Landing, the inverts have not only decimated the population of the Australian Territory but put a dent in the Asian and Saharan Territories' populations as well. A billion people—dead. And more missing. That's a tenth of the global population! At least the news has stopped lying about the death toll. With as many people who've lost touch with friends and family, there's no hiding the truth. Every Territorial Guard is fighting against them, but it's a losing battle. They can barely communicate with each other. That EMP field the inverts generate, well, it's spreading. It's all over the south-eastern hemisphere and growing, anywhere there's a high population of the bugs. It not only knocks out the digital stuff but interferes with the radio waves as well. Patricia's old colleagues mostly blame it on these small inverts that hover in the sky called antenna bugs. At least they aren't violent ones. People are dying in crazy numbers. Without Earth's support, the few hundred people living between Luna, Mars, and space are gone. Probably a better death than most of the people on Earth. I wonder if it's worse to slowly die of suffocation or starvation. Alex wakes up multiple times a night with nightmares, even though there haven't been any invert sightings in the American or Latin Territories yet. I'm so proud of the young man he's becoming through all of this. He's so much like his mother. With each day that passes, I'm more grateful I have a piece of her with me. God, we should've blown that damn thing apart the moment it entered our atmosphere.

— Darren Taggert, 2096

The experts have the Arthropod species count up to seven now including the hook beetles, bone arachnids, multipedes, and powder moths. We have the aforementioned non-lethal antenna bugs, whose EMP field makes our most advanced technology instantly obsolete. Then we have the split wings. These little bastards land on animals, decapitate them, then embed their parasitic young in their corpses. Perhaps the smallest invert, the pill bug, is mostly a scavenger but likes to explode and has been wreaking havoc all over. Worst still, the inverts seem to use the pill bug's adaptation to their advantage, detonating them strategically. It's a controversial opinion, but I'm in the camp that there's organization and intelligence to these creatures that first evaded us. I don't think they're quite as dumb as everyone in charge assumes. Earth has turned into a war-torn hellscape. They say the cities have become quite dangerous and as lawless as the old west. I remember when I thought we were in an age of unprecedented peace. Man, how naive was I? Dorothy came down with a nasty fever this winter. We still have no idea what it's from. Afraid to take her to into the city and limited to herbal remedies, we had to take shifts keeping her cool with water from the creek until the fever finally broke. The whole thing gave us a hell of a scare. Dorothy is not as young as she used to be. The whole event goes to show that the inverts aren't the only thing we have to worry about.

— Darren Taggert, 2046

*I*f I had any doubts about losing before, they're gone. The Arthropod War is nothing more than a war of attrition. The creatures breed significantly faster than we can kill them. The UTE president announced the other day that they are planning to build massive bunker cities across the globe as a last resort—a haven for humanity until the threat can be resolved. I hope to the universe it doesn't come to that. Could you imagine living the rest of your life underground? How would we even build such things? They'd have to be mind-bogglingly huge, tremendously reinforced, and the costs... The resources and manpower needed would be unreal. I don't know if the answer lies in these "pods," as he calls them, but we need to figure out a solution fast. I'm trying to be optimistic, if nothing else for Alex, but it's hard. Even Stepan, the perpetual optimist, isn't hopeful. I try not to listen when Kitty yells at him for being high so often. I don't know that I blame him. Once work is done, it's so easy to want to check out until the next morning. I can't tell you how many days I've wanted to take the radio and throw it into the rockiest part of the ravine. I can't though. Somehow it feels like our last link to civilization. I know Alex likes it too. He listens intently as he does his schoolwork. I think we'd have to be under imminent attack for Dorothy to give him a reprieve from his learning. He never had a chance at what I would've considered a normal life. Living like this, hearing what's happening out there in the world… It's hard on a person. I wish I had half of the strength Patricia did.

— Darren Taggert, 2047

Looking back, that last entry was pretty bleak. I'd love to say that I was wrong and jaded and things are much better eight years out, but nothing could be further from the truth. The five of us are still fine, but supply shortages have drastically affected our life. The last time we ventured into town (on foot, I might add) scared us so badly we determined never to go again. We're down to living exclusively from what we have on-site, and teenagers can eat! The few non-essential workers still working have been furloughed worldwide. Who would have thought, me, a survivalist? It helps that Dorothy's husband had this cabin stocked with everything you would hope to need to survive in the woods, including manuals for doing so. I've discovered that I like sticking my hands in the dirt and listening to the birds nearly as much as Dorothy does. In the cool of the forest morning, I can almost forget the troubles plaguing the planet. I've taken to hiking daily and am grumpy when I can't. We're elbows deep in canning, drying, and preserving for the long winter ahead. These cold Michigan Region winters are long when you don't have central heat. I wish Patricia could see the muscles I'm getting from chopping wood, though. She'd think they were rather dashing. I know it's weird, but sometimes I hear Stepan and Kitty making love (they have never been quiet about it), and it makes me miss her all the more. I'm glad neither of them ever bothered to read this journal.

—*Darren Taggert, 2050*

That's not weird Darren. I think it's sweet. And I'm glad that you've found the joy of gardening.

—*Dorothy Grimethorpe, 2050*

Two years out and I'm just now seeing Dorothy's response. Now I'm regretting having written that last part. So, the United Territories started construction on the pods. Originally, they were planning on building a lot more, but at the rate people are dying, that's no longer possible. Only eleven are being built. Everyone with any expertise in construction has been called in. They're even trying to build one in the last Arthropod-free corner of the Australian Territory, but I think it's a fool's errand. All combat has been moved from offensive to protecting the pod sites, which has had a pretty negative impact on the inverts' spread. They're in every territory now including ours, though not near us yet. They identified a few more species, but honestly, I stopped caring. What's another giant killing machine? Even the non-lethal species contribute to the spread of the more violent ones. It's not just the loss of a fifth of the population now that's affecting the Earth. It's estimated that the inverts have killed roughly the same percentage of the planet's wildlife too. There's no telling what long-term impacts that will have on the ecosystem, assuming humans are around long enough to experience them. Life on Earth has been irreversibly changed. Anything with microcircuitry has stopped working. We feel more isolated than ever. Thank the universe all of Winston's "technology" is older than the cabin itself. Give the radio's handle a few cranks and it works for another hour or two.

— Darren Taggert, 2052

I never did understand why your generation looked down on the simple things. I bet you've come to appreciate them now.

— Dorothy Grimethorpe, 2052

I mentioned eleven pod cities are being built. We just found out how many each will house. 250,000. Think about that. Even as big as they are, that's only enough space for 2.75 million people! I have to face the fact that a lot of people are going to die in the coming years. When I stare from this cozy rocking chair to Dorothy knitting away, Stepan and Kitty snuggling on the floor by the fire, and Alex building his wooden cart with Winston's old hand tools, I hope that it's not one of them. These cities are estimated to take sixty years to complete, and by that time, the estimated projections of Earth's population will be half of what they were! At the rate of spread, I think even that's optimistic. The news says the UTE will be providing entry on a first-come, first-serve basis prioritizing the young and healthy. They think a lottery is unnecessary given how many people will likely die before the pods can be completed. Do you realize how chaotic this will be? The area around the pods will become a lawless free-for-all, bringing out the worst of humanity as people vie for entry. Because it was a relatively local station, the news focused on the scant details of Pod Pittsburgh, our nearest haven. Supposedly, there's already a shanty town of families eager to enter. I don't know if it's the right decision, but I've got half a mind to stay put. I want to die with the sunshine on my face and my friends and family at my side. It's what I wish Patricia had been able to do.

— Darren Taggert, 2053

It's taken all my willpower to pick up this pencil. The drizzle outside is reflective of our collective mood. Dorothy passed away yesterday. She died in her sleep from what we're assuming was heart failure. We should all be so lucky in this day and age to have such a peaceful death. We buried her this morning behind her cabin on a knoll that faced the sunrise. She deserved the best treatment we could give her for taking us in. If not for her, I'm not entirely sure we'd be alive. Last I heard, Flint had devolved into a crime-ridden, dystopian landscape. We were pretty far out, but some evenings I'd lay in bed, wondering if the sounds outside were the craziness spilling out from the cities to our peaceful little stretch of the world. From what we gather, most people with the means have traveled to the pod sites, hoping like hell to gain entry. I don't know what they're going to do there, waiting for decades like sitting ducks. The four of us are still doing well enough. Between the garden and hunting, we managed to survive another handful of years, though none of us are at an ideal weight. At least we're alive. Wildlife doesn't seem quite as rampant as it once was. I'm glad to have Alex at my side. With his impeccable aim and eyes like a hawk, we rarely come home empty-handed. You have to be a great shot when you have finite ammo. At least we had a decent hoard. Once again, thanks Winston.

— *Darren Taggert, 2053*

It's about time we had something to get excited about. Stepan and Kitty had a daughter! It was completely expected. As you can imagine, not many would intentionally bring another life into this chaos. To be honest, I was becoming increasingly depressed as the news of the war became more and more abysmal. Kitty is younger than Stepan, but the pregnancy was still concerning given her advancing age. Between our little library, experience with herbs, and prioritizing her health over ours, the pregnancy and delivery had been textbook. Once Natalie was born, Stepan couldn't stop joking about his virility. It was good to see my old friend returning after so long in the dumps. Natalie is perfect, brightening up our darkening universe. We're all taking turns caring for the little angel. We're sparing as much of our food as we can for Kitty to make sure she has enough to produce milk for her daughter. She'll have a hard enough life ahead of her as it is, and she'll need all the strength she can get. I can't say I miss the crying though. I don't remember Alex crying this much. Maybe that's because Patricia took care of everything in addition to being a working mother. She really had been superwoman. I thought after so long that I'd think about her less but not at all. Not a day goes by when I don't miss her smile and her warmth.

— *Darren Taggert, 2055*

Alexander turned twenty-one this year. Patricia and I made a fine young man. He's everything I could ask for in a son. Step and I constructed a still out in the woods and made liquor from potatoes, the only thing we have an abundance of. It tasted like it'd be better suited for cleaning grease, but it did the job. What better entrance into adulthood than with a hangover? Step and I are convinced we can improve it given time. That's one thing we have, for now at least. I'm not sure Alex ever wants to drink again. I don't know why we didn't try this before. I enjoyed having a project to dive into. You can only read the same forty or so books so many times before you're just done. Stepan is already trying to teach Natalie to read using Dorothy's old romance novels. It's that or Winston's survival manuals. I need to see if I can find the old sci-fi novels we packed up when we got here. She's a little ball of energy. We take shifts chasing after the little spark, and it's all us old flames can do to keep up. Between playing with Nat on the floor and gardening, my old knees are feeling the strain of age. The next few years should prove interesting. Step and Kitty have been unsuccessfully trying to get me to join their yoga routine for fourteen years. Now I'm wondering if I should've listened. Well, it's a little late now.

— *Darren Taggert, 2057*

I killed a bear last week! I can't tell you what a relief it is to have so much meat to smoke and salt for the winter. Stepan and I were out hunting deer, and we surprised it as much as it did us. The bear must have stumbled on our creek and realized how regularly fish swam by. Step was so excited he missed his shot. Fortunately, I already had my rifle at the ready and took it out before it could run off. When we went to make sure it was dead, the damn thing convulsed, scratching me. It was nothing more than an involuntary spasm, but it gave me a pretty good gash on my calf. It hurts like hell. Natalie has been coming by my bed playing doctor. I have to say, our moonshine may not be enjoyable to drink, but it makes a great antiseptic. There's so little to do when you're anchored to a bed. Days like today, I really miss having a wall screen. Let's be honest though, would I still enjoy any films made before the Arthropod Landing? Humanity had been so blissfully naive. I do regret that I never got to show Alex all my favorite old films. He's probably glad he dodged that bullet. I think by now I've told him the story behind every one of them. I still catch myself quoting my favorite lines with only Step being able to appreciate them.

—*Darren Taggert, 2060*

I'm struggling to hold onto this pencil and my mind. My bear scratch got infected, despite all attempts to prevent exactly that. Nothing we had could slow the spread once it took hold. I'm dying. I've never believed that there is anything after this, but I have to admit, I would love to see Patricia again.

—*Darren Taggert, 2060*

CHAPTER 33: HUCK

What I had initially thought was a bunker was, in fact, a tunnel. Judging by its ragged appearance, the tunnel had been built around the same time as the pods. The dank confines showed similar wear and tear to the underground city I'd grown up in, but the heavily reinforced concrete had stood the test of time. Unlike the pods, its construction appeared far more hasty. With little help, the people of Darwin must have taken their safety into their own hands. *Who could blame them?* The only pod on the continent was on the far side of the Hive and the next nearest pod was across the ocean we'd just traversed. Humanity might have had advanced transportation before the bugs had intervened, but that didn't mean everyone could make it to safety. Frankly, I was surprised that there weren't more haphazardly constructed underground refuges like this around the world.

Artim led us through so many turns that I lost count, walking kilometers in near-pitch darkness. Occasionally, tiny shafts of light from ventilation pipes in the ceiling illuminated other chambers and corridors. I couldn't help but notice that Artim's fingers never left the wall. *He knows this place by feel. How many times has he done this?*

Brave kid. After a long stint of walking, I saw the proverbial light at the end of the tunnel. A faint orange glow trickled through a slat in the wall, guiding our way towards the exit. The light's source wasn't the hue of evening sodium lamps so prevalent in the pods, but the warm flickering orange of torchlight. Artim reached forward, operating the mechanism that opened the heavy metal door. At the sound of the squeal, a man wearing hand-crafted metal armor jumped to greet him.

"Artim!" the man said in a barely contained whisper. "I expected you back hours ago. If your parents find out that I'm letting you venture out, they'll have me strung up by my toes."

In his reaction, he hadn't noticed us until a moment later. When he saw us, he gasped as his eyes grew wide.

"Who are you lot?" he asked, his voice quavering as he lowered his polearm into an awkward battle stance that revealed minimal training.

Artim reached up and placed his hand over the guard's. "They are friends, Dane. I wish to take them to Prior Jacobi."

"Prior Jacobi?" he asked, voice shaky. "If you do, he'll know that I've been letting you go to the surface. You'll be strung up right next to me. What type of guard am I if I allow them to pass without question?"

"What they have to share with us is of far more importance than the comfort of our toes," said Artim, laughing it off. "I will assume any responsibility for their presence."

Dane sighed. "You always were a good judge of character."

Dane introduced himself to each of us, taking time to greet each one of us directly. There was a certain degree of propriety to this place, but it came from a place of humble pride. None of it felt inauthentic. I found myself enjoying the formal language and time-consuming customs that would have felt antiquated elsewhere. With Dane's reluctant blessing and under his watchful eye, Artim led us deeper into the colony through the empty corridor.

No sooner than we were through the door, the walls changed from hastily constructed concrete to hand-carved red sandstone. Aside from the flat floor, every surface from the columns to the doorways to the alcoves holding candles assumed a rounded, organic form. *Not a hard edge in sight.* Up in the ceiling were more ventilation holes that the wisps of smoke floated up through, though I saw no incoming light. *That tunnel must have sloped more than I thought.* Something still felt out of place, though I struggled to put my finger on it.

"That's it!" I said aloud, inadvertently capturing everyone's attention.

"Care to share with the group, Huck?" asked Omar, smirking.

Artim stopped and turned, making me feel a little embarrassed.

"There's no technology here," I said. "Of course not advanced tech, but I haven't seen so much as a motor or electric light."

"You won't find any, either," said Artim. "Shortly after the founding of the colony, news came saying that technology attracted the dark ones. The founding citizens destroyed their technology, opting to never use it again. That tradition continues to this day."

I looked down at our bomb. Artim read my thoughts.

"We have nothing against your technology," he said. "You'll be expected not to use it here."

"That isn't exactly something you want used here anyway," said Omar.

"That's why you didn't know about the other pods!" said Krista.

"Being voluntarily closed off like this, are you sure this Prior Jacobi will be okay with our presence?" asked Ariadne.

"He's a wise leader and will listen to reason," said Artim, "but I don't know how warm your welcome will be."

"That's okay," said Hemant. "We're not used to those."

We wound our way through a few more lengths of tunnels before emerging into a large space. We found ourselves surrounded by market stalls and people hawking their wares, eerily similar to any of the market districts we'd visited. The high-ceilinged room was packed with bodies, bustling by as they went about the day's business. The residents wore long, flowing garments in a variety of colors—all simple fabrics or furs. In the middle of the space was a large column with children dancing around to music flowing from a band playing wooden instruments. *We arrived in the middle of a celebration!* No wonder we hadn't seen a soul in the tunnels. Everyone was here. Masking the smell of sweat were the far more pleasant mouth-watering odors of fried food, proffered by the stall keepers on sticks.

"Yum!" said Ariadne.

"I have to get one of those," echoed Krista.

I was about to comment when the music ground to a halt with a discordant noise. All the chatter ceased as every head turned to face the strangers in their midst. I dry swallowed, knowing the next few minutes had the potential to dramatically affect our future.

"What is the meaning of this?" boomed a voice through the crowd.

An older, brown-robed man with thinning gray hair pushed through the crush of bodies, emerging in front of us as a coterie of helmeted guards took their places around us.

"Artim. Why am I not surprised to find you at the center of this?" he said, sighing before turning to us. "You may be guests of Artim's, but if you value your safety, I'd ask that you disarm yourselves. You find no need for weapons here."

"Will we get them back?" asked Omar.

"That depends on the reason for your presence and your conduct as are our guests," said the man. "Do you hold any ill intentions towards any one of us?"

"We do not," I said, loosening my belt and lowering my sword and dagger to the ground, nodding at the others to do the same.

"Please take the utmost care with that," I added, pointing to the nuclear weapon. "It's very delicate and critical to our task."

"And what task is that?" asked the man.

"To destroy the dark ones' Hive," said Hemant, using Artim's term as he carefully passed the device to a pair of guards.

There was an audible gasp from the cluster of people packing the space.

"Then we will do everything we can to aid you on your quest, provided it doesn't endanger my flock," he said. "I haven't forgotten my manners, but I have to look after my people first. Allow me to introduce myself. I am Prior Jacobi. Welcome to Zephyr's Hope!"

With that, there was a boom of cheers followed by the music's return, this time far more upbeat. People took the prior's welcome as permission to speak with us and began flocking our way but were shooed off by the guards.

"There will be time to shower them with your questions later," said Jacobi, his arms uplifted. "I'm sure they are hungry and weary from their long journey. Let us show them what our hospitality is like."

Market vendors began clustering around us, handing us morsels from their stalls and refusing all compensation. The procession of food was endless—deliciously fried fowl on sticks, fresh fruit bursting with sweetness, soft buttery cheese, bacon-wrapped vegetables, and dark ale to wash it down. I watched as Ariadne laughed with Krista and Trivia; all of our hardships were momentarily forgotten. She beamed with satisfaction as our gaze connected from across the room. I couldn't put into words how content I felt. For that moment, everything was perfect. *This is how life should be.* By the end of the food parade, even Ondo, who possessed the largest appetite of us all, couldn't eat another bite. Between my stuffed belly and the ale, I longed for nothing more than a soft bed and time for a nap.

"It appears that we've worn out your friends, Artim," said Jacobi, smiling. "Why don't you show them to Leoric's old dwelling?

It should have ample space for Huck and his companions. If you'll forgive me, I will take my leave. I would like to meet with you in the morning and discuss matters further. I bid you good night."

"Thank you," I said, inclining my head. "Your hospitality has been heart-warming."

Artim led us deeper into the tunnels, steering us this way and that, all the while descending. I tried to ignore just how deep in the earth we were. Concrete might not have been warm and inviting like the earthen walls, but it did provide a certain degree of security.

"It's lasted this long, Huck," said Trivia, reading my apprehension. "I don't think it's going to cave in the moment we arrive."

"Your hospitality has been heart-warming?" asked Hemant as we entered a flight of hand-hewn stairs.

"What?" I asked, shrugging. "I was trying to be grateful and speak like they do."

"I thought it was cute," said Ariadne.

"Regardless of how he said it, those people were awesome," said Ondo. "I just wish Fen could've been here to enjoy it with us."

A somber cloud descended on the group and my smile disappeared.

"Fen wouldn't want us so grief-stricken that we stop enjoying life," said Trivia, slipping her hand into Hemant's. "She and Mego were all about living while you can. If she could talk to us from beyond, she'd tell us to live it up."

"Do you think people from the beyond can talk to us?" asked Artim.

Omar smirked at the conversation we'd inadvertently begun.

"I don't think so," I said. "I've never experienced it, though some say they have."

"Sometimes I like to wander down into the catacombs where we place our dead. I swear I hear voices in the darkness. Dane tells me it's my imagination. He doesn't like me going down there, but I think it's mostly because he's afraid."

The hair on the back of my neck stood up at Artim's mention of voices. Hemant's eyes widen with the same concerns. *Are there mantis wraiths in Zephyr's Hope? If so, why haven't they killed everyone here?*

"Sounds like we need a trip down to the catacombs," said Omar.

"I can take you there!" said Artim. "Tomorrow after you speak with Prior Jacobi, we'll tour the city from top to bottom."

"I'm not sure I want to go down there weaponless, though," whispered Hemant. "The last thing I want is to—"

Hemant lost his train of thought as we walked into a vast atrium, three, maybe four stories tall, packed with lush trees and plants, irrigated with fresh water coming from the walls in carved troughs. Indirect natural light filtered down from a large opening in the ceiling.

"But how?" muttered Trivia, spinning as she stared up.

"Mirrors," said a small-statured man with close-cropped hair. "Sulien is my name. I am the keeper of the gardens. Who are your friends, Artim?"

"This is Huck, Ariadne, Krista, Omar, Hemant, Trivia, and Ondo," said Artim, rattling off our names like he'd known us forever. "They are here to destroy the Hive of the dark ones!"

Sulien looked up with surprise on his face. "Is this true? Artim has been known at times to be a little… fantastical."

I nodded.

"Thanks be!" he said. "Our people have lived underground for far too long. Though I find the idea of living on the surface mildly terrifying, it is where we rightfully belong. I have long dreamt of a garden under the sun, sticking my fingers into real dirt."

"What do you grow here? How do you get the light inside without giving the dark ones access? Where does the water come from?" asked Trivia, all signs of weariness fading.

"My, aren't you a curious one," he said, laughing.

Omar yawned over-dramatically as Trivia gave him the side-eye.

"I'm keeping you from your rest," said Sulien. "I will happily answer all of your questions before you leave. You have my word."

With a wave goodbye to Sulien, Artim continued leading us to our lodging, which wasn't too far away from the beautiful gardens that sustained the underground city's populace.

"These were Leoric's chambers," said Artim, leading us to a wooden door nestled into the side of the corridor. "He was a good man. He was one of my favorite teachers."

Teachers? The wonders never ceased. It was a fully functioning society underground, run far more effectively than the pods had ever been.

"What happened to him?" asked Ariadne.

Artim looked confused. "It was his time."

"Oh, he died of natural causes," said Ariadne.

"No," said Artim. "He'd reached the Age of Passing."

It was Ariadne's turn to look confused. "I'm sorry, Artim. I don't understand. The Age of Passing?"

"There aren't enough resources for everyone, so when people reach the Age of Passing, they drink the Passing Tea. It puts them into a sleep from which they never wake. Sometimes they give the Passing Tea to people who have broken the Three Understandings."

"Doesn't that bother you?" asked Krista.

Artim shrugged. "It's the way things have always been done."

"Why am I not surprised?" said Omar. "Same crap everywhere."

Ondo squatted down to look Artim in the eyes.

"Maybe we can change that."

CHAPTER 34: ARIADNE

I lingered in bed for as long as I could stand it after having the best night's sleep in ages. I reluctantly left the comfort of Huck's arms and the mound of fur blankets. I'd never touched fur before leaving Pod Horizonte, where only the upper echelon possessed it. Out on the surface, it was fairly commonplace as we hunted rodents, though they were never so large as to produce clothing or blankets. If they had, we wouldn't have had the time to cure it. Not that I wanted to. The last thing we needed was the smell of animal hide attracting more Arthropods.

I shivered at the cold, running my hands up and down my chilled arms. At this depth, feeling the consistent cool temperature, I understood why we'd seen so many people in furs. The cool air was a welcome reprieve from the unrelenting heat of the surface. I used the one remaining candle still flickering from the night before to light several others around the room. Then I slipped on my jumpsuit while Huck watched, grinning.

"You're beautiful by candlelight," he said, propping up on his elbow.

"I hope I'm beautiful by any light," I responded, slinging a down pillow at him.

He pulled me down into bed next to him and began caressing my cheek. "I want to wake up by your side forever."

"Maybe we can work something out," I said, peeling the jumpsuit back off.

••••••••

"About time," said Hemant, waiting with the others in the atrium. "What took you so long?"

Huck and I looked at each other with bashful grins.

"Oh," he said, awkwardly. "So… Everyone ready to go see the prior?"

"Been ready for a while, man," said Omar.

"What are we waiting for?" asked Artim, excited to go.

Though Omar was being his usual abrasive self, I could see him soften every time he looked over at Krista. Hemant and Trivia were just as lovey-dovey as before. Everyone seemed to have a little more pep in their step after the restful night.

"Did you get up to any trouble last night, Ondo?" I asked.

"Nah," he said. "Omar and Krista made it hard to fall asleep and since I didn't have anyone to keep me warm, I wandered around for a bit."

Omar nervously scratched the back of his head. "Yeah, sorry about that. We can get a little carried away."

Ondo brushed it off. "This place is truly amazing. It's set up like the pods are, but far more efficient. Who would've thought a bunch of guys with little more than shovels and seeds could build an ecosystem more sustainable than the UTE."

"Prior Jacobi always says that we have the wisdom and resources to face any problem that faces us," said Artim, leading us back the way we came. "He's a great leader and teacher. He's never steered us wrong."

"That's great to hear," I said. "We've seen our share of leaders. Most of them were pretty selfish."

"Not in Pod Baghdad though," said Huck. "Halima and Ekon were the best. It was a shame that she died the way she did—so unfair!"

"Direct it back into the mission, Huck," said Hemant. "Some days I feel like I run on Arjun and anger."

"And me," said Trivia, elbowing him in the side with a grin.

"Prior Jacobi teaches that anger eats us from the inside. Every Gathering, we discuss ways to improve ourselves and our existence."

"Reminds me of Mama Cass," said Ondo. "Every Sunday, like clockwork, she'd have us sit down and listen as she read passages from her special book, then teach us some life lesson. Some of her stories were strange, but I learned some good lessons from her. She's the one who taught me there was something watching over us. Is that what you guys do?"

Artim shook his head. "Lessons, yes, but he's never mentioned anything watching over us. He teaches us that we are responsible for our destinies."

"That's my philosophy," said Omar, as we arrived at a large wooden door with hammered iron hinges. "Plus, if something was watching over us, it's not been doing a great job."

Trivia snickered, attracting the attention of the two unarmed guards flanking the door.

"Well, we may not agree, but I enjoy having something to talk to that's bigger than me or any of my problems," said Ondo. "If nothing else, it gives me peace."

"That's all any of us want, isn't it?" said Prior Jacobi as we came through the door. "Please, come in."

Inside the prior's large office, the walls were lined with shelves overflowing with old books, making the space double as a library. Countless candles bathed the room in a warm glow as the hot wax dribbled down their sides. Instead of a desk, the only real furniture in the room was a wide wooden table, littered with papers, maps, and hand-drawn schematics.

"I've never seen so many books!" said Trivia. "I changed my mind, Hemant. I want to stay here."

Jacobi let out a hearty laugh. "I'm pleased that someone is as entranced by knowledge as I. As long as you are our guests, you are welcome to peruse the collection, provided you take care of them. These books are quite delicate, many waiting for nothing more than a careless breath to turn them to dust."

"You have my word," she whispered, awestruck.

"So, my friends," he began as the guards brought in chairs for each of us. "Tell me your story, and I will tell you ours."

After a long morning, fueled by the colony's excellent coffee, we'd shared our story in great detail as Prior Jacobi clung to our every word, stopping periodically only to ask for elaboration. He listened intently, even tearing up each time we mentioned of the loss of one of our companions. Trivia threw in the occasional comment but spent most of her time sitting on the floor, legs crossed, her nose in a book. I couldn't help but think about how excited Arjun would be in this room.

"You have experienced far more stress and loss than anyone your age—or my age for that matter—should ever have to endure," said Jacobi. "Now, a promise is a promise. You've shared your story and I owe you ours. Where should I begin?"

"Why is the city called Zephyr's Hope?" I asked. "Was she the founder?"

"No," said the prior, gesturing towards a large book resting on a podium. "I suppose that's as good a place as any to start. Zephyr was the inspiration behind our city. Her story intertwines deeply with our history." Jacobi became distant, lost in thought.

"Umm, Prior Jacobi?" asked Huck.

He jerked back to the present. "I apologize. Her messages still inspire me to this day. Sometimes I can't help but wonder what she would think of what we've built. In many ways, we owe our survival to her."

"Must have been some woman," said Ondo.

"Oh, she was."

"Can you tell us about her?" I asked.

"Of course," he said. "Her messages began about sixty years after the dark ones, what you refer to as the Arthropods, arrived. At the time, radio signals were becoming sporadic. According to the records, most of the world's technology had ceased to function wherever the dark ones were present in large numbers. Only the most basic electronics were unaffected. Out of nowhere, a little girl, with more wisdom than you can imagine, began broadcasting messages of hope. Sadly, some of them were too garbled to understand, but the ones that weren't repeaters retransmitted around the world. It's said that Zephyr herself never knew the early messages got out."

"What happened to her?" asked Huck.

"It's unknown," he said. "She perished like everyone else, I imagine, though I like to think she died from old age. As an adult, she learned of the nepotism and inequality regarding how the pods were populated. She made it her mission to transmit messages of hope and advice to all who could hear until the Arthropods' field made it utterly impossible. It was her messages to dig in that kept the first inhabitants of our city alive. All this occurred well before my time but had been carefully documented in that great tome. Every time I reread her messages, it's like a conversation with an old friend. I always walk away with something new."

I wiped the tear rolling down my cheek. "She sounds like an incredible woman."

"How *did* you dig in?" asked Trivia, gesturing to the space. "How did you build all of *this*?"

"We owe everything to Zephyr. If not for her, my ancestors would've been killed by the dark ones. Over the years, she slowly passed on all of her knowledge of survival. What she didn't, we've gradually pieced together over the centuries. These elaborate tunnels were built over decades. We gradually dug deeper and deeper. We propagated seeds using mirrors to route light safely from the surface. We constructed channels to route water from aquifers for irrigation, plumbing, and drinking. We raise goats, pigs, and geese who eat our food scraps and in return provide us with food, warmth, and fertilizer. Everything we've built will be sustainable for centuries so long as the dark ones can't breach our walls. Our only issue is maintaining the population."

"Which you do through poison," said Omar.

"To put it crudely, yes. It is an unfortunate necessity. We limit our birth rate to that of replacement. Once citizens reach a certain age, death is expected. It was a system derived long ago and has become our cultural norm. The only exception is myself and our council."

"Of course," said Omar.

"It's not what you think, my jaded friend. We are immune from the Age of Passing only so long as we hold our offices with dignity. The moment the people consider me or any member of the council ineffective leaders, we are ousted and subject to the same fate as all others. No one is above the law here. We all exist to serve the community at large."

Omar still appeared skeptical, but I was pleased by the prior's response.

"If what you say is true, then that means there could be more people dug in around the world," said Huck. "We've run into tiny pockets of people who've survived on the surface, but I think they owe their survival to happenstance. There could be more people still alive!"

"I believe so, my friend," said the prior. "Which is why your mission is all the more important. I cannot tell you how much the world will value what you are doing. If there is anything I can do to contribute to your success, tell me."

"Can you protect us all the way to the Hive?" Hemant said in jest.

"I'm afraid not," the prior said, chuckling. "We aren't warriors here, as I'm sure you've noticed. We make rudimentary armor for our guards, but their weapons are limited to wooden staffs with various metal ends, used only when the need is greatest. When it is time for you to leave, we will load you down with as many provisions as you can carry. You are welcome here as long as you require rest."

"Thank you, Prior," I said.

"Could we have our weapons back," asked Hemant.

The prior began to decline, but Hemant continued before he could.

"We know your stance on weapons, but Artim told us something that bears investigation. I think it would be in the interest of everyone within Zephyr's Hope. We will need our weapons."

"Assuming what Artim says is true, I will do whatever it takes to protect my flock. However, I must know what it is that you plan to do."

Krista brought Artim in from outside the office. He explained what he had heard as we went over its implications. Prior Jacobi listened, taking the information in stride.

"I see no alternative but to allow you to investigate," he said. "I will see that your weapons are returned to you in your quarters. I would ask that you carry the weapons only to the catacombs and back. There is a direct route that I have no doubt Artim has discovered. I beg of you, do not engage any threats unless you are in undeniable jeopardy. Your actions have the potential to detrimentally affect this entire colony."

"You have my word," said Huck. "We'll bring news as soon as we have it."

We pulled a reluctant Trivia away from the books and made our way out of the office and into the corridor.

"I think the grand tour is going to have to wait, little man," said Ondo, tousling Artim's hair.

"That's alright," he said. "What we're doing sounds much more exciting."

"We?" asked Omar.

"He's right, Artim," I said. "We cannot risk any harm coming to you. Your parents would never forgive us."

"But I—"

"No," said Huck. "I'm sorry. We need you to lead us to where you heard the noises, then we are going to ask you to return home."

Artim's head dropped. "I understand, but one day I want to be a warrior like you guys."

"I pray that you never have to be," said Ondo.

CHAPTER 35: HEMANT

Even in the safety of Zephyr's Hope, I appreciated having my war hammer back in my hands. Artim led us down through the winding city's tunnels towards the entrance to the catacombs. Unaccustomed to seeing weapons aside from staves, the scattered inhabitants gave us more than one curious look. Many parents shifted their children inside, shutting the door quickly behind them. I got the impression that most of the population was excited by our presence, but many felt like we were bringing the war to them. Who could blame them? This place was amazing. They were living happy, peaceful lives in relative comfort, and we didn't exactly have a clean track record. Death and destruction had hounded us every step of the way from Pod Horizonte.

At seven, our group was the smallest it had ever been. The last thing I wanted was to lose anyone else. Artim was right, anger did eat me from the inside. If I lost many more friends, I'd be a shell of a man anyway. At that point, what was the good in surviving? Sensing my dark thoughts, Trivia placed her hand over mine. *Okay, I still have several reasons to outlive the inverts.* I returned her smile and she let her hand drop. She was good for me. She and Arjun both.

Each had a habit of seeing what I couldn't. I thought about my twin, envisioning the look of betrayal on his face the last moment I saw him. Whether it was healthy to run on anger or not, I was. I hated the inverts for picking our planet to mess with, and I hated Kolya for messing with us. I wanted both to endure the wrath of my hammer. And having lost Marie—Kolya was mine.

Artim led us deeper into the depths, the tunnel narrowed until it was not much larger than I was. With each step down, the air became increasingly damp, the torches doing little to dry the air. Ondo rubbed his fingers on the wall, which came back glistening with moisture. With so much natural light, the city above was open and peaceful, despite being underground. Here in its depths, the cave-like atmosphere was its inverse, sending tendrils of dread down my spine.

"We're here," said Artim, stopping in from of a wide pair of wooden doors recessed into the end of the low-ceilinged shaft.

Artim lifted the rusty rod holding the door shut from its nest in the floor and swung the door wide. Immediately, the smell of mold and decay wafted from the chamber. The earthy smell wasn't as bad as the rotting smell of death but neither was pleasant.

"And you came down here for fun?" asked Krista, pinching her nose.

Artim shrugged. "There's only so many places in the colony to explore. It's not bad unless you come after an Age of Passing ceremony. Once I got bored of everything underground, that's when I started exploring the surface. There's a whole world up there!"

"There sure is," said Ariadne.

"One day I want to see it like you have," he said, eyes glistening with hope.

"I hope that one day you can," said Huck.

"Though without the inverts," I added.

"What exactly is down here, Artim?" asked Omar, craning his neck under the lintel and scanning the area.

"There's a maze of tunnels lined with recesses for our dead. In the center is a pit where we place the bones of the old, making room for the new," he said, handing me and Omar a torch. "You'll need these. Torches aren't kept in the tunnels for safety. You should be fine though, no one has been buried recently."

"What are you talking about?" asked Krista.

"You don't want to know," answered Ariadne.

"Then I'll take your word for it," she said.

"Then this is where we part ways, little man," I said. "We'll see you when we return."

Artim sat on the stairs with a *"Humph."*

The kid had been taking crazy risks long before our arrival, but I couldn't bear the guilt I'd carry if anything happened to him on my watch. *Such a cool kid, filled with unspoiled curiosity and optimism. I hope he never loses that.*

Holding a torch aloft, Omar led the way into the tunnel, naginata pointed out in front of him. The place gave me the creeps. I'd been around more dead bodies than anyone should have in a lifetime, but this place was different. It was their resting place, and we were disturbing it. The cool air made goosebumps crawl up my arms. Every hair stood on end as my inner voice did its best to keep me calm. *Dude, hardened warriors aren't afraid of ghosts. Put on your big-kid britches and suck it up.*

"I don't like this place," said Ariadne.

"That makes two of us," I said.

"I think it's all of us," whispered Omar, the usually unshaken. "I can't see further than the torchlight carries. I don't like it. Something could be on top of us before we know it."

"If they're wraiths like we suspect, light won't make much difference," said Huck. "Too bad we don't have Leisel and Marie to deal with their ilk."

"Well, we don't," said Omar. "We're all highly-trained, experienced combatants. We'll handle this just like we have everything else."

I flexed my fingers on the haft of my hammer as I heard Trivia nocking an arrow behind me. We needed to be ready for anything. We crept around the labyrinthine catacombs for over an hour, finding nothing more than the moldy, wrapped corpses of the city's dead.

"There's nothing here," whispered Omar, as if the dead would take offense to loud noises. "Or at least, there's not now."

I leaned against the rough, damp stone lining the cavern, next to a cluster of dead branches haphazardly shoved into a built-in wall vase. *What's that smell?* I leaned over to the branches and pulled off a whithered leaf, rubbing it between my fingers and letting out a hearty laugh, distracting everyone from their discussion of what to do next.

"What's so funny?" asked Omar.

"It's neem," I said, still chuckling and shaking my head. "Everywhere we find survivors, we find this damn plant. If I ever have a place on the surface, I'm planting a forest of the stuff."

"It's got a stout smell when it's fresh," said Ariadne as everyone laughed with me. "They probably use it to mask the smell of the dead. If there are Arthropods down here, it may be all that's been protecting them."

"Dumb luck," said Omar. "There's nothing down here."

No sooner had the words left his mouth than we heard the all-to-familiar sound of chittering, coming from the center of the maze. My blood ran cold. It was the direction of the pit we'd passed. *Of course, they were coming from the pit!*

"Should we go and fight them?" asked Krista.

"No," said Huck. "We promised we wouldn't draw unnecessary attention. Maybe they don't know we're here."

"Huck's right," said Ariadne. "The neem has protected the city this long. We can reassess and return later."

"You don't have to tell me twice," I said, turning to hastily leave the catacombs.

Then we heard a scream.

"Was that—" began Trivia.

"Artim!" said Ariadne. "He followed us! We have to help him!"

I took off in the direction of the pit. I guess it was too much to hope any trip to the catacombs on a mantis hunt would be straightforward. *Why didn't he listen?* I let the irrelevant thought fade. We couldn't let anything happen to the kid, especially after all he'd done for us.

We clamored into the pit chamber where we found Artim pinned to the wall through a bloody shoulder by an invisible force. In the torchlight, I could make out the faintest distortion of the wall, hinting at the slender body of a mantis wraith. Then we heard the chittering of a second to our right. *Why the hell was Artim still alive?*

Trivia loosed an arrow down the darkened corridor to the right and we heard the shriek of a hit. Huck and Omar leapt over her and disappeared into the darkness, blades swinging to finish off the creature. At the same time, Ariadne had lined up a headshot for the wraith on the wall but had yet to fire. I saw her trembling with fear—something I'd rarely seen from the ever-composed woman. I followed her gaze to the creature. It had dropped its camouflage, something I'd thought they only did on death and was positioned with its razor-sharp claw against Artim's neck. Artim was doing everything he could to brave through the moment.

The worst feeling in the world—being powerless. The same feeling I'd felt when that twisted snake pulled my brother away from me. The same feeling I'd felt when Halima died under a pile of stone. The same feeling I'd felt when my brain was addled by Dust.

The same feeling I'd felt when I watched nearly everyone I knew die on Release Day.

I pivoted forward barely a millimeter and the mantis wraith pushed the claw into Artim's throat just enough to send a drop of blood rolling down his neck. It was playing us. Gone were the days when I assumed they were big, dumb brutes. These were conniving bastards. If there was any opportunity to take it down, it wouldn't be like this. Ever so slowly, I lowered my weapon to the ground as the others followed suit. Maybe the action would give us time to think. What did it want? How were we going to kill—

A sword flashed from the darkened tunnel with lightning speed, slicing both claws off of the beast. *Huck's dao!* Its screams were short-lived. Ariadne sent an arrow in one eye and out the other, an easy shot at such close range on a visible wraith. Artim dropped to the floor, moaning. Trivia took Ariadne's bow as she rushed to administer aid.

"Thankfully, it's only through his shoulder muscle," she said. "He'll be sore, but he should regain full mobility once he recovers."

I breathed out a sigh of relief as I fetched Huck's weapon. I still couldn't get over how fine of a sword it was, from Yanus' private collection. Under normal circumstances, the Wuhanian weapon would belong in a museum, but the finely crafted blade was being used for what it was intended—protecting others.

"Thanks," he said as I handed it to him.

"You know you're not supposed to throw your weapon, right?" I asked, half-serious.

"If you won't tell Trainer Diogo, I won't either," he said, grinning.

"We should block this pit," said Omar, wiping the blade of his naginata clean with what was likely part of a burial shroud. "Artim, is there anything around here that would work?"

He shook his head.

"We need to inform Prior Jacobi immediately," said Huck. "If he could send workers down to fill it, we could stand guard. Maybe we could prevent any others from coming through."

"I have a better idea," said Ariadne. "but you're not going to like it."

•••••••

"You're probably right, Ariadne, but the level of risk is…," began the prior.

"Insane?" I suggested, back in his office with the others.

"I was going to say undeniable, but insane may be an apt choice as well."

We'd left the catacombs in a hurry, stopping by the gardens and suggesting they immediately begin keeping the catacombs stocked with fresh neem. Ariadne had shared her plan with us on the way to the prior's office. It was half suicidal and half crazy.

"What do you think, Trivia?" Huck asked.

She was the most knowledgeable among us. I'd come to trust her wisdom as much as Arjun's. She was on the floor, examining a book that we hoped would support Ariadne's idea.

"I think she's right," she said, closing the old tome gently. "There have been underground colonies of native insects that have extended twice the distance and the Arthropods are far larger than they are. I'm surprised the entire world isn't one big underground tunnel system already."

"Who says it isn't? asked Ondo, arching an eyebrow.

"Damn," said Krista. "That's going to help me sleep tonight. I was hoping you were wrong, no offense."

"None taken," said Ariadne. "This is quite the risk."

"And you're sure you want to do this?" asked Prior Jacobi.

"What choice do we have?" I said. "We barely made it a few kilometers on the surface. This territory is unlike anything we've seen before. The skies are dark with inverts and the land is teeming with their patrols."

"If we do this, there's no turning back, possibly until we reach the Hive," said Huck.

"Was there ever a turning back point?" I asked.

"No. I suppose you're right."

"Then it's settled," said the prior. "I'll have my people work through the night for your morning departure. Until then, I implore you to get some rest. You have a lengthy road ahead of you."

We filed out of his office, heading back to our quarters.

"Are we doing the right thing?" I asked. "We're putting a lot of lives in danger."

"I see no alternative," said Ariadne. "We can't survive a trek to the Hive on the surface. There's no way. At least this would give us a fighting chance."

"Then I'm with you, every step of the way."

It was settled. In the morning, we were going to embark on the most dangerous part of our mission yet. Once stocked with provisions, we were going to descend into the pit and follow the creatures' tunnel, which according to Trivia's research, would eventually lead us to the Hive. The people of Zephyr's Hope would fill the pit behind us, leaving us with no option for escape. This was a one-way trip into a nightmare.

CHAPTER 36: ARJUN

The clank of a turning key in the rust-bound lock awoke me from my troubled sleep. I'd spent the night tossing and turning, sleeping in nightmare-driven fits. The rough wooden door creaked open, revealing two unfamiliar Demented blocking the way. There was no sign of breakfast this morning, only a large wooden vessel in the hands of the smaller of the pair. Without greeting, the one with the goblet approached me, grabbed my hair, and yanked my head back so hard that I heard my spine protest with a pop.

"That hurt!" I yelled, barely finishing the sentence before a thick, warm liquid was forced down my throat.

I coughed it all over the sandy floor, sputtering for air as I splashed it across the Demented's face. The fluid was rich black. *Hemolymph!* Taking this as defiance, the second shoved me against the wall, tightly holding my mouth open as the first repeated the pour. Nearly choking me, they managed to pour the vile contents of the cup down my throat. Simultaneously, they released their grip, allowing me to collapse to the floor, gagging. The thought crossed my mind to retch it up, but I knew the unpleasant process would only be repeated. Once I regained control of my breathing, the pair jerked me up and shoved me in the direction of the door. As we walked, I realized that I was being led back down to the Queens' audience chamber. They escorted me back down the spiraling, ornately carved path into the depths of the Hive.

When I entered, the Queens had already emerged from their alcoves and assumed their watchful positions, eying me menacingly. My knees trembled with fear as I stared at the vacant slab, wondering where Kolya's body had been taken and expecting the same to happen to me. *Soon I'll be nothing more than food.* Taking a deep breath, I raised my head. The trembling noticeably subsided. If I was going to die, I would face death with my head high.

"Why am I here?" I asked.

My voice echoed off the high parabolic walls of the chamber, making me feel infinitesimally small among the royalty of our enemies. The Queens sat, staring in silence. From the direction of the queen of the split wings, mouthparts softly clacked against each other.

"Am I to be a feast for you?" I asked, calmly. "Why am I here?"

At this, the bone arachnid queen's legs began to tap rhythmically on the stone, like someone anxiously drumming away on a tabletop. All of the Queens appeared restless, even the bulbous blood midge's queen preened with her sucker, making such a disgusting noise, I considered scolding her like a child. I was losing my patience. *For what, Arjun? Death?*

High above, that familiar sound of the Queen of Queens—Samrajni—emerging from her elevated nest, ready to descend to pronounce her judgment. Unlike the day before, I had no misgivings about disrespecting her and craned my neck up, still sore from the Demented's forceful jerk.

Near the bottom tip of the gray, metallic stone of the meteorite, the wasp-like mud raptor Queen of Queens emerged from her lair, spiraling down to the point of the rock, looming far above my head. Just when I was beginning to wonder how she'd come down, her legs released and she fell like a stone in water, slower than one would expect. Only a few meters above the ground, her wings sprang to life, fluttering softly, just enough to bring her to the ground gently—and silently.

"What do you want from me?" I asked with newfound courage. "What did you do with my friend?"

I thought for a moment and realized that Kolya was no friend at all, yet the potential desecration of his corpse still bothered me.

Silence.

I was about to repeat my question when a strange sensation came over me. The walls of the sanctum, like the walls in the tunnel were covered in those same, unrepeating swirls. The swirls began to spin with a vibrancy I didn't expect. With heavy feet, I made my way to the wall, feeling its texture. *So smooth. So still.* How could fixed rock move? I removed my hand, feeling the pulse in my hands. Had it always felt that way? *Adrenaline. It must be adrenaline.* I walked back to my position in front of the dais, my feet scuffing on the floor. Now there were several Demented, Jigna and Neesh among them. Had they always been there?

"Neeeeesh," I said, the words sounding funny in my mouth. "What's happening?"

Neesh shook his head. That looked like sadness. I recognized that one. I stumbled towards him and felt the side of his face. It was callused and scarred, having been cut and scraped more times than I cared to count. The Demented way, I suppose. What made them behave like animals? Cannibals? Those are strange words. Animals. Cannibals. What else rhymes with cannibals?

There was a loud *whump*, and suddenly I was staring at the ceiling. *That sound was me. Strange. I feel no pain.* The Demented surrounded me, the biggest one I'd ever seen, dusting off his hands. He must have thrown me to the ground. Each Demented grabbed an appendage and they carried me to the slab. Kolya's slab.

"She's going to cut up my brain, isn't she?"

Jigna looked down at me with that same sad face that Neesh had. I was going to die. This was the moment. I thought back to being hurled onto the ground. It hadn't hurt. At least this probably wouldn't hurt. Probably. The brain doesn't have pain receptors. The skull feels pain though. The realization finally hit me. *The hemolymph!* I'd been drugged for the procedure. *Why hadn't Kolya been drugged?* They lowered me to the slab, more gently than I'd been brought to the ground. I let out a giggle. *You're about to die and you're laughing?*

As the Demented backed away, I had a much better vantage of the torch-lit space. The flames cast fierce writhing shadows across the walls. I could almost hear music to accompany them. Music. It'd been so long since I heard music. Was it my imagination, or had I heard some in Pod Bandung? *Hemant! I have to warn Hemant!* I began to rise, but my body was so sluggish. So heavy. *Maybe I'll just rest first.*

I closed my eyes for just a moment and felt a rocking sensation. It reminded me of standing on Mueller's boat so long ago, cruising across that vast lake with Ciro. *My companion. My love.* I felt a tear burn on my cheek as I swayed, thinking back to all the nights Ciro and I had stayed awake debating possible evolutionary scenarios for the Arthropods' existence. He had stirred my deepest feelings. I missed his presence. *Wait! I'm not on a boat.* I opened my eyes, taking significant effort to focus on the present. I was being tied upside-down onto the abdomen of Samrajni. It hit me. I was to be her next interpreter. Her next host. I opened my mouth to scream as I felt a hard, fast *thunk* into the top of my head. *So much pressure! I can't turn my head!* I stared a Jigna. *Was that a tear?* Foreign memories flooded my mind. I shook my head as much as the restricting bonds would allow, violently trying to dispel them. Trauma. Vengeance. Megalomania. In the swirling confusion, I tried desperately to hold on to my thoughts. *I...* Ciro... *am...* Hemant... *Samrajni.*

I. Am. Samrajni.

Chapter 37: Dorothy's Journal

*I*t's a strange sensation, writing in this book. Whenever Dad thought about it (which wasn't often), he'd sit down and write whatever came to mind, so in a way, it always felt like *his* book. Reading back over his entries, he spoke at length about how the world was changing. The Arthropods landed when I was so young, this has been my world. If what I write in this falling-apart journal is all I leave to the world, I want to dwell on what we have, not what we've lost. My father, Darren Taggert, died from an infection almost a year ago. The bear that he was so thrilled about taking down had some nasty claws. He lasted a few months, and only that long because of the powerful antibiotics we'd saved for an emergency like this. We hardly have any left, so let's hope there's not another emergency. We had almost amputated his leg before we realized it was already too late. Once the infection spread to his blood, it was over. He spent his last moments muttering to Mom. I wonder if there was anything there. I don't guess it matters. We buried him on the hill next to Mrs. Grimethorpe. I dug the grave myself. Everyone cried the whole time, even Natalie. Hell, we live in an isolated small cabin, we can't help but be extremely close. When you only have each other, relationships are everything. *Humph.* So much for not focusing on loss.

—Alex Taggert, 2061

*T*oday marks our twentieth year at the cabin. Well, maybe not Natalie's. At this point, we operate like a well-oiled machine. Stepan and I mend whatever new thing has broken, whether that be something on the house, the shed, or the pens. We tend to the livestock and the hunting. Natalie and Kitty tend to the food by harvesting and weeding the garden or cooking and storing the produce for the long winters. On the days when someone is ill, we all cover the slack. When Kitty is sick of dealing with food, sometimes I'll find her, hammer in hand, repairing the fence. When I get fed up with hunting, I'll go pickle some vegetables. I don't remember much about life in the city, but living off the land out here feels so… natural. It hard to imagine the conveniences that Stepan and Kitty still talk about. Cooked food delivered to your door. (Admittedly, that sounds pretty nice.) More hours of entertainment than a human is alive. (*Hah!* Come live in the woods, there's no shortage of things to do.) Robots to do the hard, repetitive work for you. (No, thanks.) Thank the universe Mrs. Dorothy had been so knowledgeable and generous. Without her, I hesitate to think about what my life would look like. These people around me taught me all I know, and I've learned a few things from experience myself. Part of me wants to stay here forever, like Dad, but the other part of me knows that could be tantamount to suicide. It's only a matter of time until the inverts reach this area. Right now, there's nowhere to go. I'd certainly rather live here in the woods than that filthy shanty town around Pittsburgh.

—Alex Taggert, 2063

As the situation worsens, humanity is slowly losing its collective sanity. People are becoming more selfish and vile by the day. Stepan and I were forced to kill three raiders a few months back! These people found us, way out here in the middle of nowhere. Before you think poorly of me, we had no choice. They were prepared to kill us for our food and our weapons. Ten-year-old Natalie included. We've worked too hard for everything we have to let it be squandered by predators. These people are ruthless. When our radio works, we're hearing more and more reports of roving bands—stealing what others have earned. It's too bad that Winston's plants don't repel criminals. A twelve gauge will, but I hate that it's come to that. After we shot those men, I spent the next three weeks plagued by crying fits and nightmares. It was awful! Information these days is limited, but we can get a clear enough picture of what's going on in the world. None of it's pleasant. So many dead. These inverts devour anything and everything in their path. At least they don't care for plants. Otherwise, humanity would really be in trouble.

—Alex Taggert, 2065

The radio says the inverts have constructed a central hive in the desert where the meteorite landed. Before the scientists lost touch with the satellites, they said the mound was the biggest animal-made object on Earth. How will we ever defeat these guys? That's not even the worst of it. Pod Wagga, the underground city in the Australian Territory was destroyed before it was even partially completed. It makes me wonder how many of the pods will be finished. Best case scenario, we're down to ten pods. That's only space for two and a half million people. The UTE says it's temporary—to buy us time to find a solution, or so they say. I think this might be the end of us. Of humanity. I'm not giving up, but

I don't see a way out of this. I miss Mom and Dad. Mrs. Dorothy too. I still don't see any reason to leave the safety and comfort of our home. I don't think Stepan or Kitty will be around long enough to see the pods. Every time one of them is sick, they take longer to recover. Our medications are pretty much limited to herbal remedies. Thankfully, Stepan has a talent with those. They cure a number of minor ills but taste horrendous. As Natalie gets older, I can tell she feels like something is missing from her life. I remember the same feelings as a teenager. Family doesn't always fill the space in our hearts for friends. After all the years, I've resigned myself to the fact I'll never fall in love. I hope different for Natalie.

—Alex Taggert, 2071

Kitty didn't make it. She got a cough that never would quit. We've tried every herbal remedy and what meager medicine we still had in our possession. Nothing worked, so at great risk Stepan and I made a trip back into what used to be Flint to look for pharmaceuticals or medical texts. We planned to hit up all the pharmacies on the side of town closest to us before disappearing again. The trip was a disaster. The inverts haven't reached Flint yet, but the city was rife with crime and every building we saw had been looted or burned. Gangs patrolled the streets. We never even got close to anything important before we were spotted. A guy yelled something in a language I didn't understand and discharged an automatic at our feet. A ricochet hit Step in his shoulder. The guy was taken aback by the accident, which gave me time to shoot him. I couldn't hesitate. As he illustrated, hesitation is death. I'll never feel right taking another human's life, but I do what I have to do to defend myself and my family. It took forever, but I managed to lug Step back to the cabin. By the time we arrived, he was pale as a sheet. He's well over sixty, far too old for this sort of thing. He died that night from blood loss. Breaking the news to Kitty was the hardest thing I've ever done. I held Natalie all night as she bawled. In the morning, I had to dig two graves. Despite that nasty cough, I will always believe that Kitty died of a broken heart. It's been just me and Nat for a while now. I'm struggling to keep her fed. Do all teens eat this much?

—Alex Taggert, 2074

*I*t's been thirty-six years since those bastards brought their ilk to Earth. Their presence affects us more with each passing month. Preceding their wake of death and destruction are waves of panic and desperation that aren't contained in the urban centers. As much as I'd like to say the worst is over, it's anything but true. The pod's construction is progressing, but at a snail's pace when compared to the Arthropods' advance. Signal is getting worse. We only catch an audible portion of a broadcast once every few weeks. We keep the radio on low all day until it gets to the point neither of us can stand it, and we switch it off for a few days. Natalie knows to scream for me whenever a broadcast comes through. Call me old-fashioned, but I like her staying in the house while I go out. It's safer there. Don't think she's all ladylike. I've taught her every skill I know. Natalie can shoot and skin a deer as well as she can gather mushrooms and berries. I taught her how to fight too. After a raider broke in and almost had his way with her, I made sure she'd never be in that position again. We found one of Winston's old manuals for hand-to-hand combat, which neither of us have any experience in. You should've seen the hilarity that ensued those first few nights. I doubt we'd hold up against someone with real training, but I think we could stand our own against the average threat. Step and Kitty can rest easy. She saved herself that first time, it wasn't even me who'd intervened. From all the hunting, she knew exactly where to plunge the knife into her assailant. Him we didn't bury, just rolled his body down a ravine a few kilometers from here. Maybe it was serendipitous because when we did, we found a flock of guinea fowl and netted them. They've been a source of food and our alarm system ever since.

—Alex Taggert, 2078

The news says in the next twenty years, the Arthropods will cover the Earth. Think about that. That's ten years before the pods' scheduled completion! I hope there's enough time, not just for us, but for humanity. Frankly, I'm surprised they haven't reached us already. Every foreign sound we hear has us up and alert, guns to our shoulders. I haven't slept straight through a night in ages. We're encountering raiders far too often. They've become trickier in their desperation—feigning injuries, starvation, fleeing "threats." I'll be honest, I don't know how much longer Natalie and I can stay here. I'm not getting any younger, and I can't abide the idea of something happening to me and leaving Natalie all alone. I don't know where we'd go or that it'd be any safer. The nearest pod is far from finished. I wish she had better company than this crotchety old fool. I did find something new in the cabin even after all these years. When I was repairing the stonework around the fireplace, I found another of Winston's hidden compartments. His paranoia may not have served him, but I couldn't be more thankful for it. Behind the secret panel was a plastic-wrapped analog ham radio in surprisingly good condition. I'm afraid to use it, but I turn it on now and then. Nothing but static. It's funny. We've lived here decades, and we are still discovering Winston's secrets. I regret I never knew the man.

—Alex Taggert, 2082

*W*ell, it finally happened. After hearing about them my entire life, I saw my first Arthropod last week. They are *so* much bigger than I expected. The hook beetle's sounds scared the living hell out of us, but I managed to keep my cool long enough to take it down. Imagine a stag beetle the size of a compact car with a hooked beak that could rip steel plating. Natalie and I were out hunting, and we saw it in the ravine. Being downwind, chance worked in our favor, giving us the drop on the beast. I shouldered the old lever-action rifle and fired the medium-caliber round into what I figured was its brain. I guess it worked. The creature collapsed immediately. Thankfully the "hooks" are slow movers. I don't like to think about what would've happened if the situation had been reversed. The thought crossed our minds to eat it, but it smelled so rank that we left it for dead. I still wake up in cold sweats thinking about it. It was only the first. More will follow, of that I'm sure. Now, every time one of us is working, the other stands guard. If it was up to me, I'd probably stay here until I died, but this is no way for Natalie to live. Maybe it's time to start thinking about leaving.

—Alex Taggert, 2089

*N*atalie has turned into a formidable, supremely intelligent person. The last time I was out chopping wood, more raiders stumbled onto our property. She dropped the three men and a woman before I knew they were there. I'm proud to have her watching my back. Maybe it's the fatherly instinct in me that's reluctant to let her hunt alone, but she'd be fine. We carried their bodies to "Bandit Ravine" as we'd taken to calling it, rolling them onto the picked clean bones of the others. That pile was bigger than I remembered it. I didn't cry like I used to, but I always resented them for forcing us to defend ourselves. On our way back, we found the bandits' camp where they had a hostage they'd kept behind during the attack. His name's Gabriel. You could tell he was a handsome young Latino, even through the bruising, bleeding, and scars his captors had given him. I don't want to know what their plans were for him. He shied away from me when I approached him. I guess I am a pretty scary-looking guy when I think about it, despite my age. I'm big, dark, and hairy. I don't smile much anymore either. The second Nat came out from behind me in her hand-sewn dress and long, strawberry locks, he was smitten. She's been nursing him back to health a lot lately. Either he was really unhealthy or she likes being around him more than this old fart. Who could blame her? I'm acting like I'm still on the fence, but I'll let him stay. He's a good man. We haven't seen any more raiders since. I think the inverts are killing them off. Strangely, they don't seem to bother us at the cabin. I thought we'd be sitting ducks.

—Alex Taggert, 2085

I officiated Gabriel and Natalie's wedding. It was fantastic to have something so happy for a change. Let this notation serve as the official record, not that I'm ordained in any way. At this point, do we still have a government to care? I've never eaten so many honey cakes in my life. It's nice to have someone willing to brave the local beehive. I wanted to give them as much of a honeymoon as I could, so since the weather was pleasant, I endured the shed for three days. I didn't mind the smaller space, but I'm not sure my back will ever forgive me for the wooden floor. Their time alone must have been successful. They've since had a daughter, Zephyr, who's just turned six months old. The precious little bundle is like the granddaughter I never had. Every time I hold her in my arms, I forget about everything outside of this cabin. I wish Dad, Natalie's parents, and Mrs. Dorothy could see her. I wouldn't have recommended bringing a life into the world, but they couldn't imagine not doing so. Gabriel said the joy of life was one of the few things that the Arthropods couldn't take from us. I've been thrilled to have him around. Not only is he a font of positivity, but he does the chores my old frame has more difficulty doing these days, like finally fixing those shingles on the edge of the roof that I wouldn't let Natalie do. I can't believe I turned fifty this year. Natalie made me strawberry shortcakes since I don't want to see another honey cake as long as I live. God, where does the time go?

—Alex Taggert, 2086

We're still over twenty years out from the pods' completion. Pretty soon, I think leaving the cabin will be inevitable. We're seeing less and less wildlife, but the further out we venture, the more likely we are to stumble on an Arthropod. One is easy enough to take down, but with each additional one, they become exponentially harder to take down. We've been eating a whole lot more poultry and eggs in recent years. Radio broadcasts are harder than ever to come by. Sometimes we go months without hearing one. By the time these damn pods are completed, I wonder if there will be a few million people left to fill them. The last death toll I heard was estimated to be around three billion. Earth had just shy of ten billion when the meteorite hit. The inverts had whittled us down to seven billion people and no telling how many animals in a matter of decades. Zephyr runs around without a care in the world as Natalie and Gabriel look on proudly. I've taken to carving little people for her. No matter how many I make, she always begs for more. I'll do anything to protect her innocence as long as possible. She'll have the rest of her life to face the real world. For now, let her play.

—Alex Taggert, 2089

I'm not sure how much longer we can stay here. We're killing a dozen inverts a month, but we're running perilously low on ammo. We wouldn't stand a chance if they ever attacked in a group. Dorothy's husband had been somewhat of a prepper and left us with a staggering supply, but after seventy years, even that's dwindling. It's curious. They still won't come near the cabin. All I can figure is that it has something to do with Winston's plants. The hook beetles move slowly through the forest, the split wings are easier to shoot than a quail, and the polies, well, just let them mosy on. You'll only be stupid enough to shoot them once. The day Gabriel did that, I thought it would be a forest fire that drove us from home. Thank the universe the bone arachnids prefer warmer climates. Lack of ammo isn't our greatest concern. Game has become so scarce in the region, that our diet has transitioned to largely vegetarian. At least we have the fowl to help lighten the hunger, but they can't breed or lay fast enough. Any thoughts we have about expanding our livestock go largely ignored, we're too afraid additional animals would attract more of the inverts. Zephyr discovered Winston's old ham radio a few weeks ago, it's hand crank like Dorothy's old FM one. She talks into the thing day and night, often about silly six-year-old things, other times about hope for the future. I don't have the heart to tell her no one can hear her.

—Alex Taggert, 2092

*T*he FM radio has stopped working since the antenna bugs have begun dotting the sky. At first, it was just a few, but as the months go by, their grid gets tighter. You can see their little purple-hued exoskeletons dotted across the sky in an eerily equidistant arrangement. With the binoculars, you can see their long black antennae extend well past their bodies, giving them their name. They just hover, all day, every day. If you watch them long enough, you can see them swap out. It's like they're watching us. Their presence doesn't stop Zephyr from continuing on the ham. She spends so much time with it, that the three of us discussed putting it away for her mental health. In the end, we just couldn't go through with it. As best as we can figure, it's not hurting anything. It's become her outlet, the childhood friend she'll never have. She speaks at length about hope, I think mostly to herself. Sometimes we'll sit outside her door and listen, needing her youthful optimism. Her wisdom is well beyond her years. She'll need every bit of it if we're going to make it to Pod Pittsburgh. By our reckoning, the pod should be nearing completion and it's almost time to head that way. It's no longer a question. Zephyr is a tough little eleven-year-old who can undoubtedly make the trip. It's me I'm more worried about. Natalie and Gabe are both in their forties and are in great shape. I cry in bed with more frequency than I care to admit. The idea of leaving my home and dad is just… unbearable.

—*Alex Taggert, 2097*

The turn of a new century and we have nothing better to report. We had a small celebration. Gabe and I ground flour while Zeph and Nat made a strawberry jam sweetened with honey from the beehive in the old stump on the ridge. Calling the dense, wood-fired cake a success would be generous, but it was sweet and delicious. We even shoved an oversized candle in the middle for good measure. It reminded me of my childhood, so long ago now. For a few moments, I felt like a human again. It's the little things that make all the difference in the world. At Zephyr's request, we tried to stay up until what we figured was midnight, but she was the only one who saw the new century in awake. The next morning Gabe and I decided to reactivate Dad and Stepan's old still, but the metal was too far gone. Well, it was worth a try. At least we had the cake. Every night since, we've pulled out every old map we could find in the cabin, trying to map our way to Pittsburgh as carefully as possible. We have no idea what we might encounter, be it bandits, Arthropods, or any other unknowns. The journey would be a challenge under the best of circumstances. My bigger concern was what would we find when we got there.

—*Alex Taggert, 2100*

Just for the hell of it, I cranked up the old FM. After leaving it running for a few days, it paid off. I caught just a few phrases that weren't garbled beyond understanding. "…half of the population…," and "…pods on schedule…" I'm assuming the former to mean that half of Earth's population is dead. I have no reason to think any more optimistically. Bastards. As far as the latter, I am continuing on the knowledge that the pods will be finished in July 2112 as they were supposed to be. If we can hold out at the cabin for a little longer, We'll leave in June for Pittsburgh. It couldn't be soon enough. We lost the last males in our flocks, meaning no more poultry once these are gone. The chickens and guinea fowl should make eggs long enough to see us out of here, but it'll be pushing it. It's getting harder as the years go by to help in the garden. The others do the work willingly, but I can tell it's an extra burden they don't need. I hope I'm not a burden on the trip. They'd never consider letting me stay. That's the good thing about family.

—*Alex Taggert, 2104*

Sometimes months pass, and I stare at this journal every night. I tell myself I'm too tired from other tasks to write, but the reality is I don't want to. The more years I go without writing, the harder it is to pick the thing up. Who would've thought a book could be so intimidating? But how many times can I say the situation is bleak or that we survived another year? Zephyr puts me to shame. Every night, without fail, she seats herself in front of that damn radio and does her whole production about hope. The second she's done with her chores, she disappears up to her room to write and prepare for her "broadcast." The other day I caught her curled in a ball in the middle of the hallway, sobbing. I lowered myself to the fraying rug that covered the worn wooden floor, groaning the whole way down. It had been ages since I sat on the floor. Zephyr was questioning why she continued when not a soul had ever responded to her messages or pleas for contact. After thinking for a moment, I asked her if her messages benefited one person, would it be worth it? She nodded, clearing away the tears, and I told her what they had meant to me. The next night she was back at it, hard as ever.

—Alex Taggert, 2109

*T*he time has come. I can't tell you how hard that sentence was to pen. We're leaving in the morning. The exact date was chosen for us. A pill bug running from something found its way onto the property and got into the fowl pen. When it just went crazy trying to escape, it wrecked the walls, bringing the whole structure down on top of the stupid invert, detonating it. The explosion burned down the shed, killed half the plants in the garden, and destroyed most of our tools. With no more food than what we had canned and the seeds that wouldn't sprout anytime soon, we had no choice but to leave. Tomorrow, we head to Pod Pittsburgh and see if we can get in. God, I hope it's not as bad as they say. Supposedly, it's one of the most crowded being so far from the Landing site. What alternative do we have? The next nearest pod is Monterrey, in the Latin Territory. That's nearly 2,000 kilometers further! Zephyr's furious that we aren't taking her radio. The damn thing weighs six kilos. That's a lot of food we'd have to leave behind and five hundred kilometers isn't exactly a short distance. In a way, I feel as though I'm making her leave a friend. I hope one day she'll forgive me.

—Alex Taggert, 2112

CHAPTER 38: HUCK

"Are you ready for this?" asked Hemant, looking up from the pit that swallowed the torchlight.

I nodded. "As ready as I ever will be."

A shiver ran down my spine as I gazed into the hole circumferenced by the city's deceased, so anxious to consume us as well. I was thankful for the few nights of sound sleep. *Who knows when the next one will be, if ever?* Wearing our patched gray jumpsuits overlaid with our repaired light armor and carrying our full battery of weapons, we were as prepared as we'd ever be to enter the outskirts of the Hive's tunnel network—a network that spanned a continent. Hemant shrugged, muscles bulging as he adjusted the heavy load on his back, the heavy burden weighed him down in more ways than one. Declining Ondo's regular offers of help, Hemant insisted that the responsibility was his to shoulder. It dawned on me just how much faith we were putting in Dieter's device. *After all this effort, it better work.*

Ariadne, Hemant, and I had convened alone late last night. Knowing from this point on, we were technically in the extremities of the Hive, we had reached a difficult agreement. The conversation was still playing on a loop in my mind.

"With every step, our mission has become more dangerous, but the reality is that it's about to get exponentially worse," Ariadne said. "We are about to face some tough decisions."

"I know where you're headed," I said. "I've been thinking about it too."

"Care to share?" asked Hemant.

"She saying we might find ourselves in a situation with no escape. Our duty—"

"Oh," said Hemant as the implications hit him.

Ariadne put her hand on Hemant's knee as he sat on the bed across from us. "You know how much we care for Arjun, but we have a mission to see through."

Hemant nodded, eyes unfocused, gaze towards the stone floor worn smooth by years of occupation.

"We've always known how this could end," I said. "Obviously, we'd like to avoid that and each of us live into old age on an Arthropod-free planet, but that may not be our destiny."

"I know," Hemant said, meeting our gaze with tears in his eyes. "It's what Arjun would do. If the time comes, I'll do what needs to be done.

Before breakfast the next morning we shared our thoughts with the others. We unanimously concurred. If it came down to it, the last person standing would blow the device, regardless of where we were. If destiny was even remotely on our side, we'd be close enough to the Queens to do some irreparable damage. The last thing any of us wanted was to add a pointless crater to the Outback. If that was the outcome, our entire mission would be for naught. Despite the agreement, no one was feeling exactly chipper as we stood by the pit, readying our harnesses for the short descent.

"The people of Zephyr's Hope will ensure that the world knows your story," said Prior Jacobi.

"You say as though we're not coming back," said Omar. "I have every intention of walking out of the Hive as it burns and collapses behind me."

The prior nodded, saying nothing.

I couldn't blame him. How many people have set out to destroy the Arthropods and their Hive over the last four centuries? Just because we'd made it further than possibly anyone in recent memory, it didn't mean we would be successful.

"Thank you, Prior, for all of your hospitality," I said. "I hope one day we can repay you."

"You can repay me by ridding Earth of this pestilence," he said with a sly smile.

Ariadne embraced him as surprise flashed across his face. *I guess priors don't get hugged much,* I thought, laughing to myself. Something was endearing about the grandfatherly man. Unlike so many of the leaders we'd come across, he was a genuinely good person. The world of the future needed more like him.

"Can we get a move on?" said Omar.

"I was hoping to say goodbye to Artim," said Ondo. "I'll miss that little dude."

I took a deep breath and turned to face the pit.

"Wait!" yelled a young voice, echoing through the catacombs.

Shadows danced on the wall, cast by the torchlight, hailing Artim's arrival.

"Wait!" he said, running into the chamber on the verge of tears, trying to catch his breath. "I couldn't sleep all night! When I finally dozed off, I overslept! I was afraid you'd left without me."

"Oh, Artim," said Trivia, wrapping him in her arms. "I'm so glad you came to say goodbye."

"I didn't come to say goodbye," he said, pulling back.

For the first time, I noticed he had a bag slung over his shoulder.

"Absolutely not," said Omar. "I'm not a freaking babysitter."

Krista gave him an angry look. "What he means is that it's way too dangerous for you to come. He just isn't used to being polite."

"But I—"

"I'm sorry, Artim, but no," I said. "We have years of training and months of experience. It's unbelievably dangerous, even for us."

"You don't understand! I can help!"

Several others walked into the small chamber, filling it with more life than I imagined it had seen in years. Save for Artim's friend Dane, I recognized no one. With the additional torches, the room was brighter than before, making the evil maw that much less inviting.

"Which of you is Huck?" asked a middle-aged man.

The man had wisps of gray around his temples and judging by the dirt under his fingernails, spent most of his time working the underground soil. Presumably, his wife stood at his side, her arm wrapped in his, long hair cascading down her back.

"I am," I said, coming forward.

After shaking my hand, the man introduced himself. "I'm Yosef, Artim's father."

"Then maybe you can talk some sense into him," said Omar, followed by a grunt as Ondo drove the haft of his hammer into Omar's ribs with a sly grin.

"On the contrary, I'm here to request that he be allowed to accompany you."

Ariadne's mouth fell open, a reflection of my own. Before I could protest, he continued.

"I can imagine what you must be thinking. I assure you, we couldn't be more reluctant to part with our only child. It's true that he may not be able to fight, but despite my protests, he's become very good at avoiding the dark ones and navigating his way underground. He's got a gift, and it would be selfish not to share it with those who need it most."

"Sir," I began, "I can't begin to tell you—"

"Forgive my interruption, but we are well aware of the dangers despite our humble appearance. This has been the hardest choice of our lives, but we believe his destiny lies with you. I hope you will accept that."

I opened my mouth to respond but felt Ariadne's tender touch on my arm. "Then we will honor your wishes," she responded.

Yosef and his wife nodded, tears of gratitude and sadness pouring down their faces as they hugged their son goodbye, likely for the last time. My eyes stung thinking about what these people were sacrificing in the hopes of our success. Omar groaned but was smart enough not to say more in reach of Ondo's hammer.

"I will guard him with my life," said Ondo.

Unable to speak, the couple nodded in appreciation.

"If Artim's going, I'm going too!" said Dane, making his way to the front of the small crowd.

"Billman Dane," said Jacobi, "are you presuming to give me commands?"

Dane stopped in his tracks. "Umm... No, Prior Jacobi. It's just that—"

"I'm well aware that you and Artim are fast friends, *and* that you have been letting him out into the wilds from time to time."

Dane looked abashed as he sulked back toward the group.

"That being said, you have performed your duty honorably. I release you from them so that you may accompany Artim, should Huck accept you."

Dane spun to face me. *What was one more novice?* Maybe he'd help keep an eye on Artim. I gave my approval. I doubted that he would be so excited once he came to face with his first invert.

"Thank you!" said Dane, bouncing with excitement.

"Now, we must get you on your way," said the prior, clasping both of my shoulders. "May fortune favor you and the task that lies ahead. Is there anything else you need before you go?"

"A stiff drink," said Omar.

Ignoring him, I shook my head. "I'm sure I'll think of something immediately after you fill in the pit behind us.

"Let us pray that you don't," he said, smiling. "Godspeed."

I turned to face the abyss, home to the bones of countless Zephyr's Hope residents. In a way, we'd be buried with them but hopefully would emerge from the ground again. A sense of dread overwhelmed me as I realized that the last time I felt sunshine might have been the final time. I pushed the idea from my head as soon as it had arrived. Thoughts like that would kill hope faster than the Arthropods. Omar was the first to descend into obscurity.

I wrapped my arms around Ariadne. "I love you."

She pressed her lips firmly against mine. For a moment, nothing else existed but us. I let myself melt into that kiss, cherishing that last moment of safety. We'd stayed like that until Ondo loudly cleared his throat. When I looked around, I realized that we were the only three who hadn't climbed down. The residents anxiously waited to backfill the hole after enduring our prolonged kiss. Avoiding eye contact, I grabbed the rope and flipped my legs over the side. There was no sign of the bottom. If Artim could do it, so could I. I scooted off the rocks lining the edge and was consumed by darkness.

The first few shovels of rocky earth were disconcerting, hearing the clinks and pops as it rained down on the copious bones littering the bottom of the shaft. I watched as the last traces of torchlight from above vanished as the dirt covered the top of the breach we'd climbed through. We were standing in a rounded tunnel, no more than two meters in diameter. The sides rippled with the tell-tale signs of Arthropod construction. As best as I could tell, we were alone—at least for the moment. We had packed our jumpsuit pockets full of neem leaves in hopes it'd stave off at least the small ones. In the tight confines of the enemy tunnel, I'd take every advantage I could get.

"Guess that's that," said Krista, staring at the mound of dirt and bones that had followed us into the tunnel. "I hope no one's claustrophobic."

I raised an eyebrow at Hemant, who'd broken out in a cold sweat. "You okay?" I asked. "I bet Ariadne could give you something to put you at ease.

"Nothing that wouldn't affect my reaction time," he said. "Let's focus on the mission ahead, okay?"

It was still odd to me that someone so formidable on the battlefield could be brought to his knees by such phobias as water, heights, and enclosed spaces. I knew it wasn't just the mission that kept him going, but the unconditional love he held for his twin brother.

I didn't have any known phobias, but the infinite darkness that sprawled ahead of us didn't exactly put me at ease. Our flashlights barely sufficed to pierce the veil, failing to illuminate any threats with adequate time to prepare for an ambush. As a result, those of us in the middle would carry the lights while the front and rear marched with weapons ready. Instead of stopping to recharge their power cells when they ran low, we would give them a gentle shake periodically as we walked to limit their sounds from thundering down the shaft and hailing our arrival.

"I don't like this," whispered Omar, pulling damp fingers back from the shiny tunnel wall.

"A little late for that, don't you think?" said Ondo.

"I was clear when I told you the risks," said Trivia, daring Omar to argue back.

"Would you rather be on the surface?" asked Ariadne. "I wasn't imagining the hordes of inverts so thick they obscured the sun, was I?

"No, you weren't," muttered Krista. "Artim saved us."

"At least here they'll bottleneck if they come at us," said Dane, upbeat given the circumstances.

"No one asked you," barked Omar and Krista in unison.

"Lighten up," said Hemant. "We're all here to kill some bugs. The last thing we need to do is waste our energy fighting each other."

"He's right," I said. "We've got a hell of a long road ahead of us and regardless of what you think, Artim and Dane are part of our team."

Omar grunted. I hoped that would be the last we'd hear about the matter from him, but I doubted it. According to Trivia's best-case scenario, we were looking at two weeks of tunnel exploration, though how we'd tell day from night was beyond me. It hadn't occurred to me to bring a pocket watch.

"Then we better get a move on," said Artim, taking the lead, his finger already bouncing along the curvature of the wall.

"You're right, Artim, but you'll be navigating us from the middle where you're safer," said Ariadne, gently tugging him back by his collar.

We'd only made it a few hundred meters when we came to an oblong cavern several times wider than the tunnel. Entrances to other tunnels dotted the room, veering off in every conceivable direction—a lotus pod of choices. The holes lining the bottom of the room drove straight down into the earth.

"Now what?" I asked, looking at Trivia.

CHAPTER 39: ARIADNE

"**W**ell that sucks," said Ondo. "How do we know which way to go?"

"We're heading south. We'll just use the compasses. They've worked since the aerials fell."

"They won't account for elevation, but that's not a bad idea," said Artim.

"Smart kid," said Trivia. "But it also doesn't guarantee that any tunnel we chose will take us in the direction we want. The thing could meander for hundreds of kilometers, slowly taking us further and further away from our objective."

"The compass is worthless anyway," said Krista, looking up. "Look, the needle keeps spinning."

"Damn," said Hemant. "Never a break."

"That doesn't surprise me," said Trivia. "We're getting closer to their epicenter. If they have some sort of magnetic interference, it'd be strongest here. I bet the radio is useless too. That's probably a factor in why Zephyr's Hope never readopted technology."

"What kept the inverts from burrowing into the city from a different tunnel?" asked Hemant.

"I was thinking about that too," said Trivia. "My best guess is that they mentally blocked off the area. When some native species encounter an obstacle, they block it out of their minds as unattainable. Those wraiths knew how far they could go, but never ventured further."

"Are you saying their… uh… hive mind simply ignores our colony?" asked Dane, drawing out the words. "Like if we could see a map of tunnels throughout the territory, there would be a big blank spot."

"That would be my guess," answered Trivia.

"Jeepers," he said.

"I wish I had a map of this place," said Artim. "How do the dark ones navigate this place?"

"Pheromones," I said. "That one *I* know. If we could see this place like they do, it bet it would look like the equivalent of color-coded trails."

"As cool as this trivia session is, none of that helps us pick a tunnel," said Omar.

"Straight ahead," said Artim. "We're still going south, and as best as I can tell, we haven't changed elevation."

"You heard compass kid," said Ondo, tussling Artim's hair. "Let's go."

The "floor" of the room was less a floor and more a concave field of bottomless craters. Little passable space stood between each entrance. Making matters worse, the undulating ground was smooth and damp, offering little traction. The edges of the pits—razor sharp.

"How are we supposed to do that?" asked Krista. "If Hemant falls with the weight of his equipment, there's no saving him."

"Mountain climbing!" Huck blurted.

"What?" I asked.

"People used to climb mountains for fun."

"Why would they do that?" asked Krista.

"To prove they could do it," said Trivia. "People did a lot for recreation before they were solely focused on survival."

"So how does that benefit us?" asked Hemant.

"One day after training I found some guys arguing over an old page in a book," Huck began. "They were making fun of the way people used to dress and failed to recognize it for what it was. It took more ration points than I care to admit, but they eventually forked it over. I dreamed about the mountains and trees in that image for years."

"And your point is…?" said Omar.

"The climbers would tie themselves together for safety. If one or two lost their grip, the others would keep them from plunging to their death."

"Smart thinking," said Ondo. "Omar, still got that rope?"

"Like I'd ever leave it behind," he said, fishing it out of his bag. "Ondo and Hemant should take the ends. We need the heaviest of us as anchor points."

If either of the pair was offended, they didn't show it. Over the next few minutes, we linked ourselves together in a line. Everyone would follow Hemant while Ondo stayed put. With any luck, we had enough rope to cross the expanse to the tunnel on the far side. Once Hemant and the bomb were safely in place, Ondo would bring up the rear. We'd have to untie in the tunnels between these types of chambers in case we ran into trouble, but I hoped there weren't too many of the lotus-like chambers between us and the Hive. Two weeks was beginning to sound extremely optimistic. At this rate of travel, it would take months. We were well stocked on food, but not enough for more than three weeks—at most. A pit, not unlike the ones below opened in my stomach. *How the hell were we going to do this?*

Hemant took the first tentative steps down the slick bank of rock and immediately lost his footing, sliding down between two tunnel entrances and barely coming to a halt before falling into a third. Tether or no, on his face was a silent scream.

"You okay?" asked Trivia.

"I'm fine," he said, taking a deep, shaking breath. He angrily wiped the sludge from his armor as he stood. "I couldn't get any traction. I don't know how I'm going to climb the other side. Not to mention, if anyone interrupts this party, I'm little more than defenseless."

"Then pray we aren't interrupted," said Omar, furrowing his brow as he fed Hemant some slack in the rope.

Hemant carefully made his way to the other side, grumbling all the while. The next few followed him with a similar lack of grace. Fortune had somewhat favored us with a small recess in which Hemant could place his boot, giving him just enough height to hoist himself up into the next tunnel.

"That sucked," he said, leaning down to clasp Trivia's hand, easily pulling her small frame up.

Next to last, I followed Huck down into the chamber with Ondo at my heels. Slippery didn't begin to describe it. It was like trying to walk up a lard-covered sheet of polished steel. By the time Ondo and I reached the opposite side, we were filthy from all the muck we'd collect each time we'd fallen.

"I don't know how sustainable this is," I said, placing my foot in the recess to climb up.

"I'm inclined to agree," said Huck. "Why don't we see if we can find an outlet to the surface and reassess our route."

Behind me, Ondo fell again. I began rolling my eyes when I was jerked down with him. When my chest hit the ground, the air was knocked from my lungs, preventing me from warning the others. Huck and Dane were pulled down ahead of me, before Omar and Hemant dug in, preventing anyone else from falling. For the first time since the fall, I heard Ondo's voice—screaming. My lungs burned as I took in a deep, painful breath and turned to look behind me. *Where's Ondo?!* Only the rope leading over the nearest edge was visible.

"Pull us up!" I yelled. "I can't stand!"

"We're trying!" yelled Hemant.

The veins in his and Omar's heads bulged from the strain. Omar was taking deep gasps, relentlessly trying to keep his footing, but still, the pair slid forward. Then Artim followed Dane back down into the chamber as Hemant and Omar slid forward. *The tether is working against us!* I tried to dig in my boots but felt nothing but empty air. Less than a meter and I would be over the edge with Ondo! Time stalled and sound ceased as I turned to see the strained faces of my friends fighting a losing battle with our weight. Each one lingered on the brink of exhaustion as all but my head slipped over the edge.

"I'm sorry, Huck," I said, tears rolling down my face. "I love you!"

His eyes grew wide. Before he could respond, I sliced my dagger through the air, severing the rope tethering us to the others, and Ondo and I plummeted into the all-consuming darkness.

•••••••••

When I came to, every part of my body throbbed with pain. Not like fall-down-a-flight-of-stairs hurt, but rather tumbled-in-an-industrial-dryer-for-hours hurt. There was no telling how long it had been since we'd fallen. I was alive, which was more than I'd expected on the interminable way down. I tried to lift my left arm, but intense pain radiated from my shoulder into my brain.

"Ahhg!" I screamed, blinded to all other thoughts than searing pain.

"Ungh," moaned something at my feet.

"I think I'd rather be dead," I said to the darkness as everything flooded back to me.

There wasn't so much as a pinprick of light. My back was arched over my pack, which probably meant everything inside that could be crushed, was. If not for the unbearable pain coming from my lower extremities, I would've questioned my spine's integrity.

"Ondo?" I asked through painful breaths. "Can you hear me?"

Another groan.

He was alive, but I couldn't say any more than that. Hell, I wasn't much more than alive. *Let's try the right arm.* Again, searing pain. The legs too. Was it possible that I had broken both my arms and my legs? Jesus. Of all the ways I thought I'd die, dying slowly from starvation or internal bleeding at the bottom of a shaft wasn't one of them. I fervently hoped Ondo was in better shape or else we were in serious trouble. He stirred and I decided to risk the pain. I smacked him with my foot. My mind momentarily glowed with the bright white light of shooting pain.

"Whaaa…" he mumbled, speech slurred. "Where eh I?"

"We fell," I said, once the inundation of pain had subsided.

"How?"

I thought about lying, but Ondo deserved the truth. I hoped he wouldn't spend our remaining moments pissed at me.

"We were dragging everyone down after us, so I cut the rope."

There was an excruciatingly long pause.

"To save them," I added.

"You wade the right call," he said, sounding strange.

What a relief. It was one thing to die, but another to feel like an asshole while doing so.

"Does it hurt to talk?" I asked.

"Little. I think why jaw is roken."

"Okay. I'll do all the talking. My jaw may be the only thing not broken. You just grunt. Can you move your right foot?"

Instead of a grunt, Ondo bellowed a loud groan.

"I'll take that as a no. We don't have to keep going."

I heard Ondo shifting. You didn't become an elite without having some serious resolve. After several more groans, we established that he was in little better shape than I was. Under normal circumstances, we would be carefully inspected by medics, medicated, and immobilized. Being the broken humans we were at the bottom of a dark shaft in hostile territory was far from ideal. When I rolled around my head, I could feel wetness saturating my hair. There was no telling how much blood I'd lost.

"I can't move to help you," I said.

Affirmative grunt.

"That means we are going to die here."

Affirmative grunt.

"I only hope the others can succeed where I failed."

Silence.

"I'm about to… pass out. If I don't wake up… I'm happy to have known you."

"We too."

All the energy left my body and for the second time, I plunged into darkness.

••••••••

My rest was filled with terror. In the nightmarish scenarios, Ondo and I were discovered and captured by torch-carrying Demented to be taken off and eaten. In the dream, we were laid on dining tables as they crowded around us with knives to cut apart their fresh prey. Thankfully before the dream reached its climax, it was once again swallowed by the merciful darkness.

••••••••

The light was faint, but I could sense it through my eyelids. It took some work since they were crusted shut, but I pried them open one at a time with some effort. When I took in my surroundings, I almost shot bolt upright, but the recent memory of pain kept me rigid on the table.

"It wasn't a dream," I said, carefully raising my head to make sure all of my body parts were accounted for.

Thank the universe I was intact! They weren't eating us, they were helping us! *Demented… helping us? How odd.* I turned my head to see Ondo, breathing peacefully. He looked like someone had worked him over from head to toe with a heavy pipe. His dark skin was made darker from the copious bruising. Over his cuts were bandages from my pack, though since hygiene wasn't a priority of the Demented, I worried most about infection.

I tried to twitch my arm to see how bad the pain still was, and surprisingly, it was tolerable. I lifted it slowly to see that it was splinted, as were my other fractures. I could smell recently-ground herbs in the poultices, flooding me with fond memories of Marie. Sadly, she had never been part of the dreams. This healing was the work of darker forces. The room wasn't too different from Marie's hut back in Evans' compound, but judging by the air's moisture and the rich smell of earth, we were still deep below the Earth's surface.

"You're awake," said Ondo, cracking an eye open.

"And you sound better."

"I was awake for some of it. They patched me up well."

"But why? These guys have stopped at nothing to kill and presumably eat us before. We were defenseless, and yet they are healing us? It makes *no* sense."

The telltale barks of the Demented echoed beyond the door, and I frantically searched the room for my bow. It was on a wooden counter built into the wall, shattered by the fall. Ondo's warhammer lay next to it, haft broken in two places. Unless he wanted to battle like a mythological god, he'd need a new weapon. Not that we were in any condition to fight anyway.

The door suddenly swung open, and four Demented lumbered in, each smelling worse than the last. Parts of their leather clothing looked fresher than others, on which I tried not to dwell. Like the others we'd come across, they were covered in ritualistic cuts and mutilations of their flesh. Instinctively, I went into a panic, reliving my capture and near assault by the twisted humans. Ondo reached out and carefully took my hand, bringing me back into the moment. I forced myself to go through the breathing exercises Grace had taught me to calm my racing heart.

After barking at each other, one with a patch over his eye grabbed a sinister-looking stinger from the table, and in one swift motion, stabbed it into my shoulder. Ondo fought his way off the table but was slammed back down by a guy covered in oozing scabs. I screamed as the pain radiated from the spot only to immediately vanish. I grew silent, perplexed until I realized that I was losing all sense of feeling from everything below my neck. *Mud raptor venom!* Unlike my time in their captivity, this venom wasn't wearing off anytime soon. I watched helplessly as they repeated the process with Ondo, making us little more than rag dolls.

The dining tables from my dreams were, in reality, makeshift gurneys. One Eye and Scabby rolled me out the wooden door into a tall-ceilinged cavern that, aside from being lit and flat-bottomed, looked no different from the tunnels we'd been traversing. When I saw what awaited us, the panic rushed back, stronger than ever, all breathing exercises forgotten. Our escorts stopped our gurneys in front of two awaiting multipedes, by the looks of things, rigged to carry us deep into the Hive. Helplessly, Ondo and I were loaded onto the backs of the pedes and strapped into place onto flat wooden saddles where some of their spikes had been filed down. I blinked away the tears, struggling to suppress outright panic. With the aid of hemolymph, the two Demented warriors hurled Ondo up to the beast's back. With a lurch, the pedes sped off down a tunnel so steep my stomach flew into my throat, leaving me with nothing but time to dwell on the terrors that awaited us.

CHAPTER 40: HEMANT

Huck was inconsolable. "We have to go after her!" he cried, desperately fighting my efforts to retain him.

Tears blurred my vision as my best friend suffered. This had to be how Huck had felt trying to hold me back when Arjun left with Kolya. However this time, I wanted nothing more than to let go. I wanted to go after them as badly as he did.

"We can't, Huck! You know that as well as I do!" I said, my heart breaking. "They were my friends too, but they just fell down a pit, man!"

"Don't you say 'were!'" he said, bawling. "There's still a chance! She could be alive!"

"No, Huck," said Omar, gripping his shoulder. "She sacrificed herself and Ondo so we could continue. Not so we'd put ourselves in further jeopardy."

"I can't leave her," he sobbed, collapsing from his knees face-first into the dirt. "We had plans. We had plans for after this was over!"

Krista came over and rubbed Huck's back. She was just as upset as he was, but putting on a brave face. "You know how tough she is, Huck. If there's any chance she's alive, she'll find her way out."

"Don't give him false hope," said Omar, ignoring her glare. "I'm not trying to be an asshole, just pragmatic."

Dane and Artim leaned against the ridged wall, not knowing what to say. Artim was crying. In the brief time they'd known each other, they'd begun to act like brother and sister. Trivia sat against a wall, her hand hadn't left her mouth since she watched them fall. As much as I wanted to console her, Huck needed me more.

"We have to get moving, Huck," I whispered, gently lifting him by his upper arm.

Huck slowly rose to his feet, wiping the snot and tears from his face, and nodded. "She's still alive," he said, turning to Omar. "Once the Queens are dead, I'm going to tear this continent apart until I find her." He pulled the ornate dao from its scabbard and gestured down the tunnel. "Even if I have to single-handedly kill every damn bug between us and them."

"That's the Huck we need right now," said Omar. "Help me kill the Queens, I'll help you search."

"Me too," said Krista, followed by everyone else in the tunnel.

••••••••

The next several days were a blur with us carefully threading our way through similar tunnel interchanges at least two to three times a day. We went left. We went right. We went up. We went down. The enemies we ran across were in groups of five or fewer and were usually more surprised by us than we were by them, making them relatively easy to dispatch before they could summon reinforcements.

Our new recruits more than pulled their weight. Artim's innate talent for determining direction was fascinating. What Dane lacked as a fighter, he made up for with his incredible hearing. On more than one occasion, the route Artim would've led us on was an active tunnel, something only Dane was able to hear. I supposed during all that time on guard duty, he had subconsciously highly honed his hearing.

We slept in short stints, none of us getting much rest. We barely knew up from down, much less day or night in that abysmal hellhole. We gave in to sleep only when we were too exhausted to travel further, circadian rhythm be damned. We tiptoed when we felt the rumbling of inverts in nearby tunnels, knowing it would take nothing for the beast to claw through the soft stone if they detected our presence. We sprinted through the tunnels when conditions allowed, hoping to gain the time we'd lost. Not only did we have our food-imposed deadline, but Ariadne wasn't far from anyone's mind.

"We're going up," said Artim on what we figured was the fourth or fifth day in the tunnels. "It's been climbing for the last hour."

"Why didn't you say something?" I asked.

"I thought it might go back down, but I'm starting to doubt it."

"Is that a problem?" Huck asked.

"Not if we want to see the surface," said Dane.

"It would be good to verify our bearings," said Trivia. "With any luck, maybe we can figure out how far we've come."

We continued up the tunnel until the smooth surface began to make the inclining passage more treacherous. Dane could hear the faint vibrations of nearby enemies, further slowing our pace as we pressed on cautiously. Eventually, I could see traces of light ahead, but the loud scratching and foul stench reigned any excitement the glow may have provoked. Intuition told me that we were coming up on a larger group of hostiles than we'd faced so far in the underground network. Omar motioned to crouch, and we steadily trundled forward until we could evaluate the looming threat.

"What in the fresh hell…?" Omar whispered.

The tunnel's mouth emerged a few meters above the floor of a sprawling, steep-walled chamber. As I peered over the edge, a sweeping range of emotions flooded my mind. Recessed into the floor were numerous pits in which non-Demented humans were crawling over each other like animals. In each, the people were barely clothed in scant strips of fabric as they climbed through their own filth, pleading and screaming with their captors in languages or gibberish I didn't understand. Between the pits roamed Demented guards armed with spears, and more alarmingly, bone arachnids and hook beetles. Trivia stifled a squeal of terror and disgust. A human farm—the most detestable thing I could imagine.

Everything clicked into place. That's why the inverts could sustain such a large population. Sure, they were killing and eating the participants in the Release Day heats, but the survivors must have been brought here and forced into this sick breeding program. That's why the Demented could live on the surface unmolested. *The twisted humans are teaming up with the bloody inverts!* I couldn't take my eyes off the vile scene below where a guard jerked a woman from the nearest pit by her hair and dragged her off—her enslaved companions beaten mercilessly for trying to help.

My throat filled with bile. Krista quietly retched into the dirt, spitting the last bit with barely restrained fury. Omar was gripping his naginata so fiercely, I thought he'd break the bladed weapon in half. We crept back from the opening just enough to reassess our approach.

"I'll kill them all," I said, face flushing with raw, unbridled anger. "And if Arjun's down there, I'll rip them apart with my bare hands."

"We have to keep our heads," said Huck, driving his fist into the ground in frustration. "When the hell did they start working together?"

"How are we going to detonate the bomb now?" asked Krista, wiping her mouth on her sleeve. "We're still pretty far from our target, but what if there are more of these... *breeding grounds* in the Hive itself? We can't kill a bunch of innocent people."

"We'd be putting them out of their misery," mumbled Omar, face cold and hard, ready to kill. "This is no way for anyone to live."

I'd been in such a big hurry to use the weapon against the inverts that I hadn't given any thought to collateral damage. Our "clear" objective was growing murkier by the minute.

"Let's get to the Hive proper," I said. "With more insight, we can determine the next step."

"We need to reach the surface," said Trivia. "If we know where we are, maybe we can send help."

"Are we not going to do anything to help these people now?" asked Dane, pleadingly. "Some of them wear the pattern of Zephyr's Hope. We can't leave them!"

"We have no choice," said Huck, drops falling from his eyes onto the tunnel floor. "We could fight small groups, but there must be thirty Demented down there and half as many inverts. If we could isolate them, maybe, but that's not an option. I'm sorry, Dane, but the mission must come first. I don't like it any more than you."

We made our way back down the tunnel, recalling a split where another tunnel had also risen in elevation. With any luck, it would lead us to the surface. When we'd nearly reached the intersection, a scream reverberated down the shaft—not one of terror, but of rage. Instantly, my worst fears were realized.

"Where's Dane?!" I said, panicking.

Without responding, Omar sprinted back up the incline, diving down onto his belly and sliding to the end. I followed suit and watched helplessly as Dane slayed one Demented after another with his bill. Anger may have proved a comparable ally to training, but he didn't stand a chance once the inverts came to the guards' aid. An eight spun its saw-toothed carapace into him before he knew what was coming. The noble knight fell in two halves before disappearing among a cluster of monsters.

Artim whimpered. He'd not only lost a close friend but watched him brutally murdered in front of his eyes. From experience, I knew that wasn't something you forget. Trivia consoled him. We were so preoccupied and distraught that we didn't hear our attackers until it was too late. The last thing I saw was the butt of a spear flying at my face.

•••••••

"Hemant! Wake up you bastard!" shouted Omar.

Judging by his face, he'd put up more of a fight than I'd been able to. I shook off the dreariness and examined the bamboo cage in which I was imprisoned. *There's some irony. Our journey began in the Bambu restaurant, and it might end in a bamboo cage.*

"Thank the universe," said Huck. "We've been yelling for over an hour!"

"Wait, where is Trivia? And Artim and Krista?" I said, searching for any sign of their existence in the cavern which held only our cage.

"They separated us while we were unconscious," said Huck, a rivulet of dried blood running down from a gash above his eye.

"We have to do something!" I shouted, tugging at my bonds fastened to the base of the bars behind my back.

"It's no use," said Omar. "I fought the guards while they tied them, so they lashed us down extra tight. That's the last thing I remember."

Having insight into what the Demented did for entertainment, I wasn't about to let Trivia fall victim to their scourge. The bulk of the backup weapon hidden under my leg drew my attention.

"Huck, can you reach my dagger with your boot?" I asked. "They must have missed it."

"I'll try," he said.

Stretching as far from the bars as his arms would allow, he began kicking at my leg.

"Sorry," he kept saying.

"I don't give a damn how bad it hurts if you get that dagger into my hands."

He had it out and on the floor of the cage in a moment and was struggling to get it into my hands.

"Fling it through the air," I was suggesting when six guards walked in.

I quickly concealed the exposed weapon with my leg. Three guards entered the cage, while the other three loosened our bonds. I desperately wanted to take advantage of the opportunity, but the Demented were smarter than I'd given them credit for. They'd tied a pair of bonds. One to the cage and the other between our wrists. The three inside hoisted us up with strength only attained by invert hemolymph, an addiction that eventually drove them mad.

I glanced forlornly at the dagger left behind that may have been our only chance at escape. For the first time since I'd awoken, I realized I no longer had the nuclear weapon.

"Where's the bomb?" I said, panicking.

"We don't know," said Huck, groaning at his rough handling.

The men led us out of the previous space and into a larger chamber to an awaiting cart harnessed to a bunch of polies. Thankfully, Trivia, Artim, and Krista were already loaded and waiting for us, unmolested as best as I could tell. *Thank god!* I thought to a flood of relief. Even our gear was strapped into the rudimentary vehicle.

"This isn't what I expected," said Omar. "I expected our final stop to be those pits."

"I wouldn't rule it out yet. You forget that we are on the Hive's Most Wanted list," said Huck. "I'm pretty sure the Queens have some extra special hell for us."

As if to punctuate his statement, three eights bustled in the room. Our guards dragged us to a nearby set of rusted rings chained to the floor, binding each of us to one.

"I don't like this at all," I said.

I couldn't feel more vulnerable—more exposed. The eights crawled towards us, their needle-sharp legs clicking on the carved ground. I clenched my eyes shut. I couldn't watch those fangs disappear into my chest. I anxiously awaited the death blow, but an attack never came. Instead, a strange tickling sensation overwhelmed my body and opened my eyes.

I should've kept them closed. The eights were coating us with musky threads from tiny orifices in their backsides. The sticky webbing tickled, but dried iron hard. By the time I was coated and the beast had moved on to Artim, I was cocooned with only my head exposed. When the deed was finished, it was the eights, not our guards, who moved us to the wagon with uncharacteristic delicacy. *Add being handled by an eight to my growing list of phobias.*

"I guess the Queens' precious prey is not to be harmed," said Omar, as he was laid in the wagon next to our bomb. "They must want us alive when they greet us with rainbows and butterflies."

"Leave it to you to be a smart-ass in a situation like this," I said. "You okay, Triv?"

"Never better," answered Trivia.

"Where are they taking us?" asked Artim in a voice about to crack.

"To the Queens, I imagine," said Huck. "We are heading to the exact spot we've been trying to reach for months, though bound, unarmed, and in their possession wasn't part of the plan."

"Am I going to die like Dane?" he asked. "I'm old enough. Please tell me the truth."

After a long pause, Huck spoke. "That's a very real possibility."

CHAPTER 41: ZEPHYR

2112

"Everyone ready to go?" Uncle Alex asked, struggling to pull the heavy pack onto his shoulders.

I helped get him situated, noticing his already heavy breathing. It wasn't too hot, but sweat dotted his dark forehead, and his gray hair practically glowed in the sunlight. I looked longly at the cabin where I'd spent my entire life. It was quite different from the aged picture on the mantle, now spotted with the hodgepodge of repairs done by less than experienced hands of those who'd come before me. As much as I'd miss it, we were starting a new chapter, a chapter that would give us a chance at a future.

"You ready, little sprite?" Mom asked, straitening my shirt like I was still a child as she fought tears.

"I *can* take care of myself, you know," I said, chiding her. "You know I can outperform you and Dad both. *And* do it with a radio in my pack."

I gave Uncle Alex a side-eye. I was still bitter about leaving it behind, but I knew he was right. Even if no one besides my family listened, it was my outlet, my way of contributing positivity to the universe. I supposed talking to the wall would be as effective, but using the radio made it feel real.

"We're well aware that you are in better shape than us, but I don't want the extra weight slowing you down," said Dad, checking his bootlaces for the third time in the last few minutes. "This will be a perilous journey. Regardless of what you think, stay close. You know how dangerous the inverts are."

"I've grown up with them, Dad. I've killed three myself," I said, gesturing to where I'd scratched the tally on my stock.

"But we've always had the safety of the cabin to fall back to," said Uncle Alex. "The trees Mr. Winston planted are the only explanation for our survival. That explains your bag's odor. I used all the oil I harvested to coat them. Keep your bag near you at all times, and we might stand a chance."

"So that's the smell," I said, jokingly pinching my nose.

"Do you have a round chambered, Zeph?" asked Mom.

I gave her my trademark look.

"Just checking," she said. "You can't blame a mother for worrying."

I'd been holding a rifle as long as I'd been reading, always sleeping with a loaded .30-30 in arm's reach. I could group three rounds at 100 meters with iron sights while moving. That's what you do when you're raised under the threat of hostiles. I'd never known a life without the Arthropods. Not even Uncle Alex really did. He was a kid when they'd arrived and had come out to the cabin shortly after. I never knew his dad, Darren, or my grandparents, Stepan and Kitty, but the adults showered me with stories every night until I fell asleep on the bear rug that covered the floor in front of the fireplace.

In a way, I'd been raised by three parents, their varied cultural backgrounds made me as much of a hodgepodge as the cabin I was so reluctant to leave. Dad had even taught me to speak Spanish.

Mom could understand a little, but Uncle Alex didn't see the point. I loved the way it flitted off my tongue. With only Dad and me speaking it well, it felt like a secret code. I always came to Dad with my problems. We would chat for hours knowing the others couldn't understand. I knew full well he would always share our conversations with Mom afterward and sometimes with Uncle Alex, but for that moment, it was *our* secret. Sometimes I even spoke Spanish on the radio, hoping another language would bring responses.

Soon things would be different, safer. Today, we were setting out for Pod Pittsburgh, the bunker city for our corner of the world. For the first time, I'd be around others. That made me more nervous than some overgrown alien bugs. Transitioning from over two decades of nature-bound isolation to a densely-populated underground pod would do that to anyone. Though excited about the change, nightmares of being buried alive plagued my rest, waking me up in a cold sweat. Underground seemed more like a prison than a haven, but I reminded myself that it was only temporary. We couldn't let the inverts have the best part of Earth. Mom and Dad held hands as they soaked in the last moments at the cabin, Mom's fair fingers intertwined with his bronze ones. Each of us was happier outdoors than in, making this sacrifice so that humanity could live on. I made up my mind. If living underground was what we had to do, I would do it with my head held high.

I'd have plenty of time to acclimate to the idea over the 500-kilometer trip. We'd planned our route after long nights of staring at Mr. Winston's old topographical maps. The others let me have input, though my idea about boating across Erie was turned down for fear of exposure. The terrain, surely changed from the outdated map, should still only take a week of hiking to traverse. I kept telling myself that it would be no different from hunting, only longer. I'd never spent a night outside of the cabin. Despite my pleas, I hadn't even been allowed to sleep in the treehouse I'd built between the cabin and the coop when I was a teenager. We'd be "roughing it," as Uncle Alex was fond of saying. No tents, just a brown, dry-rotted tarp. Hopefully, it would be enough to keep some rain off our bedrolls. Our packs were jammed with as much food as they could hold, maybe enough food for two weeks if we stretched it. Ammo was a different story. We each had three or four boxes, some not even full, but it was everything we had. My parents and Uncle Alex each had a long gun and pistol. They only let me carry my rifle.

It was hot enough that we'd need to find plenty of fresh water and had plotted our route accordingly. I had unshared concerns about the weight of my pack even without the radio, but as we ran out of food, my load would get lighter. I refused to show weakness. If Uncle Alex could make the trip in his seventies, I could do it in my twenties. He wanted to stick to the woods, fearing open land would reveal us to the inverts and open roads to any bandits that may have survived this long. I'd only seen one raider in my life. The woman stumbled into our camp, begging for food. Something about her wasn't right. Mom wanted to turn her away, but Dad caved. When he held out his hand with a palm full of potatoes, she jumped him, like she wanted to bite him more than the potatoes! Mom said I was imagining things, but Uncle Alex ended it. Shot her with his revolver. We left her body in the ravine a few hills over for the inverts. That night I spoke through sobs about how terrible it felt to see the end of another human's life, even a threatening one.

My childhood wasn't exactly *Little House on the Prairie*, Mrs. Dorothy's favorite story when she was a little girl. I lost count of how many times I read its crumbling pages in my treehouse. I felt a connection to the woman every time my thumb brushed the graphite of her cursive notations in the margins.

"We're losing daylight," Dad said, tussling my short hair.

I would always be his little girl, no matter how old or independent I became.

"Oh, Gabe, I don't know if I can do this," said Mom, staring at the cabin like Uncle Alex.

"Mom, when I'm your age, I hope to have half of your strength. And you're leaving behind a lifeless shell. All the warmth of our home is coming with you," I said, hugging her tightly.

"I love you, my daughter," she said, holding my cheek in her hand, wiping the single tear rolling down. "And I wish I had half of your optimism right now."

I laughed, stroking her beautiful long hair. "I love you too."

I'd never cared to have hair as long as Mom's, whose chestnut locks hung down below her shoulders when it wasn't bound in a bun. I had Uncle Alex cut mine using a mixing bowl as a guide. Mom always cringed. She said my hair was too beautiful to be so short. Hair got in the way. So did skirts like mom preferred, though she claimed to have killed plenty of bandits while wearing one. She made all of our clothes, but I wore overalls and a shirt like Dad and Uncle Alex. Didn't see a good reason not to.

"Well, they're not going to keep the door open forever," said Dad.

Uncle Alex nodded, and after a brief pause at the graves, we departed. With a pack on my back and a rifle in my hands, we took our first tentative steps off the property. It started like any other trip, minus the return. The warm day and heavy pack had my back sweating long before my brow, but the cool of the woods made it a pleasant hike. I kept my mind sharp by naming the trees. Any bumpkin could identify a pine, oak, or maple, but I could find the basswood, hackberry, and hornbeam. The real benefit came from identifying wild food sources. I'd been gaming and gathering since I could walk, and aside from an almost catastrophic accident when I almost ate a destroying angel, I'd become quite adept. Between rabbit, juneberries, and oyster mushrooms, I was confident we'd reach the pod with food to spare. Aside from the pine needles that made footing on rocks treacherous, the passage wasn't difficult. I basked in the wind and sun, knowing the day was coming when I couldn't. Just before lunch, Dad froze in his tracks.

"What is it, Gabe?" whispered Mom, a look of fear shadowing her face.

He slowly shouldered the pump shotgun, turning to face the woods behind us. *Something's following us.* We stood, waiting. I felt my hands grow cold and gripped my rifle all the tighter. A snapping branch! My eyes frantically searched for any sign of movement, not just ahead, but from the sides as well. The sneaky bastards liked to ambush. Dad saw something I didn't and fired. Even expecting the noise, I jumped. Something about this trip had my nerves raw. A deathly screech came from the woods as a multipede rushed towards us, carapace glistening with its black blood in the morning sun. He got off a second and third round, planting three slugs in the creature's forehead without flinching. The pede ground into the dirt meters ahead of his feet. We waited silently for over a minute before someone spoke.

"That was a close—" Uncle Alex started.

The forest filled with the sounds of crunching feet rapidly converging on our position. As practiced, we backed up against each other and fought off the attacking inverts. Surrounded, I fired as many shots as I had to, matching the fire rate and reload speeds of the adults. I took down two young hooks before a chomper tried to take my head. Dazed by the chemical essence on my pack, the split wing retreated, and I dropped it with my rifle. A rifle, mind you! Normally anything other than shotguns was impractical for the split wings. Finally, the firing ceased and Mom said the first "Clear," echoed by myself and the others.

"You ever seen anything like that, Nat?" Gabe asked, catching his breath as he gazed at the pile of dead inverts.

She shook her head. Sweaty strands of hair clung to her freckled face.

"Me either," said Uncle Alex. "And I've been in these woods a long time."

"Something drew them," I said. "The more I fired, the more came."

"Zeph's right," said Uncle Alex. "Maybe we've never seen it like that because their local population was too low."

"So what do we do? Not shoot?" asked Gabe, sarcastically.

"We have no other way to defend ourselves. We have no choice but to shoot," said Uncle Alex. "Just keep in mind, shooting will have consequences. Let's avoid that, shall we?"

"*Por Dios,*" muttered Gabe.

We nodded. No one questioned Uncle Alex's wisdom. He'd seen us through all these years in the woods, practically raising my mom and saving my dad. If anyone knew survival, it was him. We lingered a few minutes longer to make sure there weren't more surprises, then moved out as fast as our feet would carry us.

•••••••

The week of traveling was more of the same. We'd use every bit of our abilities to avoid the Arthropods, but when they showed up, we had no choice but to shoot. If I had any doubts about the need to move underground, they were gone. By the morning we expected to arrive at Pod Pittsburgh, we were nearly down to the ammo in our magazines. It was a pointless thought, but I couldn't help but wonder if crossing Lake Erie would've been the safer choice. The circuitous trip had taken far longer to avoid the cities and open terrain, but now that we were closing in on Pittsburgh, the city was the only path forward. Surely it wasn't as bad as Uncle Alex feared. Since my Grandfather Stepan's death, he'd been adamant that he'd never set foot in another city, save for this one, as long as he lived.

The eleven-day trip challenged even my optimism. We'd survived, but with every attack, I knew one slip-up could have proven fatal. The survival skills I was so proud of hadn't kept my belly full. I had imagined we'd hop from one patch of food to the next, but we kept a steady pace, never deviating far from the route to forage anything that wasn't next to the path. We'd nearly exhausted the food in our packs by the time we reached Pittsburgh's outskirts. All signs of wild food vanished, likely picked over by those waiting to enter the pod.

"What is it?" Dad asked Uncle Alex as he carefully lowered himself to a concrete slab.

"Nothing," he said, shrugging it off.

It was obvious he was reaching his physical limitations.

"Come on, Uncle Alex," I said, pulling him up after a moment of rest. "Are you going to let Dad show you up?"

He laughed. "Your Dad's a lot younger than I am."

"Pish posh," I said. "Age is only in the mind."

He shook his head laughing, rising to his feet with my help. "Maybe I've got a little something left in these old bones."

For hours, we pressed on through what had been houses—overgrown, collapsed, and worse—eerily preserved like its inhabitants had only left the day before. When Mom started crying at the sight, so did I.

"Whoa," I said, reaching a multi-story pile of rubble.

That crumbling edifice had been a towering building in its past life, now no more than a web of stone and steel. Before our trip, the largest construction I'd ever seen had been our single-family log cabin.

"This is nothing," said Uncle Alex. "Look over there."

I turned and saw the remains of several looming towers, now broken, menacing jagged fingers reaching to scratch the sky.

"They used to be twice that tall, at least," he added.

"Have you seen them?" Dad asked.

Uncle Alex shook his head. "Maybe, but I would've been too little. My mother, Patricia, had to come here sometimes for work. I remember my father talking about it."

Mom rested her hand on his. For a moment, I could almost see six-year-old Alex staring wide-eyed at the spanning city from a train window. I wondered what life would've been like in such a sprawling metropolis, so different from the forest I grew up in. With the cityscape bringing up memories, Uncle Alex began to speak of devices and foods that sounded as fanciful to me as Mr. Winston's old Asimov books.

I scanned the horizon for other interesting buildings as Dad and Uncle Alex unfolded the moth-eaten paper map. We had no idea exactly which direction to go, only that the pod was within the city's border. The problem was that it included nearly 200 square kilometers according to the atlas. *Surely, there are signs.*

"Where do we go from here?" asked Mom, fighting exhaustion.

"Puedo ayudarte con eso," said an armed man with a complexion like my dad's, then repeating the sentiment in English, "I can help you with that."

As much as I hoped the stranger could help, his toothy grin made my insides knot.

CHAPTER 42: HUCK

Time immobilized in the cart's bed drifted by as slowly as its incessantly creaking wheels. Unable to so much as flinch, I passed the ride staring at the high ceiling that the torchlight did well to reach or dozing off until awakened by the next violent jolt of the wheels. Occasionally, I caught sight of other Arthropods making use of the tunnel, ignoring the foreigners in their midst, dismissing us as no longer a threat. *It's like a slap to the face.* Every time we'd speak, one of the cart's Demented drivers would smack us with the same whip used to urge on the polies. Within an hour, we'd given up on any hope of conversation. If there was any benefit to our captivity, it was that the wooden vehicle's steady pace and direct route would have us to the Hive in mere days.

After a while of being trapped in the same position, the miserably bumpy ride had my muscles cramping so strongly that they challenged the webbing's integrity. My over-expanded bladder lingered on the cusp of exploding. When I couldn't hold it any longer, I gave in to the urge and felt the blessed relief as I flooded the floorboards with urine. Between the horrendous smell of the inverts and Demented, no one would notice a little pee. It was a wonder we weren't gagging our way to the Queens. After losing

Ariadne, my emotions were numb, distant. Resignation haunted my thoughts. Only dredging up my anger over the loss of Ariadne kept me focused on the task ahead. How we were going to accomplish it in our current state was beyond me.

After ages, we came to a jerking stop, a puff of dust nearly choking me. The Demented barked at one another, and we were unloaded haphazardly onto the ground, knocking the wind from my lungs. Surprisingly, we were rolled onto smelly, hay-filled pads. I thought our guards might not be completely blind to our comfort, but realized their purpose was to keep the noise of our hard cocoons to a minimum. Our captors built a little fire around which they ate jerky of questionable origins and shared a canteen. Judging by the black ooze dribbling down their chins, there was no question as to the vessel's contents. They were making haunting grunts of laughter, so distracted that when we spoke, no one bothered to smack us with anything.

"After all this time, tell me it hasn't only been one day," said Hemant.

"They don't get as tired as us," I said, barely invested in the conversation. "Not running on hemolymph."

"I'm not running on anything," said Omar. "I'm so hungry, I'm tempted to eat whatever they are."

"For all we know, that's human jerky," said Trivia.

"There goes my appetite," he responded.

"Do they really eat… humans?" asked Artim.

Trivia let out a sigh. Sometimes we forgot how young our companion was. "I'm afraid so. The Demented eat just about anything."

"What's hemolymph?"

"The blood of the dark ones," I said. "It's like a drug, clouding their minds and bringing out their primal instincts. They do things no person in their right mind would do. They all need to die."

Omar smirked as Hemant sighed. I didn't care. After what I'd lost, I would've blown the bomb with no regard for the inverts, the Demented, or even myself.

"There's a level of cooperation between the Demented and the Arthropods we've never seen before," added Trivia. "I suspect the hemolymph has something to do with that."

"Are you suggesting mind control?" asked Krista.

Trivia shrugged as much as she could in the hardened web cocoon. "At this point, what I know seems… useless. The deeper we go into the Hive, the less we understand about our enemies."

"We'll know more about them when we're dropped at their leaders' feet," said Omar. "Nice, stinky presents soaked in our own waste. We're only missing a pretty bow."

"Could we activate the bomb before our arrival?" asked Artim. "I saw it in the wagon."

"Not unless we can escape these personal prisons," said Hemant.

I tuned out the rest of their conversation. I couldn't do anything but think of Ariadne's mangled corpse lying at the bottom of a shaft, waiting to be found and devoured by inverts. In my heart, I wanted to believe she was alive, but my mind doubted it. *I will avenge you, Ariadne. I promise.*

As the campfire burned down, one of the Demented checked our webs with a swift kick to each of our sides. Still hard as rock. The only effect his kick had was to make me wobble back and forth slightly. With muscles asleep from the long confinement, I'm not sure how much I would've felt his kick even without the webbing.

Nestling down to sleep in an active Arthropod tunnel with Demented and polies to one side and eights to the other was wrong in so many ways. When I finally drifted off to sleep, my troubled dreams kept me from getting much rest, my mind playing the scene of Ariadne's face as she fell over and over again.

•••••••••

I awoke before anyone else and stretched my arms out. *Wait! How did I do that?* I blinked a few times, trying to dispel the darkness, but was surrounded by pitch blackness. I could move my arms freely, but still felt the crunch of the webbing encasing my shoulders and legs. I quietly flexed my shoulders until I heard the strands cracking and sloughed off the remaining portion. I repeated the process with my legs. My muscles tingled painfully as the feeling returned. I felt disgusting in my filth, but I was free. *What do I do?* I was blind, surrounded by enemies, and my friends were still trapped as far as I knew.

Destiny had provided the unexpected opportunity, but I was perplexed at how to take advantage of it. The second I tried to sneak past either the guards or the inverts, I was dead. As it was, I was hoping the eights weren't already watching my every move. *Arachnids sleep right?* In the quiet, I heard subtle scraping sounds reminding me of stray pod dogs' twitching legs as they dreamed. I felt a slight smile imagining the giant spiders making half-audible barking sounds in their sleep. The smile vanished when I wondered what they dreamed about.

I racked my brain, desperate for any action that would benefit my friends before I finally pieced together an idea. I remembered where the rope was located in the wagon and as quietly as possible, made my way to the rear and felt around for it. My fingers drifted over the cool metal casing of the bomb. I could easily activate it here, but there was little point. I'd kill tons of inverts and Demented, civilians and friends and yet wouldn't touch the Queens. Within a few months, their population would return to its previous numbers. Eventually, my hand landed on a dagger. I quietly pulled it between the wooden supports of the cage-like wagon and slid it into the sheath still attached to my leg. Replacing my hand, I moved my hand until my fingers closed on a strand of the rope. *Jackpot!* I pulled it slowly out between the bars. When I had it almost completely out, it snagged on something that fell with a *plunk*. I froze. It probably wasn't enough to wake any human, but I could almost feel an eight breathing down my neck. I waited for an eternity before the fear subsided, and I finished the job.

With the rope and the dagger, I proceeded with my little plan. I dropped to my knees and crawled under the wagon, feeling my way along its frame. Between the front and rear axle was a support, no more than ten centimeters wide with clearance a little more than double that between it and the bottom of the wagon. It was going to be a tight fit and a miserable ride. I carefully hoisted myself up into place, trying desperately not to make a sound. When I was comfortable (using the word very loosely), I slowly threaded the rope around and around my body over and over, painstakingly lashing myself into place. With so little space, I would have to keep my head turned to the side. I was going to have one hell of a neck cramp when this was over. As I was tying the knot, I heard the first grunts of stirring Demented.

With what sounded like flint scraping metal, a guard reignited the fire going as a second one inspected the prisoners. I braced myself. This was the moment they'd notice my empty shroud and panic. I fervently hoped they would be too stupid to check under the wagon. If I was too much of a pain in their ass, protected or not, they wouldn't hesitate to kill me. I heard the panicked bark. Recognizable language or not, I could hear despair in the grunt. The others jumped up and began running around the darkened campsite, searching frantically for any sign of my trail. The polies restlessly jerked against the wagon in the chaos. The eights were up and scurrying to and fro, hunting me.

"What's going on?" shouted Artim, his young voice failing to mask his fear.

"Huck's gone!" said Krista.

"What?" said Hemant. "Wait! I'm loose!"

"Me too!" said Trivia. "Our urine dissolved the web! Everybody, tear off your webbing!"

Commotion raged beyond the wagon, but I could see nothing. My companions were grunting, hurriedly shedding their prisons before the attention of our captors returned. It was in vain. With the frantic barking of a Demented warrior, warning the others of their prey's escape, there was a scuffle and then all was quiet. I clenched my eyes shut, doing little to stop the tears. *Oh, god. If they died because of me...*

"Put me down, you bastards!" said Krista. "Omar, wake up!"

I breathed a sigh of relief. If anyone was dead, she'd be screaming about it.

"What did you assholes do with Huck?!" she said before I heard a thunk.

There were no human voices after that. As each of my unconscious friends was loaded into the wagon, the space between my perch and the wagon's bottom narrowed. By the time it was fully loaded, I couldn't manage a full breath. They hadn't bothered to reweb my friends, so I assumed everyone above was simply bound. *If only the slats in the wagon's bottom were a smidge wider!*

The angry grunts of the Demented guards told me that they were arguing about my getaway. I knew they'd given up the hunt when they eventually remounted the driver's bench and with a lurch, the wagon began pulling forward once more. I wasn't sure how active the tunnel had been while I'd slept, but I imagined that they'd conclude that I wouldn't stand a chance alone in a dark, sprawling, invert-infested tunnel. Judging by their agitated barks, the escape had put them in a poor mood.

Unlike the ride in the wagon's bed, every bump was pure agony riding the beam underneath. *Forget a neck cramp, I'll have a broken rib after this.* We bounded along at a decent speed, the polies' tiny legs churning faster than a human could walk, possibly even run. I'd seen pictures of old wagons, pulled by animals so large that I couldn't fathom standing next to one. Since the Arthropod's arrival, any animal of size had been hunted to extinction. Even after regaining the surface, Earth would have to rebalance with all of the gaps in the food chain. Life would figure that out, my job was to give it a chance. How I was going to do that tied to the bottom?

As opposed to the previous day, my choices were to stare at the wall instead of the ceiling and instead of seeing the tops of the passing inverts, I saw their legs. Thankfully, the sides of the wagon reached low enough to shroud my hiding place, otherwise, a random polie might have revealed my existence. I nodded off a few times, but it was impossible to rest. Eventually, Hemant stirred above me. He must not have been the first one awake.

"You think they killed him?" he whispered.

"Doubt it," said Omar.

It was a struggle to listen to their conversation between the thundering of the wheels and their soft speech.

"How could he escape?" asked Trivia.

Initially, there was no response. I could almost see Omar shrugging. "Maybe he ran off to search for his girlfriend."

"No," said Krista groggily. "He's crazy about her, but he wouldn't abandon the mission for her. Not yet."

There was a loud snap followed by a moan from Krista. The guards had noticed their conversation and smacked her with their whip. Omar stirred, but thinking better of it remained still. I desperately wanted to tell them where I was, to prod them with my finger, but any hint that I was underneath the wagon could reveal the only hand we had to play. I wasn't sure how being down here would help, but it was better than nothing. I tried to devise a plan, but I knew nothing of the situation we were headed into. I did resolve one thing. If I thought we were close enough to the Queens, my friends safe or not, I would detonate the weapon.

CHAPTER 43: ARIADNE

I had no way to discern the passage of time during my paralyzed captivity on the back of the multipede, thundering along in the darkness with a smooth cadence at speeds matching the tram in Bandung. The pedes flew up inclines and dove down cliffs, often curving so hard I thought I'd sling off into the wall. My heart pounded against my ribs as my mind swirled with fear and uncertainty. At this rate, we'd be in front of the Queens in less than two days but in no condition to fight. I wish I'd known how long it'd take for their paralytic to wear off. Since our drivers were so focused on the tunnel ahead, if it did, I could untie myself, roll off, and escape. *No.* Ondo and I were in rough shape. We weren't up too high, two meters at most, but a fall from even this height at speed would reinjure us, maybe put us permanently out of commission.

It's not like I could see anyway in the all-engulfing darkness. I could only assume that the Demented drivers were either completely blind and letting the multipedes lead them or the hemolymph had granted them enhanced senses to observe their surroundings. *Have the Arthropods and Demented always collaborated, or is this a recent development?* I missed Marie's experience or Arjun's intelligence, the loss of both filling me with anguish. Marie was gone, but if fate had a conscience, it would reunite us with Arjun. The Demented's consumption of hemolymph benefited their strength, healing, pleasure, and resolve, but at the cost of their sanity. The questions now were: Does it have more side effects we're unaware of? Did consuming the viscous fluid bond them to the inverts? Would I ever know the answers?

Turning to the pede at my side, I checked on Ondo, wincing as each bump caused him pain through the paralytic. I wanted to spend more time developing an escape plan for us, but thought and focus were difficult to maintain. We were paralyzed, moving at gut-wrenching speeds, riding a murderous creature, flying towards the most dangerous place on Earth. Wherever Huck and the others were, I hoped they were fairing better than us. If Ondo and I were a lost cause, maybe it'd be better if he thought us dead. Then he wouldn't hesitate to blow the Hive and their damn hierarchy to hell where they belonged.

Another jerk shocked me to awareness as my pede powered up another incline just shy of vertical, jostling my stomach hard enough to relocate it. The beastly inverts operated on another level, their abilities in many ways superior to ours. Under any other circumstances, the alien species would prove fascinating, but when they threatened my species with extinction, the naturalist in me was replaced by the warrior, and right now—the warrior was pissed and biding her time until she could do something about it.

At the edge of my vision, I could make out faint outlines of the pede's spikes protruding from the beast's carapace below. Wherever we were heading, the tunnel was growing brighter by the second. What began as a glow dimmer than a candle transitioned into blazing orange sunlight as we flew out of the tunnel and onto a rocky outcropping, temporarily blinding me. With only the minimal movement of my head afforded by the paralytic, I couldn't observe my surroundings aside from the fact that we were on the ledge of a reddish, sandstone cliff illuminated by the setting sun as it fell towards the horizon. *Cliffs here? The Outback is supposed to be flat!* Two Demented untied me and lowered me down to the ground as I wrestled with my confusion. Annoyingly, they never once changed my orientation, keeping me ignorant of my surroundings. Within seconds, Ondo was on the ground next to me.

"Where are we?" he whispered.

"Other than on a high rocky outcropping where the terrain should be flat, I have no idea. The only significant mountains on the continent are on the opposite side from where we landed."

"We were moving insanely fast, but we can't have gotten that far."

A sharp kick to my side by One Eye silenced me. I felt nothing other than the jolt through my body, but I would have a painful bruise when I regained feeling in my extremities, something our guard undoubtedly knew. *This is* not *how this mission is supposed to be going!* I thought, fighting back tears of anger, directed at myself more than anyone. We were supposed to be together, fighting our way through the Outback to reach the Queens and blow them back to space where they come from. God, I hope Huck is having more luck than we are.

A soft whoomping sound came from above my head, pulling me from my self-pity, but I couldn't determine its origin. A crunch of loose gravel and the sky filled with eye-burning red dust announced the arrival of a new creature. Needles pricked the end of my fingers, causing me to twitch my arm. *Sensation is returning!* I would've told Ondo, but I was hoisted up by my captors and for the first time saw the origin of the noise. Four powder moths patiently waited on the cliff edge.

"Oh, hell no," boomed Ondo, for which he received a club to the gut, which may not have hurt but knocked the wind out of him nonetheless.

What is it with big guys and heights? I wondered, but no sooner had the thought than I realized I was about to fly on the back of a giant bug. All of a sudden, my stomach shot into my throat. *Okay, I get it.* It had been a daunting enough experience to fly in a plane but on an animal?! The guards threw me on the back of one of the dusters, this time on my stomach. The creature's fur was incredibly soft but had a stomach-churning, pungent, musky odor. Two of the four Demented guards jumped back on the multipedes and vanished into the tunnels while One Eye and Scabby lashed Ondo and me down on the dusters, tying our arms and legs with ropes draped around the inverts' bodies.

With mobility slowly returning to my neck, I propped my chin up on the duster's flat back between its wings to look at the horizon. With any luck, I could figure out where we were in relation to the Hive. What the waning sunlight revealed took my breath away as surely as if I'd been clubbed in the stomach. *Holy hell!* The landscape was dramatically different from any old topographical map we'd set eyes on—far more than the planet's natural tectonic activity could explain. The horizon was inundated with monstrously large red mounds towering up to the heavens, composed of the same material as the one on which we were perched. *Each mound rivals Pod Horizonte in size!* In the direction we were pointing, the impossibly big towers grew taller and taller until they vanished beyond the curvature of the Earth.

And the sky… The sky was dark with Arthropods, swirling and circling above in their ominous ballet. At lower altitudes, the creatures shot in and out of the mounds, always returning with something dangling in their clutches, a never-ending convoy of death. At higher altitudes, the inverts swarmed in a massive orbit of a distant, unseen object—the Arthropod Hive. Just the thought sent icy shivers rocketing down my spine. Fear nearly overwhelmed my senses as I stared at the daunting sky. We weren't remotely ready to fight our way through this. No one could be. As much as I wanted to be optimistic for Huck, his chances of making it through the inverts' defenses were as slim as the fine hairs covering the powder moth under me. I was on the verge of tears when without warning, our mounted escorts shouted a command, and the four dusters sprang from the cliff edge and into a steep, nausea-inducing dive.

We plummeted towards the earth where a few native trees still scattered the Australian Territory's original landscape. The tower flew past beneath me in such a blur that I thought I was going to become a permanent part of the terrain. At the last moment, the duster's wing snapped open and we hurtled up to a far more reasonable altitude. I couldn't remember the last time I'd eaten but had anything been in my stomach, I would've retched it up. I shot a glance at Ondo who was doing just that, sending bile down the opposite side of the duster from me. The situation was so bizarre that I couldn't help but laugh, my mind at a loss for how to respond.

"What could possibly be amusing?" he yelled over the howling wind.

"I think I'm going crazy," I yelled back. "Everything is so messed up, I couldn't help but laugh at our predicament."

Ondo cracked a smile, shaking his head. "You're right about that. I'm sure it could get worse, but I'm not sure how. I mean… look at all of them."

There was little point in trying to count, the sky held tens of thousands of the inverts, their numbers were far greater than I'd ever beheld. The antenna bug network didn't hold a candle to the sheer volume of hostile enemies fouling the territory's sky. I did my best to release the terror and found the flying sensation to be quite pleasant as I floated across the sky. Under different circumstances, I wouldn't want to land. There was something indescribable about seeing the Earth—*our* planet—from above. As the sun's blaze disappeared, the first stars began to shine their way through the darkening sky. All fear melted from my mind as I was awestruck by the beauty of what sprawled before me. If I was going to die soon, at least one of my last memories would be one hell of a view. Eventually, exhaustion overwhelmed all other senses and I fell asleep on the soft mat of hair lining the powder moth's body.

•••••••

"Ariadne! Ariadne!" yelled Ondo, pulling me from my dream of future humans riding tame powder moths.

I wiped the drool from my mouth and looked over at my friend, still draped across the back of a duster. With one finger, he pointed ahead. I followed his gesture and when I saw it, my mouth fell agape. *Dear god!*

We'd crossed most of the terrain stretching between us and the Hive overnight. The mounds had grown in height and width until they were double, maybe even triple the size we had seen the day before, but that was nothing in comparison to what lay in the distance. It couldn't be anything other than the Hive. I don't know what I expected, but this wasn't it. It wasn't just some mound like the others. *The Hive is a damn mountain!* The nightmarish creation sprawled from one end of the horizon to the other, climbing so high that I couldn't see the top for the clouds. The orbiting inverts' pattern was tighter, centered around the foreboding edifice looming in the distance. The air vibrated with all of the activity. Any euphoria from the night before had vanished without a trace.

We flew for more than an hour before we reached the fringes of the Hive. Neither Ondo nor I could form coherent thoughts gazing at what would likely be our final destination. The Hive was spattered with countless small openings, each guarded by one or two of the most aggressive Arthropod species. Our dusters headed for an opening with a large platform where the four creatures could land side-by-side with room to spare. As the inverts on the platform stirred at our arrival, a deep reverberating trumpeting pierced the air. With unprotected ears, it was all I could do to bury my face in the musky cushion of the duster to escape the noise. I felt powerless before the sound, vibrating me inside and out. With something as trivial as a noise, they were demonstrating just how much power they held over us. Briefly, I felt stupid for having the arrogance to think humans could defeat this enemy.

"I will not cower," I said to myself.

The powder moth's wings came to a dead stop and we fell towards the platform. Just before the moment of impact, it thrust out its wings and came to a soft landing. Our Demented escorts untied us, and for the first time I realized that my body was again my own. The dark pair let us slide off of the creatures' backs on our own accord and left us unbound.

"They know there's nowhere for us to go," said Ondo eying One Eye and Scabby. "Aside from flinging ourselves off this edge, there's not a damn thing we can do other than follow where they lead."

I cocked an eyebrow at him.

"Relax, I'm not taking the easy way out of this. If this is the end for me, I'm facing it with everything I have and hopefully taking a few of them with me."

"Good. If they want us bad enough to heal our injuries and fly us here under a personal escort, I'm pretty sure they'd catch you before you hit the ground anyway."

Ondo gulped. "What do you think they want with us?"

"We've been a pain in their ass since we set foot out of Horizonte and made it further than possibly any human being in recent history, save for Arjun and Kolya. Whatever the Queens have planned is not something we're going to like."

Two mantis wraiths emerged from the cave-like opening in the mountainside, their skin intentionally in the visible spectrum. Just behind them, a small band of Demented female slaves, driven by a male handler with a whip, rolled a cage assembled from bone (hopefully animal) towards us. One of our guards opened the door and the wraiths positioned themselves behind us, clicking as they raised their bladed arms toward our backs.

"You're right," said Ondo, reluctantly stepping into the cage. "I don't like this. Not at all."

CHAPTER 44: HEMANT

I preferred the bonds to the immobilizing webbing, but after Huck's escape, they weren't taking any chances. Our guards had tied the course rope so tightly that I might permanently lose some of my hands' functionality, if not the hands themselves. At least I could flex my legs now and again in the cramped wooden wagon. *Where the hell did Huck go?* I still couldn't figure that out. His webbing must have dissolved overnight like ours, but how he snuck past the inverts and where he went was a big question mark. Judging by the look on Krista's face, I was pretty sure she felt abandoned, but I knew my friend. Huck would never do that. Hell, half the reason he was here was to help me rescue my brother.

"Is it getting more humid?" Trivia asked in a whisper.

I nodded.

The air had taken on a mustier, damper quality as each hour ticked by. Like the last few days, I still couldn't be sure of the time, having only the flickering torches on the front of the wagon for illumination. There had also been an uptick in traffic joining our tunnel through the various branches as inverts carried all manner of things about, including deceased humans. My revulsion at the invasive species only grew as we neared the central hub. Whether or not it was the Hive was another question.

Before long, the faintest green glow lit the edges of the tunnel mouth. The others perked up at the change in scenery, everyone anxious to see what the source of the new light could be. Even from a distance, I could tell the space we were entering was quite enormous. The source of the glow appeared to be tiny green lamps dotting the walls. *How the hell did they create green light?* The wagon reached the end of the tunnel and the cavernous space opened around us. Next to me, Trivia gasped.

"It's beautiful," she said as our guards hopped off to confer with a Demented so large that he reminded me of some of the ancient human lore.

"Nothing from these monstrosities is beautiful," said Omar, spitting into the dirt. "You saw those people they carried through the tunnels."

On closer inspection, I could tell that the green lights were not lamps, but rather some sort of larvae, scurrying around to provide light for the workers, Demented and invert, as they carried out their abhorrent tasks.

The cavern ascended to a pinprick of natural light high above. As far as I could see, the walls were lined with large mushrooms. The ant-like toadies, normally found near water, busily harvested the mushrooms piece by piece, sending chunks raining down to awaiting Demented below who carried it away.

"They eat mushrooms?" asked Artim.

"Fungi," said Trivia. "It must be an alternative food source."

"If they can eat fungus, why the hell can't they leave us alone?" I asked.

"Probably doesn't give them all of the nutrition they need," answered Trivia. "That's why they still hunt animals."

"That's a shame," said Artim. "If they could live on fungus, maybe we could have gotten along."

"No, Artim. They're an invasive species," said Trivia. "Even eating fungus, harmony would be impossible."

"I still have every intention of ridding the Earth of their ilk," said Omar.

"How are we going to do that?" asked Krista. "I'm pretty sure our captors are taking us to the Queens and I doubt they are going to let us anywhere near—"

She was cut off by loudly arguing Demented. Bigfoot, presumably their superior, was pissed. He reached out, grabbing each of our drivers by their necks and simultaneously, lifting them off the ground as their feet flailed in the empty air. From the wagon, I could hear them gasping for breath before I heard the sickening crunch of bones. The pair went still as we looked on in fear. Krista cradled Artim's head, turning him away from the disturbing sight. The giant marched towards the wagon with lethal resolve. I positioned myself in front of Trivia and the others. He wasn't going to touch her without going through me!

When he reached the rear of the wagon, he swept me aside like a bag of rotten produce. With one hand, he easily grabbed the bomb and carried it back to two awaiting Demented females who looked more fearsome than our previous guards ever did. After barking orders, they nodded and jumped on the cart, spurring the polies on. The warrior disappeared into a nearby tunnel with the nuclear weapon, taking any chance of destroying the Queens with him. The loss hit me harder than the loss of my brother. Mission failed. I started to weep. Not like a few tears running down my cheeks, but a deluge with sobbing and groans. I collapsed into the wagon's decking as Trivia rubbed me with her calf, the only comfort she could provide.

•••••••

Once I finally regained control of myself, I wiped the tears and snot from my face with my shoulder. I felt like a disaster. My face was drenched, I smelled like piss and worse, and now we were likely headed for a painful, lingering death with nothing to show for it. I let my forehead drop back to the rough-hewn boards and realized I was staring eye-to-eye with Huck through a crack. I lurched back in surprise, grief momentarily forgotten. *Of course!* He'd been there the whole time.

"What is it?" Trivia whispered, scared to aggravate our menacing guards.

I glanced at our escorts to make sure they weren't paying attention and mouthed "Huck" to the group, subtly pointing down. Everyone did their best to conceal their excitement. After the loss of the bomb, it gave us some much-needed hope. I knew that he wouldn't have abandoned us, but his presence was more comforting than I could put into words. *If he could go after the bomb…* I rocked myself back to my seat. One of the drivers looked back at me and bared her sharpened teeth, warning me to stay put. The one with the dreadlocks never looked back. Now I had hope. It wasn't much, but right now I'd take anything.

As the fungus chambers passed, one after another, I couldn't tear my eyes away from that spot on the floor where Huck had hidden under the floorboards. *It can't be comfortable down there.* It all made sense. I couldn't figure out how he could've escaped. That was just it—he didn't.

Eventually I dozed off, but a sharp elbow to the ribs woke me. My head sprung up, not knowing what to expect. Out of habit, I frantically searched for my war hammer. Unlike the bomb, our weapons were still in the cart but inaccessible. Bound together and under a thick blanket, they might as well be with Bigfoot. We'd arrived at a new room that dwarfed the fungal farms. If this wasn't the Hive, I didn't know what it could be. Above me, a shaft stretched up until I couldn't make out anything but a pinprick of light. Like the farms, the rooms were dimly lit by a different fungus, one that glowed a soft blue.

"That has to extend for kilometers!" said Artim, then looking towards the drivers, waiting for a smack that never came.

Apparently, these two could care less if we talked.

"And down for just as many," Omar said, leaning back in from his glance over the edge, looking a little pale.

The shaft was packed with inverts bustling up and down the length of the room, many carrying small white objects.

"Are those eggs?" I asked.

Trivia nodded. "We're in the center of their reproduction. Do you realize what that means?"

I paused for a moment to let the implication set in. "We made it! We're in the actual Hive."

"It'd be more exciting if we could do something about it," said Trivia.

A smirk crossed Omar's face. "Part of me thought we'd never make it but another part of me knew that we could. I wish Carvalho was alive so that I could throw it in his face. He did *nothing* to help others. To think his son made it to the Hive." He leaned back looking pleased with himself.

If there wasn't a significant change in our fortune, our impressive feat would do little to change humanity's plight. Our wagon took a slow wind down, descending further into the depths of the Hive—something that didn't seem possible. There was no telling how impressive this place must be above ground if below was any indication. It would take a well-placed nuclear weapon to even make a dent in this place—a weapon we no longer possessed. I forced the sense of defeat from my mind. This wasn't over until I was dead. I'd sacrificed far too much to give up now when I was so close to my goals.

"We've got to do something! I doubt we'll ever see the bomb again, but I'll take the Queens out with my war hammer. Hell, I'll do it with my damn hands if I have to," I said. "We're being taken directly to them, right? Arjun said they probably weren't too much bigger than the inverts we're used to fighting."

"He's probably right," said Trivia. "They may not even have the defenses the others do."

"*If* we are being taken to them, which alone isn't a certainty, I doubt we'll be in a position to waltz up to them and smash their brains in," said Omar. "They may have us tortured and killed without us ever setting eyes on them."

Artim whimpered and Krista gave Omar a look that could kill. *If only we had* that *superpower.*

"Look!" said Trivia.

Surrounding us were small cavities carved directly into the earth that the inverts carefully placed eggs into. Once deposited, each depression was packed with a viscous, pearly liquid from an adult's mouth before the sequence was repeated. In other cavities further along in the creature's development writhed the shapes of future killers. Though innocent now, I would dispatch them without hesitation before they grew into the violent species they'd become.

As the path corkscrewed ever deeper into the Hive, the species gradually changed from one into the next. Scarier still, I spotted some larvae that I didn't recognize. It stood to reason that traveling around the planet close to the equator as we had, we hadn't come across the inverts adapted to other environments. Trivia had been captivated by one such creature which looked like an ant had mated with a rattlesnake. The two-bladed whips on the hind end of its white carapace were barely visible in the similarly colored fluid surrounding it.

"It's white as snow," said Artim, aghast.

"How do you know what snow looks like?" said Krista.

Artim gave her an incredulous look. "We had books in Zephyr's Hope."

"Astute observation, Artim," said Trivia. "I bet it's evolved to live in cold climates where it would blend into the ice and snow."

"Is there anywhere in the world without the dark ones?" he asked.

"Our future," Omar said, matter of fact.

For the first time since entering the Hive, our positivity began to return. Shortly thereafter, we reached the base of the winding shaft, where the sprawling veil of darkness was only parted by the iridescent glow of larvae and fungi. Surprisingly, the bottom of the shaft was covered in pools of the same white goo we'd seen higher. Royal jelly, Trivia had called it. I watched as more servile Demented tended to the vats, agitating them gently with large wooden paddles as some inverts siphoned the fluid and others expelled it.

"Disgusting," I said, my stomach churning. "So a product of the inverts' backsides is regurgitated as food for their young?"

"Bingo," said Trivia.

"Nurses, right?" asked Artim, who beamed when Trivia nodded.

"Wow," said Omar as the wagon took a short tunnel out of the shaft. "It's even more disgusting after you explain it."

The wagon pulled to a stop in a lamp-lit, high-domed room with several roughly constructed wooden doors recessed into the walls. The Demented women unceremoniously dumped us from the wagon in front of the eights that had escorted us down with no concern for bones' integrity. Thankfully, I had only endured some bruising, but Omar broke a few fingers when he landed. I rolled up to a seated position in time to see the scarier of the pair approaching me with a dagger as sinister as Marie's. Before I could voice concern, Razor slit my bonds and proceeded to Trivia. Confused, I massaged my wrists which throbbed painfully as the blood tingled on its return trip after its extended absence.

The other, Dreads, pulled the wagon past the large brazier at the center of the room and into an alcove with several other small carts before detaching the team of polies and leading them off. The eights' legs clicked away as their bone-white bodies passed back through the tunnel. Our weapons and gear were still in the wagon with Huck! As Razor flung open the crudely-constructed doors, a trickle of dust fell from the ceiling onto my shoulder. Looking up, I saw nothing. Something about this place put me ill at ease—considerable depth and terror-inducing predicament aside. After a moment, Dreads returned and we were corralled into the small rooms with no concern over pairing. Trivia and Artim were shoved into the first, Omar alone in the second, and Krista and I in the third. The second the door shut behind us, the scrape of iron on iron quelled any doubts as to our imprisonment. We wouldn't be escaping—at least not without help.

The spartan room hardly held anything aside from two hastily constructed beds, a basin of water, and a hole for waste. Below two candles was a plate of unfamiliar, half-eaten fruit. Krista and I dove for it, caring less who'd eaten the other half. It wasn't enough to be satiated, but it was something after our lengthy fast.

"I know it's the least of our worries, but what I wouldn't do for a shower!" I said, sitting on the unmade bed, drumming my fingers impatiently.

"Or clean clothes," added Krista. "At least we all stink to high heaven."

"With any luck, Huck can sneak out of the wagon and bring us our stuff. I'm ready to tear this place apart to find Arjun."

"I wouldn't count on it."

"What do you mean? He's right out there! All he has to do is wait for Dreads and Razor to leave, and then we can escape and gear up."

"Dreads and Razor?" she asked, shaking her head before moving on. "You mean I caught something you didn't?"

"What?" I asked, dragging out the word.

"They left us unbound because they weren't worried about us escaping. There is a pair of mantis wraiths clung to the ceiling out there."

"Crap. We need to find a way to warn Huck."

"You don't have enough faith in your friend's prowess. Huck didn't get this far without being highly observant."

"I hope you're right," I said, collapsing on the bed.

"Get some rest. We don't know how long we'll have to ourselves."

She was right. Krista had become quite an adept warrior in her own right through the course of our journey. Initially, she was a stray puppy nipping at Ariadne's heels, but Zeke's death had changed her. She'd come into her own while she and Omar were stranded outside of Pod Kano. I laid down and turned to my side. Just when I was about to close my eyes, I saw it. The smallest tuft of white fabric. I'd recognize candidate jumpsuit stitching anywhere! I bolted upright, scaring the ever-loving hell out of Krista.

"He's here!" I screamed. "Arjun is here!"

CHAPTER 45: ZEPHYR

2112

The bronze-skinned man slyly smiled back, as though knowing something we didn't. I'd yet to meet a single stranger with good motives, but that hardly meant they didn't exist. The danger of bandits had been deeply ingrained by my family before we'd set foot off our land. As much as I wanted to believe everyone was inherently good, I'd be naive to think that was the reality. If not for the sour feeling in my gut, I might have been willing to trust the man.

"No, thank you," I said. "I believe we have all the help we need."

Mom gave me a warning look accompanied by an almost imperceptible shake of her head, advising me to say no more. Dad slightly hoisted his rifle to his shoulder, no more than a few millimeters. The subtle movement was enough to draw others from the nearby, vine-coated rubble, all armed.

"There's no need for that, *amigo,*" the man said. "We're in a position to help each other. It would be… *mutually beneficial.*"

"We're not here to cause trouble," said Uncle Alex. "We're just trying to reach the pod."

The man laughed. "You, *viejo?* You think they'll let an old timer like *you* in?"

The others joined a chorus of laughter, their voices echoing down the abandoned street. Mom, Dad, and Uncle Alex passed a confused look between them.

"Oh, the wilders don't know," the man said, smirking. "Sounds like you need to meet the Boss. Follow us."

No one took a step. The men made to flank us, guns raised.

"I never said it was a choice," he added.

The men marched us several kilometers. The band's leader introduced himself as Costco because he could get anyone anything, a joke he thought was hilarious but was lost on us. Each of the strangers, self-dubbed the Peacekeepers, was covered in ornate tattoos. The inkwork was gorgeous. Had they not been our captors, I would've excitedly asked about their meaning. We'd survived attacks from the Arthropods along the journey only to fall prey to our own species. *Maybe I'm wrong about them. But if they are trying to help, why are they doing it at gunpoint?*

The Peacekeepers eventually led us to the bank of a sprawling river wider than any I'd ever come across in the woods near the cabin. The wind stirred up small waves in the lazurite water, generating the most peaceful sound I'd ever heard. After the sweaty march through the city, I was tempted to fling myself in, almost not caring where the current carried me. The bridge spanning the water had seen better days, rusting and even broken in places, but still passable. The men escorted us across, some walking on the railroad tracks, challenging each other in a contest of balance. I couldn't resist and joined the fun, doing it longer than the rest. When I started laughing with them, Dad pulled me to his side and forced me to walk with them. Like a child.

When we were closer to the small island, I could make out what was left of a towering power plant, once supplying invaluable electricity to the city's inhabitants, now silent save for the lapping of the river and the tweets of the birds. Aside from the antenna bugs above, our escorted march through the streets had been free of the invaders, having likely been cleared by the Peacekeepers. *Though what type of "peacekeeper" kidnaps people?* On ends of the island, away from the largely derelict structures, farm fields were lush with life and teeming with workers.

"Is that how you survive out there?" I asked, pointing towards the fields.

Costco nodded. "We work the fields, we fish the rivers, and we take donations. In return, we protect our people."

I questioned what he meant by donations. I had little doubt we'd find out soon enough. Finally, they led us off the bridge and to an office building lined with cracked windows adjacent to a giant collapsed warehouse. The interior was filled with men, women, and children, living in a camp-style arrangement scattered throughout the old cubicles. I waved to a few of the kids. Having never played with young ones, I was excited to see them. Their caretakers turned them away or scolded them when they returned my greeting. As we made our way through the makeshift town, we came across a burly guy giving a tattoo. *So that's where the Peacekeepers get them!* He was filling in the scales of a dragon, but what caught my eye was the fiery phoenix on his wall. I ran my fingers over the plastic protecting the art, inspecting the exquisite detail. Mom practically jerked me away. I kept turning my head over my shoulder as the image burned into my mind. Costco escorted us to a large, wooden-walled office where a tall, white-bearded man sat reading a book.

"Found these four coming in from the northwest, Boss Gruber," Costco said. "They're like all the others. They don't know the limitations."

"Thank you, Costco," he said in a grandfatherly voice as he gently closed his book and placed it on his desk. "That will be all. You and your men may have double rations today."

The men cheered and vanished through the nearest door, leaving us alone with a man who I was tempted to describe as Saint Nicholas, but thinner and shorter in beard.

"I apologize for how you were brought before me," said Gruber, coming around his desk to face us. "It's important to me that everyone understand not only how things work at the pod, but to a greater extent, how I run Pittsburgh.

"You? Run Pittsburgh?" asked Uncle Alex, voice dripping with doubt.

"The United Territories is far too preoccupied with their precious underground city to focus on the needs of the greater metropolis. Without my guiding hand, it would've fallen into chaos like so many cities nearby. If they won't let everyone in, those turned away need something they can turn to. They need hope."

"What do you mean, they won't let everyone in?" asked Mom.

"There's an age limit, my friends. That's why we've planted ourselves here on the island."

My stomach did a flip. *Age limit? Did that mean Uncle Alex couldn't come? Is that why Costco called him an old-timer?*

"But they exist to protect everyone, not just the people they deem worthy!" I said. "What about the children out there? How are they supposed to defend themselves once the Arthropods overrun the city?"

"We're survivors. Peacekeepers. It's my duty to make sure that everyone is taken care of when the United Territories shuts us out. You are welcome to proceed to the pod. I'll even provide an escort. But when they reject you three, you'll still be welcome here," he said, closing the distance to my mother. "We could use more field hands."

Dad stepped forward but was halted by raising guns from Gruber's guards. The man backed away, avoiding the confrontation. His grandfatherly manner disappeared as quickly as Costco's men had. One-on-one, Dad would prevail, but any action on his part would likely get him killed. Mom stepped closer to Dad, putting her hand on his forearm.

"What's the age limit?" she asked.

"Thirty, unless you have specialized skills," said Gruber. "What's left of the Territorial Guard will not admit anyone into the receiving zone without the Board's approval."

That means Mom and Dad too! Frantically, I racked my brain to come up with any special skills they had. All three adults were excellent hunters and gardeners. They'd learned all sorts of medical skills from books. Surely the Board would let them in.

"What skills?" asked Uncle Alex.

"Doctors, fabricators, chemists, botanists… People you'd need for long-term survival. Those government types don't appreciate real-world skills like you undoubtedly possess to have survived this long. If you're over the age limit, they'll want documentation of skills."

"What does that mean?" I asked.

"Diplomas, certifications, degrees…" said Gruber.

"The things no one can get anymore," said Dad.

"It's an exclusionary tactic, nothing more. The Board lets in those they choose and casts off those they don't. There are alternate means of access—bribery, nepotism… *favors*," he said, looking at Mom in a way that made my skin crawl.

"There's always the other pods," he continued. "They're distant, but much more accepting since so much of their local population has already died off. Last I heard, Pod Bandung was begging for people to work their shipyard."

"You mean murdered by the inverts," corrected Dad, growing more heated by the moment. "You know as well as I do that we can't travel that far. It's suicide!"

"Your son—" he began, gesturing towards me.

"Daughter," corrected my mother.

For the first time, it occurred to me how androgynous my favored appearance was. Neutral clothes, neutral hair, neutral face, and breasts so small that I could easily pass for a male. The realization had never occurred to me growing up in the woods, barely sparing a glance at a mirror. Every aspect of my image was focused on functionality, attraction hadn't even been an afterthought.

"Your *daughter* should be granted asylum due to her age, but you will not be fortunate enough to accompany her. With a proper haircut and gender-appropriate clothing, she would prove quite suitable for some young lad. Perhaps one of my Peacekeepers. The Board makes some exceptions for marriages spanning the age limitations.

"She's not marrying one of your forty-year-old men!" yelled my mother.

"Why not? They are honorable men. With her they could produce viable offspring. That's what the Earth needs to repopulate, is it not?"

"She will choose someone if and when she's ready, not have a husband chosen for her for their… reproductive compatibility!"

"Now, there's no need for hostility," he said, calmly. "I'm simply explaining your options."

"I'm not getting married," I said, turning to face my family. "And I'm staying with you. We can go back to the cabin. We've fended off the inverts before. We can do it again."

"We can't ever go back there, little sprite," she said, calling me the pet name that as an adult I found so condescending. "Even if the cabin isn't already overrun with Arthropods, they've likely eaten any game that survived the explosion. Your only hope is the pod. We'll take you to Pod Pittsburgh, then we'll stay here with Boss Gruber. I'm sure we can reach an arrangement that we are all content with."

"No," I said, crying. "I can't. I won't leave you."

For a moment, everything in the world froze, leaving only me and my mother. A tear lingered at the corner of her eye, glistening in the sunlight coming through the clouded window.

"Everything we've done has been for you," she said. "Eventually, the city of Pittsburgh will fall, just like all the other cities. We *will* die, but we will be okay knowing that our only daughter is alive and safe."

"But I can't," I said, falling to my knees. "I can't live without you!"

"You've been independent your entire life. Everything will turn out okay. With any hope, they'll find a solution to all of this mess soon. I dream of a day when you walk the Earth again, without cause for fear. You'll be one hell of a person, I only wish I could be there to see it. Be strong, little sprite, for me."

I nodded, wiping the slow stream of tears on my stained sleeve.

"What are your names?" asked Boss Gruber.

"I'm Alex Taggert. This is Gabriel and Natalie Sanchez, and their daughter, Zephyr."

At the mention of my name, the man's bushy white eyebrows rose to his wrinkled forehead.

"Wait. Zephyr as in "Zephyr's Hope?""

My mouth hit the floor in shock. How could this man possibly know about my broadcasts? Uncle Alex was always saying how the antenna bugs prevented any signals, even from Winston's ancient tube and crank ham radio. I had fervently hoped someone out there could hear me, but I had dismissed it long ago as impossible. Still, I had soldiered on, if for no one else, for me.

"Um… yes," I stammered, turning to my perplexed parents as the stream of tears matched the river outside. "But I never knew anyone was listening."

At this, Gruber's attitude completely flipped. His hardened features softened and his grandfatherly manner flooded back. He knelt next to me, brushed the loose strand of hair behind my ear, and wiped my tears with his mint-scented handkerchief.

"My sweet young one, you have no idea, do you?" he said, kneeling to the floor where I had fallen to my knees. He took my hands. "You have given us hope since your first broadcast crackled over the airwaves so long ago. My god, I can't believe it's truly you! As you can imagine, your signal was frequently interrupted, and at times unintelligible, but we tuned in nightly hoping to hear your sweet voice. There's not a soul in this encampment who hasn't benefited from the optimism of "Zephyr's Hope." At times I even doubted my calling, but your wisdom held me on this path. In a way, *you* are responsible for this city's existence. We even retransmitted your messages so that they might reach others."

Uncle Alex, Dad, and Mom traded looks of astonishment.

"Your messages gave us the much-needed hope that we could all survive regardless of what life threw at us. We've expanded your philosophy to our existence outside of the pods. So many here owe you thanks. They would've given up, save for your precious words. If it is still what you wish, I will personally escort you to Pod Pittsburgh and speak to the Board on your behalf. With any luck, they will let your mother and father in as your caretakers. I apologize for your Uncle, there are no exceptions for his age."

"But I don't understand," I said, wiping my eyes again. "I ended each broadcast pleading for a response. No one ever contacted me. How is it that so many listened, but no one reached out?"

"My dear, we did," said Gruber. "We tried every night for years, but you never answered. We assumed our messages couldn't get through."

I turned to Uncle Alex, who was shaking his head in disbelief. "I always figured the aerials' electromagnetic interference blocked the reception. I never considered the receiver might be faulty."

I groaned as my face flooded again with tears. Mom dropped

down beside me and wrapped her arms around me, filling my nostrils with her piney scent. I'd spent my youth sending signals out into the universe, praying that someone out there was hearing them but doubting anyone was. Finally, I had what I had what I'd wanted all those years: to know I had accomplished something. Helped someone. I turned to look up at Boss Gruber.

"Thank you," I said, sobbing. "Thank you so much!"

"No," he said, lifting my chin. "Thank you."

●●●●●●●●

Boss Gruber insisted that we stay the night, giving us his personal loft. The old station manager's office looked down onto the partitioned ground floor where families now dwelled in pseudo-privacy. Word about who I was spread like wildfire, but they were kind enough to allow us to rest that first night. *Who I was. Who was I?* A day ago, I was a just silly girl talking into a microphone, then to find out that not only have people been listening, but they've thrived from my messages of hope! In a way, I felt exposed. Like someone had been reading my diary, scrutinizing my imperfections and naivety. I looked down at the people milling about, crammed into the tight confines. Many rested reading and talking as the morning's sun bathed the interior in a burnt orange glow through the high banks of windows. A little boy looked up and saw me. He smiled and waved, revealing his browning teeth. I waved, back, wondering if he knew who I was or was simply being kind. I never thought I'd be somebody. A soft knock roused Dad, who woke Mom. Uncle Alex was already on his feet.

"Yes," Dad asked as he opened the door.

It was Gruber, Costco, and an elderly woman holding a tray with dark coffee and slices of bacon that smelled like the ambrosia of the gods.

"Good morning," said Gruber. "I hope you don't mind some food and company."

Dad shook his head and Gruber made himself comfortable. Costco leaned against a wall while the woman served coffee and left. Each of us took a cup. I'd never had any, but judging from the way people talked about it, I was anxious to try it. I took my first sip and almost spit it out.

"It's quite bitter if you're unfamiliar with it," he said, laughing heartily. "Perhaps try adding some cream and sugar. The cream comes from our own dairy cows."

I added the proffered ingredients and the rich liquid tasted delightful in compliment to the crispy, greasy bacon. Within moments, I was ready to seize the day with my newfound energy. Dad and Mom's eyes were wide with enjoyment. Uncle Alex sat back and sipped his black coffee, savoring each pull.

"I am a man of my word," he said, after sitting pensively for a moment. "Now that I know who you are, Zephyr, I would like you to remain here, but I will not force you to do so. Once you all have collected your belongings, Costco and I will personally escort you to the Board office as promised. Before you leave, I would ask that you give one more message of hope to our people."

I nodded in agreement, feeling suddenly nervous.

"Thank you," said Mom, grabbing Dad's hand and putting on a strong face.

The night before when they'd thought I'd fallen asleep, I heard them crying softly together. They were struggling to come to terms with our upcoming separation, which was quite likely according to Gruber. *Would the Board know who I was? More importantly, would they care?*

CHAPTER 46: HUCK

From my cramped perch under the cart, I could hear Hemant's muffled yells of excitement. He must have discovered evidence of Arjun's presence. I couldn't believe that we were on the heels of Arjun and Kolya. So close and yet so far. If they were here, where were they? I finished unwrapping the rope from around me, wincing as often as not from the pain of being so restricted in my movement for days on end. The Demented guards had left, extinguishing the oil lamps on their way out, leaving only the flickering light of the brazier to illuminate the room. *They can't have left us unguarded.* Something raised my hair on end, but I couldn't quite put my finger on it. Guards or not, every movement was done as stealthily as possible.

As far as I could tell, all of our equipment remained in the wagon above. *It's got to be a trap.* Either that or the Demented were stupider than we realized, but I doubted it. I'd seen alarmingly crazy behaviors from the rotten-minded humans, but nothing that led me to believe they were idiots. The Arthropods that ruled over them weren't either.

I slowly slid myself out from the precarious position, doing everything I could to avoid my cramping muscles dropping me to the dirt floor like a sack of rice. Despite the protests from my body, I managed to lay flat-backed on the floor and silently stretched, bringing feeling and intense pain back to my extremities. As predicted, my neck felt like that giant Demented had tried to wrench it off. I resisted the urge to groan as the agonizing pain peaked. Once the majority of the discomfort had subsided, I gazed past my feet to the iron bars locking my friends into their rooms, the hammered metal reflecting the torchlight. In theory, all I had to do was run over, throw open the doors, and we would be armed and relatively free. *Nothing about this scenario is right.* Training honed one's intuition and I wasn't ignoring mine.

A test! I scraped my foot on the floor, barely audibly. *Nothing.* I made a slightly louder scrape. Again, nothing. I ran my hands along the smooth ground and located a pebble. *That'll work.* I flung the pebble out into the room, listening intently as it tapped rhythmically across the stone floor. Instantly, scrapes emanated from the walls. Across the sprawling area, I could make out two separate distortions between me and the low flames. *Wraiths! Why did it have to be wraiths?* They must have concluded that the pebble had fallen loose from the ceiling. No sooner had I identified them, they vanished back up the wall. *Note to self, they can climb inverted surfaces. Great, they needed to be more daunting.*

What to do? Part of me longed for my old crossbow. The silent killer could bring one of them down in a hurry, not that I'd have time to load it again, thus why I abandoned it for a faster weapon. Retrieving a weapon now would be tantamount to ringing a gong. Not to mention, my enemies could see far better than I could in the dim light. I couldn't do anything under a wagon, so I shimmied out as silently as I could manage, taking my time. An idea hit me. It was approaching suicidal, but what part of this mission hadn't been? I took a deep breath, gathered my courage, and sprinted towards the doors with as much speed as I could muster from my over-tight muscles.

Clank. Clank. Clank. Each iron bar announced my presence as I sped past the doors, unlocking my friends. I couldn't stop. By now, the wraiths were after me. I could hear their chatter gaining. *Now for the hard part.* I jerked an oil lamp from the wall, snapping its rope, and sped toward the brazier. As I made a spinning turn, a claw grazed my back. *A tenth of a second slower…* I poured on all the speed I had, then turned and flung the lamp with all my might towards the open flames. Out of the corner of my eye, I could see my friends emerging from their rooms, shock across their faces. After a split-second hesitation, they launched toward the cart with our weapons. I watched as the oil vessel fell in slow motion as it descended towards the brazier and exploded, bathing the wraiths in flaming liquid. *I can't believe that worked! Thank the freaking gods!* I celebrated too soon. The creatures released shrill, spine-tingling shrieks as they clawed at the flames devouring their bodies.

"Burn you sons of bitches!" said Omar, tossing me my dao.

I caught the sword in midair and was attaching it to my back when I heard the barks of Demented, storming towards our location.

"We've been found out," said Krista.

"That way!" yelled Artim, pointing toward the opposing tunnel.

The kid's exceptional navigation skills had been reliable so far. I took off in his suggested direction as the others followed closely behind. I had little other plan other than to escape and track down the big guy who'd stolen our bomb. I had no idea how we were going to do that. The Hive was multiple times larger than Pod Horizonte, and it wasn't like we could ask for directions. More growling ahead preceded the faint glow of torches. We'd been flanked by two groups of Demented. I had succeeded in nothing. If we fought, we would be cut down. Judging by the number of voices, we didn't stand a chance. I slowed to a halt.

"I'm sorry, guys," I said. "I thought I was helping."

"You did what you could, man," said Hemant, squeezing my shoulder. "If we die, then we'll die together."

When the Demented coalesced around us, it became more apparent that we stood no chance of fighting our way out of the situation. The two wagon drivers shoved their way to the front of the crowd to face their prisoner.

"Razor. Dreads. So nice to see you again!" Hemant said with a smirk.

It was funny how staring inevitable death in the face gave Hemant an atypical sense of humor. Razor punched him so hard I heard his jaw snap. The one Hemant had called Dreads immediately began barking orders. Our weapons were confiscated and once again, we were excruciatingly bound with course hemp. This time, we weren't escorted back to our rooms. Instead, we were marched deeper into the Hive as the throngs of Demented behind us chanted with palpable fervor at what I could only assume was our upcoming demise.

Down we spiraled, trudging along on reluctant feet and muttering to each other as we went. Once again, hopelessness drove away all traces of optimism. I'd encountered the surreal feeling before and somehow we had always escaped, usually at the cost of someone's life, but this time felt different. As we continued deeper on our death march, the walls subtly changed from smooth, undulating forms, to spiraled sgraffito carved for... beauty? *That can't be right.* It was one thing for the Arthropods to have some level of intelligence, but another for them to be expressing creativity. Attention to aesthetics meant something deeper. We were dealing with a highly evolved species, one that if left unchecked could easily replace us.

The lower we ventured, the more the tunnel grew in size and the more intricate the carvings became. They were beautiful swirling shapes that mesmerized the mind. Like so many things in the Hive, they would've been far more fascinating had circumstances been different. Each of us was mesmerized by the ornate walls, a pleasant reprieve from the fear surging through our veins. Finally, the end of the tunnel opened up into a grand audience chamber, the walls endlessly carved as I craned my neck to gaze up. If it could've fallen that far, my jaw would've hit the floor. Looming far above was the sharp tip of a strange rock descending from the ceiling.

"The meteorite," said Trivia in awe.

"We're here," said Hemant. "Now what?"

"Look down," said Omar, voice quaking in anger

We'd been so distracted by the meteorite's presence that we failed to see what was directly in front of us. My heart sank. Laying on the floor in front of a large throne-like stalagmite was Dieter's nuclear weapon. The device that Hemant had lugged from one side of the world to the other, the device that we had protected as much as our friends, lay disassembled on the floor. Every single component was neatly spread out on the slab, far beyond even Trivia and Arjun's combined talent to reassemble.

"It's over," said Krista, sobbing.

Omar ground his teeth loud enough that I could hear it over Krista's sobs. My face flushed with righteous anger. I'd lost Ariadne and now I'd lost our weapon—the crux of our entire mission.

"No. It's just begun," said Artim with surprising composure. "You've done what no one else could. You've proved their defenses aren't impenetrable. We may die, but we've paved the way for others. It's only a matter of time before someone else brings them down."

"I wish I had your optimism," said Trivia, poorly masking her disappointment. "I *knew* we'd be successful. It's so aggravating!"

"My mission isn't over," said Hemant, as Trivia stroked his side with a bound hand. "I still haven't found my brother. I have to find Arjun!"

"Not to drag you down, but if you found him now, it'd only be to die together," said Omar. "You can't seriously think there is a way out of this alive."

"Fine," said Hemant, face burning. "Then we'll die together, but I will *not* let him die alone!"

I knew how he felt. As much as I wanted to believe Ariadne and Ondo were alive, I feared the worst. Maybe it was better that way considering what horrors might await us. The dream of the two of us dying of old age on an Arthropod-free earth began to dissipate like the morning fog. With the bomb destroyed and Ariadne likely dead, our mission had been a complete failure. I'd been a complete failure. I couldn't imagine. Tears stung my eyes, not in self-pity, but thinking about such a perfect human being, devoured by the inverts like any other prey. Fury seeped from my conscience. *If you're going to die, die fighting you miserable wretch! What would bring Ariadne more honor, you pining away or going down with a fight? Fine,* I answered, gritting my teeth. I'd go down fighting with my bare hands if it came to it.

Hemant's elevated voice stirred whatever nightmarish creatures hid in the darkened alcoves scattered around the room. Their soft chittering grew increasingly louder, silencing everyone and jerking me away from my internal turmoil. Slowly emerging from the nooks were representatives of each of the Arthropod species we'd encountered—and a number we hadn't. Each invert queen varied from those species that we'd encountered, slightly larger, differing markings, fewer defenses. The most noticeable difference was the significantly larger abdomen—ideal for laying eggs!

"The Queens," Trivia said above the din in a mix of intrigue and anger.

Razor and Dreads approached us from behind, forcing us down to our knees one by one. This was the enemy hierarchy we'd come so far to destroy, but at their feet, we were powerless. Our weapons and gear lined the wall only meters away, but they may as well have been in a different territory. Not only were our hands painfully bound, but a small army of Demented stood between us and our kit, ready to tear us limb from limb if we so much as flinched. It truly felt over. As the old saying goes, so close and yet so far. My nose burned as I suppressed tears. *They won't see me cry.* My shoulders slumped in defeat, and I waited patiently for whatever fate would befall us.

I don't know how long we waited silently as the Queens' chittering tapered off. When it finally ceased, I thought I felt vibrations through the floor but chalked it up to my imagination. As the tremors grew in intensity, I realized it wasn't. The others were equally confused. *Was the Hive about to come down on top of us?*

"What's happening?" asked Artim. "Is it an earthquake?"

"I think it's coming from them," said Trivia, nodding towards the Queens.

Preluded by the chittering, their vibrations increased as time passed excruciatingly slowly. Whatever ceremony this was, I wished I could've left before its conclusion. The buzzing continued until it rang in my head so painfully that I thought my eardrums would burst. Finally, without warning, it suddenly stopped as my ears rang in the silence. Nothing had happened, but all that build-up couldn't have been for nothing. I waited, trying to decipher the point, and then I heard it. Scraping coming from above. From high above. I craned my neck, squinting my eyes at the meteorite, and noticed something I hadn't before—an opening. From this distance, it looked like a tiny cave, but I was sure a closer inspection would reveal its true size. Inside, I could see movement.

Slowly putting its legs out around the opening first, a terrifying creature emerged. The sight sent jolts sizzling through my nervous system as the largest mud raptor I'd ever seen emerged from her den. From every angle, the black-striped creature was sharp as a blade and couldn't have been more petrifying. Artim's composed facade collapsed, and he began whimpering.

"Oh god," I said.

"What… the hell… is that?" said Omar.

"That…," said Trivia, voice trembling, "has to be the head queen. A Queen of Queens."

My mouth ran as dry as the Saharan desert we'd traversed as the Queen of Queens climbed down the meteorite to its furthest tip, then let go, falling dramatically. When she was meters above the earth, she snapped out her gossamer wings and landed silently behind her dais, eyeing us with hatred. Despite the exposure to her overwhelming power, I was imbued with a newfound strength. I had proudly been a thorn in her ass, even knowing that she'd pay the suffering back tenfold. *She came to my planet, killed my friends, and now she would kill me for nothing more than petty revenge. Some advanced species this was.* I straightened myself as much I could from my kneeling position and stared back defiantly. Her bulbous, unfeeling compound eyes stared right back at me. Eventually, my focus fell to the now inert nuclear bomb in pieces before me. The Queen of Queens followed my gaze, clacking her mouth parts in what had to be a mocking laugh.

"Caaannnot … kiiilll … Sammmraaajniii," she said a voice so chilling, every hair on my body stood erect. Strangely, her voice felt distantly familiar. "Serrrve … Sammmraaajniii. Slaaavesss."

Everything clicked into place. We'd caused her nothing but anguish since we'd left Pod Horizonte, destroying everything she'd thrown at us and persevering nonetheless. Up until this point, I expected my life to end with prolonged torture, but what better torture than lifelong servitude? I had no illusions that it would be a pain-free existence.

"Go to hell!" I responded, knowing that each of us agreed wholeheartedly.

The Queen of Queens slowly crawled up the back of her stone dais, and that's when I saw him. Every fiber of my being exploded in despair as I beheld the frail, degrading body of Arjun, lashed upside-down to the bottom of the vile enemy like some piece of trash. Against his will, his body provided human voice to Samrajni's thoughts which flowed through a stinger piercing his skull. Only the whites of his eyes were visible. I wanted to rip her glossy carapace apart with my bare hands.

"ARJUN!" screamed Hemant with unbridled fury and agony.

CHAPTER 47: ARAIDNE

After being forced into the cage, the slaves rolled our boxy prison down a gradual slope to a large room lined with other similar empty cages. Disconcertingly, each cage had copious amounts of blood splatters, mist, or splashes. I shook off the chill that wasn't from the red-walled cavern's cool temperatures. I semi-successfully suppressed my fears as the team of Demented slaves rolled our cage next to the others before turning to leave.

"Hey!" yelled Ondo. "You just gonna leave us here or what?"

One of the Demented, a lanky woman with matted curly hair turned to look forlornly back at us. Her eyes only held hints of the sickly yellow-red of the others. Her body had far fewer scrapes and cuts, and her stride still resembled that of a human, as opposed to the primal stride of those fully Demented. Her handler barked orders, gesturing wildly with his whip, and she promptly turned away and followed the others out of sight.

"Did you see that?" I asked.

"I sure as hell did. You think she's kind of like Marie, not completely controlled by the hemolymph yet?"

"It's certainly a possibility. Marie insinuated that there's a transition period. With any luck, she has enough compassion left to let us out."

"If she's caught doing that by that slave driver, I'm pretty sure he's going to punish her with more than that whip."

"It's a long shot, but I can't give up hope. We're in the Hive for chrissakes! Hopefully, Arjun's here somewhere, and Huck's not far behind. We have to escape and eradicate these bloody inverts for good."

"You do realize we're in a blood-soaked cage made of possibly human bones, in a maze of invert-infested tunnels, and weaponless, right?"

I couldn't help but chuckle. "I've faced worse."

"I'm glad you think our predicament is humorous. I certainly didn't come this far to wimp out," said Ondo, tugging at the tight, dried sinew that held the bones together. "I don't suppose you still have your dagger."

"No. They took that when they were healing us."

"And one dose of that stuff won't turn us into Demented, right?"

"Right."

Ondo sighed with visible relief, then promptly punched the bars with all his might. They didn't so much as crack. He jerked back, cradling his hand.

"I don't understand," he said, slowly flexing each of his fingers. "I've broken other cadets' bones accidentally during training exercises. These bones are like iron."

"I think that answers where they came from—Demented."

"Demented bones! You've *got* to be kidding me. These guys have zero regard for human life—parading around in human leather, slicing all over each other, eating other people… You guys are sick! Do you hear me? Sick!"

"Shush! You'll only make escape more difficult bellowing like that."

"Well, we're sure as hell not going to escape by punching through these bones, and I can't reach the latch. Got any better ideas?"

I was about to start offering suggestions when I heard a footstep. Ondo heard it too, his eyes darting towards the sound's origin. Around the arched entrance, peered a pair of not-quite-Demented eyes. *Yes!* I didn't know how much United she could understand, so spoke using gentle tones.

"Hi," I said, beckoning her with slow motions. "It's okay. Come talk to us. We're friendly. I'm Ariadne. This is Ondo."

The woman took a few tentative steps toward the cage and froze, touching her busted and bruised lip as she contemplated further punishment.

"What's your name?"

The woman paused, silently debating between speaking or fleeing. After a moment, she shook her head as if dispelling clouds from her mind.

"I… I don't remember," she stammered. "I think… people called me Fee. It was short for something, but…" Fee started crying. "I don't know why I can't remember. I can tell from my body that I've borne a child, but I remember nothing! All I remember is horror."

Her crying became choking sobs. Fee shattered my heart, and I began sobbing with her. Ondo had to keep wiping his face on his jumpsuit.

"If you help us, we will help you escape too."

"There is no escape," said Fee, wiping her face on the inside of her sagging burlap shirt. "The creatures guard the exits by day and seal them at night. And these perverse humans… they act as eyes for the creatures. There's no hiding."

"Then we'll just have to evade detection," said Ondo. "Do you have any weapons?"

She shook her head. "No, but your friends' weapons were taken to the throne room with them."

"My friends?!" I asked, jumping up so quickly that Fee shied back. "I'm sorry. I'm very worried about them."

"If the six others are the friends you seek, they are in grave danger."

That had to be them! The only explanation for them arriving so fast was in captivity like us. Maybe we could reach them before they blew the Hive to smithereens. *What about Arjun and Kolya? Had they made it this far?*

"When have we not been in grave danger?" muttered Ondo.

"You don't understand," said Fee. "They'll be Samrajni's royal slaves. She will drown them in the Darkness. It heals the body so she can torture them endlessly."

Any leftover fear was replaced with seething rage. We had to do something before we were indentured royal slaves for this Samrajni.

"Who is Samrajni?" asked Ondo.

"She is the creatures' supreme monarch, the visage of evil. She forces the lesser creatures and the perverse to build this tower to space. She wants to spread their wickedness throughout the universe."

"Dear God!" said Ondo, jumping to his feet. "Fee, let us out! We have to stop them! I don't know how, but we have to!"

Our intensity must have spurred Fee. She was toying with the latch when we heard a deep growl. Eight angry Demented greeted me. Fee spun, explaining her actions in the Demented's guttural language. I felt a tapping on my knuckles and glanced down to find her proffering a small stone knife. I snapped it up, hiding it in my palm. Squeezing the blade tightly, the edge felt as sharp as any metal dagger I'd ever used. The leader of the Demented, a gigantic human approached Fee. He sneered with a look of disbelief before his bulbous hand encompassed her head and lifted her off the ground.

"Don't hurt her!" I screamed.

The giant stared me in the eye, smiled devilishly, and crushed her skull in his bare hand. I screamed and screamed as Ondo held me tightly in his arms, unable to pry my blurred eyes away from Fee's lifeless body. She'd died helping us! All I could think of was the heartbreak tearing my chest apart.

A Demented male jerked open the lock as a dozen crowded into the cage with us, carelessly ripping off our armor and jumpsuits, leaving us clad in only our undergarments. The men ripped the clothes from my body, bringing back the overwhelming trauma of my first attack by the vile humans, plunging me deep into despair. My brain ceased to function, my body trembled, and I bawled like a child. The Shock had sunken its poisonous talons deep into my mind, leaving me a fragile, useless shell—all of Grace's exercises forgotten. Unable to so much as walk, Ondo carried me where the guards directed. Reality blurred in front of my dissociated mind as I curled my face against his chest.

"Come on, A," whispered Ondo. "Don't give up on me now. Even if we're headed for the worst, don't let them win!"

His words did nothing to dispel the visceral fear response. So many hands, clawing at me, ripping the clothes from my body. Just like before. I'd seen how these primal urge-driven humans conducted themselves. I couldn't escape physically, so I withdrew so deep into the recesses of my mind that I may never come out again.

"Stick with me, A!" said Ondo, giving me a little shake. "I need you here."

On any other day, the independent part of me would've ordered him to put me down, but I was a wreck, a rag doll. I was no hero. The Hive was no place for someone who couldn't keep their composure through nothing worse than having their clothes torn off. I deserved to die.

We emerged from the tunnel into a large room packed with bodies—Arthropod, Demented, and human alike. *Human. Why is that important?* In the distance, screaming. Someone was furious. The anger made me bury my head deeper, but the voice was so loud, it penetrated my withdrawal.

"What have you done to her!" the familiar voice screamed. "I'll kill every damn one of you if you've touched a hair on her head! Where are her clothes, you bastards?"

Huck? Fee said there were others. Could he really be here? He deserved someone better, stronger. I slowly turned my head. The sight was one of abject horror and dismay. There were the Queens we'd fought so hard to reach. Throngs of Demented stood in huddles, hungry for our deaths. My friends masked their defeat with fury, Huck standing among them screaming, but my mind was shrouded, allowing the most ardent scream to drift in softly. On the floor was the weapon that Hemant had single-handedly dragged from the Saharan Territory—in pieces. Centered among everything on a throne-like rock formation was a colossal mud raptor, what had to be Samrajni. The malevolent being could be nothing other than the ultimate Queen. If there was any part of me unbroken, when I saw the corpse-like Arjun bound upside-down to her abdomen—it shattered.

At that moment, we could've been swept away like grains of sand on the wind, and I wouldn't have cared. Everything—the labor, the death, the heartache—it was all for naught. We had done a task worthy of the record books, and our reward—a miserable death. Four Demented ripped me from Ondo's arms. I wanted to scream, fight, and claw my way from their captivity, but I was too broken. They led Ondo and me to two large, flat surfaces raised off of the red sandstone floor, patinated with the stain of blood. I stared. *This is where I will die.*

Huck's agonizing screams pressed against my mind's veil, almost piercing the protective shroud. I pitied him for having to watch me die. At least the pain would feel distant, hopefully short. I already felt dead with so little heart left. What remained belonged to Huck, if he still wanted it after seeing me crumbled.

"Arjun?" I murmured. "Thought you were…"

"Sammmraaajniii … slaaavesss," the Queen hissed through Arjun, "orrr …waaatch … friiiendsss … diiie."

"I'll do whatever you want," yelled Huck. "Just let my friends go! Don't hurt them!"

Why was he saying that? The Queen made a strange sound akin to laughing.

"Aaalll … slaaavesss … foooreeever," said Samrajni. "Torrrturrre … uuuntiiil … agreeeeee."

Wait, this wouldn't end in death?! We would suffer as her slaves… forever? That was impossible, wasn't it? Everything Fee said rushed back. I recalled all the things Marie had told me about the creatures' hemolymph: it had life-extending properties I'd seen the results of it myself; it made you subservient to your primal nature. Judging by the way the Demented acted here, subservient to the inverts. My hand filled with the warmth of blood as my fist closed tightly around the stone dagger, the pain awakening my senses. I thought again about grains of sand on the wind, but the only thing that blew away was the fog draping my mind.

Not today. Not any day.

CHAPTER 48: HEMANT

Outrage dripped from every fiber of my being, wrung out by the sight of my brother before me. My outburst had caused several Demented warriors to restrain me. Even with the iron-hard grip owed to their gruesome habit, it took four of them to harness my fury. Adrenaline throbbing through my veins, but it wasn't enough to escape their clutches. Arjun had been reduced to nothing more than a tool for their communication. *They will pay, and they will suffer.* I tuned out the bitch's droning about us being her slaves, my face burning with resentment. *Screw that! I won't lift a damn finger to serve her.* There was nothing they could do to make me think otherwise. Tears ignited my cheeks, a combination of my twin's current state and our unresolved conflict. The thought of losing him without mending our relationship was agonizing. It was the fault of that vile snake, Kolya! Some friend he'd been, likely fleeing at the first hint of peril like the coward I knew him to be.

When I thought things couldn't possibly get worse, another group of the loathsome Demented marched Ariadne and Ondo out of an entrance on the far side of the throne room, Bigfoot in the lead. I struggled even harder against my captors' grasp when I realized that my friends' clothes had been torn from their bodies, leaving them in only their undergarments. Ondo held his head defiantly, but Ariadne… I recognized that look. *God, no.* That was how she'd looked after our first Demented attack when she'd been accosted and nearly assaulted. It had taken her weeks to shed the bulk of the Shock's symptoms, but it was back, plain as day. *What had those miserable bastards done to her?!* Somehow, my fury doubled. I was trapped in a corner with no option of escape—making me the most dangerous person in the room.

"Sammmraaajniii … slaaavesss," the Queen hissed through Arjun, "orrr …waaatch … friiiendsss … diiie."

"Okay!" yelled Huck, surprising the hell out of me. "I'm their leader. I'll do whatever you want, just let all my friends go! Don't hurt them!"

The Queen made that creepy invert laugh again.

"Aaalll … slaaavesss … foooreeever," said Samrajni. "Torrrturrre … uuuntiiil … agreeeeee."

Oh, hell no! We were all getting out of this, Huck included. I'd rather each of us die than spend one nanosecond serving that bitch's soul-crushing agenda. I frantically searched for anything that could help us and was surprised to find Ariadne clear-eyed and focused. *That's my girl!* I thought as a devious smirk crossed my face. *We're not done yet!* Amazingly, she'd pulled herself out of her trauma-induced funk like the kick-ass warrior I knew her to be. She began mouthing something, trying desperately to grab my attention.

"Night," she mouthed.

"Night?" I mouthed back confused.

"Night!" she mouthed again, subtly opening her hand and revealing a bloody blade.

Oh, knife! From her position, there was nothing she could do with the pathetic little blade, but I was directly in front of Samrajni's exposed underbelly. I had never been as skilled as Mei in knife throwing, but I could hit a bullseye with some reliability, and my seething anger gave me lethal focus. *But how could I play our card?* Not only was I restrained by four guards, but my hands were still tightly bound. I'd been so obsessed with what to do with Ariadne's knife, I hadn't noticed what was unfolding. A line of Demented females marched out, stopping in front of the six of us before Samrajni, each brandishing a human skull filled to the brim with hemolymph. Huck coming to his senses shook his head. With nothing more than a flick of her antenna, two Demented males hurled Ondo's massive frame onto the large stone slab like he was no heavier than a pillow.

"Don't do it, Huck!" he yelled. "Don't you dare drink that crap! I don't care what they do to me, don't…"

A mantis appeared out of thin air and sliced his belly wide open, allowing his entrails to roll out onto the slab, but leaving him very much alive. In a state of shock, Ondo couldn't make a sound. Artim vomited on my boots as Trivia whimpered at my side, turning away, unable to bear the sight of her squad mate's suffering. In response, the Demented in front of Huck moved the bone vessel toward Huck's lips. *It's now or never!* They wouldn't so much as shave another hair off us while I still drew breath.

"Now!" I yelled.

Ariadne flung the tiny blade into the air, arching it high up and over the Queen of Queen's dais. With an adrenaline-fueled burst, I snapped my bonds and wrenched from my captors in time for the knife to land in my awaiting hands. Before anyone could react, I hurled it directly at Samrajni's face, aiming right between those condescending compound eyes. I hadn't accounted for the Demented's superior reflexes. Before I loosed the knife, they grabbed my forearm, sending the stone blade flipping end over end towards the Queen's abdomen—toward Arjun.

"Nooo!" I screamed across the eternity it took to impact.

The blade plunged into Arjun's abdomen, almost completely vanishing. Instead of saving my friends, I'd mortally wounded my brother!

"I'm sorry," I sputtered, body limp and spirit shattered. "Arjun, I'm sorry."

"It's alright, Hemant," Arjun whispered so faintly that I had to strain my ears to catch it.

My eyes snapped up. If nothing else, the dagger had brought him to independent consciousness, even if only for a moment.

"I love you, brother," I said.

Arjun gave a single nod, the last of his life's energy waning.

He'd always been more focused on intellectual pursuits than physical training. That didn't mean he was weak. Far from it! The frail version of my twin was nothing like the Arjun I knew. Kolya was a bastard, but at least he hadn't hurt Arjun. *Some brother I am.* The wheels of my mind spun to a halt as I faced the inevitable end of our assignment. My attempted assassination of Samrajni had killed my brother and solved nothing, only delaying Huck being force-fed the hemolymph. *This is the end.* The realization was no longer a blow to my psyche, simply an acknowledgment of our failure.

I would cherish the memory of Arjun and my companions—those present and those lost—as long as my mind was my own. I would remember them not as the maimed, broken versions that they were now, but the innocent, cheerful versions they'd been when I met them. I'd always picture Arjun with Ciro. He'd never showed emotion, but when he was with Ciro, he was at his happiest. I sighed. There was no sense in fighting. I couldn't watch the same fate befall Ariadne as Ondo. We were going to be slaves to this monster—for the rest of our unnatural lives.

As the Demented cup bearers returned to their senses, they approached with the vile sludge. I made eye contact with my brother, intending to spend my last fully conscious moments with my brother. Arjun stared back and grinned. *He never smiles! What the…?* Arjun drove his fingers into his stomach and ripped out the stone knife. The mind-controlling stinger jerked from his brain as he leaned up as far as the cloth tethers would allow. Using the last of his energy, he plunged the knife as high as he could reach into the Queen of Queens' bulbous abdomen. As he collapsed backward, he let gravity do the work, shearing open Samrajni's abdomen and slicing his tethers. What happened next, no one could have predicted. Samrajni flailed, screeching violently as her hemolymph splattered all over the walls. Given her massive size, I wouldn't have thought the blow fatal, but it was causing an intense erratic reaction among the inverts and Demented.

"Take cover!" yelled Huck in the chaos. "Get your gear!"

"Arjun," I yelled, sprinting to where he'd fallen in a heap at the foot of the dais. I cradled him in my arms. "I'm so sorry, Arjun. Please forgive me!"

"Of course," he said, his skin growing pale. "I was… I was a fool for trusting him."

"He tricked us all," I said, sobbing as my brother's death drew near.

"The Queen, Sam… She killed him."

As much as I hated the man, I had no feelings left to spare. I smoothed Arjun's dark hair out of his face. It had grown so long in our travels. He never liked it long.

"Leave me," said Arjun, struggling to lift a hand to my cheek. "I released… I… the Queen's pheromones. Distraction."

"I wish I could've saved you, Arjun," I said, embracing him.

"You did, Hemant. You did."

Arjun's last words echoed in my mind as his body went limp in my hands. The blow crushed my heart. I rocked back on the sandy ground, ignorant of the chaotic scene unfolding surrounding me. I didn't understand what he meant about the pheromones, but he'd sacrificed his life to save us all. I gently lowered his body to the ground.

"I love you, brother," I whispered into his ear. "I'll never forget you. Never."

Omar dropped my gear and war hammer next to me, shaking my shoulder. "We've gotta move. Like now!"

"I can't leave him!"

"We have no choice," said Trivia, "I'm sorry, Hemant, but we have to go!"

There would be time for grieving later, right now it was time for payback! I donned my pack, eerily light without the weapon, now scattered all around the room. I reared up with my war hammer held high, ready to decimate anything in my way. As was surprised there was no one to fight. I spun around, confused. Everywhere were inverts killing inverts, Demented killing Demented.

"What the hell is happening?"

"Arjun release Samrajni's pheromones!" yelled Trivia. "It's driven them into a killing frenzy and they are all attacking each other! The Demented must be doing the same because of their link with the inverts!"

A shadow fell over me, and I jerked back just as Samrajni's gigantic body crashed down between me and Trivia, spasming as it bled from countless gashes, holes, and bites. The crazed inverts were tearing apart the lesser queens with nearly as much gusto.

"Let's get the hell out of here before they decide we are worth attacking!" I said.

"We can't leave Ondo," said Artim.

In all the pandemonium, I'd forgotten about Ondo. I rushed to his side where Krista was attempting to help Ariadne don new clothes and armor as she tended to Ondo. His shallow breathing was coming in short gasps. Blood pooled underneath his body. Without the support of his muscles, his intestines were more outside than in.

"Stop!" he bellowed, grabbing Ariadne by the wrist. Shock was likely the only thing keeping him alive as his body coped with the intense pain. "You and I both know… I'm done for."

Ariadne shook her head. "Don't say that! You still—"

"No," he said. "Leave while you can. This place… it's about to come down on us."

"I can't!" she said, bawling.

"You can and you will," said Ondo. "Take her, Huck."

"No," she said, shaking her head.

"You've done all you can. I'll never… forget that."

Ariadne stood sobbing. She fiddled with her pack before pulling out a handful of morphine syrettes and closing Ondo's hand around them.

"Thank you," said Ondo weakly. "Now get out of here!"

Huck had to practically drag her away. She couldn't tear her eyes away from him, as if expecting the gentle giant to rise and follow us out. We ran until our lungs burned, desperate to reach the nearest source of daylight. All around were dead and dying inverts and Demented alike, groaning in pain through their death throes. *More than the bastards deserve.* When we rounded a corner, the monstrous Demented who'd stolen our weapon was blocking our path. Bigfoot was shaking his head in a desperate attempt to maintain control of his mind. When he saw us, his face contorted into a terrifying grin. His teeth were jagged and broken, his skin inundated with scars. Ariadne strode forward defiantly before I jerked her back.

"This one is mine!" I said.

Every bit of roiling rage buried deep inside me oozed to the surface in a deluge. Bigfoot's eyes grew wide as he recognized it for what it was. With strength that surprised myself, I swung my war hammer with all of my might, a blow charged with fury and adrenaline. The stupefied behemoth tried to intercept it with his bare hands but only succeeded in shattering most of the bones in his arms before I buried the hammer into his ribs. The impact stopped his heart cold, bringing him to his knees. I brought the hammer up, ready to smash his head into goo when Trivia yelled to stop me.

"Don't be like them," she said. "Be stronger."

I lowered my hammer as Bigfoot's body fell lifeless to the ground.

"You're right," I said. "Let's get out of here."

We found our way back to the spiraling path that led up and hopefully out of the Hive. Neither the remaining inverts nor the Demented were interested in our escape. As we climbed, the bodies of each rained down the shaft in a gruesome downpour. By day's end, the Hive would be nothing but a hell of a graveyard. I spat on the red earth. *Screw every damn one of them.* All around, eights were killing wraiths, hooks were killing pedes, toadies were killing shinies. From here to the throne room was the exact wide-scale extermination we'd hoped to achieve. Judging by the distant explosions shaking the ground, even the polies were tearing each other apart. For the first time, it hit me. We'd annihilated the Queens and shattered their hierarchy! Our friend's sacrifices had been worth it! Any desires to celebrate were dampened by the mountain, which had begun to come down around us.

"Get me out of here before this whole thing implodes!" yelled Krista, knocking dust from her curly hair.

We sprinted past the way we'd come in, spiraling higher and higher toward the light at the Hive's peak, the only sign of a sure exit. Slowing our progress was the slick, opalescent goo draining from the larval chambers and coating our path as the viscous liquid poured over the edge like a white, mucousy waterfall. Every larva, without exception, had been destroyed. After ages of running and dodging scores of battling inverts and Demented, we finally reached the thin air of the peak. Omar and I were the first to climb out, hoisting the other up behind us as we gulped the fresh air. As we took our first tentative steps down the slope, we beheld a spectacle unlike any other. The incredible view was only topped by our accomplishment. As far as the eye could see the immense earthen towers, dwarfed by the Hive, were collapsing into themselves as warring parties spilled out of them only to be crushed beneath them.

"We did it!" Huck screamed, grabbing Ariadne and kissing her. "They're all killing each other! The Queens are dead!"

"Take that, assholes!" yelled Omar, his arm wrapped tightly around Krista.

We screamed our cheers from the peak of the unnatural mountain until the lack of oxygen at the high altitude took its toll. I passionately kissed Trivia until I remembered the loss of Arjun. When I pulled back, she knew.

"We'll give him all the respect he deserves and more once we're safe."

I nodded. I couldn't have felt more grateful at that moment. With nothing but courage, camaraderie, and a stone knife, we'd brought down the greatest threat humanity had ever faced. The seven of us slowly made our way down the Hive's exterior as it shook violently below our feet, praying it held together until we were safe. Our first stop would be Zephyr's Hope to return Artim to his parents—a hero in his own right. And then, who knows? Inverts and Demented were dying to kill each other. Any left would be eradicated by the humans returning to their rightful place on the surface. Trivia and I could settle down wherever we damn well pleased and do our part to repopulate the planet—all thanks to the lifelong friends surrounding me.

"One thing's for sure," said Trivia.

"What's that?" I asked, allowing myself to smile.

"We're naming our first kid Arjun."

CHAPTER 49: ZEPHYR

2112

Below me in the facility's cafeteria was the entire population of Bigs, the river island community Boss Gruber had founded. I stood on the second-floor catwalk looking down at everyone gathered, having just finished their breakfast of bacon and eggs, oatmeal, and coffee. The bacon, as it turned out, was a special treat reserved for special occasions, and my arrival had qualified as one. The people of Bigs stared at me expectantly, many dressed in clothes in worse condition than my own. I'd spent my life around three people, and I still couldn't wrap my mind around being a motivator of men. My audience had always been as abstract of a concept as hope, yet here they were in the flesh, as real and attentive as ever. Adding to my nervousness was the extended audience not present. Costco had informed me that they would be transmitting my message, crossing their fingers that the signal escaped.

"My name is Zephyr," I began. *Great start, Zeph. Don't you think they know that?* I took a deep breath and imagined that I was back in front of my brass-clad microphone and its fraying, fabric-wrapped cord. I envisioned it in front of me, nothing else but the wooden-slatted wall filled with my favorite quotes to stare at. *Be yourself.*

"Several days ago, I left the only home I've ever known, taking a trip in hopes of salvation to a foreign destination—Pod Pittsburgh. The place where they tell me humans will gather under the protection of earth and concrete until we solve the problem at hand. I put aside my fear and followed my family, venturing further from my comfort zone than I ever had before.

"Now that I'm closer to my goal than ever, my feelings are torn. I'm told that the pod has restrictions in place, choosing who can enter and live their life in relative safety and who will be left behind to fend for themselves as we have been doing all along. But now the conditions have changed. We're no longer living only in isolation, fearing death from climate, sickness, or starvation but rather from the enemy. The UTE claims that there's still hope, and that hope is in the pods, but what hope is there for those refused entry? My Uncle, possibly my mother and my father. What hope is there for them?

"I tell you, I see it in front of me," I let the imagery of my bedroom dissipate and continued, facing all the eyes looking up to me. "I stand in the community of Bigs, just outside of Pod Pittsburgh. I see leaders, workers, families—united together— helping each other survive. Even after learning the disappointing news about the age restrictions, I am no less filled with hope. Not from some underground city but from the people I see before me. Your leader calls you Peacekeepers, I call you survivors. There may be hope inside the pods. There may be despair outside. But I tell you this: Hope doesn't die because we do. Hope is eternal!"

I concluded my words to a deafening cheer resounding off the metal walls enclosing the large cafeteria. People chanted my name. My name! All those years of talking to the ether weren't only for myself but for everyone. With the intermittent signal, I was uncertain how many had heard my words, but even limited to our corner of the territory, I'd helped others! My heart filled with unexpected pride with self-doubt closely behind. *Could I continue to motivate those who need it under the added pressure of reality? Would those people still care what I have to say from inside the safety of the pod, assuming my signal could even escape?*

As I walked down the steps, people crowded the sides, patting my back and touching me, as if to verify that I was real. Not having been around crowds before, I suppressed the urge to flee to the nearest office and lock myself in. Thankfully, the ever-observant Gruber noticed the panic I was attempting to mask.

"People of Bigs, Peacekeepers. This has been an overwhelming morning for our visitors. Please give them space as they prepare for their departure."

The people dispersed, many saddened by the news that I wasn't staying in the city. The community stared at me proudly as I returned to our office room, their spines more erect than they had been on our arrival. I couldn't help but feel pangs of guilt that I would be safe underground as these people died at the appendages of the inverts. Undoubtedly, some would survive longer than others, but eventually, they could all be killed—Uncle Alex included.

••••••••

When the time came to leave, Boss Gruber had the warehouse bay doors open allowing the sunlight and fresh air to refresh the indoor encampment. The entire population of Bigs was lined up along the cavernous space's sides to see us—me—off. A horse-drawn carriage was waiting, making me feel more like royalty than an influential young adult. Led by two beautiful brown draft horses, the carriage was simple but well-crafted. We'd never had horses at the cabin, though they would've been helpful on multiple occasions. After reading so many books about the magnificent creatures, I was excited to see one. I reached up and let the large animal slip its muzzle into my hand.

"Her name's *Esperanza*," said Costco. "Do you know what that means?"

"Hope," I said, almost unbelieving.

Costco smirked. "The choice was intentional. Somehow it didn't seem appropriate to hook up *Viento* or *Llorona*. Instead, you have *Esperanza y Paz*."

Hope and Peace, I thought. "They're perfect."

With Gruber and Costco at the reigns, Uncle Alex, Mom, Dad, and I climbed into the carriage. I sat down, examining the sea of faces fixed on me.

"Don't stop the message!" yelled a random male voice.

"Never lose hope!" yelled another.

I nodded, speechless as tears surged forth. Cheers and applause erupted as Boss Gruber clicked his tongue and the carriage lurched forward. I felt some relief leaving the building's populace behind. Never had people been so expectant of me, filling me with anxiety like I'd never felt before. To be around so many people after years of isolation was slightly terrifying. Mom pulled me close. The sun was already beaming down, but the wind cooled my burning face as we traveled across the bridge on the opposite side of the island. Ahead, several plumes of smoke added their haze to the cloudless horizon. Dilapidated buildings lined the streets of the old city, leading towards a vast area where all vegetation and debris were removed.

"It used to be a park," said Gruber. "I visited the place when I was just a lad. When the United Territories began construction on the pods, the park was the only sprawling natural location left in the city. As big as it was, the park was only a minuscule fraction of the city's size. Even accounting for its one hundred levels, how's this 'marvel of human achievement' supposed to serve the entire eastern seaboard of the American Territory? The UTE isn't interested in saving everyone. They have never been. They're only interested in saving who they want to save."

"But there wasn't enough time or resources to build more pods or larger pods," said Mom. "There's no way they could save everyone."

"You are correct in that sense, Natalie," said Gruber. "But there are steps they could've taken. Their admission process is far from fair. And it's small-minded. The pods have been built to house a quarter of a million people comfortably, but what about uncomfortably? Would it not be better to save as many lives as possible?"

"It's a harsh reality," said Uncle Alex who'd been quiet for most of the trip. "What good does it do to house 500,000 if their resources last half as long? Would it not be better to have half that number survive than none? I will gladly remain outside if it means Zephyr will have a greater chance at survival."

"That is a valid point, but who has the right to make that decision for the rest of the inhabitants' families?" asked Gruber. "And let us not forget how many department heads from the UTE who've gained entry for themselves and their families despite being beyond the age limit and having no specialized skills. And who decides what's specialized? If the government cronies truly wanted the pods to be successful, perhaps they should sacrifice their spaces for more appropriate choices."

"A pod needs leadership," I said. "Before the invasion, the United Territories of Earth was the most successful government in Earth's history and the only successful worldwide one."

"A pod *does* need leadership, but leadership should come from within. The UTE *was* successful, but there were plenty of people who it did not favor. Many countries were annexed without choice for 'the good of the planet.' That aside, the UTE confirmed its ineptitude in its response to the Arthropod Landing. The pod system is a glorified tactical retreat—a multi-trillion-dollar way to save face. I ask you, is this who you want leading us into humanity's next age?"

"I suppose not," I said.

"I want people like you leading us into our next age, Zephyr," said Gruber. "You have an innate talent for leadership. I won't be able to influence pod politics from outside, but I have confidence that people will see your promise. Lead whomever of us survives into the bright future we deserve."

"Here. Here," added Costco.

The weight on my shoulders had increased by the hour since I'd met the Peacekeepers, making me long for a retreat back to the woods. I wanted to return to a microphone with no expectations.

"You have a gift, *mija*," said Dad. "You've inspired so many people, even me. Regardless of what happens, I couldn't be any more proud of you. All I ask is that you never stop the hope."

I hugged him tightly as we pulled up to the checkpoint. I'd been so preoccupied with the conversation, I'd missed the slums we'd driven through. The dilapidated buildings had given way to shack after tin-roofed shack, sided by broken or rotting boards as the burdened town's inhabitants milled through their troubled existence. The disparity between the shanty town's inhabitants hoping to gain entry into the pods and the residents of Bigs who'd chosen a life outside of them was astounding. As Gruber spoke with the Territorial Guard about me, I watched as women no older than my mother washed their clothes in filthy water as the men of similar age rushed the carriage to beg for food.

"Not what you expected, eh?" yelled Costco over their pleas.

"What on Earth?" Mom asked, shoving back the hands grabbing at her bags.

"Get lost!" yelled the annoyed guard, and the beggars dispersed.

"These are all the people who couldn't get in," said Costco. "They're staying here with nothing, starving, in hopes that before they permanently close the gates some might be lucky enough to enter."

It was heartbreaking. All these people, literally dying, scared to leave and miss any opportunity for entry that would be granted to others without issue. And there were children!

"What about those kids?" I asked.

"Likely sick," said Gruber, taking back some documents and moving the carriage towards a large building that said "Pod Pittsburgh Admission Board." "Or perhaps their parents wouldn't let them enter alone."

"Is it like this outside all the pods?" asked Dad.

Costco shook his head. "No. Rumor is that some of the pods closer to the landing site are having trouble getting enough people. There are far more survivors up here."

"More people left to die," I muttered.

"Harsh, but true," said Gruber, pulling to a stop. "This is us."

He helped me and the others down and led us into a dimly lit building to a long receiving line. I made for the end, but he guided me towards an office to the side.

"They know I don't waste their time," he whispered just loud enough for us to hear. "The line is for people trying to plead their way through the limitations."

He and Costco led us through a door to a poorly lit office that was sweltering, not a single exterior window. Not that I wanted to see out anyway. A metal ceiling fan did nothing to mitigate the heat. In front of us was a large metal desk covered in papers, many of which were stamped "Denied" in big, red, bold letters across them. After a moment, a sweaty man in a tan short-sleeved shirt and olive green shorts walked in, collapsing into the chair with a hiss from the cracked vinyl cushion. A whiff of foul body odor accompanied his entry. He pulled a handkerchief from his pocket and blotted the top of his bald head and his fluffy red mustache before wiping the back of his neck.

"Gruber," he said in a posh accent. "Found another stray for me?"

Costco looked at me and rolled his eyes. I snickered loud enough to draw the man's attention, but then it returned to Gruber.

"Mr. Mitchell, I have brought with me a young lady who should easily meet your qualifications," he said.

"Young lady, eh?" he said, eying me up and down. Mitchell pulled out a new file and began to scribble. "Doesn't look like a lady to me."

"There's more to this one than meets the eye," Gruber added.

The man harrumphed. "How so?" he asked without bothering to look up.

"This is Zephyr," said Gruber. "From the radio."

"That girl that people listen to?"

"The same."

The man harrumphed again, uninterested.

"Age?"

"Twenty-six," I said.

"You will speak when spoken to," said Mitchell, glaring at me.

Gruber gestured below the man's line of sight to remain quiet. Any respect the people of Bigs had for me didn't extend to this unfriendly gentleman.

"State of health?"

"Healthy and well," said Gruber.

Mitchell eyed me up and down again, figuring that was a sufficient test for my wellbeing.

"Full legal name?"

"Zephyr Fedorov-Sanchez," said my dad, using the name I'd only heard three, maybe four times in my life, purely a formality unnecessary for cabin life.

"Special Skills?"

"She's a leader," said Uncle Alex. "A damn good one."

"Any *relevant* skills?" asked Mitchell.

Gruber looked back as if to say, "I told you so." He'd been right. These people clearly had their minds made up about who or what was specialized.

•••••••

An hour later, I was standing at the entrance to Pod Pittsburgh, looking down on the largest ramp I'd ever seen. The incline descended into the dark receiving area, a maw ready to swallow me whole situated between two massive gates embedded in the pod's thick metal roof. The cavernous space was filled with people being provided uniforms, housing assignments, duty stations, and the pod-specific currency—ration points. The vaguely conical surface stretched across the landscape, its top broken up only by a windowed elevated observation deck at its center. In my hand, I held a yellow paper with my full legal name next to a bold green stamp that read "Approved."

It was hard to make out many more details through the sheet of tears blurring my eyes. Back on Mitchell's desk were two similar papers, one read Gabriel and the other Natalie, each emblazoned with "Denied." That red-faced menace didn't give a rat's ass who I was aside from the fact I was a healthy female of "breeding age," nor did he care about my parents. Never mind that they could outfight and outsurvive him any day of the week in the woods. We hadn't even asked about Uncle Alex. Every day I would see him lounging in the comfort of the pod would be a cold reminder of the inequality of the pod's entry system.

Mom gave me the biggest hug she'd ever given me and kept kissing me on the face, trying to impart a lifetime of motherly wisdom in a few moments. Mitchell had bent the rules for Boss Gruber and allowed my family to accompany me to the pod, but they were prohibited from setting foot inside. He was standing outside of his office rolling a cigarette, watching to make sure we followed his rules. Dad and Uncle Alex each gave tearful goodbyes, each telling me more in that moment than in the months leading up to it. Even Gruber and Costco were disappointed to see me go. When nothing more could be said, I took the hardest step of my life, placing my first foot down on the incline leading to below the surface of the Earth. Within six steps, I was bathed in darkness—an oppressing darkness that would surround me for the rest of my life.

"No!" I screamed, running back up the ramp to my family.

Before they could say a word, I held the yellow admission form high and ripped it into shreds, dropping it on the ground to be scattered by the wind. Mitchell stood erect from where he leaned against the awning's support, taking a sudden interest in my refusal.

"What are you doing?!" my mother yelled.

"My duty!" I said. "You heard Uncle Alex. I'm a leader! And a damn good one! And a leader doesn't lead from the safety of the fortification, a leader leads from the front lines!"

"Boss Gruber," I said, "I request permanent asylum for my family and myself in Bigs, where I hope to grow into half the person everyone believes I am."

Gruber took my hands in his. "Nothing would honor me more than to welcome you and your family into Bigs and have you lead by my side."

CHAPTER 50: HUCK

We began the long descent from the Hive's peak with newfound energy as we dodged battling Arthropods and fighting Demented while watching a horizon of crumbling mounds. Not once did we have to use our weapons. Our enemies had completely forgotten our existence.

"What about the people inside," asked Artim. "What can we do to help them?"

Before I could answer, Krista yelled, "Look!"

I followed her finger down the slope of the Hive. Hundreds, no, thousands of people were emerging from the Hive's various entrances. The freed prisoners were barely clothed, understandably traumatized, and many were injured—but they were alive.

"They survived!" yelled Trivia, bouncing up and down excitedly.

As we descended, more and more of them joined our ranks on the long climb down the mountain, offering us never-ending thanks while others stared as the Shock plagued their minds. *Would they ever recover from the trauma they'd endured?* Most of the escapees spoke United, but many others spoke in unintelligible languages that not even Trivia could understand. The looks on their faces, however, needed no translation. By the time we reached the Hive's base, there must have been more than ten thousand people behind us. The sea of faces had survived because of us—because of Arjun, Ondo, Dane, and everyone like them who'd sacrificed their lives for Guilherme's mission.

We had no other objective than to press forward towards the coast on which we'd arrived. Trivia had Om Banyu's radio on, wearing down the battery in an effort to get a response. Before the sun dropped below the horizon that first day, the ground quaked like we'd never experienced before. Hordes of people spun to face the Hive and watched joyously as the artificial mountain caved in on itself, releasing a plume of dust into the atmosphere to turn the dusk sky umber. Rifts formed like lightning radiating from the quake's epicenter as the enemy's tunnels below followed suit. If there was any final confirmation that we'd won, that was it. Everyone smiled, patting one another on the back and cheering with enough enthusiasm that the entire world could hear our victory.

"We did it, Huck," Ariadne said, resting her head on my shoulder as she held my hand, her tears of joy moistening my shoulder. "Now what?"

"Whatever we want. We have our entire lives ahead of us."

Ariadne smiled, turning up her head to give me a soft peck on the cheek.

"What should we do for all of these people?" asked Hemant. "I think between us we have a few ration bars, but I'm not that Jesus dude. How are all of us supposed to come up with enough to feed everyone in a desert? It'd be ridiculous to survive that only to die of starvation."

"CQ, CQ," crackled over the radio.

Trivia nearly fumbled the mic in excitement. "Yes?! We're here!"

The unknown voice introduced himself as Friedrich. He and Trivia continued their conversation, parsing out details of our rescue, concluding that the closer we could get to the coast before our rescuers' arrival, the better.

"We're saved!" I said, as months worth of tension lifted from my shoulders.

••••••••

By noon the next day, our upbeat march had turned into a weary trudge as the inescapable desert sun bore down on our gargantuan party. The Outback was littered with countless corpses of Arthropod and Demented already sickening the thick air. My stomach ached with hunger pangs as my lips cracked with dehydration. We'd shared what little food and water we had, but it had done nothing to relieve the suffering of the masses behind us.

"That help can come anytime," said Hemant. "Word coming from the back is we've already lost a few."

It pained me to hear, but their deaths had been unavoidable. They had lived in such harsh conditions, and then been expected to cross grueling terrain with little to no sustenance and possibly injuries.

"At least they died free," said Ariadne, in a vain attempt to comfort me.

A faint buzzing pulled my attention, but I dismissed it as a hallucination brought on by the heat.

"You guys hear that too, right?" asked Hemant.

"You've got to be kidding me," said Krista, turning to stare up at the skies. Sure enough, there were two airplanes of similar vintage to the *Sekhmet*.

"Ho-ly hell," said Omar, starting to wave. "There's a sight I never expected to see again."

If we'd had the energy, we would've jumped up and down for joy. That didn't stop us from being all smiles.

Moments later, the twin-engine planes rolled to a stop in front of us. The hatch swung open on the first and out popped a tall, lanky gentleman with close-trimmed, neatly-combed blond hair and a familiar swagger.

"We heard you guys might need some help," the man said, laughing heartily. "By Jove, I never thought I'd see the day!"

As the second plane began spilling its crew, the laughter and celebration could be heard for kilometers. The throngs of prisoners began to surround the two aircraft, never having seen anything save for inverts in the skies. The plane crews began dishing out the clothing, supplies, and rations they had been packed with, but it still wasn't near enough for the large volume of people. A lot of the freed prisoners would be splitting a bar and sharing a blanket. It wasn't much, but it was something. By the time everyone was settled it was well after nightfall. The man we'd seen approached us, weary and sweating after the long day of aid.

"I'm sorry I didn't speak with you sooner. I wasn't expecting so many," the man said, his melodic accent soothing after the long day. "A great surprise after a heroic triumph, don't get me wrong. It will take weeks, but we will get everyone back to civilization. My name is Friedrich, I believe you knew my brother, Kurt."

Ariadne rocketed up at the mention of the deceased cook and medic of the original Misfits.

"That's just like Kurt," said Friedrich, seeing her response. "Always making a profound impact on people. He will be missed by many. You gave him a funeral, yes?"

"We built a cairn for him after the duster attack," I said. "I'd be honored to show you where his grave is located."

"I would like that very much, Huck."

The look on my face gave away my surprise that he knew my name.

"Every person on these planes knows exactly who each of you are," he said, laughing like his brother. "When we found out that

Pod Baghdad had mobilized their plane, we ramped up our efforts. That Hera must have been one hell of an engineer. It's taken two dozen of our people decades to accomplish what she did in less time. Once the antenna bugs were gone, Pod Munich's engineers worked around the clock to get them airworthy. The region around the old German Region has no shortage of vintage craft and munitions, however old and dilapidated they may be. With your accomplishments, we can take these instruments of war and turn them into instruments of peace. I haven't the words to express how grateful I am, but on behalf of a grateful world, I thank you."

The flight crews that had accompanied him stood and began their ovation. At first, the survivors just stared, but row by row, they rose and joined in applause—infirm, weak, traumatized—*everyone*. Cries, cheers, and whistles filled the night air, all in gratitude for what we'd accomplished. By the time the indescribable scene settled down, each of us was crying, completely overcome with emotion. I took Ariadne's hand feeling exhausted, elated, and heartbroken but overall honored to have helped return humanity's future.

"Where can I take you, Huck?" asked Friedrich. "The world is your—how do those Americans say it?—oyster."

I chuckled at the anachronistic turn of phrase. "Since I can remember, I've dreamed of living my life surrounded by nature—mountains, rivers, forests—you name it," I looked at Ariadne and smiled. "We've talked about starting a small community and helping humanity return to the surface, a family or so at a time."

Friedrich barely hesitated. "I know just the place," he said laughing. "You forget, I'm from Munich—the most enchanting land in the world!

Ariadne nodded excitedly. I guess we'd be settling in Munich. Who knew? With the pod's specialization in medicine, Ariadne would feel right at home working with the researchers as they adapted to their new lives outdoors.

"And you, Hemant?"

"Before now, I would've said I didn't care, so long as it was with my brother," he said, pausing. Trivia gripped his hand tightly. "Arjun sacrificed himself for us all. As much as it pains me to spend the rest of my life without him, he died a hero. I couldn't be prouder."

"Everywhere in the world will honor him and the other fallen, rest assured."

"My sentiment still stands, I don't care where I live provided the people I love are at my side," said Hemant, grinning at Trivia. She didn't give him a chance to go on, grabbing his head and pulling him in for a passionate kiss, not a care in the world about who watched.

After such an incredible day, no one's spirits could be down. We'd won! *God, I still can't believe it.* When Trivia finally let Hemant loose, his head must have been reeling from the hormones. Hemant turned to Friedrich half-dazed.

"I want to help Huck and Ariadne," he said, still grinning from ear to ear. "I mean, if that's alright with you guys."

"Dude, you don't even have to ask," said Ariadne. "There's no place we would go where you wouldn't be welcome."

"Umm, Friedrich. Huck said he wanted to be around rivers, but I don't have to use a boat every day or anything, right?"

"Slays the Arthropod Queens and is still timid around water!" Friedrich said, belting out a laugh. "No, Hemant. There's no shortage of beautiful waterways, but you don't have to use them if you choose not to. Though once you reach the Alps, you might change your mind."

"I don't know, man," said Hemant, "I intend to build a cabin for Trivia and me, and after that, I may never leave my front porch."

"There are worse ways to spend your days," said Friedrich. "You, though, you have the—pardon my expression—the bug for adventure. Otherwise, you wouldn't come this far. Give it a few months, and you'll be out doing something more productive.

Humanity is a machine that needs to be rebuilt and restarted. I can think of few people who would be better equipped to guide it through that process."

Hemant chewed on the idea for a moment. "It does seem selfish to sit on my ass all day."

"Remember, you don't have to help the entire world. Well… again. Thousands of families in Pod Munich alone will need resettlement. Even something as simple as teaching surface survival would be more helpful than you can imagine."

"I know a lot about plants and medicine. I'd be happy to share what I know," said Ariadne, confirming my previous thought.

"That's the spirit," said Friedrich, slapping his leg. "What about you Omar? What does the future hold for you and Krista?"

"I'm going back home. To Pod Horizonte," he said. "I've got my father's legacy to clean up. I'm sure Guilherme and Fabrice will find plenty to keep me busy during the coming years."

"With as much time as we've spent in the jungle, it's what I know best," said Krista. "I know it'll take decades, but I can't wait for jungle life to return. Those seagulls we saw in the Indian Ocean were the most magnificent creatures I've ever seen. I can't imagine that they were the only larger species to survive. I don't know much about wildlife, but I'm excited to learn."

"You've got a keeper, Omar," said Friedrich. "Take good care of that one."

"Oh, I know," he said. "With any luck, I'm hoping she'll marry me one day."

"Are you serious?" said Krista, slapping her hands over her mouth.

Omar nodded. "I don't have a thing in the world to give you but my love, is that okay?"

Krista nodded vigorously, unable to speak as tears came to her eyes.

Friedrich pulled a necklace with a ring from around his neck and handed it to Omar. "It was my mother's," he said, the silver ring reflecting in the firelight. "I can think of no better owner than a friend of Kurt's and a hero."

Omar clasped his hand in thanks, before dropping to one knee. Afterward, even as exhausted as we were, we danced and sang, delighted for the engaged couple. The months had been filled with highs and lows, but this night I would never forget.

"What about all of these people?" asked Ariadne. "I can't just leave them behind. It'd take you years to fly all of them out in two planes."

"Who said they are the only two?" Friedrich asked, arching an eyebrow and smiling.

Ariadne didn't know how to respond.

"Once we radioed that your mission had been a success, everyone chimed in. They're all coming to help."

"What do you mean *everyone*?" asked Hemant.

"I mean *everyone*," he said, winking.

I gazed into Ariadne's emerald eyes and for the first time, humanity's future seemed as bright as my own.

EPILOGUE: GUILHERME

"How's that new wife of yours, Lawkeeper?" I asked, turning from the framed image hanging on the wall.

Overlooking my desk was a large life-like painting I'd commissioned of the group I'd dispatched to the Hive standing outside of Pod Munich as its entire population rejoiced behind them. Based on a photograph displayed in my apartment, the artwork was one of the few frivolities I'd allowed myself as the city's prime minister. The event had been both the largest celebration and memorial service the world had seen since the Arthropods' arrival. The radio broadcast had been relayed to eager ears around the world. In the image, the heroes had been treated to fresh clothes, medical care, and hot showers, but the journey's physical and mental toll was still obvious. Gone were the innocent teenagers I'd last seen.

"Krista's great, sir," Omar replied, eying his likeness in the image. "Greenskeeper Chun has taken her under her wing. The woman's a genius when it comes to Earth's native flora and fauna. Last I checked, they were beginning to log the area's native life and cross-referencing it with older texts housed in the vault. Incidentally, Krista said thank you for granting her access."

I waved it off. The knowledge contained in those old tomes belonged to everyone. In the meantime, I had assigned scribes to create copies for each town budding out from the former pod. In the months following the Hive's destruction, the ministers and I had agreed to share any information we possessed. It would take decades, if not centuries, but we hoped to eventually piece humanity's collective knowledge back together. Judging from what we'd already learned from the past, our species hadn't always taken the greatest care of the Earth. The planet had healed much of the human-caused damage during the Arthropods' reign. I hoped that if there was any benefit to the invasive species, we would learn from our past and cherish what we had.

"Is your new deputy working out?"

"Akhil's learning the ropes quickly," he said. "He's been clean since we left him behind, not just from pheromones, but everything. And we've got him the help he needs. He's mighty proud of that badge and knows he'll lose it if I ever catch him even thinking about using again. With his little one on the way, he's got plenty of reasons to stay sober."

"A new baby tends to have that effect," I said, thinking of Luca crawling around Aline's and my apartment. "You lead well. Keep it up and you might be running this place one day."

Omar's grin stretched across his face.

"And today's numbers?" I asked, turning to Fabrice.

"He'll make a far superior leader to his father," said the Deputy Prime Minister, flashing Omar a generous smile. "Yesterday the builders fell a few below projections due to the heavy afternoon shower, but they managed to complete 93 cabins. The rain didn't hamper the farmers. They cleared just under three hectares and are right on track. At this rate, we're still on schedule to have everyone in permanent housing and alloted with arable land before the two-year mark."

"Any news on the global population growth?" asked Omar.

"See, Memo. A born leader," said Fabrice. "Yes, actually. News continues to drift in of more pockets of survivors. We're conservatively estimating that there's more than double the population of the pods scattered around the planet. Since the creatures are pretty much dead, they're all beginning to emerge from their hideaways, but finding and contacting them is proving difficult as you can imagine. It would appear that the people you met in Zephyr's Hope were far from the only ones who listened to the little girl's broadcasts and dug in. It's a shame that young woman never knew the full extent—"

My aide, Niles, sprinted into the room, interrupting Fabrice.

"Sir, we've found it! We've finally found the evidence you were looking for," he said, struggling for breath. "They came from the asteroid as suspected. A scientific program called *Phaethon*. We've secured the records from the UTE Space Agency's underground vault. What the researchers have already found is… Well, it's quite disturbing, sir."

"Spit it out, Niles," I said.

"Sir, it would appear our earlier conclusions were accurate. We caused this."

Fabrice, Omar, and I stared at each other in shock. I slowly made my way to the worn high-backed leather chair. I had a seat, already tempted by a drink, despite the early hour.

"My god," I said. "How did this happen?"

"According to our documentation, the *Phaethon* mission launched various arthropod species on a probe to the near-Earth asteroid 99942 Apophis in the year 2029 when it passed close by. The mission intended to study the effects of long-term radiation on select species with the goal of mitigating the effects of radiation on human cancer patients. The probe crashed on impact and the mission went down as a failure."

"Well, something happened," said Omar.

"Why wasn't any of this part of history? Why didn't we know that we'd caused this?" I asked, raising my voice.

"The UTESA was already facing substantial controversy over their, pardon the term, astronomical spending, so they swept the accident under the rug," said Niles. "The exorbitant cost of a single space mission could meet a lot of people's basic needs. It was thought everything was destroyed in the crash. Obviously, it wasn't."

"So you're telling me that the creatures evolved? How could they become sentient in thirteen years?"

"According to the records, the sample arthropods were injected with a serum to enhance the radiation's effects. Our researchers concluded that the serum not only protected them but encouraged radiation-influenced mutations. Somehow, they survived the vacuum of space."

"They were trifling with matters they didn't understand," said Fabrice, chewing on the end of his pencil, "and humanity paid for their hubris with their lives."

"It fits," said Omar. "When I saw the asteroid, it was pocked with holes. If the asteroid had hollows, it would stand to reason that when the probe crashed, the inverts escaped into the rock and bred."

"And with their rapid reproduction cycle, it was only a matter of time before intelligence appeared, though in thirteen years... It's unimaginable," added Fabrice.

"That must be why they never suspected that we'd caused it. They thought it was a new alien species," I said. "Thank the universe they're all dead."

"Sir, that wasn't all of the asteroid," said Niles.

"You want to run that by me again?"

"99942 Apophis was enormous. Had it impacted Earth, it would've caused an extinction-level event possibly worse than the

Arthropods. The meteorite that landed was nothing more than a sliver and even then, the creatures somehow reduced gravity's effect on the object."

"There's more of the asteroid?" I asked, rubbing my temples. *There is still so much we don't understand.* "Could we develop a missile capable of destroying the asteroid before it passes again? If we have the old UTESA designs, how difficult would it be to recreate their technology? We must completely eradicate the creatures unless we want to risk their return."

"There's another problem, sir," said Niles.

"Don't leave me waiting, man! Tell me!" I said as Omar let out an exasperated sigh.

"As soon as we realized the implications, we redirected our telescopes towards where the object should have been, but it wasn't there. We found it in *our* solar system! Sir, the asteroid has somehow altered its trajectory."

"The inverts could change *that* thing's trajectory?" I asked, arching my eyebrow.

"We believe the Arthropods have influenced it. Yes, sir."

"Damn every one of those bastards to Hell! Where's it headed?"

"Out of our solar system."

I sighed with relief. "Thank the universe. With any luck, the sun will consume Earth long before their pestilence returns."

"I wouldn't say that, sir."

"Niles, if you don't tell me every last thing you know right now, I'll send *you* to Apophis!"

"Sir, they've colonized Mars."

ACKNOWLEDGEMENTS & AUTHOR'S NOTE

In the words of friend and fellow author Emma Couette, ending a series is bittersweet. The *Release Day Saga* has taken me on a wild journey. While not as impressive as traveling from Belo Horizonte to Alice Springs, it has still been quite the challenge. Few people know this, but after the third book, I had a bout with depression that almost ended my author career before it really began. Unfortunately, my experience is far from unique among writers.

That being said, seeing this series through would have been impossible without all of the support I received along the way. I'll name the most influential ones, but there are so many who will go unrecognized who contributed in less noticeable ways like providing encouraging remarks when they were needed most, screaming in excitement when they received the *Release Day Saga* for Christmas, or watching my sales booth so I could run to the restroom.

I cannot thank my wife and daughters enough for what they have sacrificed to make this series possible. An extra special thanks goes to my editor and wife, Jessica Matthews, who helps me polish my rough manuscripts into something readable. I also want to thank my beta readers: Deshea Surratt, Emily Wan, Ariel Wells, Missy Wood, Mallory Reid, and Amanda Campbell who provide me with the feedback necessary to make my death-filled story come to life. And thank you to all of the people who've purchased and reviewed my work since the beginning.

I have discovered that I love doing in-person events like shows, signings, festivals, and cons. Despite having accounts on Facebook, Threads, and Instagram, social media is not my forte, nor is it my preferred method for connecting with readers. I love interacting with you face-to-face. I don't care how popular (or not) I become, I will always try to make time for a chat.

It bears repeating: It is important to me to tell this story authentically with diverse voices from an inclusive perspective. The characters represent varying ethnicities, genders, sexualities, religions, body types, and abilities. I did my best to handle this with care and hope it is reflected. Enjoy life and respect others.

—Ryan

RYAN MATTHEWS

The Release Day Saga is the debut series of Ryan Matthews, an English as a Second Language (ESL) teacher and graphic designer. In addition to writing and teaching, he enjoys spending time with his family, taking insect and mushroom pictures on hikes, and plowing through his extensive reading list. He also dabbles in foreign languages, open-world video games, and the French horn. Ryan holds a Bachelor's Degree in Art and a Master's Degree in Education. He lives in Tennessee with his wife, daughters, and the family pets, Luna and Coda.

@ryanmatthews501
ryanmatthewsauthor.com

NEWSLETTER

For the latest updates, events, and behind-the-scenes information, visit Ryan's website and subscribe to his newsletter.

RATE & REVIEW

If you wish to support authors like Ryan, please leave reviews on sites like Amazon and Goodreads for all of your favorite books.